The Gambler

The Wedding Pact Series, Book 3

Denise Grover Swank

Chapter One

No one had ever accused Libby St. Clair of being a practical woman. Not that she cared. The practical choice was often the safe one, the boring one. Libby St. Clair had also never been accused of being boring.

She firmly believed in living life to the fullest.

Ironically enough, the fact that she was now preparing to walk down the aisle toward a man she didn't intend to marry was the first practical choice she'd consciously made, even if no one else realized it. Especially her two best friends.

"Libby," Megan gushed, staring at Libby's reflection in the mirror. "You look gorgeous."

Blair gave her a warm smile. "She's right, Libs. You're stunning."

"And just think," Megan said, fluffing Libby's tulle gown. "Not a single mishap."

That was the part that shook Libby's faith in her plan. Why

was her wedding going so perfectly?

Blair put her hand on Libby's arm and stared into her eyes in the reflection. "I confess, when you called last month and told me you were marrying Mitch three days before your thirtieth birthday, I had my doubts. I thought this might be some scheme related to that stupid wedding curse, but I'm happy I was wrong. Mitch seems like a great guy." She cringed. "Even if he's gone a little overboard with the football theme."

Libby gave her a weak smile. "He is pretty great." There was no denying it. Mitch was a fantastic guy in social situations. Of all the many boyfriends who'd come and gone in the past fifteen years, he was the only one who was both fairly dependable and accepting of her quirkiness. He even tried to understand her close friendship with Megan's brother-in-law, Noah McMillan, which was more than she could say for Megan and Blair. That had to count for something, right?

But something was *missing* with Mitch. It hadn't really mattered at first. She'd never intended to marry him. It hadn't taken her long to figure out that the woman in his life would always take a distant second to his sporting activities. But she'd needed a date to Megan's wedding, and then Blair's, and the fact that her friends kept *expecting* her to break up with him, that they were always so utterly *shocked* she was still with the same guy, started to chafe. And so she stayed with him, at first wanting to save face and prove she wasn't as flighty as they thought. Then, because she had seen the curse come to life with her friends' weddings, and she fully expected it to do the same with hers.

Back when they were kids, the friends had made a pact to find husbands before their thirtieth birthdays. They'd formed the agreement while in line to see a fortune teller, and mere moments later, Madame Rowena had assured them they would keep the pact, but their weddings would be disasters and each of them would marry someone other than their intended. The curse. Only Libby had taken it seriously, but there was no denying that Megan and Blair had both gotten married before their thirtieth birthdays, and neither of their husbands were the men who'd originally proposed to them. And God knew, the days leading up to their weddings had been filled with disaster after disaster.

Just like the fortune teller had predicted.

"In a week or two, maybe Garrett and I will have you both over for dinner."

"Listen to *you*, Blair Hansen-Lowry," Megan gushed. "Dinner parties with other couples? Marriage definitely agrees with you."

The normally hard-assed Blair actually blushed. "Now that Garrett has moved to Kansas City and we're starting our own practice . . ." Her blush deepened. "I just never expected to be so happy." Then a mock scowl crossed her face. "If you ever repeat that to anyone, I'll deny it."

Megan gave her a teasing grin, but she knew better than to make a big deal of their friend's uncharacteristic sentimentality. "Just think. When Josh and I move into our house in Lee's Summit next month, all six of us can hang out together. It'll be like old times."

Libby had to admit, Blair looked happier than she had since high school. The curse had changed her life—and Megan's— for the better.

So what in the hell was Libby doing wrong? Staring down at her bare left finger, she tried to keep from wringing her hands. Because she'd never planned to walk down the aisle toward him, she'd refused to let Mitch buy her an engagement ring. She'd bought two cheap wedding bands at a superstore to avoid suspicion. The best man now had them in his pocket.

The door to their room opened, and Josh McMillan, Megan's husband of five months, poked his head in the room. "Hey, girls."

Megan glanced up in surprise. "Josh, what are you doing here? Why aren't you seated?"

Libby looked at him with a hopeful expression. Since Mitch had a tendency to tune out anything that wasn't directly related to the Arkansas Razorbacks or the high school football team he coached and the school where he taught phys. ed., Libby had put Josh in charge of making sure the groom's side of things ran smoothly. Perhaps this was what she'd been waiting for. Josh walked through the threshold and shut the door behind him.

"Libs, I have some bad news."

"Mitch didn't show?" She tried to keep the excitement out of her voice.

His eyes widened, then he shook his head. "What? No. Nothing like that. Mitch is in the church office watching the Arkansas football game."

Figured. "Then what's the bad news?"

He grimaced, casting a glance at Megan, then back at Libby. "I'm sure you're wondering why we haven't started yet . . ."

"You mean it's not because Mitch doesn't want to miss the end of the game?" Libby asked wryly.

"Not entirely." He looked concerned. "It's because we've been waiting on one of the groomsmen to arrive."

There were only two groomsmen, and she could account for the best man, having seen Mitch's cousin only a few hours earlier. That left one person. Josh's brother. "Is Noah's plane late?"

"Not exactly..."

She waited for him to continue, trying not to get upset until she had all the facts.

"He's not coming at all."

The blood rushed from her head. "What? Why not?"

"Libs, I don't know. He said something about Donna needing him this weekend."

His girlfriend of *four weeks?*

Back in June, Libby and Noah had become instant friends in the lead-up to Megan and Josh's circus of a wedding, and the two had schemed to make sure the new couple's marriage was legit. Their friendship had grown closer over the following months, and Noah had quickly replaced Libby's two best friends as her closest confidant.

Noah was a notorious womanizer and Libby was known for her serial dating. Their relationship confounded everyone they knew. It was so unlike them, but then, maybe that was why it worked. It had only seemed natural to include Noah in the wedding party. After all, Mitch hadn't minded.

But he'd suddenly decided not to come? Just on a whim? *What the actual hell?*

Josh gave her a sympathetic look. "Libby, I'm sorry. I warned you he could be . . . unreliable."

It was true. But Libby had never seen that side of Noah. Somehow she'd thought their friendship had changed him. It had definitely changed her.

Libby put a hand on her hip and narrowed her eyes at the innocent McMillan brother. "Let me get this straight. He agreed to be in my wedding, then he decided not to come because his girlfriend of *four weeks* has something she wants him to do?"

In a show of solidarity, Megan crossed the room to her husband and placed a hand on his arm. "Josh has told me stories of Noah's epic fails in the past, but he hasn't acted like this since I've known him. And he's taken on so much responsibility with the merger of Dad's company with Josh and Noah's . . . Josh really *did* think he had changed."

Libby wiped at the tear falling down her cheek. This wedding might not be real, but Noah still should have been here for her. The amount of grief she felt over his absence caught her by surprise.

But what did it matter if they were short a groomsman? The wedding wasn't going to take place anyway. After all, there was no way that the curse would strike for both Megan and Blair and miss her. Her knight in shining armor—her one true love, her soul mate—would show up at any minute to sweep her off her feet and marry her before her birthday on Tuesday.

Only she had no earthly idea who he might be. The only thing she knew was what the lines on her palm told her—he was creative and would shower her with the love she'd longed for her entire life.

A cold sweat broke out on her forehead. What if this didn't work?

"What do you want to do?" Blair asked, her jaw set. She'd barely tolerated Noah in the past, so these shenanigans weren't bound to make her any fonder of him.

One hundred people were sitting in that church, waiting for her to walk down the aisle.

What the hell was she going to do?

Faith. Libby just needed more faith. She'd had enough faith for Megan and Blair when their lives and weddings had begun to fall apart. Since they hadn't seemed to understand what was really going on, Libby had needed to have enough faith for all three of them.

She gave them a dazzling smile. "Go ahead with the

wedding, of course."

"What about the missing groomsman?" Megan asked.

Libby shrugged. She refused to show her friends how upset she was that Noah wasn't there. "Have Josh stand in for him." She gave him a pointed glance, disappointment seeping into her voice. "Haven't you spent most of your adult life cleaning up his messes? What's one more?"

"Oh, Libby." Megan threw her arms around her friend. "I'm so sorry."

Libby pulled loose. "I'm okay. I should have known better. I just thought he was beyond this sort of thing."

"We all did."

"Does that mean you're ready?" Blair asked, holding out Libby's wildflower bouquet.

"I guess."

Her response drew worried glances from her friends, but she was too busy trying to figure out what she would do if the curse didn't work.

No. No. No. Stop thinking like that. She just had to believe.

Libby reached for the bouquet and took a deep breath. When she released it, serenity washed through her. This was going to work.

It had to.

Megan gave Josh a lingering kiss, then pulled back and smoothed his lapel, staring into his face with adoration and love. Both Blair and Libby had been jealous of their connection, even if neither woman had ever admitted it. But Blair had found that same deep love and contentment with Garrett. So where was Libby's soulmate?

Josh left to get the groom and the other groomsman up to the altar while the three girls waited. The door flew open again, this time with more force. Libby's mother waltzed in with a theatrical flounce. "They're ready for you, my princess."

Irritation set Libby on edge, quickly followed by a stab of guilt as she studied her mother. Gabriella St. Clair was a stunningly beautiful woman. Her rich dark brown hair was thick and long, and her olive complexion was flawless and nearly wrinkle-free, even though she had to be close to fifty years old, not that she'd ever admit to it. Libby had no idea how old her mother actually was since the elder St. Clair would never confess the year of her birth. Not that it mattered. Gabriella St. Clair's face and body defied time, and she and Libby were often mistaken for sisters.

And there was the rub. Gabriella preferred to be seen as Libby's sister than her mother and often did her best to make sure she was the center of attention. Even now—wearing a form-fitting *white* dress with a deep V-neck that showed off her ample cleavage—Gabriella St. Clair would not be relegated to the background.

Libby's mother glided over to her and grabbed her hand in a dramatic flourish. "You are by far the most beautiful bride I've ever seen."

Libby gritted her teeth. "Thank you, Momma."

"I'm still not sure that boy out there is right for you."

That was one of the few things the St. Clair women agreed upon, except Gabriella didn't think Libby should marry at all.

"Thank you for your concern, Momma."

Her mother patted her cheek and looked into her eyes. "No talking you out of it?"

Libby released a short laugh. At this point, if either of her friends told her this was crazy and encouraged her to back out of it, she'd probably do it in a heartbeat. But hearing her mother say it was a whole other thing. "I've made up my mind."

"Well, nothing's forever, sweetheart." Gabriella shot a wicked glance to Blair. "And you already have a divorce attorney on retainer."

Blair's mouth opened as if on a hinge, but Gabriella was already sweeping out of the room.

Blair put her hands on her hips. "I can't believe her!"

Libby shook her head, her anxiety rising. "It's my mother. What do you expect?" She took a breath. "It's time to start."

Megan took a step toward her. "Maybe you should take a moment."

"I don't care what she thinks. We've known she's a narcissistic bitch since before I found her and my first boyfriend screwing on our kitchen counter. Why would anything change in the last fifteen years?"

"Oh, Libs . . ." Megan said softly.

Megan's sweetness was nearly her undoing. "Forget my mother. There are bigger things to worry about. I have a date with destiny."

Her friends gave her a strange look, but Libby pushed them toward the door, not giving them time to respond.

They waited in the church lobby, listening for the musical cue to start down the aisle. Blair went first, followed by Megan. And soon the music switched to the song Mitch had picked for her walk down the aisle—the Razorback fight song. She'd agreed to *everything* he'd asked for, never once thinking the wedding would progress this far.

Libby cast a worried glance toward the front door of the church, wondering where in the hell her soul mate could be. After a good twenty seconds, long enough for the guests in the church to start murmuring in confusion, Libby realized he wasn't going to come walking through the door.

Which meant he was inside the church.

Relief washed over her at that thought, which was enough to get her through the door and propel her down the aisle. Her gaze swept the crowd, looking for her Prince Charming, but the only real candidate she came up with was Mitch's Uncle Earl—a forty-two-year-old confirmed bachelor and wholesale fish salesman down in Louisiana. He was a good seventy-five pounds overweight, and during the rehearsal dinner, Libby and her friends had decided he wore a toupee. He gave her a leering smile when he realized her gaze had landed on him. Then he licked his upper lip, as if he'd just spotted a particularly succulent catfish.

She'd rather marry Mitch.

Mitch wasn't so bad. Her friends liked him. And if she could learn to overlook the football fanaticism, he was sweet. Sure, Libby had done her level best to keep Blair from marrying a man *she* didn't love, but there was no denying that Mitch was a better partner than Neil could ever be. Still, Libby couldn't fool herself into thinking she was head over heels in love. After she'd announced her short engagement, Blair and Megan had quizzed her endlessly about her decision. She must have performed the role of the gushing bride-to-be a little too well, because she'd convinced them this was what she wanted. But if she went through with it, it would be until death do us part. While Libby might know the best divorce attorney in the universe, she'd never let it come to that.

Unlike her mother, Libby believed marriage was for keeps.

So what was she doing?

Maybe her white knight hadn't shown up yet. Maybe he'd gotten lost in traffic. Libby just had to keep going and believe it would all work out.

But as she climbed the two steps up the altar, panic clawed in her chest. *Have faith*, she repeated in her head. *Just have faith.*

Mitch waited for her, wearing his black tux with his University of Arkansas tie. He lifted his pants legs to reveal his Razorback socks. "Ehh?" He grinned as he dropped it. "You're gonna be the perfect wife, Libby," he whispered. "What other bride would let her groom finish watching a football game before the ceremony?" Then he winked and nudged her with his elbow. "We won! Twenty-three to twenty-one! Go Hogs!" he shouted, following up with a victory whoop—"Wooo Pig Sooooie!!!"—that his friends joined in from the pews.

Megan and Blair's eyes flew open in shock.

Welcome to the real Mitch.

Her anxiety ratcheted up five notches.

Why couldn't Megan and Blair read between the lines and realize she wasn't in love with him? Libby had recognized all the signs with the both of them. Were they so eager for her to settle down that they'd give their approval to *anyone*?

She decided to ignore the fact that *she'd* proposed to *him*. Her lame attempt to get the curse rolling.

Lost in her thoughts, she was shocked to hear the minister ask, "Mitch, would you like to read your vows?"

Oh, shit. They were already to the *vows*?

Mitch cleared his throat and reached into his jacket and pulled out a white paper. After carefully unfolding it, he held it up for everyone to see.

Oh, my God. It's a play diagram.

Sure enough, the paper was covered with circles and x's, big sweeping lines and arrows. "Libs, you and me are like when the Razorbacks played Kansas in the Cotton Bowl in 2012. The Razorbacks hadn't beaten the Jayhawks since 1967. They used this quarterback sneak play." He held it against his chest and pointed to it. "And do you know what happened?"

11

She stared at him in shock. What was *happening?*

"They whooped some Jayhawk ass and became the Cotton Bowl champions!"

Then Mitch and his friends let out another *Woo Pig Sooie.*

Had it been possible to die from embarrassment, she would have collapsed to the floor at that very moment.

"That's us, baby. You and me. We'll whoop ass and lead our team to victory. You, me, and all our little half-backs." When she didn't answer, he mistook her horror for confusion. "You know. Our kids," he added with a wink.

His friends in the audience let loose another Hogs call.

The minister gaped for several seconds before closing his mouth and swallowing. "Uh . . . Libby, do you have vows?"

Oh, my God. This was way past cold feet. This bordered on insanity.

"No."

Mitch lowered his paper, confusion in his eyes.

"No?" The minister's eyebrows shot up. "Would you prefer to recite the traditional vows after me?"

She glanced back at Megan and Blair, who stood frozen in shock, then turned to face the minister. "No."

Mitch blinked. "What's wrong with my little running back? Did you forget your vows?"

Running back . . . run . . . If she didn't get out of here, she was going to jump out of her skin. "I'm sorry, Mitch. I can't do this." She grabbed her full skirt in one hand and took off down the aisle for the exit.

"Libs?" Mitch called out. "Are you goin' out for a pass?"

She glanced over her shoulder, ignoring the horrified stares of the guests. "I'm passing all right." She ran out the doors, Megan and Blair fast on her heels as she fought her rising hysteria.

Oh, God. The curse had failed her, and she'd just run out of her own wedding.

"Libby," Megan called after her, but she raced toward the parking lot without slowing.

Guests had begun streaming out the double doors, Mitch in the lead.

"Libby? Where're you goin'?" he called after her.

What was she going to do? She had no purse. No car keys. In fact, her mother had driven her to the church. She had nowhere to hide. Humiliated beyond belief, she was like a rat trapped in a maze, only there was no piece of cheese waiting for her. No perfect soul mate waiting in the wings. Only more humiliation.

A car pulled into the parking lot, and before she could stop to consider what she was doing, she bolted for it. The car slowed down, the driver probably stunned by the spectacle. She saw an opportunity and took it. Opening the passenger door, she glanced down at the bouquet in her hand. Without thinking, she tossed it toward the wedding guests congregating on the lawn.

Megan's grandmother's eyes lit up. "That bouquet's mine, bitches!" She leapt for it just as one of Libby's college friends grabbed it too.

Gram tackled the younger woman to the ground and a wrestling match began.

Her eyes still on the melee, Libby slid into the car. "I'll pay you a hundred dollars if you get me out of here *right now.*"

Half the guests had spilled out onto the lawn now, and Mitch stood in the front, looking dazed and confused.

What had she done? She'd been so certain activating the curse would lead her to the man of her dreams that she'd ignored the little voice in her head whispering that she was callously using Mitch. But now the proof of her selfishness was literally staring her in the face.

"Only a hundred?" an amused voice answered. "My plane ticket cost more than that."

Libby gasped in relief when she recognized the voice of the driver next to her. But then she remembered he'd stood her up.

Noah McMillan was a dead man.

Chapter Two

Noah McMillan had known more than his share of women. He'd dated plenty in high school, but it wasn't until college that he started plowing his way through too many women to count. And while his easy-come-easy-go lifestyle had continued after graduation, it wasn't until his younger brother Josh joined the family business that he gave up all pretense of giving a shit.

Why should he bother when Josh gave a shit enough for the both of them?

He knew he was a disappointment to his brother and mother, but he couldn't find it in himself to make an effort. The truth was, he'd stopped caring about much of anything after his father died a week before he graduated college.

So he'd fumbled along for more than a decade, knowing that he and his brother both had their roles. Josh was the responsible one. Noah was the joke. And Noah played his part well—perhaps too well. He was the one who'd almost made them lose their business.

There was no denying that Noah had lost the plans for an esoteric part that Josh had created for solar panels after indulging in a one-night stand at a conference. A part that would breathe new life into their flailing business. But he hadn't given it another thought until their patent was denied and their big investor threatened to pull his funding unless the McMillan brothers sorted out the problem within a week. It didn't take much tracking to figure out which firm had submitted an application for the same patent a mere week before they did.

Ever responsible, Josh decided he'd do everything in his power to save the business. So he bought a last-minute ticket to Kansas City, Missouri, to confront the engineering firm and prove they'd stolen the plans. Noah wished him well, then went on a bender, never once thinking his goody-two-shoes brother could pull it off.

Less than twelve hours later, Josh called to say he'd not only met one of the partners in the rival firm, but he was currently pretending to be his daughter's fiancé. All in an effort to get closer to the firm and find proof of their wrongdoing.

Noah hopped on a plane the next morning, expecting to bail his squeaky-clean brother out of his unsavory situation. Instead, Noah teamed up with one of the bride-to-be's best friends in an effort to keep the couple together. Granted, he and Libby had started off with completely different motivations. Libby claimed Megan and Josh were perfect for each other, while Noah's sole purpose was to keep them together for as long as it took to get evidence implicating Megan's father's firm.

But soon two things became glaringly obvious. One, Josh had somehow fallen head-over-heels in love with the girl after only a few days, and two, Libby St. Clair was different than any other woman Noah had ever met. Sure, he was intrigued for all the normal reasons the first time he saw her walk into Megan's parents' house. Even a blind man could see Libby was gorgeous. It was hard to look away from her long dark hair, her rich brown eyes, and her clear olive skin. But he'd already pissed Josh off a thousand ways to Sunday; he wasn't going to risk losing him for good by hooking up with his fake fiancée's best friend. Not that Libby would have hooked up with him anyway. She made it abundantly clear that she had a boyfriend, albeit a mostly absent one. Not that she seemed to mind. But because of their mutual goal, Noah and Libby spent enough time together before the wedding to become real friends.

After Noah went back to Seattle, he was surprised to realize he missed her. So after he thought up a lame excuse, he called her, thankful when she seemed genuinely happy to hear from him. It would be the first of many near-daily calls over the next four months.

Josh's efforts were a success. The McMillan brothers not only saved their firm, but they arranged for a merger with Megan's father's office. Josh began traveling to Kansas City, but he hated leaving his new wife at home, and Megan was running out of vacation time to travel with him. The couple had decided to move back to Megan's hometown, but in the meantime, Noah started taking the trips in his brother's place. Even more surprising—he loved the added responsibility.

And then there was all the extra time he got to spend with Libby.

No one understood their relationship, not that he blamed them. Hell, some days he didn't understand it himself. A year ago, if someone had told him he'd be friends without benefits with a sexy-as-hell woman who drew the eyes of every man she walked past, well, there was no way he'd believe it.

Then one day Libby called Noah after a disagreement with Mitch. They talked for over two hours—something Noah had never done with any other woman, whether he was sleeping with her or not. Both were under the influence at the time. Libby had been drinking wine to drown her sorrows; Noah had been drinking beer to quiet his inner demons.

"We should hook up, Lib," he said, gaining liquid courage from the three beers running through his bloodstream. "We're perfect for each other."

She was silent for so long he thought she'd either passed out or hung up on him, but she finally answered. "That's a terrible idea, Noah."

The sharp stab of pain from her rejection surprised him. "How can you say that? Look how well we get along."

"And that's exactly why we shouldn't," she said emphatically. "You're probably the best friend I've ever had. I don't want to lose you."

"But you wouldn't lose me. You'd just get more benefits," he teased in a sultry voice.

"And what would happen after we break up?"

"Hey! We haven't even had sex yet. Why are you already talking about us breaking up?"

"What's the longest you've ever had a girlfriend?"

"Uh . . ." Did he really want to confess that it was shorter than it took bread to grow mold?

"My point exactly," she said. Yet he could swear there was a thread of disappointment in her voice.

"You're telling me that you're not attracted to me?" he asked in disbelief. She had to realize there was some kind of sexual tension between them, even if they'd both chosen to ignore it. He'd almost kissed her dozens of times. And sometimes he caught her looking at him with a hungry glint in her eyes.

"Obviously I'm attracted to you," she said. "Only a dead woman wouldn't be attracted to you. But what we have is special. Do you really want to throw it away for cheap sex?"

He laughed. "I'll have you know that sex with me is not cheap. In fact, a few women have offered to pay to get with this."

"Whatever, *stud muffin*. You know I'm right."

Unfortunately, he did.

Still, he wasn't prepared for her phone call two days later.

"I'm getting married!"

His angry "You're *what?*" slipped out before he could stop himself.

"Mitch and I are getting married in a month." The defiance in her tone was unmistakable.

"A month? What the hell are you thinking, Libby?"

"Megan and Josh were married after knowing each other for only four days. I've been with Mitch for six months. Why shouldn't we get married?"

"How about because you called me two days ago telling me what an ass he is."

"It was a fight, Noah. If you stayed in a relationship long enough to discover what type of toothpaste the girl uses, you might understand."

He knew what type of toothpaste *she* used, and a whole lot of other things besides, but he decided now wasn't a good time to bring that up. Still, he wasn't sure how to handle the swirling emotions in his head, let alone put a name to them. "What do you want me to do, Libby? Tell you congratulations?"

"That's the typical response, Noah," she spat out.

"*Congratulations.*"

"That didn't sound very convincing."

"You have to give me a damn minute to catch up, okay?" His chest tightened as he moved to the fridge and pulled out a beer.

"It's been ten seconds."

"I said a damn *minute*."

"How is a damn minute different from a regular one?"

A grin cracked his mouth, despite his turmoil. No one could rein him back from his emotional spirals like Libby could. He realized he had two choices: he could give her his blessing, or he could continue down the path of belligerence and possibly lose her forever. But he had to give it one more try. "Are you sure, Lib?" He lowered his voice. "I don't think he deserves you."

"Listen to you," she teased. "You're like the big brother I never had."

That only increased his turmoil. *Big brother?* Did she really see him that way? "I'm serious, Libby. Don't you want what Megan and Josh have?"

"Who says I don't?"

A rush of anger flooded his head, burning his filter to ash. "Are you serious? You can't possibly believe what you have with that guy is love! He's more enamored with football than he is with you!"

"I can't believe you just said that!"

"The proof is right in front of you, Libby. Hell, you spend more time with me than you do with him and I live two thousand miles away."

"Then maybe I should spend less time with you!"

"Most normal women who actually *loved* their fiancés would."

She hung up on him then, and he stewed in his sorrow and

unease, telling himself that he'd call her the next day to apologize and they'd be fine. And as far as her impending marriage went, surely her two friends would help her see the light. Noah might not be an expert on love, but he *knew* Libby didn't really love Mitch. How could she when the guy was so obsessed with football? According to Libby, Mitch had a room in his apartment stuffed so full with football paraphernalia, he could star in an episode of one of those hoarder shows. What semi-intelligent man could be with Libby St. Clair without being infatuated to the point of distraction over *her*?

The next morning he called her as soon as he was sure she'd be awake.

"Lib, I'm sorry. I said some things I wish I could take back." He was surprised by how easily the apology rolled off his tongue. The first apology he could remember making was the one he'd been forced to give to his mean next-door neighbor after cutting her flowers to make his mother a bouquet. He was four at the time. Apologies had been soured for him ever since. But while he hadn't been sorry about the neighbor lady's flowers, he did regret hurting Libby. She was the very last person he wanted to hurt.

Libby didn't respond for several seconds, and his heart thudded against his ribcage. Had he pushed her too far? Finally, she cleared her throat. "I want you to be in the wedding."

"*What?*" *Rein it in, Noah.* He couldn't lose control again. He softened his tone, then joked, "I'm warning you I won't wear a tacky rayon dress. I'm more of a silk guy."

"Very funny," she chuckled, but it wasn't her genuine laugh—the one that made him feel good inside just from hearing it. "You'll be one of the groomsmen."

"Does Mitch know about this?"

"He thinks it's a great idea."

That didn't surprise him. Mitch was one of the most laid back, albeit clueless, guys he had ever met.

"So? Will you?"

"Sure." Not that he ever expected the wedding to take place. Libby had stepped up twice to keep her friends from making mistakes with their marriages. They owed her big time, and surely they would see what he did—that while Mitch was a good guy, he wasn't the type who could snare Libby's heart.

Only it didn't happen that way.

When Noah brought it up to Josh at the office a week later, Josh played it off. "Megan and Libby had a good heart-to-heart talk, and Megan thinks Libby's happy."

Noah frowned. "She's taking Libby's two years of acting in college into account, right?"

Josh had looked up from his computer. "Why would she pretend to be happy? Especially when she was so adamant about making sure Megan and Blair made the right choices."

Noah shook his head. "I've heard her mention something about getting married before her thirtieth birthday. Her birthday is next month. Maybe she's feeling the pressure."

"Libby? Feeling *social* pressure? Not likely." Josh laughed. "If anything, it's that stupid curse nonsense."

Noah perked up. "What curse nonsense?"

Josh shrugged. "Megan mentioned it right after our wedding. Something about Libby believing all three of them were cursed to have disastrous weddings."

"What does that have to do with her getting married before her birthday?"

He gave Noah an ornery grin. "I confess, my attention was on other things when Megan told me, so a lot of the details escaped me."

22

Noah cringed. "TMI, dude."

"Really? This from the king of TMI? How many of your exploits have I been forced to hear about?"

"That was different. Megan's my sister-in-law."

Josh gave him a look of surprise, then continued. "Like I said, I don't remember a lot of the details, but I *do* know Libby totally believes in it."

Noah sucked in a breath, trying to quell his brewing nausea. "I don't know, Josh. I have a really bad feeling about this."

Josh's gaze narrowed. "Maybe you need to take a good look at why you have that feeling."

"What do you mean by that?"

"Maybe you need to examine your *own* life."

Here he was trying to save his friend from making the biggest mistake of her life and Josh was using it as yet another opportunity to point out what a screw-up he was. He started to walk away, but Josh called after him.

"How's the Abrahams account coming?"

So Josh really *didn't* trust him. Noah stopped in his tracks and turned to face his brother. "Great. I have a meeting with Scott next week."

"You're sure you've got this? I know you went to college with him, but I can help if you need me to intervene."

Noah tried to stifle his irritation. He couldn't really blame Josh for being cautious. After all, he had spent the better part of a decade trying to do as little as possible. Still, it sucked to be treated like a preschooler, even if he deserved it. "I think we're good."

Josh lowered his voice. "Look, Noah. We need that account. Bad. You know that, right?"

"*I know.*"

"If you get into any trouble, you'll let me know?"

"Sure," he said, still distracted by Libby and her engagement.

That night he went out with a couple of friends and met Donna at a bar. She was with several friends who joined his group. While it wasn't exactly unusual that he went home with her, he surprised himself by asking for her number and telling her he wanted to see her again.

In a way, Josh was right. Libby's impending marriage had made him realize how empty his life was. Now that she was preparing for her wedding—or more likely because of their disagreement—she no longer called him as frequently, which made him acutely aware that once she was married, he would hear from her even less. Her absence left an ache in his soul, and his typical one-night stands weren't going to fill it. Donna was conventionally pretty and model-thin—the polar opposite of Libby's exotic beauty and hourglass figure. And while Donna was a little clueless about some things, she was actually a nice woman he could take home to meet his mother.

Everyone who knew him was shocked that he'd kept a woman in his life for more than a few weeks, and while he wasn't as over-the-moon happy as Josh, he was trying to be content. For the first time in a long while, he felt like maybe he could stop blustering and be happy. But that wasn't entirely true. Libby was the one who'd made him feel that way, not Donna.

Maybe it just took time.

As Libby's wedding drew closer, Noah became more and more anxious, and Donna became more and more of a bitch over his friendship with Libby.

Noah was supposed to fly out two days before the wedding, but Scott Abrahams was a hard man to pin down. He'd postponed their meeting until Friday afternoon, forcing Noah to move his flight to the day of the wedding. But five minutes before they were supposed to meet, Abrahams called to cancel.

"Noah, you know I like your plans, but I'm meeting with someone else next week. I'll be honest—I'll probably sign with them."

Noah's stomach dropped. "Scott, I'd be more than happy to go over the schematics with you over drinks."

"I trust your schematics, and I know we go way back, but I think I can get a better deal. No hard feelings. It's just business."

He hung up before Noah could press him for more details.

Noah felt like he was going to be sick. How was he going to explain this to Josh? His brother was definitely going to blame him for losing the job. He considered waiting until after the wedding to tell him, but that's what the old Noah would do. The new Noah was taking charge. He called his brother before he could change his mind.

"That was fast," Josh said.

"There's a reason."

"He didn't sign." Josh's voice was flat.

"He canceled the meeting."

"What happened?"

The accusation in Josh's voice stiffened Noah's back. "Why does it sound like you think I fucked this up?"

"Well, did you?"

"What the hell, Josh? You know I've been busting my ass to get this deal." Still, some inner voice taunted him. *You must have fucked it up. You know Josh would have closed the deal without a problem.*

That voice only pissed him off more.

Josh groaned in frustration. "I knew I should have sat in on some of the meetings."

Noah's irritation only grew. "You don't think I can handle a meeting?"

"I'm sure you can when drinks are involved."

"So now you're accusing me of being a drunk *and* a slacker."

"You have to admit, you've fit both descriptions in the past."

"If that's really what you think of me, why the hell am I even working there?"

"Because your name's on the damn building!"

And that was the crux of it. Noah had never wanted to take the helm of the engineering firm, but after their father's death, it was just expected of him. He'd barely managed to hold it together until Josh took over, even if he'd fooled everyone else into thinking management was easy for him. Of course, he could have left then, but instead he'd coasted along, reasoning that the business owed him for single-handedly running things for a while. But then again, he had no idea what else to do.

Maybe this was the push he needed.

"Then take my damn name off, because I quit!"

Before Josh could say something else in that condescending tone, Noah hung up.

Now what the hell was he going to do?

Since he'd remained in town—apparently for no reason—Donna came over to his apartment for dinner. And since he was leaving for Libby's wedding the next day, she was bitchier than usual. To make matters worse, over the last couple of weeks she'd appointed herself his life coach. She'd started a freelance life coaching business and slowly began offering him unsolicited advice until it had increased to an annoying intensity. Tonight she dusted off her list of the areas of his life he needed to improve to find inner peace—his apartment was too small; his car was too old; his job too financially limiting. Her list was insulting, but her passive-aggressive approach made it easier for him to ignore. "Noah, don't you think you'd be happier if you talked to Terry, my stockbroker friend, about applying for that opening in his firm? You'd make so much more money."

The combination of losing the account, his fight with Josh, and the feeling of impending doom that surrounded him like a noxious cloud had him so utterly miserable he couldn't help wondering if she was right. Maybe his life really did need an overhaul.

After dinner he was emotionally beat-up, but he couldn't let the Abrahams deal go without a fight. Even if it *was* time to stop working with his brother, he wanted to just this once prove he was capable of something other than screwing up. He sat through as much of Donna's lame rom-com as he could bear before he hid in the bathroom to call Cal, his friend from college who had stayed in contact with both Noah and Scott Abrahams.

"Sorry to bother you on a Friday night, Cal, but do you happen to know if Scott Abrahams still has that cute secretary? The one he's sleeping with? Terry . . . Tobi . . ."

"Ahh . . . Tiffany." Noah heard the smile in his voice. "Yeah, she's still there, although I think she's about to cut him loose. Scott says she's been giving him grief about not leaving his wife."

Perfect. "You don't happen to have her number, do you? Or know her last name?"

Cal laughed. "You probably picked a good time to make a play for her. I don't have her number, but I know her last name is Brown."

"That's nearly totally unhelpful."

"She went to college at Oregon State."

"She went to *college*?" Noah always assumed she'd landed her position on the basis of her physical appearance alone.

Cal laughed again. "She quit her sophomore year. She's on Facebook. Look her up there."

"Will do. Thanks."

"Noah!" Donna shouted from the living room. "Did you fall in the toilet?"

"No, coming." He flushed to corroborate his cover story and ran the water in the sink before returning to the living room. He considered searching for Tiffany on his phone, but how was he going to explain to Donna why he was looking up another woman on Facebook? That would likely get him strapped to a burning stake. He'd have to wait.

"Are you even listening to me?" Donna asked, sounding huffy, as he sat down next to her on the couch.

"What?"

"You're busy thinking about *her* again. Did you go hide in the bathroom to call *her*?"

It took him a second to realize she was talking about Libby. Ironically enough, the last fifteen minutes had probably been the longest length of time in days that he'd gone without thinking about *her*. The realization only adding to his growing tempest of anxiety.

"You're either with me or you're not, Noah."

This had also been a repeated topic of discussion between them. He wrapped an arm around her back and pulled her close. "Donna, you're the one I want, sweetheart. I'm here, aren't I?"

"Only because you had that stupid meeting with that stupid man."

She knew how important the meeting had been, yet she'd

never once asked about it. But this was how normal people functioned, right? He didn't remember his dad going home and discussing the specifics of *his* job. Normal people had responsible jobs and significant others. But he couldn't help thinking that if he and Libby were still close, it would have been the first thing she would have asked him. Noah suddenly had a craving for *something more*. He'd convinced himself that normal was what he wanted. What Josh had. But if this was it, was it really enough?

"I mean it, Noah," she pouted. "It's not normal for a guy to be friends with a girl."

"Hey, all those people did it on *Friends*."

Her eyebrows lowered into a scowl. "They all ended up sleeping with each other like some exotic swingers club."

Noah wondered how he'd missed the X-rated version of the series—and where he could find it—but he suspected she wouldn't appreciate the question. "Why does it have to be either or?" he asked in frustration as he jumped to his feet, his anxiety rising to an all-time high. He didn't need this in addition to everything else. "Why can't I be friends with her and have you too?"

"It doesn't work that way."

"If you met her, I'm sure you'd change your mind. Come to the wedding with me tomorrow. I'll buy you a ticket." He wasn't sure where that had come from, but now that he'd said it, it seemed like a good next step in their relationship. It would show her that she had nothing to worry about, that he was in this for real.

She shook her head vehemently. "No. No way. In fact, if you go to that wedding, you and I are done."

His eyes widened. "*What?*"

Rising from the couch, she planted her hands on her hips,

her lips pursed like she was trying out for some lipstick commercial.

"Donna, I'm *in* the fucking wedding! I *have* to go!" But even as he said the words, he realized how much he really didn't *want* to go.

"It's her or me, Noah." Then she stomped out of his apartment.

Noah was torn. He really wanted to be there for Libby, but he wasn't sure he could bear to watch her exchange vows with the world's biggest Arkansas Razorbacks fan. Not to mention the fact that he had no desire to see his brother. He was sick to death of people believing the worst of him, especially since he was trying so hard to change. Besides, if he broke up with Donna, he'd be drowned in a chorus of *I told you so*. He wasn't sure he could handle that on top of the rawness he felt about Libby's impending marriage.

So after a long sleepless night, he texted Josh the next morning and told him something with Donna had come up and he wasn't coming. He worried about hurting Libby, but she was marrying Mitch, the man she claimed to love. Why would she care if he came or not? She'd made her choice; it was time for him to worry about his own love life.

Donna . . . he could do this. He could be in a long-term committed relationship. He just needed to make more of an effort. He picked up his phone and called her, mulling over the idea of asking her to move into his apartment. Wasn't that what couples did when they took things to the next level?

"Did you decide?" she asked in a snotty tone when she answered.

"I'm not going."

"Wise choice, McMillan." Her voice took on a husky tone. "I'll be right over."

He made a pot of coffee, wondering when he should ask her to move in. After they had sex or before?

But when he opened the door for her, apprehension sucked his breath away. Could he really spend the rest of his life with someone who only wanted him if he met the requirements of some checklist? Someone who'd asked him to cut off a close friend? Someone, he suddenly realized, he barely tolerated? He'd rather be alone and dateless for the rest of his life.

But something even more shocking hit him and the realization nearly knocked him over. He didn't want to build a life with just anyone.

He wanted it with Libby—and only Libby.

He had to get to Kansas City and stop the wedding.

Noah put a hand on the doorframe, blocking her entry. "I made a mistake."

"I know." She batted her eyelashes. "And you rectified it, so let me in." She opened her trench coat, revealing a sexy outfit of black lingerie. He felt absolutely nothing, which only strengthened his resolve.

"No. I don't think you understand." Why had he been such an idiot? "Choosing *you* was the mistake. I'm sorry, Donna, we're *done*."

She dropped the hold on her coat, her lingerie still exposed as she put her hands on her nonexistent hips. "Think long and hard about this, Noah McMillan. You're never going to amount to anything without me. I was probably your one last chance to make something of yourself."

Maybe she was right, but he was willing to take that chance. "Then I guess I'll be the low-life slacker I was meant to be, because I'm done." Then he shut the door on her stunned face.

How had he been such a fool?

He ran to his bedroom to throw some clothes in a suitcase and grab the bag with his rented tux. He hadn't canceled his flight, and if he hurried, he could still make it there in time to stop her from making the worst mistake of her life.

Thankfully, Donna had left by the time he ran to his car and sped to the airport . . . only to discover his flight was delayed. While he waited, he opened his Facebook app and found a Tiffany Brown who lived in Seattle, went to Oregon State, worked for Scott Abrahams, and was in a relationship labeled "it's complicated." He sent her a friend request, knowing it was a long shot, in the hopes she could give him inside info about Scott Abrahams and the competition.

After a delay on the ground, the plane touched down three hours late, which meant the wedding was due to start in just half an hour. But when he tried to call Lib to tell her he was coming and to hold off going down the aisle until he got there, he realized his phone was dead. The night before had been so intense, he'd forgotten to charge it.

The rental car process seemed to take forever, especially since he had to take a shuttle to get there, but he finally headed out, following sketchy directions from the rental car agent, who looked all of fifteen. Amazingly enough, the directions were good, and when he saw the church up ahead, he went over his options. It was 5:15, which meant the wedding had already started. Maybe he could go inside and object, like everyone had done at Blair's wedding.

He'd boarded the plane with the aim of interrupting the wedding, but now he couldn't help wondering what Libby would do if he objected. Would she be relieved? Would she kill him?

He pulled into the parking lot and discovered the decision had been made for him. Libby was running out the church doors, Megan and Blair hot on her heels. Noah slowed down and drove toward them, his heart in his throat.

Then Libby bolted again, running straight for his car. He hit the unlock button, watching in disbelief as she threw her bouquet into the crowd and then opened his passenger door. The sudden frenzy of women vying for the flowers reminded him of feeding time in a shark tank. Amazingly enough, Megan's gram was front and center.

The door opened and Libby scrambled into the passenger seat. The crowd streaming out of the church was growing by the second, and Mitch stood in front of all of them like he was their disgraced quarterback.

She kept her eyes on the crowd as she shut the door. "I'll pay you a hundred dollars if you get me out of here *right now.*"

She was here. In his car. And from the look on Mitch's face, she wasn't married.

"Only a hundred?" he asked, purposely trying to keep his tone light. "My plane ticket cost more than that."

Libby sucked in a breath and turned to look at him, anger in her eyes.

Oh. Shit.

Chapter Three

Noah's grin faltered, probably because he realized he was in deep shit. But getting away took precedence. She could kill him later.

Mitch raced toward the car, and even the older guests had streamed out onto the lawn. "Libby!"

Panic spiked her pulse. "What are you waiting for? *Go!*"

The car lurched forward and the tires squealed on the asphalt. "Where are we going?" he asked, clearly confused.

"I don't care!" she shouted. "*Just drive!*"

He barely stopped at the street corner before skidding around it.

Oh, God. What had she done?

"Libby?" he asked, sounding worried. "What happened?"

"Shhhhhhh!" she hissed loudly, covering her face with her hands. "Just give me a minute."

Thankfully, he knew her well enough to keep quiet.

What the hell had she been thinking? Why had she been so certain the stupid curse would work for her? Megan and Blair had been right. It was a coincidence that both of their love stories fit the fortune teller's prophecy. Nothing more. Nothing less.

She was a fool.

And now, because of her idiocy, she'd wasted several thousand dollars, broken Mitch's heart, and humiliated herself in front of a hundred people.

She'd done plenty of stupid things in her day—like the time she ran off to Monte Carlo with a mechanic who swore he was becoming a Formula One racer, only to return a week later with a sunburn and a seven-thousand-dollar balance on her Visa card. Or the time she was arrested for painting a mural with amazing anatomical detail of her ex-boyfriend's penis, right down to the bump near his testicle, on the side of his new girlfriend's house—but she wasn't so sure she'd live this one down.

"Where to, Lib?" Noah asked, his concern evident.

Where to? She couldn't go home and face all those wedding presents stacked in the corner of her living room. She couldn't face her friends, or God forbid, her mother. She definitely couldn't face Mitch, although she owed him the apology of all apologies, and it still wouldn't be enough.

The truth was, there was nowhere she could go that would make her feel any better than she felt right now in this car. It felt like the entire world had melted away, leaving behind only her and Noah, the one person she could trust to understand.

"Just keep going."

"Okay."

His warm hand covered hers, and that simple comfort brought tears to her eyes.

She blinked them back.

There would be no tears allowed for her stupidity. She leaned her head back on the seat and closed her eyes. She'd had several sleepless nights, so the lull of the car soon had her dozing.

"Libby."

"Hmm?" Something dark and heavy pressed on her mind, but how could it when she was with Noah? Noah always seemed to lift her burdens.

"I'm hungry. Let's eat."

She opened her eyes and gasped when she realized it was now dark and they were parked in front of a café.

Then the whole nightmare came rushing back.

"Where are we?"

"The exit sign said Junction City, Kansas."

"What?" She looked around, taking in the sight of cars in the lot and the street behind her. "How did we get here?"

He lifted his shoulders into a lazy shrug. "You said to keep driving. So I did."

She slumped back in the seat. What did it matter where she was? As long as she wasn't staring into the face of her humiliation. But apparently Junction City wasn't far enough, because it was still there, staring back.

"Come on," Noah said. "I'm hungry."

She sat up straight and turned to face him. "You want me to go in there?" She pointed to the restaurant. "Dressed like this?" She waved her hand up and down the front of her sleeveless silk dress. Beading and sparkles covered the edge of her sweetheart neckline and the skirt flared at her waist, creating a sea of crinoline and silk around her.

He shrugged. "I told you. I'm hungry." Then he opened the car door and walked around the back of the car and opened her door.

She glared up at him. "Go to a fast-food drive-thru."

"No. I'm tired of driving, and you have a bladder the size of a thimble. I know you have to pee."

She *did* have to pee, but there was no way she was going inside. "I can't go in there wearing a wedding dress!"

He leaned his forearm on top of her door. "Sure you can. You'll give them a thrill that they'll talk about for years. That makes you a giver. Come on."

"*No.* I've endured enough public humiliation for one day."

He slid his arm off the door and squatted in front of her. "I don't know what happened, and I want to hear about it as soon as you're ready. But don't think I forgot the stories you told me about your college days. The Libby St. Clair I know didn't bat an eye about walking into a restaurant wearing a boa, a bikini, and a tiara. Wearing a wedding dress is way classier than that."

She scowled. There was that look on his face, the one that told her any argument would be wasted breath. "You're going to make me go in there, aren't you?"

An ornery grin spread across his face. "Let's just say you're going in one way or another." He winked. "If you make me pick you up, I'll put you in a fireman's hold and tell everyone I'm carrying you over the threshold."

She groaned as she climbed out of the car. "I hate you. You're an ass."

His grin spread. "Many women find it endearing."

"Name one." She picked up her skirt so it didn't touch the dirty sidewalk, although she wasn't sure why it mattered now.

"Well, there was Christy last week, and Tina the week before that."

"What about *Donna?*" The thought of his girlfriend stirred

anger in her gut, catching her by surprise. "Aren't you supposed to back in Seattle taking care of her *thing*? Isn't that why you couldn't come to my wedding?"

"Wow. You're in rare form." He moved around her and opened the door to the restaurant. "Somebody must be hangry," he teased.

"I'm not *hangry*. Apparently, *you* are." She walked through the door and stopped in front of the hostess stand. "I have to pee."

The teenage hostess had a phone pressed to her ear. Her eyes widened at the sight of Libby's dress and she muttered, "I've gotta go," into the receiver. She hung up and stared at them for a long moment, her mouth hanging open. This was proof enough of the odd pair they made right now—Noah in his jeans, tight-fitting olive-green T-shirt, and athletic shoes, and Libby in her ridiculously opulent dress. And it was all the confirmation she needed that this was, in fact, a terrible idea. She started to turn around, but Noah grabbed her shoulders and turned her back to face the hostess.

"We need a table for two," Noah said, wrapping an arm around her back and holding her firmly in place. "Something romantic if you have it. It's her wedding night."

Libby jerked her gaze up to meet his. He only grinned.

"And you're eating at *the Golden Cowboy Café*?" the hostess asked in disbelief.

"Well . . . yeah," Noah said. "Libby here has been talking about it ever since she heard about this place. She wanted to forgo the reception and drive straight from the wedding in Kansas City to the Golden Café."

"Golden *Cowboy* Café," Libby corrected, still grumpy.

"See?" Noah held out his hands. "But first she has to pee."

"The restroom's that way." The hostess pointed to a short

hall close to the entrance.

Moments after she entered the restroom, Libby realized she had a dilemma on her hands—there was no way she could maneuver her dress on her own in the tiny stall, and even if she wanted to take it off, which she didn't, it was laced up the back.

Groaning, she peeked out the bathroom door. "Noah."

He stood in the hall, his back against the wall. When he turned toward her, her breath seemed to stick in her throat. How many times had she looked at him, up close and personal even, but this was the first time he'd taken her breath away. She knew other women found him attractive—how could they not? His dark brown hair was slightly unruly, giving him a just-out-of-bed look, and his long-lashed dark brown eyes were usually sparkling with mischief. But now—tonight—there was something different about him.

He raised his eyebrows, and she remembered he was waiting for her to tell him why she'd called him. She resisted the urge to close the door and hide. What if he realized she was checking him out? He'd never let her forget it.

"I need help," she forced herself to say.

Confusion flickered in his eyes. "How so?"

She cringed. God, this was embarrassing. "I can't deal with this skirt." She lifted handfuls of the full fabric and then dropped it to demonstrate its bulkiness.

Fear replaced confusion in his eyes. "What do you want me to do about it?"

"I need you to hold this up so I can pee."

He took a step back. "You want me to do what?"

She reached for him. "Get over yourself and help me before I pee myself. And if you dare to try and tell me it's *my* problem, just remember you'll have to ride in the car with my

39

pee-soaked skirts."

He rushed over and pushed her back into the bathroom. "What do you need me to do?"

She laughed at how quickly he was moving now. "I don't know exactly how to do this. We'll have to wing it."

"You didn't pee earlier?"

"No, I held it, which is why I really have to pee now. Aren't you the one who said I had a thimble-sized bladder?"

"Well, yeah . . ."

She turned to face him, her back to a stall door. "I'll back up and lift the skirt in the back with one hand and you hold it up in the front."

"Aren't you worried I'll see something down there?"

She snorted. "It's highly unlikely, given the fact you'll have about ten yards of crinoline in your face."

"Why are you only using one hand to hold up the skirt?"

"So I can pull down my panties. What's with all the questions? My bladder sphincter's about to give out."

He squeezed his eyes shut. "That's disgusting."

"Hey, it's biology. Let's do this." She backed up, pushing the door open as she reached around her back. "Why aren't you lifting?"

He looked startled as he followed her into the stall. "I didn't know we were lifting yet."

"Well, we are! Do it!"

He grabbed handfuls and started tugging upward. "Why are you still standing?"

"I can't see the damn toilet beneath all of this crinoline. And I'm having trouble reaching my underwear."

She could barely make out his expression from all the fabric in her face, but a sly grin lit up his eyes. "Lucky for you, I'm an expert at removing women's panties. I volunteer as tribute."

"You have your job, and I have mine."

He shrugged playfully. "Just sayin'."

Libby reached under her skirt and got her panties to her knees, but she felt unbalanced as she started to lower herself to the seat. "I'm afraid I'm going to miss."

"You think you're going to pee on my foot?" he asked in horror.

"No! I'm afraid I'm not going to land on the toilet. What if I miss the seat?"

"You've got to be kidding me. This stall is barely wide enough to hold the toilet. How could you miss it?"

She put one forearm on the side of the stall and inched herself down.

"What the hell are you doing?" he asked. Now that she was in a crouched position, she could no longer see his face.

"I told you. I'm trying to find the damn toilet."

"Would you hurry already? Someone's going to walk in here and think I'm some pervert molesting a bride."

"And this *bothers* you . . . ?" Her voice trailed off suggestively as she connected with the toilet seat. "Mission accomplished."

"You've peed already?"

"No. I'm on the toilet seat."

"You haven't even started *peeing*?" His voice rose in dismay.

"I'm working on it."

Libby heard the bathroom door hinges squeak open, then Noah's voice. "Oh, hello. Don't mind me."

The door slapped shut in an instant.

Libby released a chuckle.

Noah chuckled. "I think we traumatized that poor woman. Are you finished?"

"No. I haven't even started yet."

"*Why the hell not?*"

"You're listening! I can't pee knowing you're going to hear it."

"What the hell do you want me to do? Cover my ears? I can't exactly do that without letting go of your dress!"

"Then hum. Or sing."

"What do you expect me to sing?" he asked in disbelief.

"I don't know!" she groaned. "How about ninety-nine bottles of beer on the wall?"

"If I sing the damn song will you pee already?"

"Yes. Do it. This is getting painful."

He groaned, but then began to sing. "*Ninety-nine bottles of beer on the wall, ninety-nine bottles of beer.*"

Libby felt herself relax and began to pee.

"*Take one down, pass it around—*" He stopped singing. "Oh, my God. I think you've ruined beer for me forever."

"You're listening to me *pee?*" she shrieked.

The door opened again, and this time Noah oozed in a pseudo-cultured voice, "Good evening. I'm the Golden Cowboy Café bathroom attendant, and I'll be happy to help you with your personal hygiene needs as soon as I'm done with the current customer."

There was a several-second pause, the sound of the swooshing door, and then Noah said, "That's the second woman who has run off in horror. If I get arrested, you better bail me out."

"Unfortunately for you, I don't have any money . . . or toilet paper." She felt along the wall of the stall. "I think this stall is out, but my dress is hiding the dispenser anyway."

"What do you want *me* to do about it? I'm holding up the front end."

"Do you want me to drip dry?" she asked, annoyed.

"That's what I do!" he protested.

"Newsflash, Noah. I can't just give it a tiny shake and be done with it. That's not how the female anatomy works."

"I'm very familiar with the female anatomy." The door hinges squeaked again. "Oh, hello, ma'am. That's not as bad as it sounds, but while you're here, could I ask a small favor? Would you mind reaching into that stall and grabbing us some toilet paper? The bride can't find hers."

"Are you in some kind of trouble, dear?" a phlegmy voice asked. "Is this some kind of sex-slave kidnapping? Were you forced to marry an old man against your will?"

"Old man?" Noah asked in horror.

Libby tried to push down her rising giggles. "No, ma'am. I'm just a regular bride trying to pee."

"In the Golden Cowboy Café bathroom?"

Libby rolled her eyes, though she was aware the effect was lost on her audience. "Do you think you could grab some toilet paper for me? Noah's hands are full and I don't think I have any in here."

"The Sizzler has nicer bathrooms." The door to the next stall banged into the wall.

"The next time I get married and go out for steak while still in my wedding dress, I'll keep that in mind."

"Oh, dear," the woman said. "I hope you're not one of those polygamists."

"No, ma'am," Libby said. "I couldn't even handle one marriage. I think society is safe from any matrimonial deviancy from me."

Noah's hand reached over the top of her sea of silk and crinoline, handing her the toilet paper.

"Well, good luck, dear," the woman called out, then her voice tightened in disapproval. "And you, young man. The least you could do is take your bride somewhere decent to eat. The Chinese buffet is just down the street."

"I'll keep that in mind," Noah said in a chastised tone, echoing Libby's previous statement. Several seconds later, he addressed Libby in a whisper, "Are you done yet?"

She stood, careful to keep the back of her skirt from touching the toilet. "I'm done; now back up so I can get out." Her dress tugged her forward as Noah started to lower the skirt and she laughed when she saw his horrified face.

"Can we get out of here now?"

"I have to wash my hands first." She glanced over her shoulder at him as she made her way to the sink. "Personal hygiene. But then maybe you don't think you need to wash after your little shake." She winked at him in the mirror as she turned on the water.

"I'll have you know it's more than a *little* shake."

She laughed.

"I suddenly feel the need to affirm my manhood."

"The size of your shake has nothing to do with your manhood."

He moved behind her, lightly pressing his chest to her back. "I'll have you know it has *everything* to do with my manhood."

"Too bad for you, I'll never have it confirmed," she teased.

A few days before she proposed to Mitch, Noah had suggested a change in their relationship. She'd refused, but not because the offer wasn't tempting. In truth, she'd considered sleeping with him months ago, right after they first met. But she was with Mitch at the time, so she and Noah became friends instead. Now she marveled at everything she would have missed if she'd given in to her initial lust—the late-night talks about nothing and everything. The long walks in the park with her dog Tortoise. All the things she'd never done with a boyfriend.

Their friendship was more intimate and wonderful than any of her other relationships, but she knew who she was—and who he was, for that matter—and there was no way they could introduce sex to their friendship without ruining it. What they had was worth more than a few days—or months, at best—of what was sure to be amazing sex. But knowing it and accepting it were two different things.

When she turned off the water and reached for a paper towel, she caught his reflection in the mirror, and from the look on his face, she wondered if he was waging the same war.

Chapter Four

"Finally done?" Noah asked. "Let's eat."

Libby shook her head in disbelief. "You seriously still want to eat here?"

"Of course. I didn't do all of this just to get back in the car."

"Noah."

"Get moving." He opened the door to the hall, then grabbed her elbow and guided her out the door. He released his hold as they walked to the hostess stand.

Still wide-eyed, the hostess grabbed two menus. "You're still here. I thought this was one of those TV shows. Especially with all those women running out of the bathroom."

"Nope, just us," Noah said. "And we're starving, but remember, we'd appreciate something romantic."

"Follow me."

They walked through the Western-themed restaurant,

drawing the attention of every guest and wait staff in the joint. Noah waved to one family and then pointed at Libby, lifting his eyebrows in a *can you believe this* look.

Libby smacked his arm. "Stop that!"

"What? I told you that you'd be the talk of the restaurant. It's like being in a parade."

"Then maybe you should go see the Cotton Bowl Parade with Mitch." As soon as the words left her mouth, she regretted them. The mention of her fiancé's name—ex-fiancé's name—reminded her of her selfishness as well as her public humiliation.

The hostess stopped and motioned to a corner booth. The seat back was dark stained beadboard and a lantern with a candle sat in the middle of the round table. She turned to Noah and grimaced. "This is the most romantic table I have."

His grin spread from ear to ear. "It's perfect." He motioned for Libby to slide in and she glared up at him, waiting for him to change his mind. But his grin widened even more. Rolling her eyes, she surrendered, and he scooted around the opposite side.

The hostess placed their menus on the table. "Can I get you anything to drink?"

"He'll have a beer," Libby said with saccharine sweetness, remembering his earlier comment in the bathroom.

The hostess shook her head. "Sorry. We don't serve alcohol."

Noah shuddered. "Thank God. I'll have a water."

Libby couldn't resist a small grin. "Water too, please."

The young woman looked eager to get away. "Your waitress will be right with you."

"You frightened that poor girl," Libby said, trying to ignore all the people staring at them.

"Why? Because I cringed when you ordered a *beer*?"

"No! Me. This dress. You coming on so strong."

"Please," he scowled good-naturedly. "Why would someone be afraid of a wedding dress? I wrestled it and lived to tell the tale. Now you . . . you're on the cranky side tonight. She's probably frightened of *you*."

"I'm entitled to be cranky! I ran out on my own wedding!" The words came out louder than she'd intended, catching the attention of the people at the tables nearby—not that they hadn't been openly staring in the first place. "How did we end up in Junction City? How far are we from Kansas City?"

"About two hours."

"*Two hours?*"

"Like I said, we're here because you told me to keep going."

"Yeah," she waved her hands around in circles. "I meant drive *around*. Not take a *road trip*."

He shrugged, looking unconcerned. "I made a judgment call."

She pursed her lips and stared at the menu without really reading it, berating herself for her mistake. How could she have done this to Mitch without stopping to consider his feelings?

"Lib."

His soft tone caught her attention, and when she looked at him, she was surprised by the seriousness in his eyes. She was used to teasing and humor from Noah, not this resolute side of him.

"What happened?"

Did she really want to admit what an idiot she'd been? Wasn't the fact that she was sitting here in Junction City, Kansas, on her wedding night proof enough?

She opened her mouth, unsure of what exactly to tell him, but their waitress appeared and saved her from speaking. "Welcome to the Golden Cowboy Café. I hear you two are celebrating your wedding."

"That's right." Noah's wide smile returned. "We decided to make the wedding dinner an experience to remember."

She put her hands on her hips. "So you came to the Golden Cowboy Café?" Her tone suggested she was calling bullshit.

Noah laid on the charm thick. "I hear your fried pickles are to die for. How about we start with those. Then I'll take your eight-ounce sirloin, medium, with a baked potato, and the lovely bride will take the same."

Libby started to protest that she could order her own food. But they had eaten enough meals together for him to know what she liked. Besides, hadn't she made enough stupid choices lately to last a lifetime? Might as well let Noah decide on her meal.

The waitress walked away and Noah's grin fell, his concern returning. "Libby, what happened?"

"I made a stupid decision, okay? Does that make you happy? You tried to stop me and I blew you off. Do you want to gloat now?"

"No. God, no."

A tear slid down her cheek and he brushed it away with his thumb. She wasn't prepared for the shot of electricity that zipped through her. Of course, it wasn't the first time her body had reacted to his touch, but in her emotional state, she was worried she lacked the strength to restrain herself.

"Libby, you're my best friend. I'd rather be dead wrong than see you hurt like this." He left his hand in place, spreading his fingers to cup her cheek. "Now tell me what happened."

Should she tell him about the curse? It was obviously a

figment of her imagination. No sense looking like an even bigger idiot, but his touch was making it difficult for her to concentrate. "Megan, Blair, and I made a pact to get married by the time we were thirty." She gave him a sheepish grin. "My birthday is next week."

His eyes widened in surprise and his hand dropped. She felt a strange sense of loss without it.

"Really?" he asked, shaking his head. "Blair doesn't seem like the type of woman to care about that sort of thing."

"She's not. We were all nine when we made the pact."

"And they seriously went through with it? That's why they got married?"

She shook her head and released a sigh. "No. *They* forgot about it. It was purely coincidence that they planned their weddings when they did."

"So they got married according to the pact"—his voice trailed off as his eyes met hers and held them— "and you felt compelled to do the same."

She glanced down at the table. "Something like that."

"Oh, Lib."

"It was stupid, I know. Idiotic. Moronic. I'm the—"

"Stop. It's so you. I love it . . . even if you picked the wrong guy."

She narrowed her eyes, waiting for the *but*. "You're kidding."

"Libby, I've never met anyone with more gusto for life. I love your quirky ideas and beliefs, and I love that you believe in palm reading and pacts made by nine-year-old girls. It's who you are."

"But Mitch got caught up in this disaster. I literally ran away from the altar."

"Come on. It's Mitch. How broken up can he be? I'm sure

he'll be far more upset if the Razorbacks don't make the Cotton Bowl."

She shook her head. "Thanks for trying to make me feel better, but what I did was wrong."

"Okay, it was wrong. You screwed up, but you're owning it. If you're worried about Mitch, why don't you give him a call to apologize?"

"I don't have my phone."

"I'd give you mine, but it's dead. And in my hurry to pack, I forgot my charger."

She shook her head, remembering that he was supposed to be thousands of miles away. "Why aren't you in Seattle? You told Josh you weren't coming."

He gave her a sad smile. "Just like you, I realized I'd screwed up. I raced to make my flight . . . only to discover it was delayed. That's why I was late."

She tilted her head. "What about *Donna*?"

"What about her?"

"I thought you had a *thing* with her."

He shrugged again. "I canceled it."

"If you were planning to come to the wedding, where's your tux? You told me you were going to pick it up in Seattle because you changed your flight."

"It's in a garment bag in the trunk of the rental car. You didn't expect me to wear it on the plane, did you?"

She lifted her eyebrows. "You do realize you're talking to a woman who's wearing a wedding dress in the Golden Cowboy Café?"

He laughed and she couldn't help but laugh with him. Still, while she could live with the embarrassment, she couldn't live with the guilt of hurting Mitch. Her laughter faded and she grew serious. "I still need to talk to him."

Noah was quiet for a moment. "Do you know his number? Or is it just stored on your phone?"

"I know it."

He slid out of the booth and walked over to the nearby table. The family of five sat watching them with great interest as Noah approached him. "I have a huge favor to ask."

The wife stared up at him wide-eyed and the husband murmured, "Okay."

"Libby here," he pointed his thumb toward her. "She needs to make a phone call. And she got so freaking excited"—he stopped and looked down at the three kids at the table—"oh, damn. I just said freaking in front of your kids. Oh shit. I just said damn."

Libby started to chuckle and the wife waved her hand, her gaze shifting back and forth between Noah and Libby. "They've heard worse. Go on."

"Well, she got so excited at the idea of eating at the Golden Cowboy Café that she literally ran off and left her phone in Kansas City. Could she borrow yours? If you let her go outside and make a call, I'll stay here as her deposit."

"You can borrow mine if you'll sit with us as a deposit," shouted a woman who was sitting at a nearby table with three female friends. The other women giggled.

"Sure, on one condition," the wife said, speaking up to get his attention.

"Okay . . ."

"I want a picture with the bride."

Noah glanced back at Libby, his eyebrows raised in an exaggerated gesture.

She hesitated, her stomach protesting the call she was about to make. "Sure."

Noah studied her for a moment before turning back to the

family. "Tell you what, let's let the bride make her call first, then she'll be available for a photo after."

The wife handed him her phone, which Noah brought over to Libby. After helping her to her feet, he stooped to whisper in her ear. "If you don't feel up to taking the photo after you talk to Mitch, I'll get you out of it."

"I can't let you do that."

A strange look crossed his face. "Haven't you heard? Not following through and making up excuses are all that I'm good for. Now go make your call." When she started to protest his declaration, he gave a slight push to the small of her back. "I'll be here if you need me."

Libby walked out of the restaurant, drawing another round of curious stares from the diners. But she ignored them and stepped out the door, immediately shivering in the November cold in her sleeveless wedding dress. Sucking in a deep breath, she typed in Mitch's number and waited, feeling like she was going to throw up. He answered on the third ring. "Hello?" She could tell he was confused by the unfamiliar number.

"Mitch, it's me."

"Libby?" He sounded worried. And relieved.

"Yeah."

"Where are you? Are you okay? When no one heard from you, we all worried you got kidnapped after you hopped into that stranger's car."

She shook her head, feeling like the world's biggest bitch. "How can you be so nice to me after I ran out on you like that?"

"Libby. I still care about you. You running out doesn't change that."

"I'm sorry." She choked on the words.

"Was it the Razorback call? Or the play from the Cotton

Bowl?"

"Oh, Mitch . . ."

"It's okay, Libs. Really." There was a pause on the line, and then he added, "I was having doubts this week, but I didn't want to be that asshole who broke up with his fiancée before the wedding."

"You *were*?"

"Yeah . . ." He sounded embarrassed. "Remember me telling you about my old college girlfriend?"

"Sheila?"

"Yeah, that's the one. Well, she called me up this week . . . and I . . . I'm sorry."

So he'd cheated on her. She could hear it in his voice, yet she didn't care. It would have been hypocritical to care given that she'd only arranged to marry him in the hopes that another man would come along and destroy their wedding. "Mitch, believe it or not, I really do want you to be happy."

"So this worked out for both of us?" he asked, sounding like he didn't quite believe it.

"Yeah." She laughed, wiping a tear from her cheek. Karma was a real bitch, but this was what she deserved for treating him like crap. It sounded like Mitch had found his match, and Libby was still alone. "I suppose it did."

"I hope you find what you're looking for, Libby. I knew all along I wasn't it. I should have ended things months ago, but you were like the perfect woman, you know? Gorgeous and laid back, and you didn't even care that I was gone so much. I couldn't understand why we just didn't feel right, but I figured it would all work out in the end."

She sighed. "Me too."

"Take care of yourself. And if you haven't already, call Megan and Blair. They're flipping their shit."

She cringed. "Thanks."

She hung up and called Megan, figuring she would probably be the easier to deal with of her two friends.

"Hello?" Megan answered tentatively.

"Megan, it's me."

"Oh, my God! Are you okay? Blair's raising holy hell because the police won't put out an Amber Alert for you."

"Amber Alerts are for children."

"Everyone's told her that . . . not that she cares. She was certain you were kidnapped. Where are you?"

A sharp wind hit her, making her shiver with cold. "Junction City, Kansas."

"What? How did you get there?"

"Noah just drove—"

"*Noah?* How could you be with Noah? He's in Seattle."

"No, he changed his mind and flew to Kansas City, but his plane was delayed, which is why he was late. He was driving the car I got into."

There was a long moment of silence, then Megan said, "So you planned this?" There was a sharp edge to her voice now.

"What? No!"

Megan was silent for another beat. "Why did you run away, Libby?" she finally asked.

What should she say? "I was scared. It was all too much." Both true.

"You never intended to marry Mitch, did you?"

Oh, God. She'd figured it out. Libby's face burned with embarrassment. "How can you say that?"

"Because you believed in the curse more than any of us. And after what happened to Blair and me, of course you'd think the same thing would happen to you."

How could she respond? Megan was right, but that didn't

mean she wanted to own up to it.

"I'd ask you how far you were willing to let it go, but I guess we all got front row seats to that answer."

The condemnation in her words stabbed Libby in the heart. In all the time she'd known Megan, she'd never sounded so judgmental.

"Why shouldn't I believe in the curse?" Libby asked, wrapping an arm across her chest in an effort to block out the cold. "It worked out exactly like the fortune teller told us it would for you and Blair. She said the curse covered all three of us. It should have worked!"

"The curse isn't real, Libby!" Megan lowered her voice. "You've pulled some crazy things before, but this . . . Think about what you did to Mitch. You left that poor man at the altar, when you had no intention of marrying him at all."

"I've already talked to Mitch. His old girlfriend called him this week. Turns out he didn't want to marry me either, but he felt bad about breaking up with me right before the wedding."

"Libby, that doesn't make it right."

Anger roared in Libby's head. "You know what, you're one hundred percent correct. It doesn't make it right. Not even close. I feel like a bitch and I already apologized to Mitch. But let me ask you *this*, Megan Vandemeer *McMillan*: Who stood by you when you paraded a fake fiancé around claiming he was Jay? And who helped you realize that he was the love of your life? Me. That's right, *me!*" She stamped her foot for effect, sending pain shooting up from her heel to her shin. "I stood by you because you're my friend. I'm sorry if you think it's too much for me to ask you to do the same!"

"Oh, God, Libby," Megan said, sounding horrified. "You're right. I'm so sorry."

"Too little, too late." Then she hung up and sucked in a

deep breath of cold Kansas air. Megan's words had stung, but there was no denying they were true. She'd been irresponsible and self-centered, but there wasn't anything she could do about it now. She felt a sudden need to see Noah. He'd make her feel better. He always did. Turned out he really *was* her best friend.

Chapter Five

Noah anxiously glanced at the door for what had to be the hundredth time, wondering if he should go outside. Calling Mitch had to be difficult for her. What if she needed support? After five minutes passed this way, he decided to go after her, if only to give her his jacket, but the door opened and she walked into the restaurant with a strange look on her face.

She stopped at the table of the woman who'd lent them the phone, plastering what he recognized as a fake smile on her face. "Do you want to take that photo now?

The woman hopped out of her chair and raced around to stand next to Libby, pausing only to hand the proffered phone to her husband. "Get close up, Bill. No full body shot. I don't want my fat rolls showing." She turned to Libby. "I'm posting this on social media. No one will believe this, so I need proof."

Libby's smile widened as she faced the camera. After several clicks, Libby turned to face the woman. "Thank you so much for letting me use your phone. If you get a call from a woman named Megan, please tell her I said to go to hell," she said in a sweet voice.

Noah's blood pressure began to rise. So she'd called his sister-in-law, and apparently Megan had been a bitch about the whole runaway bride thing.

The woman's head jutted back in surprise, and then she laughed. "Will do. I'm sure there's a story *there.*" She cast a wicked glance at Noah and winked before leaning close to Libby and whispering something in her ear.

Libby's eyes widened and she shook her head, mouthing the word *no*, but the woman ignored her and sat down with her family.

By the time Libby returned to the booth, the fake smile had slipped from her face.

"Lib? Did you get ahold of Mitch?"

"What?" She glanced up at Noah. "Yeah."

"And?"

She released a heavy breath. "He's actually pretty okay. He said he was having doubts too. Turns out his old college girlfriend contacted him this week . . ." Her voice trailed off, but he thought he heard her mumble something about a curse working for Mitch.

"So he's not mad?"

"What?" She looked startled. "No. He's not mad in the least."

"But Megan is."

She shivered. "Yes. I don't know. I hung up on her."

Her shaking drew his attention to the goosebumps on her arms, and he remembered she'd been standing outside in forty-degree weather in her sleeveless dress. He scooted around to her and pulled her close, wrapping an arm around her shoulders. "You're freezing."

She stiffened at the contact, which caught him off guard. He'd hugged her plenty of times before and she'd never reacted like that. But she instantly relaxed and leaned the back of her neck against his arm.

"What did Megan say?"

"You're warm." She snuggled into him and closed her eyes.

He'd sat close to her more times than was probably appropriate given the fact she'd had a boyfriend. Somehow this was different. Libby was a stunningly beautiful woman, but tonight, in her wedding dress, she was beyond gorgeous. He'd spent so much time sneaking glances at her while she was asleep in the car, it was a wonder he hadn't run off the road. But now her face was tilted toward him, and her cheeks seemed to glow in the warm light of the restaurant. Strands of her thick, dark hair had worked loose from her non-fussy up-do. As she snuggled closer to him, her lips softened and the worry wrinkles on her forehead faded. He was staring at her long, dark eyelashes when her eyes opened, and he found himself lost in her gaze.

He expected her to pull away, but she remained still, her rich dark eyes staring back at him. She looked so serene, so beautiful, he found himself drawn to her—the force so powerful it was almost magnetic. He started to lean over to kiss her, the instinct so strong it overrode all reason.

"Here's two steaks for the happy couple," the waitress singsonged in a happy voice.

Startled, Noah jerked upright and Libby scooted out from under his arm. Had she realized what he was about to do? God, he hoped not. He wanted more with her, but now wasn't the time. A month ago, she'd made it perfectly clear how she felt about them moving past friendship, and he had to confess, she had valid points even if he hoped to persuade her she was wrong. But he'd rather have her in his life as his friend than not at all, and he'd never forgive himself if he screwed it up with her. Let him fuck up everything else in his life, but not this. Not her. As the waitress slid their plates onto the table, he was already working on excuses if Libby decided to call him out.

"Can I get you anything else?" the waitress asked. "Steak sauce? Ketchup?"

Libby looked around the table. "Where are Noah's fried pickles?"

The waitress cringed. "Sorry about that. I have to admit, you've got the kitchen staff fit to be tied. They keep poking their heads out the door to get a look at you instead of doing their jobs. They'll be right out."

Noah didn't care about the pickles. He only wanted the waitress to leave so he could assess the fallout from his near mistake. When Libby picked up her fork and knife without saying anything, he decided to ignore that it had ever happened. "So you and Mitch are okay?"

"Yeah." She kept her gaze on her plate as she sawed on her steak. "He wished me well, but then that's Mitch. He's awesome like that."

"Having second thoughts?"

"What?" Her gaze jerked up to his. "No. I didn't really love him." A tiny grin twisted her lips. "And if I had to listen to one more Razorback call, I think I may have killed him before our first anniversary. Did I tell you the wedding was Razorback themed?"

"What?" he laughed, relieved she'd let their awkward moment pass. "You're kidding."

"Nope. He wore an Arkansas printed tie and socks. Megan

and Blair wore red dresses, and he had a Hog groom's cake."
Grinning, she stabbed a piece of her steak. "In his vows, he
used a play from the 2010 Cotton Bowl game."

"Why in the world did you agree to that?" He couldn't
imagine her going along with any of it.

She shrugged. "It's what he wanted."

"Doesn't the bride typically get what *she* wants?" He
couldn't understand why she'd proposed to Mitch, but it
absolutely astonished him that she'd let him plan the entire
wedding. She loved weddings and everything about them.
Heck, she'd probably started planning her *big day* when she was
a middle-schooler collecting images cut out of magazines.
None of this made sense.

She shrugged again, not looking up at him.

"Libby."

She lifted her gaze to his.

He paused. "Yeah, Mitch is a great guy, but he wasn't the
right guy for you." He held up his hand in case she started to
protest. "And no, this isn't me gloating."

Something like regret filled her eyes. "You have every
right."

He gave a small shake of his head. "Nope. Not even a
little." He turned serious. "But one day, you'll meet a guy who
can give you the kind of love your friends have found, because
that's what you deserve, Libby. A guy who will stand by your
side no matter what, then sweep you off your feet while he's
giving you the stars and moon." He hoped that guy was him,
particularly since a band of jealousy coiled around his heart at
the notion of some other man giving that to her. The feeling
was unsettling; he'd never been jealous like this before.

Tears filled her eyes. "I don't think I'm going to find that,
Noah. It's too late."

"Bullshit. You're not even thirty yet."

"It's not that."

"Then what is it?"

A soft smile lit up her face. "You're the only man who's ever liked me for *me*."

"What does that mean?"

"Guys always see the outside. They rarely pay attention to the inside."

Guilt washed through him. How many times had he been so dazzled by a woman's beauty, he'd ignored everything else about her? And while he'd seen firsthand how many men openly gawked at Libby, it had never occurred to him to ask how she felt about it. "Not every man is like that, Lib. Look at Josh." *And me.* But he couldn't tell her that. She was still raw over her breakup with Mitch. He didn't want to be her rebound.

She pursed her lips and didn't answer.

He decided to change the subject, although he wasn't sure the one he was moving on to was any safer. "So you called Megan."

She sighed. "Mitch said she and Blair were freaking out." A grin cracked her lips. "Blair thought I'd been kidnapped and wanted the police to issue an Amber Alert."

"Wait. Isn't that for—"

"Yeah. For kids. Megan says she was irritated when they wouldn't do it."

Noah chuckled. "Sounds like Blair." He paused. "What did Megan say about you running off?"

She scowled. "Nothing good."

"I gathered that from the fact that you suggested a complete stranger tell your best friend to go to hell."

She grinned up at him, a new playfulness in her eyes. Relief spread warmth through his veins. She had every reason to be upset, but it killed him to see her that way. He'd do anything to keep her happy.

He gave her a cocky grin. "Since you were supposed to get married, I take it you've got a few days off for your honeymoon."

"Well . . . yeah. I postponed all my photo shoots for the next couple of weeks."

"Where were you going for a honeymoon?"

"We were supposed to go to Santa Fe, New Mexico, but then Mitch's high school football team made it into a playoff game. So we canceled the trip."

"But you still have time off?"

"Yeah. Why?"

"Let's go on a road trip."

Her eyes widened. "You're kidding."

"No. We're already in Junction City. Why not just keep going?"

"How about the fact that I don't have any clothes on me besides this wedding dress?"

"So we'll buy you more clothes."

"Noah, I don't have any money. Or a cell phone. Or a form of ID for that matter."

"Then I'll pay for the trip." When she started to protest, he held up a hand. "Consider it a non-wedding present. Or if you'd like, consider it your kidnapper providing for your basic needs."

"And you can take off work just like that? I thought you guys were in the middle of a merger that was sucking away all your free time."

He considered telling her the truth—in fact, he was dying to tell her the truth. She was the one person who would understand how he felt. She knew how hard he'd been trying with the family business. But this was about Libby right now, not him. His problems weren't going anywhere. He could wait.

"Lucky for you, I took time off."

She ate several more bites before looking up at him. "So where would we go?"

He grinned. "Wherever we want. In fact, I declare tomorrow Libby St. Clair Day."

"Does that mean I get to pick where we go?"

His eyes narrowed. "Where do you want to go?"

She laughed. "I don't know. I'm just trying to learn the rules."

"The rules are we don't do anything responsible. We just have fun."

Her lips pursed as she considered it, then she grinned and held out her hand. "Deal."

"Deal." He shook her hand, holding it a few seconds longer than necessary before releasing it.

She leaned toward him. "So where are we going?"

Then he knew how to make it really fun for her. He'd never met anyone who loved surprises more than Libby. "I've decided not to tell you. You'll find out tomorrow."

"You have no idea."

"I guess you'll find out." She was right, but he'd never admit it. But as long as she continued to look this happy, he'd figure out how to get her to the moon if she wanted to go there.

Chapter Six

Over the course of their dinner, Libby relaxed and tried to forget the wedding gone wrong. Several of the customers—and even the staff—grew bold enough to ask for photos with her. Some, like the woman who'd cat-called him, wanted a photo with Noah. By the time they finally left, Libby had taken a photo with almost everyone in the restaurant. The restaurant manager even offered to comp their bill if Libby would let him hang his photo with her by the entrance.

When Noah held the door to the parking lot open for her, she felt happier—and freer—than she had in months, even if she was freezing. "Now what?" she asked.

"I think we should find a hotel and stay in Junction City tonight. Your photo session took over forty-five minutes and now you're all over my Twitter feed. Did you have to give them your Twitter handle?"

"Why not?" she teased as he wrapped an arm around her

shoulders and walked her to the passenger door. "Garrett got his fifteen minutes of fame when he was on his way to break up Blair's wedding. Why shouldn't I?"

"Because, Libby St. Clair," Noah leaned close, his breath warm on her cheek, "you are a dazzling star who can't be reduced to a few tweets of you posing for photos in a Kansas steak house wearing a wedding dress."

"Cut the bullshit, Noah."

"I mean every word." And strangely enough, he sounded like he did.

Overcome with gratitude and something else that warmed her insides, she threw her arms around his neck. "Thank you."

He pulled her close, but slowly, as though she might break. "What did I do?"

"You took a miserable night and made it more than bearable."

"That's what best friends are for, right?"

She leaned back and looked into his face. "Who knew you'd be so good at this best friend thing?"

A strange look crossed his face. "Yeah. Who knew?" He broke loose and opened the car door. "You need to get in the car before you freeze."

After he got in and turned on the engine, he turned to look at her. "So find a hotel here in Junction City?"

"Yeah."

"I saw a sign for a decent-looking place when I turned off the interstate. Let's try it." He pulled out of the parking lot and headed toward the hotel, both of them keeping quiet during the short drive.

When he parked in front of the entrance, he turned to her. "Wait for me to come around and get you."

"Why?"

"It's freezing outside, and you're wearing a sleeveless dress. I'm going to pull a jacket out of my suitcase for you."

"I'll be fine." She pushed the door open and scrambled out, forgetting that it would take more effort than usual with all the material of her skirt. The next thing she knew, Noah was there next to her, offering her his hand. She looked up at him with a scowl. "I said I could do it."

"And I'm sure you can, but why not let me help you?"

How could she explain to him what she didn't understand herself? She'd always had trouble accepting help from other people, but for some reason, right now she found it even more difficult to accept help from *him*.

He helped her out and she landed against his chest. He snaked his arm around her back and pulled her closer to keep her steady. An unexpected wave of heat washed through her when she looked into his eyes. She'd learned to tame her lust for Noah after months of friendship. So why did it feel like such a struggle tonight?

She pulled free and started walking toward the entrance. Noah fell in step beside her, thankfully not mentioning their awkward embrace.

There were less than half a dozen people in the lobby, so Libby was less of a spectacle here than she'd been in the restaurant. Noah stopped and turned toward her, looking uncomfortable. "Do you want two rooms?"

Libby's heart stuttered. What was the right way to answer that? She didn't want to be alone, but she was too humiliated to admit it.

But he misinterpreted her hesitation. He nodded and put his hand on her shoulder. "It's okay. I don't mind the extra money."

She grabbed his arm to stop him as he started toward the

front desk. "No. One room is good. We can just get two beds. No need to spend the extra money. Besides," she added in a rush, "you've spent the night in my apartment before. This is no different." But it was very different and she could see he knew it too.

He studied her face with a seriousness she wasn't used to from him. "Are you sure? Maybe you just want to be alone. I understand if you do."

"The last thing I want is to be alone right now." Her voice broke and she realized that made her sound needy. She'd trained herself years ago not to appear needy. Needy women sent men running to the hills. But this wasn't *any* man. This was Noah. Her *friend*. That's what friends were for, right?

Sadness filled his eyes, and he pulled her into a hug. "Oh, Lib."

She was acutely aware that the few people in the lobby and the desk clerk were staring at them like they were a daytime soap. But she just rested her head on his chest for several seconds, amazed by the peace she felt in his arms. Everything seemed so much less hopeless when she was with Noah.

He kissed her forehead, then set her loose. "One room it is."

Noah approached the front desk and rested his forearm on the counter, ignoring the shocked look on the clerk's face. "We need a room with two beds."

If possible, the clerk's eyes grew even wider. "Uh . . ." He shook his head and tried to regain his composure. "Two beds? For your wedding night?"

"She's a kicker," Noah said with a straight face. "She kneed me in the groin only a month ago and now I'm less one testicle." He leaned his forearm on the counter and glanced around. Ignoring the openly staring couple in the lobby, he lowered his voice to a stage whisper. "I'll have you know, that was a difficult one to explain to the insurance company."

The man's gaze shifted to Libby before swinging back to Noah. He swallowed. "Umm . . . we don't have any rooms with two beds, sir. Only a room with a king-size bed. Maybe you should go somewhere else."

Noah stared down at her with an uncertain look in his eyes, but she nodded her approval.

Turning back to the employee, Noah shrugged and said with an air of resignation, "We did marry for better or worse. In sickness and in testicular injuries. I only hope she doesn't jostle the prosthesis. How quickly can first responders get here?" The clerk still appeared alarmed, but Noah shook his head. "Never mind. We'll take it."

The clerk refused to make eye contact as he quickly checked them in and handed Noah the room keys. "You're on the second floor, sir"—then he tacked on—"and congratulations." Although he seemed somewhat uncertain that congratulations were indeed in order.

Noah placed his hand on the small of her back and shepherded her toward the elevator. When the elevator doors opened, he kept his hand on her back even after they were inside. She could feel the heat of his touch through her dress. Determined not to let him know how he was affecting her, she fought to keep her breathing slow and even.

Think of something, Libby thought. *Think of something to keep your mind off throwing yourself at him.* "I made you lose *your testicle?*"

"What other reason could I give him for not wanting to sleep with my beautiful bride?" His voice was tight, but his hand remained on her back.

That certainly didn't take her mind off her hormones. *Think of something else.* "You forgot your bag," she said.

"I'll get it once you're settled in the room."

She looked up at him in surprise, but he kept his gaze on the elevator doors. Then the doors opened and he was ushering her out of the elevator and leading her down the hall to their room. She couldn't help noticing how he'd taken charge tonight—she hadn't seen him this focused once in the five months they'd known each other.

He pushed the door open and waited for her to walk through.

The first thing Libby noticed was the giant king-size bed, which didn't seem so giant when she thought about sleeping in it with Noah. As she'd reminded him downstairs, he'd stayed overnight at her place multiple times, yet the closest they'd ever come to sleeping together was snoozing on opposite sides of her sofa. She wasn't sure she could spend the night in that bed with him without acting on this . . . this whatever was happening to her tonight.

If Noah was affected by the sight of the bed, he didn't let on. "I'll be back. Are you okay here?"

His attentiveness made her smile. "I don't need a babysitter. Go already."

He paused in the doorway and glanced back her, the warmth in his eyes catching her off guard. "I just want to make sure you're okay. Part of the best friend gig, right?"

"Yeah. Right."

He pulled the door shut, and she sat on the edge of the bed and heaved a loud sigh. She may have napped earlier, but she was weary. She laid back on the bed and covered her eyes with her arm.

What was she supposed to do now?

She'd believed in the curse hook, line, and sinker. What reason would she have had for doubt? Megan and Blair's weddings had both gone according to the curse plan. But hers...If the curse was wrong, it threw everything else in her life into question.

The only way she'd gotten through her childhood was by believing in magic and fate. That she was like Cinderella and some man would finally love her. But if magic didn't exist and fate was coincidence, how was she supposed to find her happily ever after? What if she *never* found someone to love her, really love her? Her father had left when she was a baby. Her mother cared for her in her own way, but she was always too busy finding her next lay to spend much time with her. Maybe she was just unlovable.

"Lib?"

She moved her arm, surprised to see Noah was already back. "That was fast."

"It's colder than a witch's tit out there. I didn't waste any time." He sat on the bed, looking down at her. "You okay?"

Sighing, she sat up.

"I'm fine."

He grinned. "Liar."

"I am."

"Only a *true* narcissist could be fine after what you've been through. And I've always had you pegged as only half a narcissist. Don't tell me I've had it all wrong."

She laughed, and then before she realized what was happening, she started crying.

Noah pulled her to his chest, rubbing slow circles on her back. When she finally settled down, he said, "Let's get you out of that dress."

"I don't have anything to wear."

"I was about to suggest you wear nothing," he teased, "but given the situation, how about you wear one of my T-shirts?

Okay?"

She nodded, hating that she'd broken down like that. She'd brought this on herself, which meant she didn't deserve to cry. She sucked in a deep breath, then stood. "I need help getting my dress off."

His smile was a touch self-deprecating. "Lucky for you, getting women out of their clothes is my specialty."

"Save the tales of your exploits for another time." She knew he'd undressed plenty of women, but for some reason the thought irritated her. She turned and presented her back to him. He tugged on the laces at the rise of her ass.

"Good God. Is this a wedding dress or a chastity belt?" he groaned as he fought to work the laces loose.

"Megan might have been overly aggressive in pulling them tight."

"I guess she didn't want Mitch to have easy access." His hands stilled as he groaned. "God, Lib. I'm sorry."

She shook her head. "Don't be. It is what it is." What would he think if he found out she'd never intended to marry Mitch at all? Would he judge her like Megan had? She couldn't take the risk.

Once he got the bottom strings free, the rest unlaced more quickly, loosening the dress enough for her to take it off.

"Do you want to take a shower?" he asked. "I'll pull a T-shirt out of my bag and leave it on the counter while you're in there."

Holding the front of her dress to her chest, she turned and looked up at him. "Why are you being so nice to me?" she blurted out.

Surprise washed over his face. "I thought we'd already been over that. You've had a shitty day and I'm being a good friend." When she didn't say anything, he continued. "Look, today and tomorrow are *your* days—"

"You really plan to make tomorrow Libby St. Clair Day?"

He grinned. "You bet your sweet ass I do, but before you think I'm being chivalrous, consider this: Maybe I'll have a shitty day next week, and then I'll expect you to wait on me hand and foot. Paybacks are awesome."

He was almost self-centered enough to make her believe his explanation. Almost. "So you're like the ant in the ant and the grasshopper story."

He held up his hands in protest. "If I have to be a bug, I'd rather be a scorpion."

She shook her head and moved closer to him. "A scorpion is more like a spider than an insect, and even so, you're not a spider." She grinned. "More like a roly poly."

Mock anger filled his eyes. "You're dead to me, woman. I guess you'll be sleeping in the buff tonight."

She reached up and kissed him on the cheek. "Thank you."

He pulled her into a hug. "Always, Lib," he said. "I mean it."

And she could tell that he did, which made her feel bad for doubting him earlier at the church.

Maybe there was hope for Noah McMillan yet.

Chapter Seven

Noah set his carry-on bag on the bed. When he heard the water in the shower turn on, he stopped unzipping the suitcase and took a deep breath. Libby was in the other room—naked—and his thoughts raced into dangerous territory.

He wanted her more than he'd ever wanted a woman.

Part one of his plan had come to fruition without his involvement—the wedding had been aborted—but now what did he do? Libby had shot down his proposition a month ago. Could he really risk laying it on the line? The thought terrified him—what if she refused to give them a try?—but right now it didn't matter. While he might be ready to give their relationship a shot, she'd only just broken up with Mitch. This was hardly the time to make his feelings known to her.

He pulled out a T-shirt and cautiously pushed the bathroom door open. Her wedding dress lay in a giant puddle of fabric on the floor. "Lib, I'm putting my shirt on the counter."

"Thanks."

He set it next to her towel, then picked up her dress and carried it out with him, shutting the door behind him. Holding it up in front of him, he studied the silk gown. Based on what she'd told him about her football-centric disaster of a wedding, this was probably the only part of the whole affair that had truly been her. Unsure of what to do with it, he laid it across the back of the desk chair—the skirt billowing everywhere— then pulled out another T-shirt for himself.

The bed loomed in the middle of the room, teasing him. He had no clue how they were going to handle sleeping together. For one thing, Noah usually slept in his briefs, which meant he had no pajama bottoms. He'd have to settle for wearing a T-shirt over them, but the feelings of protectiveness she'd stirred inside of him were also rousing other feelings that might not be so easy to hide if they were nearly naked and close together in bed.

He'd think about that later. Right now he had to figure out where they were going for Libby St. Clair Day. What would make her the happiest?

He gasped when the answer hit him, and he pulled out his laptop to search the Internet for wacky tourist attractions. He'd made a list and mapped a few out by the time she emerged from the bathroom, her damp hair hanging in loose waves over her shoulders and down her back. Her long sexy legs peeked out from under his shirt, which hung mere inches below the curve of her ass. Every nerve ending pinged at the sight of her and he resisted the urge to jump up and show her how much he wanted her. He forced himself to act natural.

"Feel better?"

"Yeah."

He slowly stood, trying to be nonchalant.

She nodded to his laptop. "You working?"

"Working?" he teased, even though the reminder that he was no longer employed made his stomach sink. "There's no real work allowed on Libby St. Clair Day. Only play. I was planning it for us."

Her eyes lit up with excitement. "What did you come up with?"

He shook his head and closed the lid. "It's a surprise."

"That's hardly fair."

"It's perfectly fair." He grabbed his T-shirt and toiletry bag. "I'm going to take a shower now."

"All right."

He grinned. There was a cute smirk on her face—the one she always got when she was up to something sneaky. "Feel free to try and figure out the password on my laptop. It's unbreakable."

Her eyes widened in mock indignation, but she didn't try to protest. She knew he had her figured out.

When he emerged from the bathroom five minutes later, he found her on the bed, propped up against the headboard on a pile of pillows. The covers were pulled back, but her bare legs were tucked to the side and his computer was on her lap. She looked up, not even pretending to hide what she'd been doing.

God, he loved that about her.

"No luck, huh?" he asked smugly.

She started to respond, then stopped, lifting her gaze up from his legs to his face. "No."

Was she bothered by his lack of pants? The shirt he'd picked covered all the essential parts in the front, but left his briefs-covered ass exposed in the back. Libby wasn't the kind of woman to be offended by naked bodies. If anything, her art background made her appreciate the human form more than most people. So if it wasn't his body in general, did that mean she was affected by *him*?

Could she want him too?

His pulse quickened at the thought, but he told himself that he had to take this slow. She needed time, and right now she needed him to be her friend. And while it was no secret that Noah had slept with more women than was respectable, Libby had her own more-than-healthy share of short-lived relationships.

Lately he'd found himself in the strange situation of offering others advice in matters of the heart, so he made himself take a step back and fill that role for himself. What advice would he give another person in his situation? He'd encouraged Garrett to go for it, but Garrett had only had days to convince Blair to cancel her wedding. Libby had already run out of hers. He'd gotten to know Libby well enough to realize she was vulnerable now. It wouldn't take much to convince her to sleep with him, but he also knew her well enough to realize that if she *did* sleep with him, it would be as a short-term emotional Band-Aid.

Of course, a short-term fling could blossom into something more, but when they slept together, he wanted her fully committed to making this thing between them work. His thought process stunned him. He'd never before given any consideration to how a woman would feel about sleeping with him. Only that she did.

What the hell had happened to him? Of course, the answer was simple, even if it had taken him months to figure it out: Libby St. Clair.

"Noah?"

She had to wonder why he was just standing there, gawking

at her. What had they been talking about? Oh, yeah. His password.

"My laptop is more secure than Fort Knox." He moved to the other side of the bed and sat down, trying to act like sitting next to her on the bed they were going to sleep in together was no big deal.

"Is that a challenge?" Her voice rose with excitement.

"Sure, if that makes you happy. I'd prefer to call it a worthless endeavor."

She closed the computer and handed it to him. He set it on the nightstand, worried he'd stolen her playfulness, but while she wasn't bursting with happiness, she wasn't frowning either.

He started to slide closer to her, but there was a knock at the door. Libby stiffened, her body tense with anxiety, and Noah slid off the bed. "I'll check and see who it is."

He peered through the peephole, and was surprised to see a hotel employee with a room service tray. "You must have the wrong room," he said, opening the door. "We didn't order anything."

The older man dressed in black pants and a white long-sleeved shirt paired with a black bow tie cleared his throat. "Compliments of the hotel. For your wedding night." His eyes shifted to Noah's crotch, but he abruptly lifted his gaze and held out a tray with a bottle of champagne, two plastic cups, and a piece of shriveled angel food cake.

Noah tried to hide his grin as he took the tray.

"Is it true?" the man asked. "Did she . . . you know?"

Noah gave a quick glance over his shoulder before turning back and lowering his voice. "Yeah, she's vicious in bed. I can show you the foot-long scar if you like. It's still pretty fresh."

The man's eyes widened and he turned around, muttering, "No thank you, no thank you," before hurrying down the hall to the elevator.

Noah carried the tray into the room and kicked the door shut behind him.

"A foot long?" Libby commented with raised brows. "I'm sure there's some psychological delusion of grandeur there."

Noah grinned as he set the tray on the dresser, trying to think of things other than his exaggerated twelve inches and the woman on the bed. His T-shirt wouldn't hide much. "How about some champagne?"

Her smile fell. "Champagne is for celebrating and there is *nothing* to celebrate."

"I disagree." Noah twisted off the cork and quickly filled the plastic cups, then carried them over to the bed and sat down, one leg still dangling off the side. "Here."

She refused to take it. "No. I told you we have nothing to celebrate."

"Of course we do. How about the fact you dodged a bullet today? You could have married a man you didn't really love, but you came to your senses at the last minute."

He held it out to her again and she reluctantly took it this time. "That doesn't seem like something to be proud of."

He looked her in the eyes. "It took guts, Lib. Do you know how many people would have just stood there and gone through with it?"

Some emotion washed over her face, but it passed too quickly for him to register. She looked up with a smile. "How about we celebrate the fact I haven't kicked you in the other ball . . . yet."

He burst out laughing. "I'll drink to that, although I resent the tacked-on *yet*."

She clacked her glass against his, then took a healthy gulp.

He took a sip of his own champagne and said, "Looks like

we'll need more of this." He got up and grabbed the bottle and the cake, setting the bottle on the nightstand before sitting down again. "Do you want the cake?"

"Angel food?" she asked. "Doesn't sound appropriate for either one of us. You and I are more like devil's food, don't you think?" Her teasing tone removed the sting.

"Maybe it'll be a good influence on us." He picked it up off the plate and held it up to her mouth.

Hesitation flickered in her eyes for a few seconds, but she leaned forward and took a bite. She grabbed the cake out of his hand and held it up to him, lifting her eyebrows playfully.

As she held the cake in front of his face, he realized why she'd held back for a moment. Without realizing what he was doing, he'd reenacted the cake part of a wedding reception.

She put the cake on the plate, then finished off her cup of champagne. He grabbed the bottle and poured more for her.

"What do you want to do?" he asked. "Watch some TV? Go to sleep?"

"TV. I don't think I can sleep."

He reached for the remote and clicked on the TV, scrolling through the channels until he found an episode of *Friends*. The goal was to put her at ease. They'd watched plenty of movies together at her apartment, and sometime he'd sit behind her and rub her back. "I'll rub your back if you like."

"Really?"

"Yeah, turn around."

She drank the rest of her champagne and handed him the cup before scooting closer.

"Why don't you lay your head on my legs, close enough for me to reach your back."

"Okay."

She maneuvered so that she lay sideways, her head resting

on his upper thighs. His hand rested on her back. It should have been no big deal; they'd watched TV on her sofa before, but never this intimately.

He stayed still for a moment, letting her relax on him before he began to rub over her T-shirt, shifting slightly so she couldn't see his arousal at the sight of her sexy legs and barely covered ass. She sighed with contentment and soon her breathing evened, her body sagged into his, and he realized she'd fallen asleep.

To his surprise his arousal faded, shifting to something deeper—the need to make sure she felt protected and comforted. He realized even if *she* made a move, he would turn her down. That so wasn't his style, but he didn't want to blow their chance on what she could potentially see as a one-night fling.

The episode ended and he turned off the TV, then tried to decide if he should disturb her to turn off the light.

She shifted slightly, then lifted her head to look at him. "I'm sorry. I fell asleep."

"It's okay, I'm tired too." He reached up and flipped the switch, flooding the room with darkness.

She scooted off him but stayed close. "Noah? Can I ask you a favor?"

"Anything . . . well, except for buying you tampons. A guy has to draw the line somewhere."

She laughed. "You're safe there . . . for now."

He grinned in the dark. "What's your favor?"

She paused, and when she finally answered, her voice sounded unsure. "Will you hold me?"

He didn't answer, just rolled onto his side and reached for her, pulling her back to his chest, bending his hips back in case touching her aroused him again.

She put her hand over his. "You're the only one who stood by me today."

The thought sobered him. How could that be? He was the least responsible of all of her friends. He instinctively pulled her closer. "Oh, Lib. I'll always be there for you. I promise. I'm sorry I said I wasn't coming. If I'd kept my original flight yesterday, maybe I could have helped you change your mind."

Her head rubbed against his chest as she shook it. "No. You couldn't have. I was sure I knew what I was doing."

The sadness in her voice wrecked him. "It's over. Tomorrow is Libby Day and we won't mention any of this at all, okay? Just fun."

"Okay."

Soon her breath evened again, and he drifted off to sleep too, wondering if this was what contentment felt like. If it was, he knew he wanted it with her.

Chapter Eight

Libby woke facing Noah, their legs intertwined. For a few moments she was confused and horrified. Had she had sex with him? But the thought barely had the chance to form before she remembered everything. He'd only held her.

She'd slept in a bed with Noah and he hadn't made a move on her. She wasn't sure whether to be relieved or insulted. She settled on disappointed—another surprise. But sex with Noah was bound to ruin everything, she reminded herself. Yesterday he'd proved himself to be a loyal and supportive friend. She couldn't let her hormones screw that up.

She untangled herself, making him stir, then propped herself up on one elbow. "Good morning."

"What time is it?" he muttered, keeping his eyes closed.

"I don't know. I can't see a clock."

"Go back to sleep," he grumbled. "Whatever time it is, it's two hours earlier in Seattle. For me, it's like the middle of the night."

"It's not the middle of the night. The sun's out."

Groaning, he rolled over and looked at the clock on the nightstand, then groaned again.

"So what time is it?"

"9:13." He didn't sound very happy about it.

"I'm hungry."

He lay on his back, looking up into her face. He blinked as his eyes adjusted to the light. "You're worse than Tortoise." Then his eyes widened. "Hey, where *is* Tortoise?"

"Did you seriously think I was irresponsible enough to leave my dog alone overnight?"

"Well, no."

"Liar."

He looked relieved when she laughed.

"He's with my friend Steph. She treats him like a little prince."

"I miss him."

That surprised her . . . then it didn't. She'd adopted Tortoise while Noah was in town—they'd gone to the dog shelter together—and he'd teased her to no end about the name she'd given him. But he'd grown attached to the animal too, and often asked about him, as infrequent as his calls had become these past weeks.

"Hey," she said, giving his arm a shove. "Why haven't you called me very much over the last month?"

"That's a two-way street, Libby."

It was true. She'd pulled away from him after telling him about her engagement. She realized now it was because his disapproval had smarted. Even though she hadn't intended to go through with the wedding, she'd known all along he was right about marrying Mitch.

"None of that," he said, pulling her close again. "Yesterday happened in a vacuum."

It hadn't, not really. But it was nice to pretend it was true. "Maybe so, but today has its own very real problems."

He frowned. "What problems could you possibly have on your special day?"

"Remember? The only thing I have to wear is a wedding dress."

"Hmm . . . I see your point. Should I go out and pick up an outfit for you?"

"Are you kidding?" she asked in mock horror. "I don't care to spend my special day dressed like a hooker."

He leaned to the side to catch her gaze. "I'm slightly insulted by that."

"Only slightly?"

"Well, I admit, it's a legitimate concern."

She lifted her eyebrows in mock surprise.

"I have a pair of sweatpants in my bag. You could wear those."

"So I'm going to pair your sweatpants and T-shirt with my white beaded shoes?"

"Only so we can go out and find you something more suitable to wear. Unless you want to go in the buff. Or in your dress."

"Sweatpants it is."

"Thought so."

She hopped out of bed and grabbed her bra from underneath the wedding dress on the chair, then slipped into the bathroom and closed the door. She was in the process of putting her bra on under Noah's T-shirt when she saw his toothbrush on the counter.

Oh, God. She'd been talking to him with morning breath.

She could get a toothbrush while they were out shopping, but she didn't want to go that long. Looking over her shoulder, she turned on the water and grabbed his toothbrush, quickly putting toothpaste on the bristles. She'd been brushing for half a minute when Noah knocked on the door and pushed it open a crack. "Are you decent?"

"Uh-huh," she said with the toothbrush in her mouth.

He opened the door the rest of the way and stared at her in the reflection in the mirror for a moment, his forehead wrinkling. "Here's the pants."

"Thanks," she mumbled, still brushing.

His mouth dropped open. "Is that *my* toothbrush?"

She pulled it out and spat in the sink. "Yeah."

"Oh, my God!" he said in horror. "That's *disgusting.*"

"Come on," she said, cupping water into her hand and slurping it into her mouth. "You're telling me that you've never shared a toothbrush with someone before?"

"Absolutely not. Now that thing is covered in your germs."

She rinsed off his toothbrush under the running water. "It's no different than kissing."

"But at least I get something out of kissing. What am I getting out of this?"

She turned around to face him, lifting her eyebrows in a playful manner. "My charming personality *without* halitosis?"

Something happened in his eyes then, the annoyance shifting to something she didn't recognize, but it was gone just as quickly as it had appeared. "Just remember paybacks are a bitch."

A grin spread across her face as she stalked closer to him and rested her palms against his chest. "Am I supposed to be scared, Noah McMillan?"

His eyes narrowed. "You have no idea what I'm capable

of."

His tone was teasing, but the combination of their proximity, their playful banter, and the suggestive words he'd just uttered sent an unexpected wave of heat coursing through Libby.

That was the thing. She *wanted* to find out what he was capable of . . . .

Her hands were still on his chest, but her fingertips were on fire now. She inhaled sharply, trying to make sense of the war being waged in her head. Her body demanded she grab the back of his head, pull his mouth to hers, and drag him to the *very* available bed less than ten feet away, so they could have what she was sure would be the most amazing sex of her life. But her head commanded her body to stop. She had too much to lose with a spontaneous fling. It wasn't worth the risk. Even if she let herself think they might have the potential to have something long term, she had a hard time ignoring what was plainly written in her palm. She was destined for a man who was creative. She was certain an engineer who worked in an office didn't qualify.

"Lib?" he asked, concern in his eyes. One minute she'd been playing around with him, the next she'd practically turned to a statue, her hand glued to his chest.

She forced a smile and stepped back. She would *not* make things awkward between them. She needed Noah. No matter what her heart wanted, her body wanted, she couldn't afford to do anything that would risk pushing him away, especially now. She tugged on the sweatpants in his hand. "Thanks." Confusion wrinkled his brow as she pushed him out of the bathroom. "I'll be out in a minute."

When she emerged several minutes later, he was looking at his laptop again. He glanced up at her with a sly grin before closing the lid.

He wanted her to try to wrest his secret plans from him, so she gave him a haughty smile instead. "I'm starving."

"Good thing for you they have a continental breakfast here," he teased, packing his computer into his messenger bag. "We can take our things downstairs and leave after we eat."

She noticed his bag on the bed, the lid open. He brushed past her, and into the bathroom, as she turned her attention to the wedding dress he'd arranged on the bed next to it.

Noah came back out and packed up his toiletry bag. "What do you want to do with your dress? It won't fit into my bag."

"Leave it."

He spun around to face her. "You're the one who picked it out, not Mitch, right?"

She hesitated. "Yes."

"Do you love it?"

"What?"

He released a sigh, looking embarrassed. "Megan's mother picked out her wedding dress, but she had her heart set on another one. Josh bought it for her."

"I know. I was there," she teased.

He forged on. "Libby, do you love the dress?"

She tilted her head to the side and gave him an ornery grin. "If I say no, does that mean you're going to buy me a new one?"

Groaning, he grabbed her shoulders, then enunciated his words slowly. "Do you love the dress?"

She did, but she couldn't very well wear it again. What man would tolerate her wearing a dress she'd bought for her wedding to another man? She could hardly explain that her reasons for almost marrying Mitch weren't exactly honorable.

Noah grabbed the room key and walked out the door

without another word.

Had she pissed him off? She couldn't figure out what she'd done other than borrow his toothbrush.

But she didn't have long to contemplate it. The door opened a few seconds later, and Noah walked in with a clear trash bag. "Hold this open." He shoved it toward her.

There was no denying him, so she did as he'd asked. He folded up the gown and crammed it into the bag. When he finished, she looked up at him with an inquisitive gaze and he shrugged. "We couldn't leave it. If nothing else, you can sell it on eBay or make an art piece out of it."

She sucked in a breath, then released it, thrown off by an unexpected rush of emotion. "Thanks."

She slipped on her wedding shoes, then stood in front of the full-length mirror. Noah's black T-shirt hung to her thighs and his gray sweatpants were rolled up to her ankles. The drawstring in the waist was pulled so tight it looked like she had a life preserver hidden under her shirt. The beaded, two-inch white heels topped off the ensemble. "I look like I'm about to join to the circus."

Noah grinned. "You look better in that shirt than I ever did."

She'd seen him in this shirt before, and she had to admit he filled it out quite nicely. It swam on her. "You liar. You're loving every minute of this."

"Okay, you look like a homeless person who stole a bride's shoes. Happy? Let's go eat."

He insisted on carrying his bag and her dress down to the lobby. The obvious wedding dress crammed into a trash bag drew strange looks from other guests at the breakfast buffet, but they flat-out gawked at her. She was used to getting attention, but not like this.

A couple of younger women sat at a table together, snickering as they watched Libby pick up a tray from the counter and follow Noah in the food line.

"Is this some new fashion craze?" a woman behind her asked.

"Yes." Noah leaned around Libby with a serious expression. "It's taken over Lesser Mongolia and Kurdistan. It's all the rage."

"Kurdistan?" she asked in amazement. "I had no idea it was a high-fashion country."

"Until a few months ago, they had no fashion at all. They used to go around naked. Do you know how cold it gets there?" Noah asked, heaping his plate with bacon. "Let me tell you, it's not pretty. I had to draw the line when Libby tried that one." He shook his head with mock disapproval. "You can only imagine how many times I had to bail her out of jail."

The woman eyed Libby up and down.

"I can see what you're thinking, what with her swimming in these clothes," Noah said, moving to the next food station, "but I can assure you she has the figure for it. She used to walk around town and cause massive car pile-ups from all the men gawking at her. In fact," he winked at her with a conspiratorial grin, "she wasn't arrested for indecent exposure. She was arrested for breaking up so many marriages—those men got one look at her and they knew no woman could ever compare to such a goddess."

The woman's mouth dropped and she stared at Libby wide-eyed before she realized what she was doing and jerked her gaze back to Noah. "I had no idea someone could be arrested for that," the woman said.

Noah nodded. "They had to make an emergency law. It's called the Libby Law. In Hedonista, Iowa." Noah shot Libby a wide grin and moved to the other side of the room to get some coffee.

The woman kept sneaking glances at Libby, but Libby ignored her, trying to keep a straight face as she walked over to join Noah.

"Walking naked in public?" Libby whispered.

Noah shrugged.

He started to say something to her when one of the seated young women snickered, then stage-whispered, "She's so tacky. There's no way she could break up a marriage."

Noah's back stiffened as he glanced over his shoulder, but Libby simply reached for a mug and poured herself some coffee.

"I have no idea what that *fine* looking man is doing with someone like her," the woman continued.

The second woman giggled. "Must be charity work. Girls like her make guys feel sorry for them, which is why they never give us a chance."

Noah's eyes hardened, but Libby put her hand on his arm. "Ignore them. They're not worth it."

He stood still for several seconds, but then he set his coffee cup on the counter and handed Libby his plate. "Could you take this to the table for me? I'll bring your coffee over."

She tilted her head and narrowed her gaze. "Why? What are you going to do?"

His eyes twinkled with mischief. "Trust me on this one, okay?"

"Okay . . ."

"I'll join you in a minute."

Libby took the two plates to their seats and watched as Noah wandered over to the table with the two women. He grabbed a chair and pulled it over to their table, angling it between them. "Good morning," he said, pouring on the charm.

Their eyes widened and one of the women held back a giggle.

"How are you two lovely ladies this morning?"

"Good. We're good," they mumbled, their words slurring together.

If Libby hadn't known better, she would have thought Noah had gone over there to flirt with them. And even though he'd clearly stood in line with *her*, they were falling for it hook, line, and sinker.

He placed his forearm on their small table and leaned forward. "I couldn't help overhearing what you said about my lovely bride over there." He tilted his head toward Libby and they at least had the grace to blush. "Now, I have to ask you two, do I look like a fool?"

One of them turned from pink to scarlet while the other shook her head and mouthed "no," horror in her eyes.

Noah's voice took on an air of condescension. "I can assure you that Libby has more class in her pinky finger than the two of you put together, and even if I had never been lucky enough to meet her, I wouldn't have given either of you the time of day. I don't care for mean, gossipy women." He stood and grabbed the back of the chair. "Now that we've got that clear," he added, his charm restored, "you ladies have a good day."

The other hotel guests stared at Noah and several began to clap as he replaced the chair at a nearby table.

The two women hastily gathered their things and headed for the elevator.

Noah grabbed his coffee and Libby's and headed back to their table.

She pursed her lips in disapproval. "Noah, you didn't have to do that."

He picked up his fork, concentrating on his food. "Of course I did. Those two imbeciles were trash-talking you. I had to set them straight."

"You could have just let it go."

He glanced up in surprise. "I'm your friend, Libby. I can't stand by and let you get hurt. Why do you think I changed my mind about coming to Kansas City?"

His question caught her off guard. "I thought you came because you were supposed to be in my wedding."

Something unreadable flickered in his eyes and he looked down at his food. "I thought you were hungry."

"You're hiding something from me."

He hesitated for a long moment, then met her gaze and held it. "You wanted me at the wedding. I couldn't let you down."

Tears stung her eyes. "You're the only person in this whole mess who hasn't let me down." She shook her head, once again reminded of her humiliation. "I'm an idiot."

"You're not an idiot, Lib." His voice was soft and understanding. "You just got blinded by what you thought was love."

Love? The wedding had never been about that. Her *quest* for love, sure, but she'd never loved poor Mitch. She was beginning to doubt she'd ever find true love. Maybe someone like her was incapable of it. People modeled what they grew up around, didn't they? If so, she was doomed.

They ate in silence for a minute, but then Libby found herself thinking about Noah's nudist story and snorted out loud.

"How'd you come up with the town name so quickly for

your nudist story?" she asked. "That was clever."

"Well, I *am* pretty smart."

Something in his tone caught her attention. She knew he hated being treated like an idiot, especially by his brother. And she'd seen proof of his intelligence time and time again. He could add huge numbers in a flash and he was the only person she knew who could divide a five-digit number by a three-digit number in his head. While he didn't like to talk about it, she got the impression he'd started at his dad's company when he was really young. She'd always wanted to ask about it, so she wasn't surprised when she heard herself blurt out, "When did you graduate from high school?"

He gave her an embarrassed shrug. "Right before my seventeenth birthday."

She gasped. "You're kidding. I always wondered how you got your degree so young. I guess it's a good thing since your father died at the end of your senior year in college."

"Yeah." He grimaced at the memory, but he recovered quickly and shot her an ornery grin. "Ready for your big day?"

She cradled a cup of coffee in her cold hands. "Where are we going?" She tried—and failed—to keep the excitement out of her voice. She'd loved surprises since she was a little girl and her abuela would show up on her birthday to take her out for a day of surprises and fun. There'd been too little fun in her life when she was younger.

He pursed his lips, then said, "Walmart. You can get clothes and toiletries. I can get a phone charger. It's only a few miles away." She started to say something, but he spoke first, a smug look on his face. "They don't have a Target. Yes, I checked."

He knew she hated the superstore. "And where are we going after that?"

"It wouldn't be a surprise if I told you."

"Can you give me a hint?"

He laughed. "Let's just say I would never go there if you weren't with me."

She wondered what could be so repulsive to him and her eyes flew open in horror as an alarming possibility occurred to her. "Oh, God. Please tell me it's not the Precious Moments chapel in Carthage, Missouri. All those little angels with baby faces give me the creeps."

He burst out laughing. "That would serve you right for using my toothbrush."

"Maybe I'll just hitchhike home."

"Not a chance. Now that Megan and Blair know you're under my care, they'll never forgive me if I don't deliver you home safely myself."

The thought of her friends sobered her for a moment, but she would sort things out with them later. Today she was going to have fun.

"Here." He handed her his jacket before they stepped outside. "We'll try to find you a coat at Walmart." Then he snickered and led the way out to his car.

She would have preferred a thrift store, but on a Sunday morning in a small Kansas town, it wasn't likely they'd find one. So she let him drive to the superstore, which was only a couple of miles away. The selection of clothing was just as abysmal as she'd expected. She grabbed a pair of jeans and a couple of shirts, along with some panties, night clothes, and a pair of canvas tennis shoes. Noah laughed when she opted for a bulky sweater instead of a coat. He headed off to find a phone charger cord while she picked up some toiletries. A few minutes later, he found her in the deodorant aisle, holding a new toothbrush in his hand.

She laughed. "Is that for you or me?"

He shuddered. "Me."

"You big baby."

They checked out and she felt guilty when she saw the total, knowing most of it was for her. "I'll pay you back."

"Consider it payment for all the meals you've provided me," he said, keeping his gaze on his wallet.

They'd eaten plenty of meals together, sure, but they'd always split the cost of restaurants and pizza delivery. She didn't say anything, figuring she'd pay him back when she got home.

She took the bag of clothes to the restroom at the front of the store and changed. When she came out, Noah was holding the charger cord in one hand and the empty case in the other. He looked up at her, his eyes narrowed. "You didn't use my toothbrush, did you?"

"Jeez, if you were so concerned, you should have taken it out of the bag and kept it with you." She grinned. "But now that you mention it, I need to go back—"

She made a play of turning around and heading to the restroom, but he grabbed her arm. "Not a chance. Let's go."

He grabbed his toothbrush out of the bag as he ushered her out the doors.

"What's the deal with the toothbrush phobia?" she asked. "There has to be a story there."

His eyebrows rose. "If you're a good girl, maybe I'll tell it to you."

She turned around and walked backward. "Are you suggesting I'm not?"

"Asks the woman wearing a shirt that says, 'I should come with a warning label.'"

She laughed, feeling happier and . . . *lighter* than she had in weeks. "I figure it's true."

A cocky grin spread across his face. "Good call."

He plugged in his phone as soon as they got into the car, and after they gassed up, he headed west on I-70.

"Thank God," she said in a gush. Carthage was in the opposite direction. "No demonic cherubs."

"Lucky for you, Libby St. Clair Day doesn't involve torture."

They were quiet for a few moments. Then she asked, "Shouldn't you check in with Donna?" Just saying the woman's name filled her with irrational anger.

He grimaced. "I suspect I'd get cussed out if I called Donna."

"Ah . . ." She cringed, trying not to feel guilty about how much his answer gratified her. "That bad, huh?"

"Let's just say I don't have to worry about *her* using my toothbrush."

"What happened? You find someone else to replace her with?"

A grin tugged at his lips, but it looked off. "Something like that."

She wondered if she should offer him sympathy. Donna was a rare exception to his parade of women—she'd lasted nearly a month. Did that mean she had meant something to him? The thought sent an unexpected wave of jealousy through her, but she reminded herself that she and Noah worked better as friends. She had no right to feel jealous, yet that ugly emotion simmered inside her nevertheless. Today was about fun, not this guilt and jealousy, so she decided to change the subject. "What about Josh? Shouldn't you call him?"

"I'm not his favorite person at the moment either."

"Pissing people off right and left, aren't you?"

"It's what I do best." Only there wasn't any humor in his tone now.

That got her attention. "Want to talk about it?"

He turned to look at her. "Want to talk about why you asked Mitch to marry you and then let him plan your entire wedding?" He could have sounded condemning, but it was more conspiratorial. Yes, they both had baggage they'd rather not bring on this trip.

"Touché." She kicked off her new shoes and sat cross-legged. "Any other taboo subjects?"

"I refuse to discuss fracking, Obamacare, and the Dalai Lama," he said without missing a beat, then turned to look at her. "In that order."

She laughed. God, it felt good to be with him, on the road to some new adventure. "Fair enough. That leaves global warming, campaign fund fraud, and the Mormons."

He grinned and a happy glow filled his eyes. She knew in that moment that he needed this just as much as she did. But why? She knew he'd been working a lot lately—something he wasn't used to doing. Maybe he was relieved to have the time off. Or maybe he was more upset over Donna than he was letting on.

"Where are we going?" she asked, unable to stop herself from asking again.

His grin told her that was exactly what he wanted. "It's a surprise."

"Are we going to Colorado?"

He shook his head. "If I tell you yes, will you leave me alone?"

"No. I wouldn't believe you now."

"Good call."

They fell into a comfortable silence before he asked,

"What's going on with your photography project?"

"The one with shadows? I stopped working on it." She'd used him as a model in some of the photos, putting him in various poses with his face in the shadows. The idea was to capture the interplay of light and darkness with the angles of his face. He had the face of a god, with his well-defined nose and strong jaw, and the way the light loved his features made the project exciting. Since he hadn't been back in town for a while, she'd tried to use Mitch, but his features weren't as pronounced, so the images hadn't turned out as well as Noah's.

She'd given it up.

"So what are you working on?"

"Nothing."

He frowned. "Libby. The exhibit's in two months. This is your dream! To be on display in a New York art gallery."

"I know," she sighed. "But nothing seems right anymore." The invitation to display her photographs in the gallery had been a dream come true, and the project had progressed much better than she'd expected until her somewhat-fallout with Noah. After that . . . well, she'd lost touch with the heart of it.

"But it was going so well."

She shrugged. "I'll come up with something else." But she was worried she wouldn't.

"Lib." He seemed to think over his words for a moment. "I know you and I are the type of people who tend to feel suffocated by deadlines, but stick with it. You know it could be your big break."

Big break in photography was a relative term. The wedding and family photography paid the bills, but the artistic projects fed her soul. His reminder only made her more anxious.

"Change of subject?" he asked.

She nodded, wondering why she was surprised he could

read her. He seemed to understand her better than anyone else ever had. Maybe it was because they were so alike—just another reminder that they were totally unsuitable for each other. How could two completely irresponsible people, who consciously avoided the hard topics, make a relationship work? The thought only made her sadder.

"Does Tortoise still sleep with that stuffed rabbit?"

"Yes," she chuckled. "I couldn't find it last week and he moped around for two days until I pulled it out from under the sofa." She paused. "He misses you. We haven't been to the dog park since you were last around."

"Really? Are you taking him for walks in your neighborhood?" He glanced over at her, looking worried. "Your neighborhood's sketchy, Lib. It's not safe."

"Tortoise will protect me. In fact, he did a few weeks ago."

"*What?*" He sat up straighter. "What happened?"

"It was nothing bad. We were outside around midnight and some drunk homeless guy wandered up. Tortoise freaked out and scared him away." She was playing it off now, but the guy had wigged her out at the time. He'd started calling her names as he zigzagged toward her. Tortoise had released a low growl and bared his teeth, sending the tottering man off.

"Why are you going outside at midnight?" He sounded angry.

"Calm down, Noah. I had to take Tortoise outside to pee."

A scowl covered his face. "You need to move."

"My lease isn't up for another six months."

"Move anyway."

She sighed. "You know I can't afford it." She paused. "And I'm not doing the roommate thing again." Her last one had stolen her credit card. Libby was still cleaning up *that* mess.

"Then come to Seattle and move in with me."

She gasped. "What?" Was Noah interested in something more with her? Not just sex, but something serious. Moving in was so many levels above a hookup.

He looked surprised by his own statement, but he must have decided to go for it because he shrugged and said, "Why not? Seattle has a better artistic atmosphere than Kansas City."

Her mind whirled with excitement and her heart beat furiously, catching her by surprise. Did *she* want more with *him*? "But my business . . . my clients . . ."

"You'll find new ones."

She sat there speechless for a few moments, her barely used practical side vying for attention. Knowing Noah, if he were interested in a romantic entanglement with her, he would already have put on the moves. Last night they'd shared a bed and he'd acted like a eunuch. Still, something unfamiliar glowed in her chest—a spark of hope—and she decided to dig deeper.

"Noah, how's this gonna work? Am I supposed to hide in my room when you bring a girl home? Not to mention the fact that you have a one-bedroom apartment."

He scowled. "I don't like the idea of you being in that condo alone, Libby. Especially since Mitch isn't around now."

So he hadn't contradicted her. She gave herself half a second to get over it before moving on to her next shocker. While she knew he cared about her, he'd never been this protective before. What was going on with him?

"If it's money, I can help," he said. "I don't have much, but I can help you get out of your lease so you can move."

"Noah, I can't let you do that."

"At least think about it, okay?" he asked quietly.

"Okay," she agreed, if no other reason than because he sounded so worried.

They rode in silence for several minutes before she asked, "Where are we going?"

A big grin spread across his face. "Crazy."

Chapter Nine

The hour and a half drive to Wilson, Kansas, was awkward for the first thirty minutes and it was entirely his own fault. He had no idea why he'd burst out with his suggestion that she move to Seattle, but there was no reeling it back in now. Even more alarming, he'd meant every word. He *wanted* her to move to Seattle with him. He *wanted* to try a real relationship.

What the hell did he do with that?

Libby was right, of course. There was no way she could move into his one-bedroom apartment with him as a friend. Would she be willing to try it if he moved to a bigger place? Maybe living together would help convince her they had what it took for a long-term relationship. He just needed to show her how compatible they were. Besides, now wasn't the time for her to think about a new relationship. She was still devastated over her non-wedding to Mitch. She might not have gone through with it, but she was the one who'd proposed in the first place. Her heart had to be hurting. But if he was patient, if he showed her that he didn't want to date other women, surely she'd be willing to give them a try.

What was he thinking? He'd quit his job less than forty-eight hours ago. He might be inexperienced with relationships, but he *did* know he needed to be gainfully employed to prove to her that he was a grown-up. Why had he gone off and quit?

Part of it was that he felt he could never be taken seriously at the firm after all the goofing off he'd done over the years. Up until a few months ago, the job had never been more than an obligation to him, and his own father had made it clear to him how poorly he would fulfill the family legacy. But the crazy thing was, he'd recently learned he *liked* responsibility and took pride in a job well done. The problem was that he needed to convince other people of that . . . and now he'd left the company on a whim and he had no idea what to do with his life.

He wallowed in his thoughts until the atmosphere in the car mellowed, and soon he and Libby were chatting easily, as if nothing had happened. As if he'd never mentioned Seattle.

Libby was looking down at the radio, trying to find a station in the middle of nowhere, when Noah spotted a billboard advertising the place he was taking her.

"Could you check my phone?" he asked. It had been charging for over an hour, and while he'd felt it vibrate on the seat next to him, he hadn't bothered to check it. He was sure it was full of texts and voice mails from his brother, admonishing him for his irresponsible behavior. And while he didn't exactly care to deal with that right now, if Libby was busy reading over the list, she wouldn't look up and see the sign.

"Okay." She left the radio on a Latino station and checked the phone. "A text from Donna, three from Josh, two from

Megan and one from Blair. Ten missed calls. Five voice messages. Oh, and a Facebook notification that Tiffany Brown has accepted your friend request." She glanced up at him. "I didn't think you used Facebook." She sounded irritated.

"I don't."

"Yet you friend requested her." Her mouth pursed. "You haven't even friend requested *me*."

"Because I'm never on there, Lib. You know that. It's a work thing."

"On Facebook?" She sounded skeptical.

"It doesn't matter now anyway. I don't need it anymore," he said, not wanting to share the whole sorry story of how he'd lost the account and promptly quit. "This is our exit." He turned off, thankful he had an excuse to dodge the conversation.

She looked around. "Where are we?"

"Wilson, Kansas."

"Why are we here?"

"It's your first surprise." He was suddenly nervous. This had seemed like such a good idea last night. Now it seemed incredibly stupid and lame. "Close your eyes."

"What?"

"Just do it."

She covered her eyes with her hands.

He glanced over at her. "No peeking."

She grinned. "You're not planning to slow down and dump me on the side of the road, are you? I'll pretend I prefer Iron Man to Thor if it means that much to you."

He laughed. "I already told you, I can't go back to Kansas City without you. It would be a death sentence."

"What you fail to mention is that *you* don't have to go back to Kansas City at all."

Her words sobered him. She was right. His only excuse for his frequent trips to K.C. was the work he'd been doing on the merger of his and Josh's firm with Megan's father's firm. If he didn't work there anymore, he would have no reason to come. No reason to see *her*.

Libby continued grinning, unaware of his emotional turmoil, and he planned to keep it that way. "I promise you won't come to any harm on *this stop*. No guarantee for the next one." He found what he was looking for and flipped on his turn signal. "We're almost there. No peeking."

"Hurry!" she said, squirming in her seat.

He parked the car and turned off the engine, his stomach twisting with anxiety as he looked at the object he'd just driven nearly one hundred miles to show her. It was ridiculous. She was going to think he was crazy. "Okay, open your eyes."

She dropped her hands, and a moment later, her mouth dropped open too. Then she climbed out of the car.

He followed her, watching her closely as she tucked her hands under her armpits to keep warm. She stared at the giant black object that towered over them. "What *is* that?"

He swallowed. "It's the World's Largest Czechoslovakian Egg."

"*The what?*"

Oh, God. She hated it.

"It's a twenty-foot-tall and fifteen-foot-wide fiberglass egg," he explained. "The town has a large Czechoslovakian community, but it was dying off. So they built the egg to bring in tourists. A guy somewhere in Kansas made it for cost and the whole town came together to paint it." He pointed to the black egg with the white and yellow pattern adorning its sides. "They decorated it by hand."

She stood in silence. Horror stole his breath when he

realized there were tears in her eyes. "You hate it."

She shook her head as the first tear slid down her cheek. Then she turned to him and threw her arms around his neck, burying her face in his chest.

"Talk to me, Libby. Why are you crying?" He'd wanted to make her happy, but apparently this was just one more thing he'd failed at.

"I love it," she mumbled, still clinging to him.

"You're crying because you love it?"

She pulled back and looked into his eyes. "This is the most perfect gift anyone has ever given me." Her arms still firmly wrapped around his neck, she said, "How did you find this place? What made you even think to look for it?"

An older couple walked toward them from the parking lot. They gave Noah and Libby a confused look.

"She's so overcome by the symbolism of this piece," he said over the top of her head in mock seriousness. "It's moved her to tears."

The elderly man's eyes narrowed as he looked up at the giant egg, then back at Libby.

Noah shrugged with a *who can explain it* expression.

Libby broke free and wiped her eyes.

"I told you. It's Libby Day," he said. "So I looked for things that I thought would make you happy."

"Like a giant black egg?"

"Not a giant black egg. The world's largest *Czechoslovakian* egg."

A grin lit up her face and something warm and comforting spread through his chest. He had made her happy after all, and the complete satisfaction that gave him took him by surprise.

"So you like it?" he asked.

"I absolutely love it. It's perfect." She wiped her cheeks and sucked in a breath. "I want a photo."

"Then a photo you shall have." He walked back to the car and grabbed his phone. "You stand over there," he said, pointing to the sign in front of the egg.

She moved closer to it, but before he could snap the photo, the elderly woman gestured for him to stop.

"You go on over there with your wife," she said, walking over to him. "I'll take a picture of you two together."

Wife? He started to correct her, but then he glanced over at Libby and the word soaked in.

Wife.

Last night and this morning he'd pretended be her groom, but today there was no wedding dress to give them away.

"Oh," Libby spoke up. "I'm not—"

"Don't be silly, Lib," he said, handing the elderly woman his phone. "Let's get a photo together."

Libby gave him a strange glance, but he just wrapped an arm around her back, his hand resting on her hip. They fit together perfectly, and Noah didn't want to let go of her after the woman finished snapping several photos of them.

"You two are so cute," the woman gushed, her face beaming as she handed the phone back to Noah. "How long have you been married?"

"We're not—" Libby started to say.

"We just got married," Noah interrupted. "We're on our honeymoon."

She clapped her hands in excitement. "Howard!"

"What?" the elderly man asked, sounding annoyed as he walked around the giant egg and stared up at its apex.

"These cute young things are newlyweds!"

Libby gave Noah a confused look, but he just grinned.

"Mealy heads?" Howard asked. "What the hell are mealy

heads? Is that some kind of cult?"

"*Newlyweds*," his wife shouted in disgust. "Turn on your hearing aid!"

He fiddled with his ear. "What?"

"They're *newlyweds*. They just got *married*!"

"Married? Well, why didn't you say so?"

"I just did!" she groaned, then smiled at Noah and Libby. "You two look very happy."

Noah smiled and glanced at Libby, who still had that same strange expression on her face.

"Are you on your way to your honeymoon?" the woman asked.

"Yes," Noah answered before Libby could respond. "I had to bring my Libby to see the giant egg. She's a huge fan of omelets."

The woman's brow lowered in consternation.

Libby started to giggle.

The woman shook her head and wandered off toward her husband as Noah glanced down at Libby, aware that he was still holding her close. "Do you want to walk around the egg?"

A mischievous look filled her eyes. "Why not?"

He could have pulled away, but decided to see how she'd react if he continued to keep his arm around her as they began to walk. She snuggled closer.

"It's cold."

He rubbed her upper arm with his hand. "You should have gotten a coat instead of this sweater."

She shrugged and walked around the back of the egg, happiness lighting up her eyes. "So they made this as a draw for tourists."

"According to what I read on the Internet."

"Is it working?"

He laughed. "We're here, aren't we?"

They walked around to the opposite end. "*I like omelets*, was that the best you could come up with?" She laughed.

"Well, you *do*."

"So what's next on the agenda?" she asked, her eyes dancing.

He stared down at her in wonder. How could he have spent the better part of five months with this woman without realizing how perfect she was for him? But he hadn't been ready back then. He'd still had some growing up to do. God knew, he still did.

"Well?" she asked, shivering.

"You look like Rudolph," he said, tapping the end of her red nose and wrapping his coat around as much of her as he could. "You really should have gotten a coat."

"I thought keeping me warm was part of your job description. Isn't that why you have your arm around me?" she asked. "So you don't deliver me home with a raging case of pneumonia?"

He forced his smile to remain in place. "Yeah. That's exactly it."

They walked back around to the front of the egg. "It's really kind of incredible, don't you think?" she asked. "That an entire town came together to create something so impressive."

"If you think a giant black egg is impressive . . ."

She turned, her chest pressed against his as she looked up at him. "Of course it is. It's the world's largest egg."

"World's largest *Czechoslovakian* egg."

"But that's not what makes it impressive. People cared enough about their town to try to save it. Someone dreamed it up and designed it. A man donated his time to make it. Then the town came together and painted it." She pivoted and stared up at it, thoughtfulness in her eyes. "Have you ever cared about anything enough to devote yourself to it like that?"

Yes, and it killed him that he was just now seeing it. Especially when he wasn't sure she could take him seriously.

"Have *you*?" he asked, deciding it was safer not to answer.

She sucked in her bottom lip, sadness flickering across her face. "No. I don't think so. But I'd like to."

"You'll find it," he said. "Maybe it's right under your nose."

Her forehead wrinkled. "Maybe."

Some of her happiness faded, and he couldn't have that. "Are you hungry?" he asked, sounding excited. "I hear they have great Czechoslovakian food here."

She laughed. "I had no idea you liked Czechoslovakian food."

"Never had it. But today's all about adventures. We need to hurry and eat, though. Demonic cherubs await you in Carthage, Missouri."

She cocked her head and laughed. "I'm feeling pretty safe considering we're headed in the opposite direction."

"Maybe I was just trying to throw you off. You better be careful not to fall asleep in the car; we might just be there when you wake up."

"I'm warning you, if you take me there, and a demonic angel jumps out at us, I'm pushing you in front of me," she teased, then turned more serious. "No heading back east. At least not today, okay? I don't think I can handle going back yet."

He pulled her into a hug. "No heading east." He gave her a squeeze, then chuckled, saying in a commanding voice, "Go west, young woman. Into the unknown frontier."

She stepped away from him and headed toward the car. "Let's go get some Czech food."

Their lunch was leisurely and their food delicious. While he'd always loved being with her, something felt different today . . . in a good way. Was it this realization that he wanted more with her? Was it that they were on an adventure? Or was it that the universe had finally shifted and made Noah care about someone other than himself?

As he watched her over lunch, he realized it was true. For the first time in his life, it was more important to him that someone else was having a good time than that he was enjoying himself. And, weirdly, he was having a better time because of it.

They headed back into the car after lunch and Libby fell asleep halfway to Garden City, which gave Noah time to check his messages on his phone. Donna had told him to go to hell and rot there, adding plenty of other colorful language. Megan and Blair's texts were frantic messages that had been sent before Libby spoke to Megan. He paused before moving on to the texts from Josh. He could only imagine the things his brother had accused him off. Sure enough, the first text had been sent while Noah was on the plane the day before. It accused Noah of being irresponsible and self-centered, citing Noah's loss of the account and his subsequent resignation as the perfect examples, then went on to add that if there was anyone he needed to consider in all of this, it was Libby. The next text had come later that night, after Libby had told off Megan, and it denounced Noah's decision not to let anyone know he'd taken her from the parking lot. The third said Josh was giving Noah until Tuesday to change his mind about quitting or he'd tell their mother when she came home from her cruise.

Damn, how had he forgotten about his mother?

Last was the friend request from Tiffany Brown. Not only

had she accepted his request, but she'd sent a message.

Hey, stranger. I never expected to hear from you again after our crazy night at the Super Bowl Party last year . . . but that doesn't mean I'm unhappy I did. Call me.

Then she'd listed her phone number.

Oh shit.

"Where are we?" Libby's drowsy voice interrupted.

He locked his phone and set it down beside him. "We're almost to Garden City."

"Garden City? Where's that?"

"Close to Colorado."

"Colorado?"

He grinned as she spent the next ten minutes trying to guess what they were going to see.

"A Hungarian waffle?"

"No."

"A Greek taquito?"

He laughed. "No."

She was amused when he parked in front of a newer-looking red brick building. "The Finney County Historical Museum? Are you trying to bore me to death? Is this your payback for using your toothbrush?"

"Guess you'll find out." He was more nervous this time, not only because what he was about to show her was disgusting, at least in his eyes, but he suspected Libby would appreciate its eccentricity. He got out of the car and stuffed his phone into his jeans pocket while he waited for her.

"I'm not about to get a history lesson, am I?" she asked, sounding skeptical.

He laughed, motioning for her to follow. "You'll find out when we get inside."

She tagged along until she was beside him, her arms tightly

wrapped over her chest.

"We need to stop and find you a real coat," Noah said, watching her shiver. "There's a Target in this town."

"You just need to take me somewhere warmer." Then she hurried to the front door and went inside.

After he paid their small admission fee, they walked into the museum together.

Of course, she immediately made her way over to a genuine human skeleton nestled in a coffin and covered in Plexiglas.

"Oh, my God," she gushed, leaning closer to it. "Is this why you brought me here?"

Noah laughed. "Strangely enough, no."

She read the sign next to the display and cringed. "They used to carry this through the town in parades?"

He crossed his arms over his chest and shook his head. "So it claims."

"That's disgusting."

"You love every minute of it."

She grinned up at him. "I do."

"Then you'll love why I really brought you here." The museum was small, but it took him a moment to find the purpose of their visit, a brown ball nearly the size of a basketball that sat on a table. He swept his arm in an arc, pointing to the sphere. "This is it."

Her eyes widened as she read the sign. "The world's largest hairball?" She looked up at him. "Is this a Guinness World Records tour?"

He grinned and lifted his shoulder into a half-shrug. She read parts of the sign out loud. It been removed from a cow's stomach, and had originally weighed over fifty pounds instead of its current twenty pounds.

"I'd like to remind you," he teased, pointing to the bottom

line of the sign, "that you are not to play with the giant hairball."

"Ewww. Disgusting."

She cringed and giggled at the same time and Noah felt a fizzy happiness float through him. He'd been with literally countless women, but while those easy dalliances had been fun, they'd left him feeling empty and unfulfilled, ready to look for the next bright young thing. He'd only ever felt this . . . contentment with her.

"How did you find this place?"

Her question pulled him back into the moment. He unfolded his arms and let them hang at his sides. "The Internet. You can find anything there."

They parted ways and wandered around the museum. Noah was checking out an exhibit about some old cowboy at one side of the museum, while Libby was squatting in front of the skeleton again. A young woman approached Libby with an apologetic grimace. "I'm so sorry. My associate should have told you that we're closing soon. You and your husband will need to leave in ten minutes when we close."

Libby stood. "That's okay. We're almost done."

The woman leaned closer and winked. "Your husband is really hot," she said in an undertone he could just barely hear.

Libby's face reddened. "Oh, he's not my husband. He's just a friend."

The museum employee looked stricken. "Is he gay?"

Libby laughed. "No. Definitely not. But Noah . . . he's not husband material . . . if you know what I mean."

The woman nodded. "Too many of them aren't nowadays."

Libby flashed him a smile before returning her attention to the skeleton, but Noah was too caught up in her words to even pretend to pay attention to anything else.

Not husband material.

Somehow it was worse that she hadn't hesitated to say it in front of him. Well, it was sort of true, wasn't it? Up until recently, that's exactly how he'd wanted it. Unencumbered. Unattached.

Unloved.

How come he'd never realized he was lonely? Libby was like a warm ray of sunlight, and he wanted nothing more than to bask in it. He wanted more than one-night stand after one-night stand, but he didn't want just anyone. He wanted Libby. He just had to prove to her that he was suitable, that he was the type of man who could be her partner.

But first he had to get his job back. Even if it meant crawling back to his brother with a peace offering.

The Abrahams account.

He pulled out his phone and responded to Tiffany's Facebook message.

I hear your boss is on a work trip this week. Any hint where he might be?

She responded within seconds.

Las Vegas. At that stupid machine convention. I'm going with him. We arrive Monday afternoon.

Noah knew exactly where they were going next.

Vegas.

Chapter Ten

"Las Vegas?" she grumbled in disgust. "Why are we going to Vegas?"

He shrugged as they pulled onto the highway. "It sounds like fun."

"You told me you hate Vegas as much as I do."

He grimaced. "I thought we could see Hoover Dam. Remember we watched *When Fools Rush In*, that stupid movie with the guy from *Friends?* You said you wanted to see the dam after that."

"True . . ." But that wasn't why he really wanted to go to Vegas. She had no idea how he'd managed to snow so many women. She found him so transparent. He was up to something else, she just didn't know what yet.

"It'll be fun."

"If you say so." But she had to admit that anything with Noah was fun. If he wanted to go to Las Vegas, she was willing to give it a shot.

They stopped for the night in Liberal, Kansas, only an hour away. She suggested they continue driving, but Noah said he needed to plan out the next day's adventures.

"I thought it was Vegas," she said over dinner at a barbeque restaurant.

"That's the final destination," he said, typing into his phone. "We can still have an adventure on the way."

He'd spent more time on his phone in the last fifteen minutes than she'd seen him do in the five months she'd known him. That was one of his appealing traits. She'd gone through a ton of men who seemed more attached to their phones than they were to her. Noah was always totally engaged with her. Except tonight. Then the obvious reason hit her square in the face. He didn't want to be there.

"You don't have to do this, you know," she said without accusation. "You can take me home. Or even put me on a bus."

His face jerked up, his eyes wide with alarm. "Why would you say that?"

"Noah," she leaned closer and lowered her voice. "Where would you be right now if you weren't here with me in Liberal, Kansas?"

He placed his phone on the table and sat back in his chair. "If you had gotten married, probably in a hotel room in Kansas City."

"You weren't planning to take a flight back to Seattle today?"

"No." He frowned. "Josh and I were supposed to have a meeting tomorrow."

Guilt washed through her. "We need to go back. You have to go to that meeting."

He shook his head, his eyes hardening. "No we don't. Josh can handle the meeting and I was owed some vacation time."

"Just last month you told me that you'd used up all your vacation time."

He groaned, then leaned closer. "Libby. This is where I want to be. With you."

"Because you feel sorry for me."

He laughed. "*Sorry* for you? Why would I feel sorry for you? Well, other than the fact you're wearing clothes from Walmart."

The way he was blowing off her concerns irritated her. "Noah, I'm serious."

"Libby. So am I." He sighed, then put his hand over hers. "Are you having fun?"

"Well, yeah. But that's not the point."

He smiled, that dazzling megawatt smile that usually won him any woman he wanted. She'd been immune to it. Until now. Her insides warmed and her breath caught in her chest as she stared into his deep brown eyes.

"The point is," he continued, apparently unaware of the impact he had on her, "*this* is where I want to be. *With you.* There's no self-sacrifice involved. You should know me well enough by now to know that I'm incapable of *that* particular trait." He gave her a wry grin, and she decided to let it drop even though she didn't agree with his assessment of himself. But she also knew him well enough to know when it was pointless to argue with him.

She flashed him a smile. "Okay. You've sold me. You want to be here. I want to be here. We both want to be here. What are we doing tomorrow?"

He pushed out a breath, looking more relaxed. "It's a surprise, of course."

"Why? Today was my day. Tomorrow can be yours."

He shook his head. "No can do. You don't have a license, so you can't drive."

Well, shit. He was right. "Where are we staying in Vegas and when will we get there?"

"Caesar's Palace. I made reservations for Tuesday night."

She reached her hand across the table. "Let me borrow your phone."

"Why?"

"I need to call Blair."

He hesitated. "Why?"

"Since when did you start giving me the third degree? I'm going to see if she'll send some things to me at the hotel."

"Okay." He tapped on his screen before handing it over. "Do you need some privacy?"

"No," she released a mock laugh. "That went so well with Megan last time. I need a witness in case Blair figures out a way to reach through the phone line and strangle me."

"You don't have to call her, Lib. I can get you anything you need."

"Like a driver's license?" He shrugged. "Yeah, exactly."

She tapped in Blair's number, her back tense as she waited.

"McMillan," Blair answered. "If you do anything to my best friend, your balls are mine."

Libby couldn't help but grin. "What's Garrett going to say about you taking another man's balls?"

"Libby," her friend said, her voice thick with relief. "Garrett won't say a thing. I have a whole trophy case full of men's testicles."

Libby had no doubt about that. Blair Myers Hansen had made a name for herself as a hardass divorce attorney, which was paving the way for the new practice she'd opened with

Garrett.

"Where are you, Libs?"

"Ah . . ." She glanced out the window. "Billy Blue Duck BBQ."

"Maybe not *so* specific."

"Liberal, Kansas."

"When are you coming home?"

She glanced at Noah, but he was staring out the window. "I'm not sure yet. Probably not until later in the week."

"You're spending a week in *Liberal, Kansas?*"

Libby chuckled. "No. We're on our way to Vegas."

"*Vegas?* You hate Vegas."

"Yeah . . . well . . ." She swallowed. "Noah's taking me on an adventure. He's planning it all and I'm letting him."

"So you're okay?" Blair asked in a quiet voice that caught Libby by surprise. "Really?"

"Yeah," she answered. "I am."

"You know we're here for you, no matter what, right? Megan feels terrible about what she said."

"It's okay," she said, almost meaning it. Megan had hurt her deeply, but she couldn't exactly blame her for the things she'd said.

"Talk to us next time, okay?" Blair sounded insistent. "No judgment, no matter how much Megan spouted off." Not giving her a chance to respond, much less protest, Blair continued. "You did it because of the curse, didn't you?" She paused. "Your birthday."

Libby shot a glance at Noah, who was thankfully still looking out the window. She suddenly wished she'd asked for privacy. "Yeah." She saw no reason to deny it.

"I know you believe in it, but it doesn't mean anything, Libs. You can still meet an amazing guy and fall in love. You were never in love with Mitch." She hesitated. "I was too caught up in Garrett and setting up the new practice to see what was right in front of my face. I let you down. I'm sorry."

Libby gasped at Blair's confession. Her friend really *had* softened. "You don't need to be sorry. It's done. Now I'm spending the week with Noah."

He flashed her a grin, then motioned toward the restroom with his thumb.

Libby nodded.

"Be careful with him."

Libby shuddered, suddenly grateful Noah had just left the table. "What's *that* supposed to mean?"

"We both know what he's like, and you're vulnerable right now. You were seeing Mitch when you met him, but now you're available. And sometimes you don't make good choices after a breakup."

Libby would have gotten angry if Blair had said it in a haughty tone, but her friend sounded genuinely scared. And Libby had to admit it was true. She was notorious for making stupid decisions after a breakup.

"I know you like Noah, but I don't trust him for one minute."

Libby laughed, but it sounded harsh. "You think he plans to take advantage or convince me to sleep with him?"

Blair's voice hardened. "The thought had occurred to me."

"News flash: he could have totally taken advantage of me last night. We slept in the same bed and I only had on his shirt and my panties. But no worries. He was a perfect gentleman."

"I'm pretty sure that's an oxymoron when used in conjunction with Noah McMillan."

Libby sighed, not wanting to have to defend Noah to her friend. "Look, I appreciate your concern, but there's absolutely *nothing* to worry about." At least Blair didn't seem to be picking up on her disappointment. Still, Blair's worries corroborated Libby's original misgivings about her attraction to Noah. She shook her head. She could mull that one over later. "I need a favor."

"What is it?" There was a hint of the old Blair, guarded and wary.

"Do you know where my purse is?"

"I have it. We didn't know when you'd be back, so I seemed like the logical person to hold on to it."

"Then that's perfect. Can you dig out my driver's license and express ship it to Caesar's Palace? And put my credit cards in it too."

"*What?*"

"Look, I know it's an inconvenience for you—"

"It's not an inconvenience. I have it in my possession. I can ask my assistant Melissa to ship it. The question is why you *need* it."

"Do you really think it's a good idea for me to be traveling around the country with no ID?"

"When you put it that way . . . But why are you traveling around the country at all?"

"Why not? This is like my last big adventure. I turn thirty in two days and then I'll be old and boring. Let me have one last fling before I leave my youth behind."

"I'm not even going to comment on the fact that I'm already over thirty. But old and boring? You?"

Libby chuckled. "Well, I'll give it a go."

"Be careful, Libby. Just don't let your heart get hurt, okay?"

"I walked out on a wedding, Blair. I think my jaded heart is safe."

"I'm not so sure."

"Just send my stuff to Caesar's Palace in care of Noah. He made the reservation."

"When are you planning to come home?" Blair asked again.

Libby hesitated. "I don't know." She wouldn't admit that part of her was tempted to take Noah up on his offer to move to Seattle and stay with him, albeit only temporarily. She could room with him until she found her own place. There was nothing for her in Kansas City anymore, and besides, Noah was right. The art scene was much better in the Pacific Northwest.

Maybe she needed a change. Maybe it was time to reinvent herself.

Chapter Eleven

It was still early after they finished eating, so Noah suggested a change of plan. They pushed on to Amarillo, three hours away. This time the room had two queen beds. After Libby got dressed for bed, Noah tried to ignore the tantalizing fact that her pajama shorts and camisole left more parts of her exposed than covered.

When he came out of the bathroom, she was already in one of the beds, propped up on pillows, her hair spilled out around her.

She was gorgeous. He knew this, yet sometimes when he saw her, she took his breath away. But her earlier words— "Noah's not husband material"—still rang in his head. He really needed to get Abrahams to sign the deal so he could get his job back and prove himself to Libby.

He climbed into bed. "You ready to go to sleep?"

"Yeah," was her soft reply.

He flipped off the light and let his eyes adjust to the dark as he put his hands behind his head.

"Thank you." Her words were so quiet, he almost missed them.

He laughed. "For taking you to see a hairball? Most women would have taken off running."

"Just goes to show how much you really know me."

And he *did* know her. He knew that she liked her coffee with several tablespoons of hazelnut creamer. And that she hated to wear socks, even in the winter. That she sucked at parallel parking and had accrued a whopping seven unpaid parking tickets. He knew she often got so absorbed in a photography project, she'd go all day without eating. But when she did eat, she didn't pick around her food—she had a healthy appetite. He knew she had a kind and loving heart and that she'd do anything for her friends.

And he knew that he loved her.

He expected to be more surprised by the revelation, but perhaps he'd been warming up to it since the moment he'd laid eyes on her. A part of him had guessed at the truth for months. The real question was how he could make her see that they were meant for each other.

"It was a perfect day. I don't think anyone else would have guessed what I truly needed today. So, yes, a giant hairball and world record egg were perfect. One day, when you finally decide to settle down, you'll make some woman very happy."

"What about you?" he asked, deciding to go for it. His pulse quickened and he forced his breathing to remain steady, every sound amplified in the dark.

She released a soft chuckle. "I think maybe it's time for me to reexamine my life."

He mentally kicked himself. Obviously, he'd posed the

question the wrong way. "Like what?"

"I've been thinking about your offer." She rolled onto her side to face him, propping her head on her upraised hand. He could see her profile in the light filtering through the cracks of the draperies. It reminded him of her photography project and he suddenly wished he had a camera to preserve this moment. But he knew he'd never capture it the same way she would.

"Oh?" What was she talking about? He couldn't remember making any offer. "And what did you decide?" he asked, hoping her answer would jog his memory.

"I think I want to move to Seattle and stay with you."

Blood rushed to his head as he fought his emotions. Could it really be that easy?

"It wouldn't be for long," she added.

What? Then he remembered how he'd posed the offer. He'd suggested that she move in as his roommate, not his partner. He struggled to form a response, finally settling on, "You can stay as long as you want, Lib." Stupid. That was stupid.

She laid back down on her back. "I know you'd let me stay as long as I want, but you and I both know that wouldn't work long term. And your future girlfriends wouldn't appreciate me living there. Is that what happened with Donna? I noticed you two were together until right before my wedding."

Should he tell her the truth? Was it time to lay his heart on the line?

"Besides," she continued. "I've decided turning thirty alone is a good thing. I think I should give up men for the year and work on my project. If I'm in Seattle it will be easier to use you as my model."

"Alone?" he forced out. God, karma sucked. He knew he deserved this ironic twist, but it didn't mean he was any less horrified.

"Well, I won't be *totally* alone. I'll have you."

But not in the way he wanted.

"What do you think?" she asked.

"About you moving to Seattle?"

"Well . . . yeah. All of it."

What should he say? "I think moving to Seattle is a fan-freaking-tastic idea. You know I'll help you any way I can. And you don't have to hurry to find a place. You just said you don't have enough money for the security deposit for a new place in Kansas City. The cost of living is higher in Seattle."

"That's the part that concerns me. I'll be starting from scratch with my clients. But I can supplement my income with a part-time job to save for a deposit." She sighed with disappointment. "Maybe this isn't such a good idea after all."

"No, it's a great idea. But you should just focus on moving to Seattle and settling in with me. Then you can work on your project and build your client list without the stress of making ends meet. There's no need for you to hurry to move out."

"You have a one-bedroom apartment, Noah," she said skeptically. "That will never work long term."

"I've been thinking about moving," he lied. "The real estate market is improving, so it makes sense for me to invest in a bigger place. You could have the second bedroom and stay with me until you're more established."

"What about Tortoise?"

"I've been thinking about a house." Another lie, but he felt no guilt. He'd do whatever it took to get her to agree. "Then Tortoise would have a yard. We could take him for walks in the neighborhood. Besides, I miss the rambunctious guy."

She was quiet for several long seconds. "Are you sure?"

"Very." He was more sure about them than he'd ever been

about anything in his life. He'd wait for her. A year felt like an eternity, but if she wanted a year, he'd give it to her. Libby St. Clair was worth waiting for.

She was silent again. "This seems so spontaneous, but it feels right."

"To me too." She had no idea.

She was quiet again and Noah soon heard the steady rhythm of her breathing.

He lay awake for another hour, repeatedly checking his phone for another message from Tiffany. He didn't know much about Abrahams's plans in Vegas other than he was attending a trade convention that began Tuesday at Caesar's Palace and he and Tiffany would arrive tomorrow afternoon. But he did know that Abrahams hadn't yet signed a contract with the other engineering firm, which meant Noah still had time. But when he pressed Tiffany for details about his competition, she remained vague and made comments about how excited she was to see him in Las Vegas.

This was bound to get complicated.

The next morning Noah woke before Libby, a rare occurrence he attributed to all the uncertainties in his life. For a man used to coasting through life, he suddenly had quite a few things to worry about.

The top item on his list lay on her side, facing him. The covers had slipped down and her skimpy pajama top had shifted while she slept, exposing a generous amount of her breasts.

A jolt shot straight to his groin and he suppressed a low groan. God, he wanted her, and the urge to slip into bed with her was so strong he had to clench his teeth. With women, Noah was used to acting on urges, so this new restraint chafed. His surging hormones insisted on seducing and screwing her, but his heart wanted more. When his head finally chimed in, it told him his heart was right. Libby had an underlying distrust of men, even if she would never admit it. She *expected* men to screw her and leave her. He had to prove he wanted more.

He wasn't sure how to effectively do that other than to continue to be her friend. But then he risked that she would never see him any other way.

"You're awake?" Her voice was heavy with sleep, and the husky sound of it stirred him even more. "How late is it?"

He glanced at his phone. "It's around six."

"Six? How long have you been awake?"

"Not long."

She stared at him for several seconds with an intensity that made him want to squirm, but just when he was about to break and ask her what she was thinking, she sat up, leaning over her crossed legs.

"I suppose you have a plan for today," she teased.

"Of course."

"More world record sites?"

"Only time will tell."

She swung her long legs out from under the covers and stood. Her pajama shorts had been pushed up to the crease where her ass met her thighs. Of course, he knew he was only torturing himself with something he couldn't yet have—but his eyes remained glued to that long expanse of bare skin, his mind drifting to dangerous territory. He imagined those long sexy legs wrapped around his waist as he plunged deep inside her. His hand in her thick dark hair while he kissed her—

"*Noah.*"

He blinked, only then realizing she'd said something. "What?"

A grin spread across her face. "Where'd you go just now?

Thinking about our itinerary?"

If only *that* were on their itinerary. "Busy day. A lot to think about."

They were ready to get on the road within less than half an hour. His Facebook alert went off while he was loading his bag in the trunk, and he saw Tiffany had sent him a message.

He's meeting Eric tomorrow night for drinks.

Shit. He hoped that didn't mean what he thought it did. *Eric?*

The other firm.

He had to get there sooner. He had to see Scott Abrahams before he met with the competition.

When they were on I-40 headed west, Noah cast a surreptitious glance at Libby. Many of the women he knew took an hour or more to get ready, but Libby could be up and out the door in thirty minutes, looking more gorgeous than all of those women put together. Today she wore her hair up in a high ponytail. She had on a pair of jeans and a long-sleeved black T-shirt, which made her dark eyes more pronounced than usual.

"I'd like to try to get to Vegas tonight," he said, trying to sound casual. "Which means we can't stop as much today."

"Oh," she said with a frown. "Sure."

Dammit. The sooner he got to Vegas, the sooner he could try to win back Abrahams, but in the scheme of things what was one day? For the business, it could mean everything. Still . . .

"You know what?" he said with a shrug. "Screw it. We'll just take our time."

She turned to him with her dazzling smile. "How about you pick a couple of places to stop, and we'll still plan on making it to Vegas by tonight. How long is the drive?"

He grimaced. "Thirteen hours. Is that too long for you to do in one day?"

She laughed and turned back to face the road. "No. Once a guy I was with drove us from coast to coast in three days. I can handle being in the car."

Libby had talked about the previous men in her life before, and hell, he'd hung around with her and Mitch plenty of times before the wedding, so the stab of jealousy that seized his gut took him by surprise. He didn't like the idea of her being with anyone else. "Did you make a lot of stops?"

She laughed again. "If you're asking if Barry stopped so I could see giant eggs and hairballs . . . no."

"Barry?" He couldn't stop the derision from leaking into his voice.

"He was a surfer. Sun-bleached hair. Washboard abs. His legs . . ." Her voice trailed off.

"You remember his name?"

His tone caught her attention. "What's *that* supposed to mean?"

He forced himself to take a breath and chill the fuck out. Why was he this jealous of some guy who'd obviously meant nothing to her? "Nothing. Sorry. I haven't had enough coffee."

She frowned and shifted in her seat. "I flew out to L.A. to meet a friend. I met him on the beach, and the next thing I knew, I was on this cross-country trip with him and his friends, their surfboards strapped to the top of their van."

"Van?" He forced himself to laugh.

"A regular Scooby-Doo adventure minus the ghost mystery."

"What about the mask disguise?" he asked, teasing.

"Oh, there was a mask."

He wanted to ask her more, but her own tone had changed.

"Let's just say it was one more hard lesson learned."

His hands tightened on the steering wheel. "What lesson was that?"

"That most men only want one thing from me. They see my boobs and my mother's Colombian ancestry and . . . Let's just say I'd always suspected as much, but that trip confirmed it."

What had Barry the Bastard done to her? He had an urge to find the prick and beat the shit out of him. "How long ago was this?"

She sighed. "Between my freshman and sophomore years of college."

"Oh, my God, Lib. You were a baby."

She laughed. "It seems like that now, doesn't it? Now that we're supposedly adults."

She was right. His own college years seemed like a lifetime ago. Back then he'd thought he would live forever and could get away with anything.

She shrugged, trying to act nonchalant, but he could tell it was forced. "Turning thirty has convinced me it's time to grow up."

"I would say growing up is overrated, but I guess we can't all be Peter Pan."

She reached over and stroked her hand down his arm, her touch sending tingles of sensation shooting through him. "You've been trying. You've inspired me."

His eyes flew open in surprise. "*I've* inspired you to *grow up*?"

"Yeah." She leaned closer. "Megan's told me what Josh has said about you."

"Nothing good, I'm sure." He wanted Libby to base her opinion of him on her own experiences, not on half-truths and opinions she'd learned about in a game of telephone.

"You've changed, Noah. You're taking responsibility. You're helping your brother. You've inspired me."

He shook his head and said bitterly, "I'm no inspiration to anyone."

"Who would have thought Noah McMillan was capable of humility?" she teased.

But it wasn't humility. The kicker was that he was still the screw-up, even after his temporary foray into responsibility.

Who was he kidding? This trip to Vegas was a huge waste of time. He was out of a job, and the company was out of a lucrative contract. He'd lost the respect of his brother . . . again. He didn't have a shot at winning the woman next to him, and no matter how hard he tried he'd never quiet his father's last words to him: "You'll never amount to anything."

He'd spent the last fifteen years proving just that. Why stop now?

He was exactly where he deserved to be.

Chapter Twelve

Talking about Barry had put Libby into a bit of a funk, but now Noah seemed to be stewing in some emotional mess of his own. She realized she might have given him the wrong impression about what happened on the trip, but it seemed too late to clear it up now. No one had physically harmed her or even coerced her into anything against her will, but it had shaken her to her core nevertheless. Normally it was easy to leave her ugly memories in the past where they belonged, so why had she even thought of Barry? The whole curse debacle was dredging up all kinds of things, it seemed.

She was sure she'd said something to trigger Noah's bad mood, so she went over their conversation, trying to figure out where it had gone wrong. He'd reacted to her story, but he hadn't retreated into silence until she'd told him that his change was inspiring her own. Was Noah the type of guy who wanted to hang on to the bad-boy persona, even if he was changing for the better? She was trying to figure out how to fix the problem when Noah slowed down and pulled over to the side of the road.

"What . . . ?" she asked, but then she looked up. Right there in front of them, on the other side of the highway, stood multiple old-school Cadillacs. They were arranged vertically, their hoods partially buried in the ground, and covered in splotches of multi-colored paint.

"Cadillac Ranch," Noah said, resting his hand on the steering wheel as he turned to face the cars.

She'd heard of it, but had never seen it in person. "I wish I had some paint."

Noah laughed. "I read about that online, that people just go into the pasture and paint the cars. How about we stop on the way back?"

"You're not going to dump me by then?"

He swung his head to face her, looking startled. "What's that supposed to mean?"

"Aren't you irritated with me? Isn't that why you're so cranky?"

"*What?*" Noah shook his head. "No, I'm not mad at you, Lib. It's all on me. I'm sorry for being an ass." He released a long breath. "I'm not going anywhere, okay?"

"Yeah." She leaned back in the seat with a sigh. No matter how much she wanted to believe him, history had taught her that no man ever stuck around. But to be fair, she'd done her own share of bailing. "Let's go."

Noah took a long look at her before he pulled back onto the road. "We'll paint one when we come back. Unless we go straight to Seattle from Las Vegas. You can help me pick out a new place and then we can fly back to K.C. to get Tortoise and pack your things."

She wasn't sure why his suggestion filled her with so much happiness, but the idea of moving to Seattle felt so *right*. Of course, it was also incredibly dangerous. Now that her lusty feelings for him had made an appearance, she wasn't sure how well she could hold them back. Seeing Noah for several days every two or three weeks was manageable, but living with him every day . . . How was that going to work? Common sense told her that their relationship was like a carefully constructed house of cards. One wrong move and the entire thing could come crashing down. Was she really willing to risk it?

But the thought of not going filled her with disappointment. When she added it to her disappointment over the curse, her mother, her friends' blindness to the true nature of her relationship with Mitch—not to mention their own ridiculous happiness, courtesy of the curse—and her inability to finish her photography project, she felt like she was drowning in it. At the moment, moving to Seattle felt like her only lifeline in her sea of loneliness.

It turned out there wasn't much else to see along I-40. All the fun tourist sites were miles off the highway. Since they didn't have time to stop, they decided to push through and try to make it to Hoover Dam before sunset. The drive through New Mexico was long and eventless. Noah was still subdued, though he clearly didn't want to talk about it, and Libby didn't feel much better. But they'd had so much fun the day before Libby decided to push her negative feelings aside and try to regain some of their lost joy. She made him play several rounds of the Alphabet Game, which instigated a good-natured five-minute argument about the rules.

"Using license plates is cheating," she insisted.

"Libby." He spread out his hand and waved it in an arc. "We're in the middle of the desert. We have to use license plates or this game will last until we reach Las Vegas."

Next they resorted to keeping track of states on license plates. After Noah found Alaska, he grinned. "This reminds me of the trips my family took when I was a kid."

Somehow, despite all the time they'd spent together, they'd never delved much into each other's pasts. She wasn't proud of her relationship history and she presumed Noah felt the same way about his own. But it felt strange they'd never shared much about their childhoods. "Tell me a story from when you were a kid."

His eyes lost some of their sparkle. "You mean growing up as Josh McMillan's big brother."

The pain in his voice made her suck in her breath. "Noah . . ."

"What?" He glanced at her. "It's true. He was four years younger than me, but it didn't take long for me to fall into his shadow. He was like the most perfect child ever born." He shot her a grin. "But I'd made it easy for him. It couldn't be too hard to look good in comparison to me."

"We don't have to talk about it." She should have known by now that there was a reason neither one of them had volunteered information about the past, their childhoods included. Libby's past was full of regrets and betrayals. Why would she want to dredge it all up again? Obviously Noah felt the same way.

He was silent for so long she assumed that was his answer. Then he swallowed, as though he were preparing himself. "No." He turned to look her in the eye. "I think you should know. I don't want to keep anything from you, but I need to work up the courage to tell you some of it. Okay?"

She knew he was referring to something other than his childhood now, but damned if she knew what. But he was obviously trying to build a deeper level to their friendship and she wanted that too.

"Yeah." She gave him a warm smile. "Okay."

He sighed and sank back into the seat, his left arm gripping the steering wheel. "I was a pretty wild kid. My mom has videos of me literally bouncing on the furniture."

She laughed. "I believe that."

"When I was older, I was diagnosed with ADD, but not until grade school. So I went through the first ten years of my life trying so hard to be good, and never succeeding. I just couldn't pay attention or even remember to behave. Schoolwork was a nightmare. Night after night of me trying to finish my spelling and math homework. My mother was more understanding, but my father . . ." His voice trailed off.

His right hand lay on the seat next to him and Libby covered it with her own.

He took in a deep breath and let it out, keeping his eyes on the road. "My father was a good man. He just didn't understand me, but Josh . . . *Josh*, he understood. Josh was like a clone of my father. So when Josh started school—and of course excelled at everything—I think my father slowly disengaged from me."

"Oh, Noah."

"But my mother . . ." The affection in his voice warmed her heart. "My mother stood by me, no matter what. Even as I single-handedly fucked up my life in middle school."

"How could you fuck up your life in middle school?"

He tilted his head and gave her a wry grin. "You didn't see my grades."

"You're obviously intelligent—you graduated from high school early and started college when you were sixteen—so it couldn't have been that bad. Weren't you on medication?"

"Oh, yeah. Two daily doses of Adderall, but what most people don't realize, especially my father, is that medication isn't some magic spell that kills ADD. It only temporarily tames it. So while I could focus, I was still unorganized and late and left my homework at school almost daily. My mother tried to help me create systems to remember things, but my father wasn't as understanding."

"Noah. How could he have been so blind and short-sighted?"

He turned his hand over beneath hers and curled his fingers around her hand. "Libby, I don't want you to get the wrong idea. My father was a good man. He just didn't understand me. And Josh was so much easier for him to relate to than I was . . . I think he finally decided to leave me to my mother's devices and focus on Josh."

"But you were his *son*, Noah. He just gave up on you?" she asked in dismay.

He shook his head. "It's not as harsh as it seems, Lib. He stopped trying to discipline me for my grades and behavior in school. He still loved me; he just gave more attention to Josh. And really, it ended up being a *good* thing. My mother was much less heavy-handed and it made all of us closer in a way."

"It's just not right, Noah."

He squeezed her hand. "Maybe you're right, because even though we got along better after he took a hands-off approach, I was still jealous of what he and Josh had. Don't get me wrong, I love my mother, but part of me still craved my dad's attention and approval."

"Of course you did."

"When I was properly medicated—and trust me, it's hard to properly medicate a teenage boy—I could finally focus on my work and I discovered I was really good at math . . . at a near-genius level. It helped that all my math classes in high school were in the beginning of the day, when I was good and dosed. By the time we figured out I would graduate early, my father took notice. Craving his attention, I told him I had decided to major in engineering. Just like him."

"Did that make him happy?"

"Ecstatic. I was finally becoming the son he wanted, not the screw-up he tolerated."

"Noah."

"No, it's okay. It wasn't his fault. You know, I'm not sure I ever want kids. I don't think parents realize the power they hold. I've screwed up everything else in my life. I sure don't want to screw up my kid." He frowned and his shoulders slumped.

He was so wrong. He'd be fantastic with kids, even if he didn't realize it. And maybe the way his father had messed him up would prevent him from making the same mistake. But now wasn't the time to convince him. "So you majored in engineering for your dad, but did you like it?"

"By the end of my sophomore year I wasn't sure if I was in the program because I wanted to be there or because I wanted to make my father happy. But Dad was already talking about me joining his firm. His partner was thinking about retiring around the time I graduated, so I could fill his shoes. But the more my father talked about it, the tighter the noose was pulled around my neck, squeezing the life out of me. I felt like it had been decided for me."

"Did you at least tell your mother?"

A soft smile eased the hard lines on his face. "My mother figured it out before I even said a word. But when she gently brought it to my attention in high school, I told her she was wrong. I was willing to discuss it with her later, of course, but I still wasn't ready to give up my new relationship with my dad. And then my dad died."

His tone told her there was a lot more to that story, and she questioned whether she should push him to tell her. But she could tell he'd been carrying this burden around for a long time and he needed to share it. If he was like her—and she knew they were much too much alike for their own good—he wasn't used to sharing this personal, intimate information with the women in his life. It was a good rule of thumb never to share personal information with someone who won't be around long. But she sensed that this wasn't something he'd told *anyone.*

"It had to be hard when your dad died, but at least you were getting along with him, right? No regrets."

He swallowed and looked uncertain. "But we weren't getting along . . ."

Her eyebrows lifted. "Did you tell him that you didn't want to take over?"

"No." He shook his head, pressing his lips together. Now he looked like he was about to be sick.

"We don't have to talk about it, Noah."

"No." He turned to glance at her, and the fear in his eyes caught her off guard. "I want you to know. Even if . . ."

"Even if what? I run off screaming?" She turned in her seat to face him. "Don't you think there's a reason we haven't told each other much about our pasts? I've done a lot of things life I'm not proud of too. And you and I"—she waved her hand back and forth between them—"we get each other. It would take a lot to make me run off screaming. It's not like you killed anyone, did you?"

His face paled and he gripped the steering wheel tighter.

Oh, God. What had he done? Her head raced through the

possibilities. He couldn't have killed someone in cold blood. She knew him. He wasn't capable of it. But until fairly recently, he'd lived an irresponsible life. A DUI wasn't outside the realm of possibility.

She squeezed his hand. "There is nothing you can tell me that will make me run from you. We're friends, right? Friends stick together. You can tell me if you want. Or you can wait and tell me later. But I'm here. I promise. I'll listen without judgment."

"Don't be so sure of that." His words were bitter and full of self-loathing.

She stiffened her back and said forcefully, "Try me."

He took in several deep breaths. He was waging some inner war, so she held on to his hand and squeezed, letting him know he didn't have to deal with it alone.

"He came to visit me at school," Noah said quietly.

"Your dad?"

He nodded. "I had no idea he was coming. I was only about an hour and a half away, so it wasn't a long trip." He swallowed nervously, but she could tell he was settling into the idea of telling her. "His partner had given him a retirement date and I was preparing for my senior finals. So Dad had brought some papers." He stopped talking for a moment and took another breath. "He had added me to the firm. As a partner. It was dated to take effect after I graduated, but I'd been doing so well in school . . . and he thought I'd stopped taking my Adderall. For some reason, that made my accomplishments more real to him then."

"Had you *really* stopped taking your Adderall?"

His mouth twisted to the side. "Let's just say I wasn't getting it through legal means."

"Why?"

He shrugged. "Part of it was me. I hate how it makes me feel. Sure, I can focus, but part of me feels dead inside—like everything is *too* stable, like I lose part of me, as stupid as that sounds."

"No, I'm an artist, I get that. I need the emotional highs and lows to do my work."

"Yeah, well, an engineer needs slow and steady, not a fuck-up like me. After I stopped taking it my freshman year, I could tell I was screwed. But I knew I'd disappoint my dad if I went back on it, and he'd know if a doctor prescribed it to me since I was on his insurance." He glanced at her. "Like I said, my dad hated me relying on medication to do well in school. And honestly, I don't know that he would have offered me a partnership if he thought I had to live with it for the rest of my life."

Her anger started to rise. "You're *kidding*."

"I wish I was. I think he considered it along the same lines of being an alcoholic or a drug addict. My need for medication to remain on task was a weakness to him."

"And your mother stood for that?"

"There was a lot of hidden context, Lib. We compartmentalized things. My mother and I had our relationship. My father and I were mending ours. We all kept things purposely separate, probably in case my progress crashed and burned. And it was a good thing too. It's the only thing that kept my mother from turning her back on me after he died."

Oh God. The person he'd killed was his father. But Josh had told them all last June that his dad had died from a heart attack. "What happened, Noah?" she asked softly.

"Like I said, he came to see me. Just dropped by." Noah pulled his hand from hers and ran it through his hair. "But I'd set up a meeting that afternoon. In my dorm room."

He stopped and she realized he needed encouragement. "You were buying drugs."

"Yeah, Adderall. But they weren't cheap. At that point I no longer took it every day. But I had finals, so I needed more. My source told me he'd sell me twenty pills on credit, and he'd give me a discount if I sold some myself. It wasn't hard. I knew guys without ADD who'd buy it, so it was a no-brainer. But Dad was there when Vic showed up. And although none of what I just told you was even mentioned that afternoon, my father figured it out pretty fast, even if he didn't have all the facts."

"He thought you were a drug dealer."

He didn't answer, but he didn't have to.

Libby thought she was going to be sick. Poor Noah had only wanted his father's love and attention. But part of her was pissed at his dad, pissed that he'd allowed Noah to go to such desperate lengths to please him.

"I'd never seen him so angry," Noah said so quietly that Libby had to strain to hear him. "His face turned red and his veins bulged and it didn't take a genius to see he was about to stroke out."

"What happened next?"

"He ripped the document to pieces, telling me what a bitter disappointment I was and how stupid he'd been to believe I could change. He told me no drug dealer would ever be part of his business and he was still considering whether he'd disown me as a son. Then he stomped out and I never spoke to him again."

The muscles in Libby's back knotted. The rest was obvious. "When did he die?"

"Three days later."

Oh God. Only three days? No wonder he felt responsible. "And your mother? What did she say?"

"I don't think she even knew. Like I said, we compartmentalized our relationships. But some nights I wonder if I should tell her I'm responsible for killing her husband. Would she forgive me? I know Josh never would."

"You didn't kill your father, Noah."

He didn't answer, but then what did she expect him to say? He'd lived with this guilt for well over a decade. She wasn't naïve enough to think that her absolution would make it go away. "Is that all you've got, McMillan?" she asked. "Hell, my past is more riddled with shit than that."

He spun to look at her then, the desperation in his eyes breaking her heart. Maybe he thought she *could* give him absolution for his wrongs, but she'd learned years ago that she couldn't give *anyone* what they needed. She was incapable of it. But for the first time, she wanted to change. She wanted to have more with him. She wanted to share everything—past, present, and future.

But it was a huge risk. They were both fuck-ups. There was no disputing that. The chances were far greater that they would break up and when they did, it would all burn in an epic crash.

Libby was a survivor, but she knew she'd never survive a breakup with Noah.

Chapter Thirteen

For the first time since his father died, Noah felt like some of the crushing weight had been lifted from his shoulders. The guilt was still there—he wasn't sure that would ever go away—but it had eased a bit. Before today, he'd never considered telling anyone his deep dark secret. In fact, he'd planned to take it to his own grave, but somehow, he had found himself *wanting* to tell her. He suspected she was the only person who might truly understand.

Someone else might have wanted a different reaction from her—hugs and murmurs of semi-sincere sympathy—but Libby had given him exactly what he needed: she'd insisted his father's death wasn't his fault and she'd put his experience into perspective.

Her admission that she'd suffered hardships of her own wasn't a surprise. Based on the stories she'd told him about her past, he knew she had a tendency to push men away, or more accurately, she would hold them at arm's length and dump them when things bordered on serious. In retrospect, it wasn't surprising she'd stayed with Mitch for so long. He was totally different from her usual type—good-looking, emotionally distant, somewhat narcissistic bad boys.

In a nutshell, guys like Noah.

But there had to be some reason she would consistently pick men who were destined to never last more than a few weeks, and he suspected it had something to do with her cougar mother and her absent father.

Noah only wished his admission had triggered Libby to open up. But it had the opposite effect: she clammed up for over an hour after that, only talking again when they stopped for her to pee while he got gas, about an hour outside of Hoover Dam. The glances she gave him let him know that she was wrestling her own demons. His confession had stirred them up.

She started to warm up as the dam got closer. "I want to park in that area where Salma Hayek is sitting when Matthew Perry finds her."

"You're not planning to sit on that ledge, are you?" he asked in alarm. "That's a several-hundred-foot drop."

She shrugged, wearing a faint grin. "Maybe."

He wasn't sure he could stand back and watch her do that, and he was once again surprised by his protective instincts. Noah McMillan was a self-centered man. He was fully aware of it. It had ruled his life for nearly fifteen years. If he let his instincts toward Libby take full rein, what would happen to him? Would he lose himself entirely? But given the life he'd lived, was that really a bad thing?

"They would have never worked out in real life," she said.

He blinked, realizing he'd missed part of what she'd said.

"Salma and Matt? Why? What Hollywood gossip do you know?"

"Not the actors, the couple in the movie. Isabel and Alex. They were just too different."

His heart lightened. "So if too different is bad, then similar is good?"

"Yeah." She looked confused. "Maybe."

He let it drop because a sign for the dam appeared and Libby perked up and begged him for a coin.

"I want to throw it over the side when we reach the middle of the dam. Just like in the movie."

Grinning, Noah dug out a quarter and handed it to her. He would have given her a twenty-dollar bill to toss out the window if he'd thought it would bring her out of her sullen mood.

But when they pulled into the entrance of the dam, Libby's enthusiasm waned when she realized they couldn't drive over the dam.

"National security," a security officer who guarded the entrance told her when she asked. "You can thank 9/11 for that."

She was quiet when they walked out of the parking garage and toward the blocked-off road.

"It's okay, Lib. It's only slightly different. You can stand in the middle of the dam and toss it over."

She nodded, still lost in herself.

He wrapped an arm around her back, pulling her to his side as they walked. When they reached the middle, she stopped and looked over the edge.

"The water's a lot lower than in the movie."

"Drought," Noah said. "I've heard the lake is at a record low."

"So *nothing's* as I expected."

To anyone else, Libby would appear to be sulking over something trivial, but he knew how her mind worked. This was connected to something bigger and he suspected it had to do with her aborted wedding. "Sometimes that's not a bad thing."

She looked up at him, her eyes filled with sadness.

He wasn't used to seeing her so down. That was one thing he loved about her, her ability to find the good in the bad. He just needed to remind her of it now. "You know that whole saying about God closing a door and opening a window. Or is it closing a window and opening a door?" He tilted his head and raised his eyebrows playfully. "Or maybe it's like Alice jumping down the hole to Wonderland."

She grinned. "I get what you're saying. But I'm turning thirty tomorrow and look at my life."

He put his hands on her shoulders. "Yeah, look at it. You have two great childhood friends who love you enough to hunt me down and skin me alive."

"Who were completely oblivious to the fact I didn't love Mitch." He'd give her that. It had ticked him off too.

"Okay, so they've been a bit self-centered and clueless lately. But you have a career you love."

"Which doesn't pay shit and interferes with the whole responsible adult gig."

"Hey, I saved the best for last. You have me."

A strange look filled her eyes, and for a second he thought she was going to reach up and kiss him. Instead she wrapped her arms around his back and pressed her cheek to his chest. "Yeah, I have you."

"Libby, you know you can talk to me. I know something's bothering you."

"It's my birthday. I had . . . a wish I was sure would come

true, but it didn't. Now I'm questioning everything."

"Sometimes questioning everything is good. It puts you on the right track." Didn't he know that firsthand? Meeting her was what had made him question everything, and he didn't want to go back.

"Look at you." She lifted her head and grinned up at him. "Noah McMillan: life coach."

"Maybe I'll make it my new career."

Worry flickered in her eyes. "Is something wrong with your old one?"

The wind blew her hair into her face. Without thinking, he reached up and tucked the strands behind her ear. "It's always good to keep your options open."

She nestled her cheek against his chest and they stood like that for nearly a minute. He marveled that he could be this close to her without planning on how to get her into bed. Not that he didn't want to get her into bed, but that wasn't what she needed.

Was this real love? Being with someone and somehow getting something from it even if sex or talking wasn't part of it. For the first time he got what people meant about growing old with the one they loved.

In the scheme of his life, this was such a small moment, yet every preconceived notion about love was being chucked over the edge of the dam. He'd always thought true love—a love worthy of a lifetime commitment—was full of fireworks and passion. He had never suspected there could be more. His love for Libby was like a river of peace threading through his troubled soul. She quieted his demons and made him believe he could be a better person. That he had a purpose in the world. And while he wanted fireworks and passion, he now realized he needed both.

He kissed the top of her head, letting his lips linger longer than he should have. He expected her to back away and break the moment, but she hung on tight.

"I want to throw the coin together," she said. "I want to share our wish."

He wanted to share more than that, but it was a start. "What if we wish for different things?"

She shrugged, a grin lighting up her face as she looked up at him. "Then I guess the one who wishes the hardest will win."

"Challenge accepted."

She laughed. "It wasn't a challenge."

"It most certainly was. If you tell a guy something's a test of strength or will, you better believe he'll try his damnedest to win."

"Fine." She grinned as she dug the coin out of her pocket and held it up. "How do we do this?"

"How about you hold it and I'll cover your hand with mine?"

"I think both of us should touch it," she said. "Then we can just drop it."

He shook his head. He knew how superstitious she could be. He wasn't superstitious at all, but he'd agree to anything she wanted. "How about you hold out your hand." He grabbed her hand and turned it palm up, spreading out her fingers, then placed the quarter on her palm.

Her body stiffened slightly and she sucked in a tiny breath.

Noah had been around enough women to know when one had a physical reaction to him.

Could she really want him?

With his index finger, he lightly traced around the coin in her palm. "Do you know what you're going to wish?" he asked, his voice huskier than he'd intended. But now that he knew she

153

might want him physically, his body was ready to go from zero to sixty in less than two seconds.

"Yes." Her voice was low and she kept her eyes on her hand. "Now what?"

Was she talking about them or the coin? But even if she *was* talking about them, he knew he had to take it slow.

"Now I put my hand over yours." He did just that, lacing their fingers together and pressing the coin between their palms. "Then we hold our hands over the edge and on the count of three, we let it drop."

"Okay."

They maneuvered their arms over the edge and she looked up at him, the sadness in her eyes replaced with hope.

"One," she whispered.

Her chest was still pressed to his, their hands linked, and Noah realized he'd never felt more connected to anyone in his life.

"Two."

What was she going to wish for? Was it fair to hope his was stronger than hers? All he knew was what his heart wanted. Her. He'd heard love was stronger than any force in existence. His wish might prove if that was true.

"Three." By unspoken agreement, they kept their fingers linked and opened their palms. The coin dropped, but they continued to look into each other's eyes for several seconds.

Libby finally lowered her hand and released his, looking over the edge of the dam. "I need to go to the bathroom."

The change of subject was so abrupt, he chuckled. "I told you that you have a bladder the size of a thimble."

"I do not."

"I'd challenge you to prove it by holding your pee until we get to Caesar's Palace, but I don't want to pay for the rental car to be detailed."

She laughed and smacked his arm. "You're a cruel man, Noah McMillan."

"You like me that way."

They stopped outside of the restroom and she looked up at him, her eyes twinkling. "I'll never admit it."

"I'd never expect you to."

She continued to stare up at him and he wondered what she wanted. Did she want him to make the first move? But he couldn't. Not yet.

Then she disappeared into the bathroom and he pulled out his phone to call his brother. Noah suspected her thirtieth birthday wish was to be married, but it didn't make sense that she would care this much about a pact she and her friends made when they were kids. Other than Mitch, Libby had made no real attempt at a relationship. The goal of getting married by a set date didn't fit her behavior over the last decade. He hoped Josh knew something that could help him understand what was going on with her.

"I'm surprised to hear from you," Josh said, sounding condescending. "Has something happened to Libby?"

"Nothing has happened to Libby." Noah tried to remind himself once again that he'd earned his brother's distrust. "But I *am* calling about her."

"If this is about her driver's license, Gram's bringing it."

"*Bringing* it?"

Josh laughed, but it sounded like he had something up his sleeve. "Megan's grandma caught Libby's bouquet when she tossed it while running to your car. Gram heard you were going to Vegas, so she decided to head there herself to find a man for a quickie wedding. In fact, she's probably checking into Caesar's Palace as we speak."

"And Megan's mother *let her*?"

"She may be in her seventies and she may be a bit eccentric, but she's not senile. Knickers really couldn't stop her," Josh said. "Besides, when Megan realized she couldn't be talked out of it, she convinced Gram to act as your chaperone."

"Our *what*?"

"You don't mind Gram hanging around, do you?" Noah heard the challenge in his brother's voice. If Noah was up to no good with Megan's friend, he wouldn't have reason to protest. While Noah appreciated Gram's eccentricity more than most people, he wasn't sure he wanted her hanging around. Josh had him. "That works out for us. In fact, we're checking in tonight instead of tomorrow. So she came by herself?"

"No, believe it or not, she's brought Garrett's nana with her too."

"Oh, God." Everyone knew they'd hit it off at Blair's reception for the wedding that didn't happen, but a trip to Vegas together? "How'd they arrange it so quickly?"

"It's Gram. That says it all. I'll text you her number so you can arrange to meet her somewhere."

"Yeah," he said absently. "Thanks."

"Now what were you calling about?"

Noah hesitated, wondering how much to tell him. "Something's going on with Libby. She's not herself."

"Well, she *did* just dump a guy at the altar."

He shook his head, wondering how much to tell of what he knew. It only took him a millisecond to realize he didn't want to break her trust. He'd play dumb. "No, that's not it. It's something else. Something bigger. She's upset that she hasn't reached some goal by her thirtieth birthday. Do you have any idea what it is?"

Josh groaned. "It's that stupid curse."

"Yes," Noah said, getting excited. This sounded exactly like something that would motivate her. "When we talked about Libby getting married, you said something about a wedding curse. But you didn't remember the details."

"That stupid curse and pact have been about the only thing Megan and Blair have talked about since the wedding."

Noah glanced toward the restroom door, wondering how much time he had left. "So enlighten me."

"Honestly, I'm not sure I should tell you anything. You should ask her yourself."

The bathroom door opened and Libby came out, but she stopped to say something to a little girl who was walking out with her mother. Noah started to panic. He hadn't learned anything. "Josh! What about the curse? This is important."

"They all made a pact when they were girls. Megan and Blair didn't even remember it, let alone take the curse part seriously."

Libby was heading toward him now. "The pact is the curse?"

"No. The pact was that they were all supposed to be *married* by thirty. A fortune teller cursed them. She told them their weddings would be a disaster and each of them would end up marrying someone else. The person they were destined to marry."

"Thanks." He hung up, still dazed as he watched her make her way to him.

Libby had asked Mitch to marry her. She'd tried to set the curse in motion. But whom had she wanted to marry instead? Could it be *him*? But maybe not. Blair had broken up with Garrett years before her wedding to Neil, and Megan hadn't even met Josh until the week of her wedding. Both men had needed to convince their now-wives that they were meant to be together.

Libby stopped in front of him and a smile lit up her face.

And suddenly, Noah had hope they could work out after all.

Chapter Fourteen

Libby practically shrieked with happiness when Noah told her the news about Gram. "So Gram's really coming to Vegas?" she asked as they walked toward the car. "And Garrett's nana too?"

"That's what Josh said . . ."

Libby heard the hesitation in his voice, not that she blamed him. While Noah seemed to love Gram, the older woman was always trying to talk him into being her nude model in her senior citizens' art class. Lord only knew how wild she might get in Vegas. But Libby was thrilled she was coming. After Libby's abuela died when she was seven, Gram became a loving substitute grandmother. Libby was just as fond of the older woman.

"Knowing Gram, she won't be that tired when she gets there. I bet she'll want to do something tonight."

Noah turned to face her as he opened the passenger door

of the car. He seemed to be studying her more intently than usual. "You're really happy about this, aren't you?"

His question surprised her. "You aren't?"

He shook his head. "This isn't about me, Lib. It's about you."

"No, it's about both of us, right? It's *our* road trip." Libby was surprised to discover she meant it. She was willing to give in to Noah's wishes—without resentment—if being with Gram wasn't what he wanted.

A smile spread across his face. "You know I love Gram, and it's a riot to watch her and Nana Ruby together. They're like the Geritol Odd Couple. It'll be fun."

"Are you sure?" He sounded convincing, which should have been enough. Noah McMillan never did anything he didn't want to do. But she wanted to be certain.

The wind gusted and blew her hair into her face again, and Noah reached up and brushed it aside. The touch of his fingertips on her cheek shot lust straight to her core, but something else warmed inside her, and she wasn't sure what to make of it. She stuffed it down along with her rising libido.

"I'm very sure. How about we see if they even want to hang out with us. For all we know, Megan and Knickers concocted this whole thing for us to be *their* chaperones, and they'll try to ditch *us*."

She laughed and couldn't stop herself from throwing her arms around his neck. "You're brilliant."

He held her close. "Just tell my brother that."

"Surely he knows by now."

But he didn't answer, and when she looked up at him, he just flashed her a smile. "We have two silver foxes waiting for us at Caesar's Palace, ready to have a good time. We can't leave them hanging for too long, can we?"

"I love you," she said jovially as she climbed into the car. "You're amazing."

Noah stood beside the open door for a couple of seconds as if frozen in place, then teased, "That's me. Amazing. I wish more people would recognize that." He shut her door and moved around to get into the driver's seat.

She was excited to see Gram, not to mention the no-nonsense Nana Ruby, but the sun had set and her early funk had worn her out emotionally. She closed her eyes and let the lull of the car soothe her jagged nerves. It hardly surprised her that her thoughts immediately went to Noah.

Libby was glad he'd told her about his father—it explained so much about him. A part of her longed to make a confession of her own, but she couldn't bring herself to tell him about her childhood. She couldn't place her finger on the reason for that hesitation, which upset and confused her. She had no doubt Noah would be just as understanding of her situation as she had been of his. But she couldn't let it out of the lock-box of memories. It was something she hadn't even shared with Megan and Blair, and she'd known them since kindergarten.

She was still lost in thought when Noah touched her shoulder.

"Libby, we're here."

She blinked in surprise. "Where?"

"Caesar's Palace."

"What? How'd we get here so fast?"

"You fell asleep."

"But I wanted to see Vegas!"

He laughed. "Trust me, you can see as much of it as you want. But not in this car. While you slept, I made arrangements to drop it off here at the hotel. Which means we have to get all of our things out."

That wouldn't be too hard considering everything she had with her was either on her person, in Noah's suitcase, or stuffed in a clear trash bag. "You know we're going to have to carry a wedding dress stuffed in a trash bag through the hotel?" she asked, reaching for the door handle.

"Hey, it's Vegas. I doubt anyone will even notice this time."

He had a point. She got out of the car and waited while Noah talked to the rental car attendant. When she reached into the trunk for the bag with the wedding dress, Noah—still talking to the agent—moved toward her and handed her a gray garment bag with the name of a tux rental place in bold letters.

He really *had* brought a tux. Why had she questioned him before? Noah and Libby bullshitted the rest of the world, but they were always real with each other.

He grabbed his carry-on bag and the trash bag and flashed her a smile. "Let's go."

She followed him down several long halls until they entered a large marble-clad foyer with a giant statue in the middle. Noah checked his phone, then handed it to Libby. "Josh texted me Gram's number. Why don't you call her and tell her we're here? Maybe we can meet up with them somewhere. If nothing else, you can get your ID."

She took the phone and wandered closer to the statue, staring up at the painted ceiling. It surprised her that Noah had picked this place with its grand extravagance. He seemed more like a Bellagio guy. Gram answered on the first ring.

"So you ran off with my Libby, did you?" she asked with a chuckle.

Her chest warmed at the sound of Gram's voice. "Gram, it's me. The runnee herself. Libby."

"Libby, my girl. Did you run off to Vegas to get married, too?"

"Too? Who's getting married in Vegas?"

"Me, of course. I caught your bouquet." Then the older woman grumbled. "Ruby, stop getting your panties in a wad. If I want to get married, I'll damn well do it."

Good Lord. Even Gram—a seventy-something-year-old woman—was having better luck in the love department than she was. Noah hadn't mentioned this part of Gram's plan. "I didn't even know you were seeing someone."

"I'm not. I'm hoping to meet him here."

"In Vegas?"

"It seems like a great place to start. After I snag him, I can take him to an Elvis wedding chapel before he changes his mind."

Libby grinned to herself. "Elvis? I didn't know you were an Elvis fan, Gram."

"I'm not, but going through a drive-thru chapel seems tacky."

Libby chuckled. "I won't argue with you there. Noah said you brought my driver's license?"

"I brought more than that, my girl. Why don't you come up so I can show you?"

Libby laughed. "That sounds like a bad pick-up line, Gram."

"Maybe I'm trying to help you get picked up. I'm in room 1835 and you better get up here soon. Don't bring Noah."

That caught her off guard. "Why not?"

The older woman laughed. "I don't think you want him seeing some of it." Her voice was muffled when she spoke again. "Ruby, give it a rest!"

Libby had no idea what Gram could have brought that she wouldn't want Noah to see—but it couldn't be good. Especially if it had something to do with "getting picked up."

"Noah's checking in now. I'll come up to see you and then meet him in our room."

"Perfect. I'll see you in a few minutes. And on second thought, bring that boy up with you after all. I need to see if he looks just as good as the last time I saw him at Blair's wedding. I've been talking him up to my sculpting class."

Noah was walking toward her as she hung up, trailing his suitcase and the trash bag stuffed with her wedding dress. A few people gave him strange looks, but for the most part, everyone ignored them. "You get a hold of her?"

"Yeah, she's in room 1835 and she's up to no good."

He laughed. "It's Gram. That's a given."

"She says she's brought"—she made air quotes—"more than my license. At first she told me not bring you, but she changed her mind."

His grin spread wider. "That does sound like trouble."

"Especially since the main reason she wants you there is so she can make sure you look as good as you did at Blair's wedding. I suspect she's about to proposition you to sit for her sculpting class this time."

He burst out laughing. "That old woman is bound and determined to see my bare ass. Perhaps I should just drop my pants and show it to her."

Gram isn't the only one who wouldn't mind seeing your bare ass sprang into her mind out of nowhere. What in the world was wrong with her? If she couldn't control her raging hormones, she might have to ask to sleep in the grandmothers' room.

"How about we go up to Gram's room first and get your surprise? Then we can drop everything off at our room."

"Sounds good."

Noah was quiet in the elevator, but Libby wasn't feeling very talkative herself. She realized things were about to change.

It had been easy to pretend the outside world didn't exist when it was just her and Noah.

Perhaps Noah felt the same way and that's why he'd reacted so strangely to the news that the older women were crashing their party.

But before she knew it, she was knocking on the door to Gram's room, and as soon as Gram answered the door, any hesitation fell away. "I'm so glad you didn't marry that giant teddy bear," Gram squealed, pulling her into a hug. "That boy wasn't the man for you."

Libby hugged her back, instantly feeling better. "Turns out you were one of the few people who thought that way. Noah was against it from the moment I told him."

Gram chuckled as she stepped back and pinned her gaze on Noah. "Of course he was. He's in—"

"Standing right here," Noah quickly interrupted, putting a hand on Libby's shoulder. "And I'm eager to hit some blackjack tables, so how about we grab Libby's things, drop our things off at our room, and then the four of us can head out?"

Gram's gaze narrowed on him. "Impatient, are you? I didn't take you for a gambler, Noah McMillan."

"Sometimes you have to play the hand you were dealt," Noah responded.

"As long as you don't fold too soon," Gram winked.

Libby looked back and forth between the two, wrinkling her nose in confusion. "What are you two talking about?"

Noah flashed her a tight grin. "Nothing." Then he returned his attention to Gram. "You up for blackjack?"

Gram shook her head. "You two will have to hit the tables without us. We're about to head out to see a show."

"Oh, that's too bad," Noah murmured, half-heartedly.

"What are you seeing?"

Gram scowled and waved her hand. "Some old geezers' rock group Ruby wants to see. I hope they put enough denture adhesive in this time. Last night they spat their dentures out onto the stage. It was all over Twitter."

"You try singing a vibrato like that without spitting out *your* dentures," an older woman's voice shouted from inside the room. "And that wasn't a rhetorical question."

Gram looked over her shoulder. "It wasn't a question at all!" She turned back to Libby and Noah, shaking her head. "We'll do what *she* wants tonight and what *I* want tomorrow." She had a wicked look in her eyes and Libby wondered if Nana Ruby knew what she was getting herself into.

"I heard that!" the older woman, who could only be Nana Ruby, shouted.

"Then how about after the show?" Noah asked.

"After the show, I'm goin' to bed," Nana Ruby called out from behind Gram. "And let those poor kids in, Maude. They've been drivin' all day."

Gram ushered them into the spacious room with two beds. As soon as she caught sight of Nana Ruby, sitting on the edge of one of the beds in a sparkly shirt and a pair of jeans, Libby's mouth dropped open.

"I told you this shirt was a bad idea," Nana Ruby grumbled, getting to her orthopedic-shoe-covered feet.

"You keep your shirt on, Ruby O'Donnell," Gram said. Then she burst out laughing at her pun.

"You look amazing, Nana Ruby. Honestly," Libby assured her. "I'm just not used to seeing you look so . . . colorful. And sparkly."

"Maude said if we went to see The Crooners, I had to wear this shirt." The gray-headed woman scowled as she sat back down. "At least only three people know me here."

"What happens in Vegas, stays in Vegas," Gram said with an over-exaggerated wink. "Ain't that right, kids?"

Noah laughed. "I promise not to spread word of your exploits once we get home, Gram."

Her eyes widened. "What? I was counting on it. Especially if I get you drunk enough to drop your drawers. I bet your hiney's as firm as the sculptures all over this hotel." She turned her sharp gaze to Libby. "Am I right?"

Libby gasped in shock and sent an embarrassed look to Noah, but her mind was now preoccupied with wondering how firm his ass actually was. *No. Don't go there.* "I wouldn't know, Gram. Noah and I aren't like that."

She shook her head, her lips pursed. "Well that's a damn shame."

Libby's face flushed and she forced herself not to glance at Noah to gauge his reaction. He moved up beside her, and she was very aware of the warmth and nearness of him when he settled a hand on her shoulder. "You said you brought Libby more than her license?"

"Yeah." Gram picked up a black carry-on bag and set it on the bed. "I went to your place with Megan to pick up some clothes."

"Oh, God," Libby mumbled under her breath. "Please tell me Megan picked them out."

Gram laughed as she patted the bag. "I took some liberties."

Noah's shoulders shook with suppressed laughter. "I can't wait to see what you chose, Gram."

She started to unzip the bag and then pointed at him. "You wait in the bathroom."

"Why?" He sounded defensive, like a chastised little boy.

Libby found it adorable.

"This isn't for your eyes." She pointed to the door. "Go."

Noah waggled his eyebrows, pleading with Libby to let him stay, but she shrugged and smirked. "You heard the woman." Ordinarily, nothing in that bag could have embarrassed Libby, but with her out-of-control hormones or whatever was going on with her, she'd rather not have Noah around if Gram was about to pull out something risqué.

Noah grumbled about missing all the fun, but he winked at Libby as he shut the door. "Make sure to talk really loud so I don't miss anything," he said from the bathroom.

Gram lifted the lid and Libby sighed with relief when she saw perfectly ordinary items—rolled jeans, some rolled T-shirts, a cosmetic bag. It was far neater than she usually packed. It had Megan's touch all over it. "Megan grabbed your makeup bag and some shampoo and shower gel."

Libby broke into a huge grin. She didn't usually mind going so *au naturel*, but she had a sudden urge to look her best for Noah tonight, which would require her full arsenal. "What else did you bring?"

Gram gave her a mischievous glance as she pulled out several slinky cocktail dresses. "For you to go out with Noah."

Libby's pulse picked up at the thought of wearing the black beaded dress with its neckline that plunged farther south than an Antarctic expedition. "*Gram.*"

Nana Ruby shook her head and mumbled something about pneumonia under her breath.

Next Gram pulled out the lingerie Megan and Blair had given her for her honeymoon—a black lace bra and panties and an ivory babydoll with a lace bra, a sheer lace skirt, and matching G-string panties. They were French—and quite expensive. But she reminded herself that she had no business wearing them here in Vegas, even if the thought of Noah's reaction made her skin flush.

She had to pull herself together.

She feigned a sigh of impatience. "In case you've turned senile since Saturday—and I know you haven't—you know as well as I do that this is a road trip, not a honeymoon."

The older woman shrugged and tossed a pair of red lacy panties onto the bed. "Then there's this." She held up a sexy, silver, barely-there negligee.

"Um . . . Gram. That's not mine."

She winked. "I know. It was my wedding gift to you. I hope you don't mind that I unwrapped it and put it in with your things."

"Since there was technically no wedding, you don't need to give me anything at all. You should return it."

Gram waved her off. "You need this."

Need it? No. That nightie would get her into trouble faster than she could charge up her Visa in an art store. "I've sworn off men for the next year. I won't be needing that anytime soon."

"Sworn off men?" Gram asked in dismay.

"Leave the poor girl alone, Maude," Nana Ruby muttered, shaking her head. "She doesn't need a man. A year off might be good for her."

"Poppycock!" Gram exclaimed, waving her hand around as if she were physically batting away nonsense. She turned to Libby. "Why would you give up men? Have your ovaries shriveled up? Are you having hot flashes?"

She was having hot flashes all right, but not the kind Gram was talking about. "No, Gram. Let's just say I keep making stupid choices with men. Maybe it would be best if I took some time off to focus on me. Then I can figure out what kind of guy I want."

It was far easier to figure out what she didn't want—some version of Josh, Garrett, or Mitch. She'd be bored in ten minutes if she married a responsible, rule-following, white-collar guy. And that was the problem. The men who weren't like that were the ones she'd wasted the last twelve years—okay, fifteen years if she included high school—of her life on. Men like that didn't stick around.

And she couldn't begin to untangle the knot of complicated feelings she had when she thought about Noah.

But Gram was like a bulldog with a peanut-butter-filled treat. "A year? That's ridiculous. What if you meet the perfect man for you? Your soul mate?"

Gram's words sobered her. "I don't think I have a soul mate."

"Pfft." Gram waved her hand. "I know for a fact you have a soul mate."

Libby needed to change the subject fast. There was no way she wanted to spend this entire trip in some existential funk. "What else is in there?"

Gram put everything back except the black dress. "Oh, you know. This and that." She leaned toward the bathroom door and shouted, "Noah, you can come out now."

Dammit. How much had he heard? Why hadn't she taken into consideration that he could probably hear every word? Of course, she'd already told him about her celibacy plan, but she still didn't like the thought of him overhearing their conversation.

He emerged from the bathroom grinning ear-to-ear and looked around the room. "What? No Chippendale dancers? No collapsible stripper poles?"

Libby couldn't suppress her giggle. Given that it was *Gram,* those things were entirely too possible.

"This girl doesn't need Chippendales when she has you," Gram said.

Nana Ruby made a sound like she'd started to choke. If only Libby could get Gram to choke her words down.

"I've seen her dance," Gram said, holding up the dress. "She doesn't need a stripper pole. But this is a lucky dress. If you want to win at the tables tonight, you should make sure she wears it."

"Gram!" Libby protested. The dress wasn't much better than the lingerie. Probably worse. At least if Noah saw the lingerie, it would likely be with the purpose of removing it. The dress was pure provocation. She had one way out of this. "Noah isn't superstitious, Gram. He doesn't need luck."

"That's not exactly true." Noah wrapped his arm around her back and rested his hand on her upper arm. "Libby's my lucky charm. But if the dress makes her even luckier, then it's a deal."

Gram smiled like she'd just stolen the crown jewels. Nana Ruby muttered under her breath. But Libby barely even noticed because Noah's hand slid down her arm, sending flutters through her insides.

This was bad, bad, bad. He wasn't even touching her bare skin, yet his touch was igniting a fire inside her that refused to be doused with a blanket of common sense.

But Noah seemed totally oblivious to her struggle and his hand continued to make a lazy trail up and down her forearm. "If you and Ruby are going to the show, you better get going. According to the signs downstairs, it starts at seven-thirty, and this place is huge."

Given the state of her surging hormones, Libby wasn't sure losing her chaperones was a good idea, but it gave her an excuse to escape Noah's hold without looking suspicious. She bolted for the door and jerked it open, her hand slipping on the handle in her haste.

Gram chuckled as she closed the suitcase and started to zip it. "That eager to ditch us, huh? I get it."

She'd forgotten all about the suitcase. And she'd never even asked about her license. *Good God, Libby. Get it together.* "Gram, did you bring my wallet too?"

The older woman snickered as she patted the case. "It's all in here, Libby, my girl."

She started to lift it off the bed, but Noah slid over and pulled it from her. "I'll take it from here."

Gram pointed a finger at him. "You owe me a drink later. And I plan to collect."

Mischievousness filled Noah's eyes. "Just text me and I'll tell you where we are."

She gave him a brisk nod and then tilted her head toward the door. "Come on, Ruby. Let's go see some old fogies spit their dentures into the audience. But I'm warning you, I'm not throwing my Depends up on that stage."

"You don't even wear Depends," Nana Ruby grumbled as she walked into the hall.

"Damn straight, I don't," Gram said as she grabbed her purse and followed her friend out of the room. "I've got on a black piece of cloth that looks like dental floss riding up the crack of my ass, and nobody wants to see that flying anywhere."

Gram was wearing a G-string. Libby couldn't let herself picture that.

Noah burst out laughing and his eyes were twinkling when he glanced at Libby on his way out of the room, rolling both bags and carrying the dress.

Tonight was going to be a long night.

Chapter Fifteen

Noah paced the room, waiting for Libby to emerge from the bathroom. She'd been in there for forty minutes. And while she'd taken a shower, she didn't usually spend much time on makeup or fixing her hair. She didn't need to. Libby was a natural beauty—inside and out.

He hated that most of the men she'd known hadn't looked much beyond her beautiful face and body. Had he done the same thing at first? He gave himself a serious self-examination and concluded that while her physical appearance had grabbed his attention, it was her personality that had made him want to see her again.

He'd never met a woman like Libby St. Clair, and he was positive he never would again.

He sure as hell hoped this plan to make her see him in a different light worked.

"Lib," he called through the door. "How much longer are

you going to be?"

"I'm not feeling well. I think I should stay in tonight. You go ahead without me."

A momentary twinge of concern seized his stomach, but he pushed it away when he took into account that she'd protested vehemently about wearing the black dress. He had no idea what it looked like, Gram had held it in a wadded-up ball, but Libby—who was never embarrassed about anything she wore, wedding dress in a steak house aside—didn't want him to see her wearing it.

There was no way in hell she would get away without showing him.

"You're a terrible liar," he answered. "Get out here. The blackjack tables are calling our names."

She didn't answer but the door cracked open an inch.

"Come on, Lib. How bad could it be? If you look like a clown, you can change. I promise."

"It might make me look like I've made an unwise career choice, but I don't think it's a *clown* you have to worry about." The door opened more and she stepped out into the doorway.

She stood still, shifting self-consciously. Something in his brain registered that she was acting out of character—other than the wedding dress, he'd never seen her self-conscious— but all the blood that usually went to the reasoning part of his brain had rushed to his crotch.

She grimaced. "That bad?"

He still couldn't answer. He couldn't do anything at all except stare at her. From Libby's reaction to Gram's demand, he'd suspected it was a sexy cocktail dress, but nothing could have prepared him for this—a sleeveless black dress that clung to every sexy curve, the hem hitting her mid-thigh. And the neckline . . . oh, God. The neckline. The V dipped below her breastbone, cradling the sides of her breasts like he longed to do with his hands. Something in his head signaled him to lift his eyes from her cleavage to her face, but that view was just as enthralling. She'd put on more makeup than usual and had made her eyes smoky and her lips red and shiny. Her hair was in a loose up-do, similar to the one she'd worn on her wedding day, but a few tendrils hung next to her cheeks, showing off the small diamond solitaire earrings she always wore.

A groan escaped her parted red lips. "I'll change."

"No!" he barked without thinking. The only way the dress was coming off was if he stripped it off her himself.

"But I look like a hooker." She put her hand on the doorjamb and jutted her hip to the side. If anything, she looked even sexier.

Get your shit together, McMillan.

He didn't trust himself near her, yet his feet propelled him forward anyway. "No, Lib. You definitely *do not* look like a hooker."

"But—" Any further protest died on those gorgeous full lips as she stared up at him.

He stood directly in front of her now and it took every bit of self-control he possessed to keep from pulling her into his arms and kissing her. But it wasn't time for that. He still needed to prove himself.

"You're wearing the tux," she murmured. Her gaze locked with his as her fingers played with his lapels. It was a delicate, fluid gesture—like they'd been together for years and placing her hands on his chest was the most natural thing in the world.

He let a slow, lazy smile spread across his face. "I might as well get my money's worth out of it." He winked. "Thanks for picking black instead of powder blue."

She cringed, but then a grin lifted the corners of her mouth.

"I wanted mauve." Her shoulder lifted in a delicate motion that held him captive. "But I *did* let Mitch pick out everything."

"Well, thank you, Mitch," he murmured, trying unsuccessfully to keep his voice light.

Her gaze dropped to her hands and she stiffened slightly, as though realizing what she'd done. He expected her to jerk her hands away, but she kept them in place, her palms flat and her fingers splayed. "I think I should change." Her words were soft and uncertain.

"No, Lib. You should definitely *not* change." Dammit all to hell. His body was resisting this untested concept of self-control and his voice had taken on a sultry tone.

To his surprise, she pressed herself against him—only slightly—but enough to tell him that she was ready and willing.

God help him, so was he.

Don't fuck this up, McMillan.

He took a step back. "So now that we've settled that, let's go play some blackjack."

Confusion swept over her face, and perhaps a bit of hurt, but she gave him a wavering smile. "Okay."

Gram hadn't thought to pack Libby a purse to go with her dress, so she left her faded Indian print bag in the room. Noah stuck her license in his wallet in case she needed it and reached out a hand to her. "Let's go."

She hesitated before taking it, but then she let him thread his fingers with hers. He knew he was sending her a confusing mix of signals. Part of him needed to know that she wanted him physically as much as he wanted her, but his gut told him the time wasn't quite right yet. Not if he wanted his plan to work.

They walked to the elevator hand in hand, and when the doors opened, he released her and followed her into the car, moving his hand to the side of her hip.

She gave him an inquisitive glance, but the seven other people in the elevator stopped her from asking questions. She was taller tonight, wearing shiny, black, fuck-me heels that spiked his lust even higher.

Libby St. Clair was the sexiest woman he had ever known and he had no idea how he was going to keep his hands to himself all night. Let alone sleep with her in the king-size bed in their room.

God help him.

The door opened and a well-dressed middle-aged man stood in the entrance. His gaze landed on Libby's face and quickly zoomed down to her cleavage. Noah's hand tightened on her hip and he locked eyes with the asshole as the guy made a move toward Libby. The look in Noah's eyes made him hesitate and alter his course.

Libby's body sank into Noah's side, and he glanced down to see if she'd noticed the silent exchange between him the fucker who was now sneaking glances at her ass. If she had, she didn't let on.

The top of her head hit right under his chin and the smell of her shampoo filled his nose—jasmine and a faint hint of apples. It was *her* scent and he realized now that he'd missed it the last couple of days. The complimentary hotel toiletries she'd been using smelled fine, but this . . . well, this was the essence of Libby St. Clair.

The elevator reached the first floor and Noah kept his arm around her as the doors opened, then ushered her into the hall and toward the gambling area. Several people from the elevator followed them, including the guy.

The fucker was still checking out her ass.

Noah tensed, about to turn around and confront the

bastard, but Libby looked up at him, her mouth pursed in disapproval. "I have no idea what's gotten into you tonight. Just ignore him."

His eyes widened in surprise.

"Yes, I know when guys are checking me out. It's a survival skill," she teased. "Ignore him."

"But—"

She pulled him aside and waited until the guy passed them, giving Libby a slight backward glance before rounding a corner. Noah jerked against her hold, but her fingers dug into his sleeve. "Noah, I think it's sweet how you've taken on this protective role, but beating the shit out of someone in my defense isn't going to help a thing." She gave him a dazzling smile. "Now come on. You promised to spot me a few games of blackjack."

Sweet? Protective role? He forced himself to calm down, surprised at how outraged he was on her behalf. How many times had he himself checked out a woman? It had to be equivalent to the number of breaths he'd taken since his birth. But this was his Libby—she was a person with feelings, not some mannequin to be ogled.

Dammit, taking a good look at himself in the mirror sucked donkey ass.

She reached up and kissed his cheek and then rubbed the spot with her thumb. "Don't let this ruin our night."

"You said you hate to gamble."

She stared into his eyes for several seconds. "It depends on what I'm gambling on."

Before he could respond, she grabbed his hand and pulled him along. Could she be talking about him? *Them?* Was she thinking about a quick fling or something more? Maybe she was talking about moving to Seattle. Or even choosing a new deodorant. The possibilities were endless.

He barely registered where they were going. The truth was, he hated Caesar's Palace, but Scott Abrahams was staying there, and as massive as Vegas was, it made sense to stay in the same place. He hadn't heard from Tiffany, and that had him more than a little worried. He still hadn't let her know he only wanted information from her, but he'd deal with that when the time came.

Libby headed for one of the blackjack areas, but Noah pulled her back. "We should eat first. You have to be starving."

She shook her head. "No. I'm not hungry."

"We have to eat sometime tonight and we're all dressed up. How about I make a reservation somewhere? We can play for an hour or two and then have a late dinner."

She pondered it a moment. "That's a great idea. Maybe Gram can join us."

Gram. He'd almost forgotten about her. So much for a romantic dinner, not that it was going to be one. His current plan was to woo her until they got to Seattle, then tell her how he felt. Her one-year celibacy plan was an issue, but he was pretty sure it was only a protective measure. If she insisted on following through with it, he'd respect her wishes and wait.

He pulled out his phone and looked up a contact. "How about if I make reservations at Blue Willow for four at eleven? If Nana Ruby decides not to come, it'll be no big deal to go from four to three." When she seemed to hesitate, he added, "I ate there last time I was in Vegas, and it's pretty nice."

"But is it expensive? With the hotels and the food . . . I know we're splitting the cost, but I spent a lot of money on the . . ."

Her voice trailed off and he knew she was talking about the wedding. She'd mentioned that she'd paid for most of it herself, without her mother's financial or emotional support. She'd barely let Mitch pay for anything, which seemed odd considering she had given him everything he wanted. But she hardly had any money in the first place, so she had to be broke now.

"Don't worry about the cost. Tomorrow's your birthday. You only turn thirty once. Consider it my birthday gift to you."

The mention of her birthday sent a dark shadow over her face and she turned toward the gaming area again. "I need a drink."

"What do you want? I'll get you one."

"I can get my own drink," she said defensively. "You take care of getting chips."

The memory of the asshole in the elevator was still fresh in his mind. "I think we should stick together."

She laughed, but the sound was devoid of any humor. "I know how to handle men, Noah. Just like you know how to handle women. It's what we do best."

His mouth gaped open. It was the truth, but it was hard to hear it put so bluntly.

She shoved his arm. "Go on. I'm going to flag down that waitress. What do you want?"

Beer wasn't going to cut it tonight. "Gin and tonic."

She lifted her eyebrows, but something was still off. "Going for the big guns tonight, huh?"

She cut off his response by flagging down a departing waitress. When she noticed he was still standing there watching her, she mouthed *go* with an exasperated look.

After he made the reservation for the restaurant and bought a hundred dollars' worth of chips, he found her sitting at a blackjack table. She had the rapt attention of the two men who sat to her right. They looked to be in their thirties and both were fairly good-looking and obviously interested in her. Libby was playing with a small stack of chips in front of her, picking them up and letting them drop into a stack with a rhythmic clink.

"Mississippi, you say?" she asked, her voice sultry. "I've never been to Mississippi. Is it as hot as they say it is?"

She was flirting with them.

He stuffed down his anger and jealousy. As far as she was concerned, they were nothing more than friends. Still, he'd never tried to pick up women when they were together. He'd told himself it was out of respect for her, but now he knew it was because he'd loved her all along. Apparently she didn't feel the same limitation now that she wasn't with Mitch.

Noah stood back and watched her, surprised she didn't realize he was there. It was obvious the two guys hadn't put it together that they knew each other. She leaned forward, batting her lashes, and put her hand on the hand of the man closest to her.

He'd never seen her this way. She'd always been real with him, even that first weekend before Josh and Megan's wedding. Still, he'd always suspected she was an accomplished flirt. Her current performance confirmed it. This wasn't the woman he knew, and dammit, it was hard to see her this way.

"Libby," he said, trying to keep the tightness out of his voice. "Where'd you get the chips?" He already knew, but dammit, he wanted her to admit it.

She turned and flashed him a brilliant smile, but there was something dark in her eyes. "Craig here was kind enough to loan me a few. Wasn't that sweet?"

The two men were now giving their full attention to Noah. He glared at the man on the end, whose reddening face identified him as Craig.

Craig slid off his stool. "We didn't know she had a boyfriend, man. She told us she was waiting for her friend. We thought her friend was a *she*."

Both men grabbed their chips and Noah said, "Hey, don't forget this." He tossed a twenty-five-dollar chip across the table toward them.

They scurried away and Libby looked up at him with a lazy grin that didn't reach her eyes. She pushed a glass toward him. "Here's your drink."

He reacted before he had time to think it through. "What the hell was that?"

"What?" she asked innocently. "Are you going to play or not?"

The dealer's eyes narrowed, waiting to see how this played out.

This wasn't how he'd hoped things would go at all. "I thought you'd sworn off men for a year."

A sheepish look covered her face.

What had made her go from welcoming his touch minutes ago to practically blowing him off for two strangers? Then it hit him.

She was terrified.

She was scared to admit she wanted something more with him. So her instinct was to prove she didn't need him by finding some guy for a meaningless one-night stand.

He was still upset, but he forced himself to see this as progress. He smiled even if he didn't feel like it, then reached for her chips and slid them away. "These are luckier," he said, replacing them with part of his stack.

There was worry in her eyes when she met his gaze, but it vanished in an instant, replaced with another performance. "And what do you have for luck?"

His smile turned more genuine. "You." Then he added, "Gram said your dress was lucky, remember?"

She nodded and turned her attention to the table.

They put some chips down and the dealer dealt them their hands. After fifteen minutes, Libby was twenty dollars richer and Noah was ahead by fifty. "I told you it was our lucky night," Noah told her with a wink.

A waitress passed their table and Libby got her attention. "Another mojito, please."

Libby shot Noah a questioning glance and he shook his head. "I'm good."

They spent the next thirty minutes at the table, both of them winning some and losing some, then Libby finished her drink and stood. "Let's go do something else."

They scooped up their chips and moved away from the table. Libby wobbled slightly, so Noah took her arm. "Why don't we get something to eat?"

"What time is it? I thought you made dinner reservations for eleven."

"It's around nine-thirty, but we haven't eaten since this afternoon. I'm hungry. Let's get a snack."

"I thought you wanted to gamble."

"Let's sit at the slot machines. We can grab something to eat while we play."

"Okay. But first I have to go to the restroom."

"Of course you do," he chuckled. "I'll go get something to eat and meet you at these slots right here, okay?"

She studied him for a moment. "Afraid I'll ditch you?"

His breath caught. "Should I be?"

A small smile lifted the corners of her mouth. "No, you're safe for now."

Chapter Sixteen

Libby went into the restroom and took care of her business, then washed her shaking hands and looked at her reflection.

Why had she flirted with those guys? It wasn't like she was interested, but if she was going to act on this impulse to sleep with someone, it would be better to do it with a stranger she'd never have to see again than to sleep with Noah and lose him forever.

But it made her feel slimy and unworthy of Noah's friendship.

She wasn't sure why his reaction to those guys had surprised her. She couldn't ignore what was right in front of her face. Noah wanted to sleep with her. There was no misinterpreting that. She wasn't sure she could be strong enough for the both of them.

He was waiting at a slot machine with a bowl of nachos and a couple of bottles of water.

She sat down next to him, grinning. "You realize how ridiculous this is, right? I'm wearing this dress and you're in a tux, but we're sitting here eating chips covered in processed cheese in front of dollar slot machines."

He grabbed a chip and took a bite. "It's kind of more us, don't you think?" He held up the container toward her. "The nachos, not the machines."

She took a chip and leaned over the container so she didn't drip cheese on her dress. "Yeah, I suppose."

"How come you've never read my palm?"

The question came out of nowhere and caught her off guard. "Uh . . . I don't know." But that wasn't true. She realized that now. She'd been worried about what she'd see, or more aptly, what she *wouldn't* see.

He took another chip and looked into her eyes. "You've read the palms of just about everyone we know, yet you've never asked to read mine."

"First of all, we hardly have any friends in common, and second, you've never *asked* me to read your palm."

He set the tray of nachos down and held out his palm to her. "Libby," he said in a husky voice. "I want you to read my palm."

Her heart began to race, and she fought to keep her breathing even. She started to reach for his hand, then stopped. What was she so afraid of? Confirmation of what she already knew? Noah McMillan wasn't the man destined for her. "You don't believe in it."

"Maybe I do. *You* do. And you were right about Josh."

"I thought you said it was a lucky guess."

"What difference does it make if I believe or not? I want you to read my palm."

She took a deep breath and grabbed his hand, the contact

sending a jolt of desire straight to her core. Trying her best to ignore it, she cradled his hand in hers, using her right index finger to trace the lines.

"What does it say?"

Her nerves were on edge and she could hardly concentrate on the grooves in his hand. "You have a deep life line. You're very healthy."

"True." Her eyes were still on his hand, but she could hear the grin in his voice.

"It's also very long. You'll live a long life."

"So you're saying I can take up dangerous sports without fear, like sky diving or rope-free cliff climbing."

She grinned and snuck a look at him. "No."

His eyes held hers and she felt a new connection to him. What was it? It was at once deep and unnerving and . . . comforting. Then it hit her.

Love.

She loved him.

Not just *you're my best friend* love. She was head over heels *in* love with him.

"Go on," he coaxed softly. "I want to hear about my love line."

Oh, God. This was *terrible*. What did she do with this knowledge—this *yearning* for him? Noah was bound to freak out if he knew she felt anything for him other than friendship and primal lust. If he even got an inkling, he was sure to take off running. That's what he'd done with all of his past relationships.

Get it together, she told herself. *Don't let him see anything's wrong.* She took a breath, trying to steady her nerves. "I'm not done with your life line."

"All right."

With great difficulty, she tore her eyes from his and looked down at his palm. "There are several hash marks on your life line indicating major life events." She lifted his hand closer to her face. "The first was in your very early twenties."

"My father's death," he murmured. "When I took over the company."

"Another in your mid- to late thirties." She paused and took a closer look. "Several, actually."

"Bad things?"

She pursed her lips. "No, not necessarily. The way some of these are smaller and close together suggests they might be marriage and children."

Nausea stirred in her gut as she thought about him with someone else. A wife who wouldn't understand their relationship . . . and would be right not to.

She took another breath, hoping her hands didn't start to shake, and decided it was safer to move on. "This is your head line." The pad of her index finger rubbed over the line running above his life line. "You're very intelligent." She glanced up at him through her lashes. "But we knew that already."

A gleam of reassurance filled his eyes. He always joked about being an idiot and a fool. It shocked her to realize that part of him actually believed it, his academic achievements in his teens and in college notwithstanding.

"See how it curves and is so long?" she asked, waiting for him to look. "That means you're a creative thinker and problem solver." Creative thinker, but not necessarily creative. What did she make of that?

"And my heart line?"

"Why are you so insistent on your heart line?" She was scared to study it.

"I want to know what my future holds."

"Sometimes surprises are good."

"What does it say?" he prodded.

She dragged her gaze from his again. She'd looked into his eyes for months without feeling this way, though she'd noticed from the start they were the perfect color—a warm golden brown. Why was she so drawn to them now? "It says . . ."

Noah's phone rang and they both jumped, caught by surprise. He groaned and reluctantly pulled his hand from Libby's. "I better check to see who it is." Then he groaned again and rejected the call.

"Anything important?" she asked.

He frowned. "No, just some work thing."

"Shouldn't you take it?"

"No." His answer was firm as he held out his hand. "Are you going to finish with my love line?"

She gave him a sad smile. "We both know how that one goes."

"No, Lib. You don't."

Was he right? Could they really work? Because she knew that's what he meant. The real question was what he wanted. A quick fling or something more? What if he didn't run away from her if she told him she loved him? Could she really take the risk? She was terrified. She'd lost so much. She couldn't lose him too.

"Why did you propose to Mitch?"

"What?"

"Libby." He was more insistent. "I know about the curse."

She looked up at him, blinking in confusion. "What?"

"The curse. You told me about the pact, but Josh told me about the curse."

Humiliation burned her face. "What do you know?"

"I know you want to uphold the pact you and your friends

made when you were girls, and I also know you believe you were cursed by a fortune teller."

She closed her eyes. "And?"

"I'd rather hear it from you." His voice was soft and understanding.

Her eyes opened. "You want to hear that I asked Mitch to marry me so the guy I was supposed to marry would show up?"

"Who was supposed to show up, Libby?"

Tears filled her eyes. "It's stupid, I know. But the fortune teller said our weddings would be disasters and each of us would marry someone other than our intended." She sucked in a breath. "It worked for Megan and Blair, so why wouldn't it work for me? Especially since I was the one who believed in the curse the most. So I proposed to Mitch, expecting *him* to show up."

His eyes hardened. "*Who*, Libby? *Who* did you expect to show up?"

Her voice broke. "I don't know."

His shoulders sagged, then he took her hand and cradled it between both of his.

She gave him a half-shrug. "Megan met Josh on that plane and Blair never thought she'd see Garrett again. Neither of them expected to marry the men they married. Megan didn't even know Josh." She paused. "I thought something like that would happen to me."

"So that's why you let Mitch plan the wedding and wouldn't let him pay for it." He seemed to be saying it more to himself than her. "You never wanted to marry him?"

"You must think I'm a total bitch."

He slowly shook his head. "No, Lib. I love that about you."

"That I intentionally hurt Mitch?" she asked in disbelief.

"No. That you believed in something so much you risked everything to make it happen."

"Fat lot of good it did me. Tomorrow's my birthday and look where I'm at."

"You're with me." He studied her face as he wiped a tear from her cheek. "Libby, did you ever really think about who you were supposed to marry?"

She shook her head, but a little voice inside her head was screaming that the answer might be right in front of her. But her palm told her differently. Which did she believe? The curse or the lines on her palm? Could she believe in one without the other? She swallowed the lump in her throat. "It doesn't work that way. I wasn't supposed to know."

"Think about it *now*. Tomorrow's your birthday. Who are you supposed to marry?"

Was he saying what she thought he was? "The curse isn't real, Noah."

His gaze held hers. "I think it is."

"You're not superstitious," she whispered.

His finger lightly traced her jaw, sending shivers of need down her spine. "I am now."

She wanted this more than she'd ever wanted anything in her life, but now that she might actually have a shot at it, the fear that she would screw it up terrified her. She jumped off the stool. "I want to play poker."

His eyes widened. "*Poker?* Right *now?*"

"Yes."

"You hate poker."

"I want to play anyway, but I need another drink first."

She flagged down a waitress and ordered another mojito. Noah watched her for a moment before ordering another gin and tonic.

Her life was shit. She might as well get drunk.

She knew it was stupid and irresponsible, yet that's what she was. Irresponsible. Just ask anyone. No wonder the curse hadn't worked for her. She didn't deserve it.

Chapter Seventeen

"I need to go the bathroom before we play poker."

She'd had several drinks and she really did have to pee often, but he recognized what she was doing. He held on to her hand when she tried to pull away. "Don't run away, okay? Promise me you won't run away."

She looked into his eyes. "You're still safe."

For now hung in the air as he dropped her hand and watched her walk into the restroom.

Noah's phone rang and he reluctantly pulled it from his pocket. Tiffany had called earlier. He knew he needed to set up a time to meet her, but he didn't want to think about Tiffany when he was with Libby. It might have been different if he hadn't slept with Abrahams's assistant earlier in the year. It felt disrespectful to call her while he was with Libby, but how could he hope to make a life with the woman he loved if he didn't have a job?

He needed to talk to Tiffany, as much as it killed him to do so.

But Tiffany wasn't the person on the other end of the phone. Noah wasn't sure whether to be irritated or thankful. "Hey, Gram. I thought you were at that old geezers' show. They spit out their dentures already?"

She released a belly laugh. "Ruby was snoozing in her chair."

"I was not!" Garrett's nana shouted.

Gram snorted. "Yes, you were, old woman. I can't help if it you have the napping hours of a farm hand."

"I own a damn farm!" Ruby protested.

"*Why do you think I used that analogy?*"

"Gram," Noah asked. "Am I on speaker phone?"

"Seemed easier this way." She cleared her throat. "Obviously, we left. How are things goin' with you and Libby?"

"Fine. She's in the restroom." He couldn't very well tell her what was really going on.

"Fine?" she barked. "Is she wearing that little black thing?"

"Uh . . . yeah . . ."

"And things are just *fine*?"

"What does that mean?"

"It means I don't know what it's going to take to get the two of you to hook up if that dress didn't do the trick. Do I have to lock you in a room?"

"Is it that obvious?"

"Of course it's obvious," Ruby cut in. "A camel dying of thirst in the desert would spit his last sip of water to put out the damn fire between you two. Why do you think we're *really* here?"

That rattled around in his head for a few seconds.

"So?" Gram demanded. "What the hell are you doin' to get the girl?"

"Maybe Libby should be the one trying to get me," Noah said. "I thought you were a feminist, Gram."

"Damn straight I am, but you and I both know that girl's even more of a commitment-phobe than you are."

"I said that too!" Ruby shouted.

"Commitment-phobe? But she planned a wedding . . ." Noah said. "She believes in the curse."

Ruby laughed. "Boy, you got a lot to learn, don't ya?"

"Yes, ma'am?" His voice rose, uncertain that was the right answer.

"Good boy. Admittin' you don't know everything is the first step to pullin' your head outta your ass."

He couldn't help but laugh.

"Libby's like a kid who wants to go to the amusement park and ride a rollercoaster," Ruby said. "She's excited to get there, but she starts to chicken out before getting on the ride. She just needs some encouragement."

Noah grew indignant. "I'm not pushing her to do anything she doesn't want to do."

"You take me for an idiot, boy?" Nana Ruby barked.

Noah jumped even though the woman was on the phone. "No, ma'am."

"Nobody said anything about dragging her onto the damn ride and tying her in."

"Unless she's into that *Fifty Colors of Gray* BS stuff," Gram said. "Then she might like to be tied in."

"It's BDSM," Ruby corrected. "Not BS."

"Oh, yeah. That's what Megan said. How'd *you* know?" Gram asked.

There was a pause before Ruby answered, "I might have

read it."

"*Might* have?" Gram asked. "How did you *might have* read it? Did you whack your head and get amnesia after you finished?"

"No, dammit!" Ruby shouted. "Okay, I read it. Then I joined MatureSingles.com."

"And?" Gram encouraged.

"I met a man! Are you happy? Don't you dare tell those prude daughters of mine that I found a man who's into spanking."

"Okay!" Noah interrupted. "That's TMI!"

"Only if she leaves her jaw open too long for oral sex," Gram said. "Do you, Ruby?"

"Oh, my God, Gram!" Noah shouted, drawing the looks of the people around him. He wasn't sure he'd ever get that mental image out of his brain. "That's *TMJ*, not TMI."

"Oh, then what's TMI?"

"Too much information," Ruby supplied.

"How'd you know that?" Gram asked.

"I got a Twitter account."

"I have one too and I still didn't know that."

"My grandkids taught me to use it," Ruby added smugly.

"Huh," Gram said, then returned her attention to Noah. "So is Libby into BPM?"

"I give up," Ruby groaned.

"I don't know if she is or not. It hasn't come up in discussion." Noah's face was burning. "I haven't even kissed her yet."

"What?" Gram shouted.

"Maybe he's old-fashioned," Ruby said.

That seemed to appease Gram since she swung the conversation a different direction. "Are you like those fundamentalist Christians who think they should fill their baskets full of kids?"

"*What?*"

"Their quivers," Ruby said. "How do you get everything so *wrong?*"

"Quiver? I *bet* those kids are quivering with lust. They can't even hold hands or hug before they get engaged, and they don't kiss until the wedding. I bet they don't last thirty seconds on their wedding night. You don't want that happening with Libby, do you?"

Noah stifled a groan. How was he having this conversation with two grandmothers? "*Look*, I appreciate the advice, but I know how to handle women."

Both women started cackling.

"What?" he asked defensively.

"There's a difference between handling tarts and handling the woman you want to marry," Ruby said. "And it's plain as day that Libby's scared to make a commitment. Now how are you going to deal with that?"

"My plan was to give her all the space she needs . . . but that dress . . ."

Gram chuckled. "That's why I called it a lucky dress. It'll help you two get lucky."

But he still didn't think that was what she needed from him. She needed to know he was going to stick around. "I just did everything short of flat-out telling her I love her and want to marry her, and she jumped up like I'd shot her and said she wanted to play poker."

"Libby hates to gamble," Gram murmured.

"I know."

"She's gonna go looking for another man," Gram said. "That's what she does."

"She already did," Noah said, trying not to sound defeated.

"But she didn't do anything."

"That's good," Gram encouraged. "That sounds like progress."

"She told me she wants to take time away from relationships. If that's what she wants, I'm going to give it to her."

"While you play with your strumpets?" Ruby asked.

"No," Noah said firmly. "I'm going to convince her that she's the only woman I want. Ever."

Gram chuckled. "There may be hope for you two yet."

Chapter Eighteen

Noah was stuffing his phone into his pocket when Libby emerged from the restroom. He must have noticed her questioning glance because he said, "Gram. I told her about dinner. They'll meet us at the restaurant."

"Okay." But Libby's anxiety was making her skin feel too tight. Noah seemed more reserved as they made their way to the poker tables, yet his eyes never left her, making her more and more anxious.

Don't blow this, Libby. Don't lose him.

She still had no idea what he wanted. A fling? Something more long term? Their earlier conversation had insinuated he was interested in the latter . . . maybe even in marriage. But this was Noah, a man who'd informed her months ago that he was allergic to marriage. She would have chalked her confusion up to the alcohol she'd consumed, but she couldn't do that since she'd barely even had a buzz all night. The drinks here must be watered down.

She knew she should just ask him, lay all the cards on the table, but when she started to ask, her throat squeezed tight.

They sat at a table with another couple and a middle-aged man with a Texas drawl. Noah was right—she hated poker— but you couldn't really talk to your tablemates, so she had some time to think. But half an hour later, she was a hundred dollars poorer, totally sober, and ready to move on.

"What do you want to do?" he asked. "Tomorrow *is* your birthday."

"My birthday," she sneered. "A pox upon my *fucking* birthday."

He looked amused. "Someone's been binge-watching *Game of Thrones.*"

She curled her upper lip and looked for another waitress. Getting drunk sounded like an even better idea than before they sat down the poker table. She'd gotten sidetracked with her plan by the game.

"Turning thirty's not so bad." He shrugged and grinned. "I survived it with very little scarring."

"I was supposed to have my life together by now, Noah."

"What do you think is missing?"

"I wanted to have an exhibit."

"You're working on it. You just need to get back on track. Once you get to Seattle, you'll be able to devote all your time to it."

Seattle. Over the last few hours, she'd forgotten about moving to Seattle. If she moved to Seattle, what if they tried this and it epically failed? She couldn't bear watching him sleep with woman after woman.

Now she was even more depressed and confused.

"What else you got?" he asked.

The pact. The curse. She knew it was stupid and juvenile, but she'd thought it might mean someone would love her enough to stick around.

"Libby." His voice was gentle and coaxing. "Why are you so upset about turning thirty?"

"My life sucks giant donkey balls."

He chuckled. "How giant? Anything like the Czechoslovakian egg? Because *those* would be some impressive balls."

She swatted his lapel. "Don't make fun of me, Mr. I-have-my-life-together-and-I-had-a-fucking-girlfriend-but-I-don't-need-her-because-I'm-sexy-and-all-the-women-in-the-world-throw-themselves-at-my-feet."

"That's a very long name," he murmured. "It's really weird that I don't remember changing it. And where's this line of women? It's the men who are lining up for you, Libby St. Clair."

"Who cares?" She didn't want to talk about all the women he'd screwed. Then she had an idea. "It's my birthday. I want to play a game."

Hesitation filled his eyes. "What kind of game?"

"A drinking game." She grabbed his hand and led him to the counter of a nearby bar. As soon as she had the bartender's attention, she ordered six shots of vodka.

Noah cringed and rubbed the back of his neck. "You're planning to get totally shit-faced, huh? At least it's not tequila."

"Vile stuff." Back in college, she'd lost a few nights to tequila.

"So what's this game?" he asked.

She laughed at the fear in his voice. "Truth or dare."

His eyes widened slightly before focusing on her. "Okay." He didn't sound any less fearful. "But I have to warn you that this seems like the wrong place for it. It's kind of a classy joint. Maybe we should go somewhere else."

She shook her head. "Nope. This is us. All dressed up fancy but keepin' it real."

The bartender started to pour the shots, and when he finished Noah stopped him before he walked off. "Can we have some shot glasses with water? Say six? And a draft beer."

"Sure." The guy shook his head muttering something about weirdos as he left to fill the glasses.

Libby was about to pounce on him, but Noah held up his hand in defense. "Since I've turned thirty and become an *old geezer*," he teased, "I'll pass out after three shots. Let's make it last longer."

"Where's the fun in drinking water?"

"We'll mix them up so we won't know if we're drinking vodka or water. Like a drinking Russian roulette game."

"Okay." She had to admit it was a good idea. "And the beer?"

"Hey, beer goes with everything. So how's this work?"

"We get to ask each other a question. If you answer my question, I have to drink the shot. If you pass, you do."

"What can we ask?"

"Anything."

He pondered it for a moment, then the corners of his mouth lifted slightly. "What about the dare part?"

"Drinking the shots is the dare."

He shook his head. "Nope. I'll only play if daring is an option."

What was he up to? What did it matter? She was the one who'd suggested the game, and she'd done it because she wanted answers.

After the bartender delivered Noah's draft and their shot

glasses of water, Noah mixed up all the shot glasses, then gave her a wink before he took a sip of his beer.

She squared her shoulders. "Okay. I'll go first."

Noah grinned. "I'm ready."

"Truth." She gave him a sexy smile and leaned forward. "Why did you break up with Donna?"

She studied his eyes, but he gave nothing away as he rested his forearm on the counter. "Many reasons. She was a bitch. She tried to change me. She hated my apartment. She wanted me to get another job, preferably investment banking . . . and she hated you."

"She hated *me*? She didn't even know me."

"She was jealous of you. I think she knew that she and I would never be as close as you and I are."

The giddiness she felt over Noah's misfortune filled her with guilt, yet it was undeniable. But she could understand why Donna hadn't understood their friendship. Right now she struggled to understand it herself. Better to focus on the other reasons. "She wanted to change all those things about you? What a *bitch*."

"She had her moments," he said with an air of self-deprecation. "My turn."

"Okay." She picked up a glass and drank, feeling it burn down her throat. Vodka.

"Do you have any birthmarks or interesting freckles?"

She set the glass on the counter. "Really? That's your question?"

"Hey, we're just getting started. Gotta start with the easy ones and work my way up. So? Do you?"

"You already know I have that brown spot on my leg."

He leaned forward, his hand resting on her exposed right knee. His fingertips made a slow path up her inner thigh, then under the hem of her dress and up a couple more inches. "Right here?" His hand stopped, his fingertips gently caressing her skin. "I saw it last summer when you were wearing that pair of jean shorts you love, the ones with the frayed ends. The ones that make your ass look amazing."

He'd checked out her ass that long ago? *Focus, Libby*, but it was hard with his hand so close to other parts of her that wanted to be touched. "You said it looked like a map of Australia."

"For the record, I was referring to your birthmark at the time, not your ass. Any more marks?"

"One."

His fingers stroked a lazy pattern on her inner thigh in the area of the mark. He must have studied it extensively to find it so accurately without looking. The thought that he'd spent time studying her legs turned her on even more.

"Go on."

"It's on the underside of my left breast. A red spot."

His gaze dropped to her cleavage. "You know I want proof."

"Maybe later."

His eyes smoldered with desire. "I'm going to hold you to it."

What were they doing? They were ruining everything. "That's all of them," she forced out as she slid a shot glass toward him. He removed his hand from her leg to lift it to his lips.

This is a dangerous game, she thought to herself. But she was tired of fighting the way she felt for him. This wasn't just untethered lust she felt—she wanted to sleep with *him*. Alcohol would give her an excuse.

He downed his shot. "I want a dare."

She laughed. "Nope. I get to pick. Truth."

His gaze drifted to her lips, making it hard for her to concentrate.

"How old were you when you lost your virginity?"

A slow smile spread across his face. "Sixteen, in the back of my car with Penny Lindquist."

"Was she your girlfriend?"

"For about a week. Apparently she had a crush on me, and when she found out I was graduating early to go to college, she propositioned me."

"You're kidding."

"Nope. Thus began a long line of women in my life." For a moment it looked like he was about to say something more, but then he grinned. "My turn."

"I have to drink first." She grabbed a random glass and gulped it down, regretting the move. Vodka.

Noah turned his smoldering gaze on her. "Dare."

"I don't want a dare."

"You get one anyway." He leaned forward again, his eyes hooded and darker than normal.

She sucked in a breath, sitting back on her stool. "What is it?"

"Kiss me."

Her gaze landed on his lower lip and her heart pounded against her chest. She couldn't remember the last time she'd been this nervous about kissing a man, but this was *Noah*. There were so many reasons to think this through more, but the alcohol was beginning to cloud her judgment.

"Are you sure?" she asked him quietly.

"Very. But only one kiss."

Only one? Was he testing her first? Did he want to see if she was a good kisser before deciding whether she was worth the risk?

Did it matter? She wanted this too, so what was holding her back?

He sat on his stool, his right forearm draped along the counter. His legs were separated, so she spun to completely face him and tucked her legs between his. She leaned toward him, her face inches from his. "You didn't say what kind of kiss. How do you know I won't give you an innocent peck?"

"I don't. The anticipation of what you'll do is part of the thrill."

She touched his lower lip with the tip of her finger, skimming it lightly while she held his gaze, their lips inches apart with only her finger separating them. His tongue darted out to lightly lick her finger and an electrical current shot to her core.

He grabbed her hand and kissed her fingertip before pulling it down to his lap. "Are you going to torture me all night, Libby?" he asked, his voice deep and husky. "Or are you going to kiss me?"

"Is this torture for you, Noah?" she asked in a whisper.

"You have no idea."

She moved her hand to his cheek and lowered her mouth to his, her tongue resuming the path her finger had taken. He gasped into her parted lips before she pulled his bottom lip between hers, raking her top teeth across it. He tasted of beer and vodka and the promise of so much more. His hand was suddenly on her neck, pulling her closer. The kiss deepened, and her seductive playfulness vanished, replaced with want and raw need.

And then he pulled back, his breath coming in quick pants, his eyes wide with wonder. "That was by far the best dare I've ever given."

She had a new appreciation for the dare aspect of their game too. She picked up a shot glass and held it out to him.

A grin lit up his face. "We are *so* going to regret this in the morning."

Was he talking about the kiss, the drinking, or both? But they'd just boarded this runaway train, and she didn't see any way off at this point. "We'll worry about that tomorrow. I want my twenty-nine years of living to go out in a celebration. Truth."

"I want a dare. Just like the one I gave you."

"You don't get to pick either. Truth."

His eyes danced with playfulness at her response, relieving her anxiety that he'd be upset with her. "What deep dark secret do you want to know this time?"

"Have you ever been in love?"

His playfulness faded slightly. "Once."

That surprised her. From what he'd told her, he'd never been with a woman long enough to fall in love. "Who was she?"

He shook his head.

"You're not going to tell me? Why not?" Was it Donna? Had he cared for her more than he'd let on?

He picked up the shot glass. "I haven't had near enough of these to tell you yet." He downed the drink, slammed the glass down and pounded the counter, then turned his attention back to Libby. "Have *you* ever been in love?"

She didn't need to consider her answer. She just picked up a glass and downed it. Vodka. There was no way she was admitting she loved him and only him.

"Damn," he murmured, his gaze drifting from her mouth down her neck and hovering at her chest. "That bad?"

"Not enough of these." She waved the empty glass and set

it on the counter.

The whole thing was making her sad and she didn't want to be sad. Tomorrow would be sad enough. She tilted her head to the side and grinned. "I think it's time for a dare."

His eyes lit up, which didn't surprise her. He was more a dare man than a truth man. That thought sobered her. Man after man had lied to her, but she'd always counted on Noah to not be on that list. But what if she'd gotten that wrong too?

"Do you tell me the truth?" she asked, surprised the words blurted out without a filter. Maybe this drinking game had been a bad idea after all.

His head jutted back in surprise. "What do you think I'm lying about?"

She waved her hand wildly. "Nothing. Anything."

"So you're not accusing me of lying about anything in particular, or just in general."

She was ruining their fun again, but she had to know. "Everybody lies, Noah. Parents lie to kids—the Tooth Fairy, Santa Claus. People tell little white lies to make someone feel better—yes, your singing voice is beautiful. Your baby is the cutest thing *ever*. But I'm talking big lies."

He took her hand in his. "I have never lied to you, Libby. At least not intentionally."

That didn't make her feel any better.

He grunted and pulled her hand closer. "I told you I was coming to the wedding . . . and then I said I wasn't. Maybe you saw that as a lie, but it wasn't. I truly intended to come when I said I would. I simply changed my mind."

"Then you changed it back again."

"So you could actually say I lied about *not* coming."

She shook her head. This was so confusing. What she really wanted to know was if she could trust him, but she couldn't ask him that. What was he going to say? No? But he'd always been there for her—the late night calls. The long talks. The encouragement with her photography. Maybe she should just trust the feeling in her gut. The one that told her she could rely on him.

"What's the dare?" He took a sip of his beer and then set the glass on the counter, rubbing his hands together in anticipation. "I'm ready."

She grinned. "You have to stand up and sing."

"What?" he said with a laugh. "There's no music in here, Lib."

Her grin turned smug. "You were the one who wanted a dare."

He shook his head, took another gulp of beer, and stood.

"I want you to sing 'Like a Virgin,'" she said, laughing.

"Oh, no." He rolled back his shoulders, smiling. "You only said to sing. I get to pick."

He grabbed his phone and tapped on the screen. "I'm not really an a cappella singer," he explained, glancing up at her. "Karaoke's more my style."

He leaned over the counter and grabbed an empty glass, then pressed play and tucked the phone into it. She could barely hear the music over the murmur of voices in the bar, but she burst into laughter when she recognized the tune.

"*Dog goes woof. Cat goes meow,*" Noah belted out in a loud tenor.

"Oh, my God," she said trying to catch her breath. He was singing "What Does the Fox Say?"

He continued, grinning ear to ear. He nailed most of lyrics in the first stanza and only stumbled over a few animals.

"I have to admit it frightens me that you know the words!" she shouted at him.

He just beamed and launched into the chorus. *"What does the fox say?"* He shimmied his shoulders and his hips and continued to sing.

Libby could hardly catch her breath from laughing so hard.

The bartender came over with a frown, shaking his head. "Sir, I'm afraid we'll have to ask you to leave."

Libby continued giggling as Noah feigned indignation. "Why? Are the other guests jealous of my performance?"

The employee's frown deepened. "There are other places to go if you want that kind of entertainment." He took Noah's phone out of the glass and pressed the screen, turning off the music. "The patrons in this lounge prefer a less rambunctious atmosphere."

Several couples were shooting them condescending glares, but a few were laughing.

"Not a problem." Noah winked at Libby and stuck his phone in his pocket. The bartender brought the bill and Noah signed for it, still grinning. He picked up two shot glasses and handed one to Libby, then clinked it with his. "To getting kicked out of bars."

"Hear, hear!" She downed the shot and slid off the stool, nearly falling on her ass. Water.

Noah grabbed her elbow and pulled her upright. He kept her steady as they walked out of the bar.

"Let's go sing karaoke," Libby said, holding on to his arm.

Without warning, he leaned over and kissed her, his tongue coaxing her lips open before it plunged into hers. His lips made her almost delirious, and the alcohol only added to the effect.

When he lifted his head, he looked into her eyes. "Marry me, Lib."

Her eyes flew open. "What?"

"We can go right now. Get married in a chapel. We still have time to do it before your birthday."

"Noah . . ." She shook her head. The three rapid shots—or was it four?—were all slamming into her bloodstream at once, making it even harder to focus.

"Just say yes."

There were reasons she shouldn't, but damned if she could come up with any right now. She'd never had as much fun with a man as she did with him.

Besides, what if the curse had worked? What if Noah was the man she was supposed to marry? God knew she loved him, but did he love her?

"Yes."

"Yes?" he asked in disbelief.

"Yeah."

He kissed her again—much shorter this time, but just as passionate—then lifted his head and shouted, "We're getting married!"

A few people stopped to stare at them and a group of women in cocktail dresses started clapping. One of them catcalled, "Snatch him up, honey. He's hot!"

"Isn't that sweet?" an older woman asked the man next to her. "A young couple in love."

Her husband squinted in disgust. "Them and half the people in this damn town."

The crowd added to Libby's giddiness. This had to be a dream. She was marrying Noah. This was happening.

"Let's go get a taxi."

He tugged her toward the hotel lobby, but she dug in her feet. "Wait! I need my dress."

He stopped and eyed her, his hand skimming from her waist down the curve of her hip. "Why? You look absolutely *perfect.*"

"If I'm getting married, I need my wedding dress. I can't get married in black. It's bad luck."

"The girl needs her dress," the older woman tsked.

"Lib, it's ten-thirty. We'll have to hurry if we're going to make it by midnight. And we still have to get a marriage license."

"What?" Of course they needed a license. How could she have forgotten that?

"It's open late. We can still get it, but we have to hurry."

He pulled her down the hall to the elevator bank to their wing.

She looked up at him, blinking to make him more in focus. "I can't believe we're really doing this."

"Neither can I."

Chapter Nineteen

Something in the back of Noah's head told him to slow down and think this through, but the alcohol encouraged him. He loved her. This was what he wanted. Why wait?

When they got to the room, Noah pushed her against the wall and kissed her again.

"Maybe we should get married tomorrow," she said in a breathy voice, bringing him to his senses.

He took a step back and rubbed the top of his head. "No! We have to do this tonight." He grabbed the trash bag off the floor and dumped her dress onto the bed. "How do we get this back on you?"

Her eyes widened in disbelief. "I'm not putting it on *now*."

He shook his head. "What are you talking about?"

"You can't see me in the dress before the wedding. It's bad luck. I'll change there."

"But I've already seen you in it!"

"You haven't seen me in it before I walk down the aisle to you!"

If this was what she wanted, he'd make it happen. "Okay."

She started stuffing the dress back into the bag. "Come on. Help me."

They crammed it back into the bag and then ran to the elevators. The doors to a car opened and a group of men stared at them, then at the bag in Noah's hand.

He lifted it a few inches in greeting. "We're getting married."

It must have been the shocked looks on their faces that made Libby giggle as she leaned against him, resting her head on his upper arm. The love and joy in her eyes sucked his breath away.

He couldn't believe this was actually happening.

A parking attendant greeted them at the entrance of the hotel. "Where to?" Then he looked down at the clear trash bag and his eyebrows lifted in understanding. "Oh. Which chapel?"

"We don't know, but we need a marriage license," Noah said. "And we need to be married before midnight."

"Okay. Here's what you do," the man said. "You get your license, then you go to Little Heaven. My aunt Angelica owns the place. I'll tell her you're coming so they'll be ready for you. Sound good?"

Noah looked down at Libby for confirmation. Beaming up at him, she nodded.

He grinned. "Sounds perfect."

The parking attendant nodded and led them to a cab and opened the back door. He leaned his head into the open front passenger window. "This young couple needs to get a marriage license. Take care of them for me, will you?"

"Sure thing, Ned."

Noah helped Libby into the backseat and climbed in beside her.

"But stick around and wait for them. They're on a tight deadline. They need to go to Little Heaven afterward. They have to make it before midnight, capiche?"

"Got it."

The bag was still outside the car, but when Noah tried pulling it in, he couldn't fit it through the door. He gave it a tug, then fell backward, his head on Libby's lap. He looked up into her surprised eyes. "Your wedding dress is kind of a bitch."

She burst out laughing.

"Here, let me take that," Ned, the Caesar's employee, said, unprying the bag from the door.

"We need that!" Libby shouted, shoving Noah off her lap.

He righted himself before he fell to the floorboards.

The man leaned over and grinned. "I'm only putting it onto the front seat, miss. My friend Paul here will make sure nothing happens to it, right, Paul?"

"You got it, miss."

Ned shut both doors and banged on the roof.

The taxi driver pulled out of the circle drive and headed toward the strip. "Where are you kids from?"

"Seattle."

"Kansas City," Libby said, "but I'm moving . . . to Seattle."

"Aww . . ." he chuckled. "A long-distance relationship. How long you two been together?"

"Five months," she said. "But I was with another guy until last weekend."

The driver shrugged. "Hey, this is Vegas. You wouldn't be the first cheaters to get married."

"Oh, no," Libby protested. "I didn't cheat. We were just

friends." She turned to Noah. "You wouldn't cheat on me, would you?"

His eyebrows rose in shock. "Cheat on you? God, no, Lib. Never. I respect you too much to hurt you like that."

"Are you going to ask me the same question?" she asked.

He slowly shook his head, a soft smile on his lips. "I already know the answer."

"Hey, no worries," the driver said. "No judgment from me. I've seen crazier things happen in this city." He handed them a bottle of water and winked. "You kids look a little thirsty."

Noah screwed off the cap and handed the bottle to Libby, watching her mouth as she drank down several gulps. He was still in shock that she'd kissed him. He'd kissed her and it was even better than he could have hoped. How much better would the rest be?

The ride to the courthouse was faster than Noah expected, but they'd finished the water as Paul pulled up to the curb. He glanced at his phone to check the time. 11:05 and he'd a missed text from Gram.

Oh, shit. He'd forgotten all about the dinner reservation.

He helped Libby out of the car and quickly called Gram.

"I'll be waiting right here," the cab driver said, starting to pull away.

"My dress!" Libby shouted.

Noah lowered the phone from his ear. "We're not getting married here, Lib. Just picking up the license."

"But what if he drives off with it?" Worry filled her eyes. "I can't get married in black."

He gave her a quick kiss. "He won't. I haven't paid him yet. Come on."

He heard Gram's muffled voice. "Noah! Did you butt dial me? If so, I hope that butt's naked."

Shit. He put the phone to his ear as he held the door to the office open for Libby. "Sorry, Gram. No, I didn't butt dial you, and no, I am not naked."

"That's a pity," she grumbled. "Still haven't made progress with our girl?"

"Actually, we're walking in to get a marriage license, then off to Little Heaven Wedding Chapel to get married."

"You're *what?*"

A woman at the counter pointed to her ear and shook her head at Noah. "Gram, I've gotta go. Thanks for all your help." He hung up and stuffed the phone into his pocket, ignoring the new round of vibrating. He'd deal with Gram later.

There were two couples ahead of them. The first couple at the counter looked barely eighteen. The girl kept glancing around as if she was waiting for her parents to show up and ground her. Maybe she was.

He looked down at Libby, his chest burning with love. He couldn't believe he'd proposed. He couldn't believe she'd accepted. Could it really have been this easy all along?

No, neither one of them had been ready until now.

Next was a gay couple. They looked like total opposites. The man who did the talking was stylishly dressed and had a take-charge personality, while his soon-to-be-husband wore jeans and a soft sweater. But when they looked at each other, the love in their eyes was unmistakable.

Is that what people saw when they looked at Noah and Libby together? He glanced at the clock on the wall. 11:15. He tapped his foot impatiently. He had to make sure her dreams came true. Getting married before she turned thirty was important to her and he was determined to make that happen.

Finally it was their turn and Libby practically bounced to the counter.

"We're here for a marriage license," Libby said, the excitement in her voice unmistakable. "We're getting married." She looked up at Noah with wonderment on her face, like she couldn't quite believe this was happening.

He knew exactly how she felt.

The clerk rolled her eyes. "Then you're in luck. Marriage licenses are what I do here."

They filled out the form, showed their IDs, Noah paid the fee, and then they were climbing into Paul's cab. The clock on his dashboard read 11:22.

"We're going to have to hurry."

Paul looked over his shoulder, sporting a huge grin. "Don't you worry. I never back down from a challenge. I'll get you there with plenty of time to spare."

"It's okay if we don't make it," Libby said, leaning her head on his shoulder. "If we're off by a few minutes, it's okay."

Noah turned to her and lifted her chin so he could look into her eyes. "No, it's not. We'll do this. We'll make it work."

He kissed her to show her how much he loved her, but then he realized he'd kissed countless other women. It hadn't meant anything to him other than a prelude to getting laid. Could Libby tell the difference? He could. Just holding her hand gave him more of a thrill than he'd felt with any other woman.

"Noah?" she asked softly, and he realized he was staring at her. "You okay?"

"Never better."

"Really?" she asked hesitantly. Her eyes were more focused. She was obviously sobering up a bit. "Are you sure you want to do this?"

Was she about to change her mind? Had she agreed only because her judgment had been impaired?

"Yes." He kissed her again, partially in desperation, and partly because he couldn't believe he could—that she was so willing and accepting.

"We're here," Paul said cheerfully.

When Noah looked up, he saw they were parked in front of the Little Heaven Wedding Chapel. He fumbled with the door handle and scrambled out, pulling Libby with him. He dug out his wallet and handed the driver a handful of cash.

"Thanks for the ride. You've been a lifesaver."

Noah started to turn away, but Paul called after him, "Hey! Don't forget the dress!"

Libby gasped and wrestled the bag through the door. If they had time, he'd love to watch her try to wrangle the dress that was nearly as large as she was, but the clock was ticking, so he took it from her, grinning. "Let me wrestle with it now, you can wrestle with it after you get it on."

There was a saucy grin on her face as she handed it to him. "Then we can wrestle it together when we get back to the room."

The thought of taking it off her again was distracting, shuttling blood away from his brain to his other thinking appendage. But he had the rest of his life to think about taking her clothes off—now he needed to make sure they made the midnight deadline.

The rest of his life.

With every other woman, Noah had considered marriage akin to a prison sentence. He hadn't been able to fathom committing to one woman. Until Libby. He hoped to spend the next fifty or more years with her, and he was certain it wouldn't be long enough.

But what if he was rushing her? In the cab, she'd asked him if he was sure. He'd never asked that same question of her.

He grabbed her hand and pulled her to a halt. "Lib, wait."

Worry flickered in her eyes.

"You asked me if I was sure, but are *you* sure?"

Her eyes lit up. "Yes. Very."

"Then let's get married." He put his hand on the small of her back and guided her to the door.

As soon as they entered the lobby she stopped in her tracks. "Oh, my God," she whispered. "You really did bring me to demonic cherub hell."

He wasn't going to argue with her assessment. Cherubs were everywhere. Painted on the walls, the ceilings, the doors, and even the floors. Cherub statues lined the walls and sat on pedestals. A cherub statue cheerfully peed in the pool of the fountain standing in the corner. A counter with a glass display case was on their left.

Noah gawked in horror. "Oh. My. God."

"I guess we know why it's called *Little* Heaven."

Noah had started to turn around when a woman called out with a thick accent he couldn't place. "You must be the couple my sweet Ned told me about. Welcome. Welcome. We have everything already prepared. I am Angelica. I hear you're in a hurry." She emerged from the dark hallway directly across from them and glanced down at Libby's impossibly flat stomach. "A little one on the way? You need today's date to match a due date?"

"What?" Libby gasped.

"No," Noah said with more force than he'd intended. "We want to be married before Libby's birthday. Which is tomorrow. But she needs to put on her dress. Is there somewhere she can change?"

Libby glanced around the room, pressing her back to his chest, then looked up at him with a hesitant look in her eyes.

He leaned down and whispered in her ear. "We don't have to get married here."

"We don't have time to go anywhere else."

She was right.

He turned her around and put his hands on her shoulders, bending at the knee so he could look her in the eyes. "I know this probably isn't how you imagined it." He gave her a sly grin. "But you're probably the only woman in history to have two themed weddings. Now we'll have plenty of material for cocktail parties when people ask us about our wedding. No boring stories for us."

"Oh, Noah." She threw her arms around his neck and buried her face in his chest. "How do you always know just what to say to make me feel better?"

He had no idea. It was probably the only thing in his life that had ever come naturally to him. Only further confirmation they were perfect for each other.

"Come, come," Angelica said, tugging on Libby's arm. "We must get you dressed."

The woman snagged the bag from Noah and grabbed Libby's arm. "I'll get her ready," she said, tugging Libby down a cherub-lined hall. "You pick out the extras."

"Extras?"

The door to the dressing room closed and Noah jumped when a man's voice sounded behind him. "Flowers. Rings. The like." He had a deeper accent than Angelica. It sounded like a bizarre mix of Italian and the Deep South.

Noah spun to see a plump, bald man walking through a curtain behind the counter. The man tightened the sash of his white satin robe. Had he just gotten out of bed?

"I'm Tito and I'll be happy to assist you. So what will it be?" the man asked, his voice sounding like it was on autopilot.

His head bobbed as he spoke, drawing Noah's attention to the tufts of thick chest hair peeking above the V of his robe. "We offer several flower options." He led Noah to a refrigerator full of bouquets and boutonnieres. "What does your bride like?"

"Uh . . . nothing too fussy." The bouquets in the case looked like the ones Megan and Blair had carried—roses and lilies in formal arrangements. That wouldn't work. "What about those?" He pointed to a pile of flowers at the bottom. A mix of yellow daisies, pink rosebuds and some other flowers in pinks and purples covered the floor of the cooler.

"Those?" Tito shook his head, chuckling, then explained slowly as though Noah were a simpleton. "*Those* are the leftovers. The ones that weren't good enough to be in bouquets."

Didn't that describe him and Libby? Never feeling like they were good enough? He knew these were the flowers she'd want. "We'll take those."

"You don't understand," the bald man said, enunciating each word. "Those aren't for sale. They're at the bottom because they were the leftovers."

"Then why are they in the case?"

The man groaned. "Because Angelica gives them to her mother to make sachets."

Noah gave him a blank look.

"You know, those little bags full of flower petals that stink up drawers."

"I still want them."

"They're just loose." He opened the door and snatched them up. "See? They're not even in a bouquet."

Noah reached around him and grabbed a roll of twine. "So just bundle them together and wrap this around them."

The man lifted his hands in the air in defeat. "Take them if you want. You can have them for free. But your bride is going to walk out on you the minute she sees them."

"You don't know my Libby." *His Libby.* He marveled at his words. She was his. She was actually his.

"Do you have rings?"

"Oh, shit. We don't have *anything.*" No wonder Libby had been so stressed over the last month. Even if Mitch had come up with the ideas, he knew she'd organized it all. Turned out there was a whole lot more to this wedding planning gig than two willing participants.

"Not to worry." A smug smile lit up the man's face. "We can take care of *everything.*" He moved over to a glass case full of rings. "We have a nice selection of rings over here that will fit anyone's budget. From the bare basics to the high rollers."

Noah seriously doubted high rollers got married here unless they were drop-dead drunk. But the selection ran from simple gold and silver bands to large diamond rings that he suspected might actually be cubic zirconia.

"Let me see those." He pointed to silver bands—his and hers. The larger band was thick and the smaller band daintier, but both were smooth silver with tiny beading at the edges.

"After the bouquet decision, I'm not surprised," the man grumbled under his breath. "These are part of our budget selection."

Noah had to admit the design wasn't much, but he was certain Libby would love them. He'd get her a diamond engagement ring later . . . from a more reputable place.

The man's gaze zoomed in on Noah's crotch and then moved slowly up his chest and stopped at his face. "What size are you?"

Uh . . ." What the hell was he talking about? Cup size? Then it dawned on him. "I already have a tux. See? I'm wearing it."

"Not for the tux. The ring." He pointed to Noah's left hand, which rested on the counter. "What size ring do you and your bride wear?"

"Uh . . . I don't know." Noah hadn't bought a ring since his class ring in high school, and ring sizes had never come up in conversation with Libby.

The man rolled his eyes and reached over to grab Noah's hand. He shoved the ring on Noah's left ring finger.

"This is all so sudden . . ." Noah joked. "And I'm already taken."

Tito scowled and moved the ring around on Noah's finger. "Lucky for you, it fits perfectly. Now we'll see if the other one fits your bride."

"What else do I need to get?" Noah asked, glancing over his shoulder at the door and wondering what was taking her so long. He reminded himself that the dress was a monster to maneuver. They'd be lucky if they were married by midnight. But he couldn't shake the worry that she might change her mind.

"Professional photography? Minister? Music?"

"We have to pay for music?"

The man gave Noah a look that read *cheap bastard*. "We have a deluxe package that will provide it all and include a few extras."

"Fine. Yes to all of it."

The man grinned and then turned to his cash register to total everything up. "That will be nine hundred and ninety-nine dollars."

Noah knew he was getting screwed, but he handed over his credit card willingly enough. He'd pay a hell of a lot more than that to marry Libby. He wanted it to be perfect for her, but he reminded himself that there were demon cherubs watching their every move. "What are the extras that come with the deluxe package?"

Tito smiled as he handed Noah the receipt. "Our top-of-the-line service, including an audience."

Noah put his credit card back in his wallet. "Wait. An audience?"

"We're ready!" Angelica shouted from behind the door.

A sigh of relief escaped Noah's lips and he started for the dressing room, but Tito stopped him. "Where do you think you're going?"

"To see my bride."

He shook his head. "Oh, no you aren't. Give me that ring and march yourself inside the chapel and wait up front."

He pulled the ring off his hand and handed it him. "But . . ."

"You don't want to see her before she comes down the aisle." He picked up the bouquet Noah had tied together with the twine. "I'll give this to the bride." He leaned to the side, partially covering his mouth. "And I'll give you a heads-up if she takes off after seeing it."

"Ha. Ha," Noah mumbled, but his nerves were kicking in now that the majority of the alcohol had left his system. Libby had to be sobering up too. What if he was wrong about the flowers? What if she changed her mind about everything?

He really wanted to talk to her one last time, but as much as it killed him to admit it, Tito was right. Given how superstitious Libby tended to be, he didn't want to press his luck by forcing his way in to see her. He pushed on the double wooden doors that bore a placard reading *Holy Seraphim Chapel,* took one step inside, and froze, completely unprepared for what he found there.

The chapel looked like it had been cobbled together by a drunken construction worker fired from Caesar's Palace. They had tried to emulate European chapels with the domed ceiling, Corinthian columns, and stained glass, but on a much smaller scale. The effort had failed miserably.

The back wall was encased in an arch and a backlit stained glass window filled most of the space. It might have been pretty if not for the design. The panes were covered with the figures of grown men sporting short stubby wings and flowing fabric wrapped around their johnsons, which made them look like they were wearing diapers. Naked women surrounded them, gazing up in adoration. All the male figures were identical, as were the female figures, and to make matters worse, they had clearly been modeled after Angelica and Tito.

Oh. Fuck.

Crooked columns held up the arch and the platform floor in front of the window was painted a faux gray marble, as was the short aisle leading to the altar. The front of the room had held Noah's attention so long he realized he'd missed the rest of the chapel. There were three arched niches on either side, all filled with concrete angels, which thankfully bore no resemblance to the two owners. The insides of the arches appeared to have been spray-painted a metallic gold.

The mural on the ceiling was composed of multiple scenes of a naked angel bearing a remarkable resemblance to Tito, although Noah was certain the artist had over-exaggerated the man's penile girth and length. Angelica was there too, with wings this time, and there were multiple images of her and Tito in the throes of passion. One particularly memorable composition showed the two fornicating on a bench in a garden, with Tito thrusting from behind wearing a shit-eating grin.

Holy hell. Some things couldn't be unseen.

Noah took several hesitant steps down the aisle, telling himself that Libby would probably love it. He suspected she was the only person on the planet who would.

It wasn't until he stepped onto the small platform that he realized the back row of folding chairs was occupied by six men, most of whom appeared to have been plucked from a holding pen at the police station. One man wore a grungy knit cap and slurped from a can of Campbell's soup, while another leaned his head against the wall, releasing a small snore.

"We're all ready," Angelica singsonged as she entered the chapel through the double doors, her hands pressed together at her breasts as if in prayer. "Your beautiful bride is ready. Shall we begin?"

He nodded, finding it difficult to push out a yes. His chest was so tight with nerves he could hardly breathe. He noticed a clock on the wall over the entrance, the hands in the shape of angel wings. 11:49. At least Libby hadn't taken off yet.

Angelica glided over to a stereo system in the corner and pressed a button. Music poured into the room and the double doors swung open as if by magic.

Libby filled the doorway, Noah's bouquet in her hands, looking more beautiful than he'd ever seen her. Their eyes locked and everything else fell away. However strange and unconventional this was, it was right. It was them.

The first lines of the song "Teen Angel" played on the speakers overhead—the original recording from the 1950s, from the sound of it.

"Oops, wrong song," Angelica murmured, pressing a button that stopped the music. "That was from the last couple."

Libby's eyes widened and she held back a giggle.

God, he loved her.

Tinny piano music filled the room, reminding Noah of something from the 1980s. Then he realized it *was* something from the 1980s—his mother had listened to this song over and over when he was a kid. "Angel Eyes". Was it destiny that they played his mother's favorite song?

Angelica gave Libby an exasperated look. "Well, what are you waiting for? Tito's about to start singing."

Sure enough, Tito's voice floated around them, but there was still no sign of Tito. *"Girl, you're looking fine tonight, and every guy has got you in his sight."*

Noah had no idea where Tito could be, but he didn't care. Libby was walking toward him with a soft smile on her lips. But then she stopped halfway down the short aisle, her eyes wide and her mouth slightly agape.

His heart skipped a beat. Had she changed her mind?

Sensing movement behind him, he looked over his shoulder. "Oh. My. God."

Now he dearly regretted paying for the top-of-the-line service. And to his horror, he now realized why Tito had been wearing a robe.

A hole had opened in the arched ceiling and a pair of bare, hairy legs dangled from the opening.

Tito continued to sing, putting emotion into his words as he belted out the rest of the stanza.

Noah considered grabbing Libby and running the hell out of there, but his feet were frozen as the horror continued to unfold—the lower part of Tito's abdomen was now visible, including his fabric-draped groin.

Libby burst into hysterical laughter.

Angelica planted her hands on her hips and gave Libby a dirty look. "Shh!"

Libby covered her mouth and gave up all pretense of walking gracefully down the aisle, instead rushing over to Noah as he stepped off the platform to meet her. She grabbed his arm and whispered, "What in the hell is happening?"

"I have no fucking idea." His gaze had found its way back to the still-emerging man. Tito's bare chest was now visible, as was the small golden harp he held in his hands. He dropped another couple feet, then remained in place as his feet began to kick the air.

"I told you no demonic angels, Noah," Libby whispered.

His stomach clenched and he turned to apologize, but her grin spread from ear to ear.

"Did you request this?"

"You actually think I *would*?" he asked in dismay.

"Asks the man who took me to see a giant hairball," she countered in a whisper.

"Shhh!!!" Angelica hushed louder.

One of the homeless-looking guests sat up and pointed. "Hey, that man's wearing a diaper!"

Angelica stomped her foot. "*Shh!*"

But Tito was too caught up in his performance to notice the commotion. He kept belting out the song as he descended, and to add gravitas to the occasion, the front of the chapel darkened and two spotlights flashed on, bathing Tito's now visible and very hairy chest with a warm glow. As soon as his shoulders cleared the space, two wings unfurled from his back, both covered in white and silver feathers with sparkles that caught the lights. One of the wings caught on the wire holding Tito in the air, tilting him sideways. His arms flapped and his legs kicked as he hung there, suspended three feet off the ground. He released a little yelp, but almost immediately continued to sing and strum his harp.

Libby broke into giggles again, burying her face in Noah's arm to muffle the sound.

A true showman, Tito jiggled enough to free his wing and landed gracefully on his feet. Without missing a beat, he turned his attention to Libby, crooning with even more earnestness as he repeated the chorus.

"Hey." Another man in the back shook the snoozing guy next to him. "You gotta see this."

The younger man roused, then blinked. "Dude, what was in that weed?"

"I don't know, but we gotta get some more."

"Shh!!!" Angelica snarled as she grabbed their arms and pulled both them out of their seats.

"Hey! I want to see the show," one of them protested, but she pushed them out through the doors. The four remaining men looked startled.

"I think I should get a refund on the deluxe package," Noah mumbled.

Libby giggled again. "Is this guy performing the ceremony?"

"Meet Tito, and I'm thinking that's a yes."

"Oh, my God. We're getting married by a man wearing a diaper."

"Nothing but the best for you, Libby St. Clair." He grinned. "At least it's not a skirt. And in case you're wondering what's underneath . . ." He motioned his head toward the ceiling.

Libby looked up and gasped, followed by a new round of giggles.

Tito finally stopped singing and cast an unamused glance at Noah and Libby. "You'll have to come up onto the stage so I can perform the ceremony."

Oh, crap. How much time had they lost to Tito's theatrics?

"What time is it?"

"What?" Tito asked.

"Is it midnight yet?"

"It's 11:55," Angelica shouted from the back of the room. "Tito still has time for another song."

"How about Tito sings after he pronounces us husband and wife?" Noah asked, trying to curb his impatience. He took Libby's hand and helped her onto the platform in front of Tito.

"You're carrying the bouquet," Tito said, scrunching his nose. "I tried to convince him to use a real one."

Noah started to explain, but she smiled up at him. "It's beautiful. But you don't have a boutonniere."

"I don't need one, Lib."

She gave him a short scowl. "Yes you do."

Angelica climbed up onto the platform, taking photos with a small click and shoot camera, but from the looks of it, she was putting more of Tito in the frame than the bride and groom.

Libby ignored her and plucked a daisy from her bouquet and stuffed the stem into Noah's coat pocket. "It's not perfect, but it will do."

"It fits this crazy wedding."

She looked up at him, her face radiating happiness. "It fits us."

He beamed with his own happiness. "Yeah, it does."

"Are you ready for the vows?" Tito asked, sounding annoyed. "I have a beautiful service prepared for you."

"I'm kind of curious what he's got," she whispered to Noah.

"Then by all means, let's do it."

Libby bit her upper lip, probably to hold in her laughter.

"Yes, we're ready for the vows. But can we do our own after?"

"Well, I guess." Tito sounded miffed, but he lifted his chin. He leaned over and set the harp on the floor. "Angelica. The vows lighting."

Angelica had been moving around getting photos, but now she hurried to the back corner.

Tito was still spotlit in his golden glow, but two softer spotlights now shone on the floor in front of him. He curled his fingers and motioned for Libby and Noah to move to their positions.

"I feel like I'm in the plot of a horror movie," Noah muttered. "And it doesn't end well."

Libby burst out laughing again.

Tito's forehead furrowed into a deep frown, but he took a deep breath and lifted his hands at his sides, holding his arms horizontal to the ground, palms up. A light shot out from behind him, putting him in silhouette as a bright light surrounded him. He closed his eyes. "And lo, I descend from above to join you two in holy matrimony."

Libby grabbed Noah's hand and held tight.

"Do you Elizabeth . . . uh . . ." He pulled the top of his loincloth away from his stomach and looked inside.

Noah leaned close to her and whispered, "If he takes that thing off, I'm leaving, Lib."

She lifted her hand to her mouth and bit the side of her index finger. "Deal."

Tito looked up and cleared his throat before returning his arms to their previous positions. "Do you, Elizabeth Gabriella St. Clair, take this man, Noah Michael McMillan, to be your husband?"

She looked up into Noah's face, her eyes dancing. "I do."

"To have and to hold in the angel's glowing light?"

She took a deep breath, her shoulders shaking with suppressed laughter. "I do."

"Will you stand by his side until his aura fades?"

She grinned. "I will."

"Will you let his wings spread wide so that he can take flight?"

She tilted her head and gave Noah a mischievous grin. "It depends on where he's flying off to."

Tito's head jutted back in surprise. "Oh."

"I'll take it," Noah said, squeezing her hand. "I'm not planning to fly anywhere without her."

Tito looked confused by the alteration to his vows.

"Noah Michael McMillan, do you take Elizabeth Gabriella St. Clair to be your wife?"

The words filled him with more hope and joy than he thought possible. "I do."

"To have and to hold in the angel's glowing light?"

Her eyes twinkled with mischief. God, he loved her. He never suspected he could ever love anyone this much. "I do."

"Will you stand by her side until her aura fades?"

He shook his head, lifting his hand to cup her cheek. "Her aura will never fade. Impossible."

Her eyes glistened as she looked up at him with unabashed love. "Oh, Noah."

"Um . . . okay . . ." Tito fumbled, clearly unsure what to do.

"I've got this, Tito." Noah reached for Libby's hands and held them gently in front of him. "Libby, I'm so grateful Josh tricked Megan into letting him be her fiancé."

Tito's eyes widened. "Huh?"

"If he hadn't tried to steal information about her father's business, we might never have met."

Tito's eyes widened even wider.

"I've had more fun with you in the last five months than in the previous four hundred and ten combined. But more importantly, I've found my best friend. You make me a better man, Libby St. Clair, and I can't wait start our lives together in Seattle—you, me, and Tortoise."

She smiled up at him, tears in her eyes. "Noah, you've been there for me when everyone else almost gave up on me. Thank you for the last two days, which were exactly what I needed. You're the only one who's ever really understood me. But more importantly, you're the only person in this world I can completely trust. Thank you."

"Oh, Lib." He brushed away a tear. "I promise I'll never let you down."

"I'm counting on that."

Tito studied them for a moment and shrugged, then picked up his harp. "The rings."

Noah tilted his head and grinned. "If he pulls them out of his diaper," he whispered into her ear, "I'm not using them."

"We have rings?"

Tito began strumming an unrecognizable tune on the harp, then said in a theatrical voice, "Release the doves."

Angelica opened a small cabinet door on the wall and two white birds flew out and swooped around the room.

Noah's mouth dropped open. "You have *got* to be kidding me."

Libby started laughing again. "It's perfect!"

"Hey!" one of the men in the back shouted. "It pooped on me!"

The birds swooped around the room a few times before finally landing on the top of Tito's harp, the rings dangling from their feet with strings.

"Come get your rings," Tito said, nodding toward the doves as he continued playing the instrument.

"Is now a bad time to mention I hate birds?" Noah grumbled, inching his way forward.

"I'll do it," Libby said as she stepped around him, slowly reaching for the string on the first dove. She handed Noah the ring—hers—then untied the other ring and moved back in front of him.

The back doors burst open, spilling light into the darkened chapel, and Noah wondered what Tito and Angelica could possibly have planned next. Startled, the birds went crazy, flapping their wings and taking off into flight, swooping over their heads.

Noah put a protective arm around Libby and pulled her to his chest, but then he realized the two older women standing in the doorway had nothing to do with the Little Heaven Wedding Chapel deluxe package.

"Sweet baby Jesus!" Gram shouted.

"No," Nana Ruby said in disgust. "That's not Jesus. It's just a hairy man in a diaper."

Tito stopped strumming and shot them a glare. "I'm sorry, but we're in the middle of a service. Feel free to sit and watch or wait in the lobby, and we can marry you next."

Ruby snorted. "He thinks we're getting married."

Gram chuckled. "You've got it wrong there, Mr. Diaper Man. She's got herself a man who's into BMI, and I'm on the prowl." She paused and took in the mural on the ceiling. "Although I may have found him." She turned back and appraised Tito with a gleam in her eye. "Is this one of those Costco things? I didn't know you kids were into that."

Noah burst into laughter. "I think you mean cosplay, Gram. And we're not. This is everything that comes with the deluxe package."

Gram nodded as though that explained everything.

Tito shuddered and looked down his nose at Noah, which was difficult since Tito was a good six inches shorter. "You know these women?"

"They're our grandmothers," Libby explained with a shrug. "Kind of."

Tito waved them forward. "Then come in and sit down. We're in the middle of their vows."

"Wait!" Libby said, holding up her bouquet. "You're not here to object to the wedding, are you?"

"Object?" Gram asked in disbelief. "Why would we object? I've been shipping you two since you first laid eyes on each other."

"And I could see your connection at Blair's wedding shower for my sorry excuse for a grandson, Neil," Ruby added. "Let's get this going."

The two women sat down as Tito lifted his arms and stared up at the hole in the ceiling. "Let us resume."

"What time is it?" Noah asked.

Nana Ruby looked at her watch. "Eleven fifty-nine."

Noah grabbed Libby's hand and shoved the ring on her finger. "Lib, if you don't like this, we can get you a new one." Then he held his hand out to her and she slipped the other ring on his finger.

"It's perfect."

Noah turned to the shocked Tito. "Quick. Declare us man and wife."

Tito looked dismayed. "But we have more service first. We haven't gotten to the dancing angels yet."

Libby's mouth dropped open. "Dancing angels?"

"Maybe later!" Noah shouted. "Declare us man and wife!"

Tito shook his head. "Okay, I declare you man and wife, you may—"

Noah pulled Libby into his arms and placed a hard kiss on her mouth.

"—kiss your bride," he finished in defeat. "You ruined the wedding."

Libby pulled back and stared into Noah's face. "No, it was the most perfect wedding ever."

Chapter Twenty

"We did it," Noah said beaming. "Happy Birthday, Libby."

She stared into the face of her husband. *Noah's my husband.* "I can't believe we did it."

Worry wrinkled his forehead. "Are you sorry?"

Their decision had been impulsive. They'd made it while they were drunk. Noah hadn't even said the words *I love you*, yet she knew he did, just as she knew they hadn't made a mistake.

She shook her head. "No."

"Say cheese!" Gram said, holding up her phone.

Tito stood behind them, posing with his harp as Gram and Angelica snapped photos.

"We need a picture with you and Nana Ruby," Libby told them. "Angelica, can you take a photo of all us?"

"Photos are included in the deluxe package," Noah said, when Angelica started to balk.

"Come on, Gram," Noah said.

"I gotta send this tweet first." She tapped on her phone and looked up at them with a grin. "Done."

They spent the next five minutes taking photos. Libby insisted the paid wedding guests be in the photos and Noah found the two men who'd been kicked out, sitting on the floor of the front room, and invited them back in.

Tito took center stage for all the photos. One of the men kept grabbing at Tito's loincloth and the pseudo angel kept smacking his hand away. Libby giggled through it all, wondering how everything could be so perfect.

Then just as Noah predicted, a bright light shone from the hole in the ceiling and Tito rose back up into the air, his wing catching on the edge of the hole.

"Angelica! Lower me back down!"

Angelica kept pushing a button on the wall by the stereo system. "It's stuck."

Noah ushered the three women toward the exit, snagging Libby's hand in his as they moved. "Let's get out of here."

"Tito!" Angelica cried out, hurrying toward the platform. "I'll get the ladder, baby."

"How'd you two get here?" Libby asked the grandmothers after they'd made it into the lobby.

"We took a taxi," Nana Ruby said, covering her mouth as she yawned. "It's waiting for us outside, and I think I need to get back and go to bed. I haven't been up this late since Nixon was in the White House."

Gram curled her upper lip. "That's a crock of bullshit and you know it. You were up late on that cruise you went on last summer. The one with the used tire salesmen convention."

Nana threw up her hands in exasperation. "That was one night—*one night*—and I was drunk, besides." She leaned closer to Gram. "And when I told you last week, you said you'd carry

239

it to your grave."

"I haven't given up anything, you old fool. You've given yourself up."

"*Never mind.*" Nana released a huge groan. "Maude. It's time for *both* of us to go back and go to bed."

Gram didn't look pleased. "I wanted to take Noah and Libby out for their wedding dinner. And wedding cake."

"I suspect they have other things on their mind," Nana said with a sly grin. "Especially after what Noah told us earlier."

Libby swung her gaze up to her new husband. "What did you tell them?"

Noah gave the two women a small shove toward the front door. "Thanks for coming to the wedding and I'm sorry about the dinner reservation. Let's try it again tomorrow night. Say around eight?"

They nodded as they hurried into their waiting taxi, Gram pausing to shout, "You kids have fun."

Noah and Libby stood outside Little Heaven, still holding hands. She glanced up at him, surprised to see he was staring back at her with a look of amazement on his face.

"What?" she asked, feeling self-conscience.

He slowly pulled her into his arms. "I can't believe you're mine."

A slow smile spread across her face as warmth filled her chest.

He kissed her, but this time it wasn't full of fire and passion. It was soft and gentle, like a welcome home. Tears burned her eyes and she smiled up at him. "Let's go back to the hotel, Noah."

He nodded and was about to flag down a taxi when Paul, the cab driver who'd brought them there, pulled up to the curb.

He leaned across the front seat and looked up at them through the passenger window. "I figured you two would need a ride after you got hitched."

"Thanks," Noah said as he opened the back door for Libby. He gathered up her skirts and helped her into the car. Then he settled in beside her and took her hand.

"Where to?"

"Caesar's Palace."

"Sure thing." Paul glanced at them in the rearview mirror as he started toward the hotel. "Did you get the big show?"

Noah laughed. "Yeah, I got the deluxe package." He tilted his head with an amused gleam in his eyes. "You could have warned us."

"And spoil the surprise? Nah . . . But I'm surprised Tito and Angelica didn't see you off. Tito likes to walk couples to the curb, strumming his harp."

Libby broke into giggles. "Tito was a little stuck when we left."

"Tried to go back up in the ceiling, huh?" He shook his head in sympathy. "He hasn't got that one perfected yet."

Paul pulled up in front of the lobby and the parking attendant, Ned, greeted them and opened their door. "Did you go to Little Heaven?"

"We sure did," Noah said as he helped Libby out of the back.

"It was a wedding you'll never forget, am I right?" he asked.

"Not even when we're old and senile." Noah grinned and leaned over to pay the cab driver.

"Good luck!" Paul said, sliding over in his seat and poking his head out the passenger window. "Getting hitched is the easy part, staying hitched takes work. But I've been married to my Annie for nearly forty years and I wouldn't trade a single day for all the money in the world."

"Thank you," Libby said, giving him a small wave.

"What room are you kids in?" Ned asked as a group of three women climbed into Paul's cab. "We'll send up a little congratulatory gift."

Noah took Libby's hand as he gave him the number.

Ned winked and sent them off with more good wishes.

They didn't say a word as they walked into the hotel lobby, although Libby's dress drew quite a bit of attention. She realized she was still holding the bouquet, so she lifted it and motioned as if to throw it. A group of women saw her and started squealing with excitement as they formed a group. Laughing, Libby turned her back to them and threw the flowers over her shoulder.

"I got it again!" Gram shouted.

A collective groan echoed inside the marbled foyer.

Libby spun around to see the older woman lift the bouquet over her head like she was a champion boxer. "How . . . ?"

Noah laughed and shook his head in disbelief. "She and Nana Ruby walked in the door just as you threw it. I never would have believed it if I hadn't seen it with my own eyes." He called over to the two women. "Maybe you really *are* destined to get married in Vegas, Gram!"

Libby had to wonder if Noah might be right. "Congrats, Gram! I can't wait to meet your groom."

Nana Ruby scowled. "Don't encourage her."

The two grandmothers wandered off in the opposite direction, which was probably for the best considering several of the younger women in the crowd looked like they wanted to tackle Gram.

They walked to the elevator in silence—the only sounds around them were the voices of the people passing by and the swish of her skirt. A sudden sense of dread filled Libby as she thought about the taxi driver's words. To her horror, she realized he was right. She'd spent so much time thinking about getting married, she hadn't stopped to consider marriages could be ended. They might be married now, but he wasn't permanently attached to her. He could walk away at any time.

Blair and Garrett's profession was proof enough of that.

Noah's hand squeezed hers. "Lib, you okay?"

The elevator door opened and she was surprised to find an empty car. They walked inside and she kept her gaze on the doors as they closed, her stomach tying into knots.

"Lib, talk to me." The anxiety in his voice caught her by surprise.

What should she tell him? That she was still scared to lose him? Did she really want to sound so pathetic on their wedding night?

She put her hand on his cheek and looked into his eyes, searching for answers to the questions she was too scared to ask. She lifted up to kiss him and he covered her hand with his.

"Lib?" He was more insistent this time, and his face was pinched with worry.

"I just can't believe you're mine," she repeated his words. He pulled her into his arms, kissing her so senseless that it took her several moments to realize the doors had opened and an older couple was waiting to get into the car.

"Sorry," Libby said as Noah pulled her to the side.

He grinned down at her. "I'm not," he whispered.

She smiled back. This was Noah. Her Noah. She knew they were perfect for each other—that she couldn't find a man who would suit her better.

Even if her own palm told her differently.

Sometime between Megan and Blair's weddings, she'd

fallen in love with him. She'd been too foolish and scared to admit it to herself, but some part of her had known for a while.

Now that the curse *had* worked out after all, should she worry about the destiny on her palm? Was their marriage already destined to fail?

The elevator stopped at their floor and Noah tugged her off the car and toward their room.

She had a choice—she could let her worries consume her and ruin their night, or she could let it go and consummate her marriage to the man she'd never thought she could have.

She chose to celebrate her new life.

Noah held the door open with his foot, and with a wicked gleam in his eyes, he bent down and swooped her up into his arms.

"Noah!" she squealed, laughing. "You're going to break your back!"

"Not a chance." He grinned, looking down. "The bigger threat is me tripping on your dress and crushing you."

She pulled up the fabric and shot him a wicked look of her own. "I prefer to have you on top of me in bed."

The intensity of his kiss caught her by surprise. So much so she barely noticed Noah swinging the door shut behind them and lowering her until her feet touched the floor. Her arms still clung to his neck and he pulled her so close she couldn't catch her breath.

She dropped her hands and unbuttoned his jacket, spreading her palms across his chest, the cotton of his shirt rough under her fingertips. She wanted to feel his bare skin. She wanted to taste it. She wanted to feel it pressed against her own naked body.

He groped at the rise of her ass and she realized he was fumbling with the lacings of her dress. He cursed under his breath and she couldn't help laughing.

"You'll never get it like that." She turned around and presented her back to him. "It'll go faster if you can see what you're doing."

He paused for a moment, then she felt his hands at her lower back. "You and this dress are going to be the death of me, Libby St. Clair. I'll die from oxygen deprivation because all the blood that goes to my brain has gone somewhere else."

"Maybe it's Libby McMillan now."

"Not helping," he grunted as he turned her around and kissed her again. One of his hands cradled the side of her face as the other worked on the strings at the base of her spine.

She pulled back, grinning. "Who knew changing my name would make you so happy."

"You can keep St. Clair if you want, but I have to admit I like the idea of you taking McMillan."

"Why?"

"Because it would be just one more piece of proof that you're mine."

She gave him a gentle kiss and then spun around to show him her back. "Let's get this off so you can see more proof of what's yours."

He sucked in a breath, and within moments his hands were at her ass again, tugging on the strings, but he moved slower than she expected. She was about to ask why when he bent down and placed a kiss over the skin exposed by the loosened dress.

It was her turn to suck in a breath of surprise as he continued to loosen the laces, his mouth following the trail. When it was halfway up her back, he stood and slipped his hand into her dress, reaching around to her abdomen, his fingers light on her skin. The tips skimmed down to the top of her panties, making slow circles, before dipping slightly underneath the lacy fabric and rising back up to her stomach.

"I think you're trying to kill *me* now," she murmured, her eyes closed.

"No dying yet," he said, his tongue tracing circles on her back. He rose and his mouth found the base of her neck and moved up to her ear. His one hand was still inside her dress, but the other had abandoned its task of loosening her lacings. The hand in her dress rose to the underside of her breasts, as high as the fabric would allow. He blew cool air below her jaw, then licked and kissed the spot.

"Noah."

"I've studied this spot for months, did you know that?" His voice was rough-edged with desire. "When you wore your hair up this summer, I wanted to lean over and taste it. And now I can."

"You can taste a lot more if you get this dress off of me."

His hand stilled under her breast, then moved to her breastbone and slowly slid down over her belly button, continuing its descent over her panties and between her legs. His mouth concentrated on her neck, finding the spot that made her squirm as his fingers concentrated on gently stroking the cleft between her legs.

She gasped. Intense heat spread throughout her body, burning hottest between her legs. Her knees weakened and his free arm circled around her front and cupped her breast, his thumb brushing her nipple over the fabric of her dress. His mouth stilled.

"You're not wearing a bra."

"I didn't have one," she gasped while his fingers between her legs focused on the spot that drove her crazy. "My black dress . . . the front . . . I couldn't wear one." Something in the back of her head reminded her that she'd left the dress at the wedding chapel, but she didn't care. She had more important things to worry about.

The hand between her legs slipped inside her panties and she moaned at the direct contact.

"You're so wet," he murmured against her neck.

Rather than answer, she reached behind her and found his erection, rubbing the heel of her hand over the zipper of his pants.

He pressed himself against her and released his own moan.

She fumbled with his zipper and then the button on his pants, finding it hard to concentrate with the sweet torture his hands were performing.

"Noah. Dress. Now," she panted as she climbed higher.

"Not yet. I rather like making you squirm."

"So you're a sadist," she teased. "Maybe this should have come up before the wedding."

"No. I just like knowing I can make you so wet." His finger slipped inside her as though to prove his point.

She gasped again. "I don't want to come on your hand. I want you inside me."

"You can come over and over again tonight, Lib." His teeth nibbled on her earlobe. "I'll make you come as many times as you want."

His words turned her on even more. "Not the first time." She moaned as his finger moved in and out of her, the heel of his hand pressing against her mound. "I want you inside me the first time I come with you. I want you to make love to me."

His hands stilled and his mouth stopped. For a moment she worried she'd somehow offended him, but then he pulled his hand out of her dress and gently turned her to face him, and the adoration and love in his eyes was undeniable. He cradled her face with both hands and kissed her, his thumbs brushing her cheeks.

The love in his eyes, in his touch, was nearly her undoing. This seemed like a dream. She was married to Noah. He was hers. She clung to him, worried she'd lose this perfect moment with him, worried she'd lose *him*. That he'd come to his senses and realize this was all a terrible mistake.

His hands glided down her neck and over the thin lace on her shoulders, and then reached behind her and started loosening the laces, all while they continued the kiss, his tongue performing a slow dance with hers. Suddenly she felt cool air hit her naked back as he pulled down the dress to expose her shoulders, but it stopped at her upper arms.

He lifted his head to look down at her. "You have to let go, Lib."

She hadn't realized she was clinging so tightly to him, but she couldn't bring herself to let go.

He cupped her cheek and whispered, "Trust me."

But he wasn't just talking about what they were doing physically. He was asking her to hand him her heart.

He reached up and pulled her hands down, kissing her knuckles and skimming kisses over her wedding ring. Then he lowered her arms to her sides and continued the task of undressing her. He was slow and precise, lowering the dress a few inches at a time, pausing to place kisses on her shoulders, her collarbones, over the swell of her breasts, in the valley of her cleavage. She watched him until she was lost in sensation, closing her eyes so she could enjoy the feeling of him worshipping her.

The edge of the dress brushed over her bare nipples, making them even more erect. Then his mouth found one and his fingers teased the other. She moaned, tangling her hands in his hair.

The dress lowered to her waist, his mouth following, then over her hips. After it fell to the floor, leaving her in a puddle of silk and crinoline, his mouth continued its descent, placing kisses over the band of her panties. He rubbed his chin over her mound and she moaned again. Need coursed through her, stronger than she'd ever experienced it.

He rose and stood in front of her, and as they stared in each other's eyes, his hands reached behind her and started pulling pins from her hair.

"God, Libby. You're so beautiful," he whispered as he removed the last pin and her hair tumbled down her back. "I love your hair up, so I can see your sexy neck, but right now I want it down." He kissed her again, still gentle but more insistent than before.

She realized she was completely undressed except for her panties and her heels, while Noah was still completely clothed. She reached inside his jacket and pushed it over his shoulders, letting it fall to the floor. Breaking free from his kiss, she looked into his dark eyes as they watched her—the expression in them turning her on even more. She was surprised her fingers made quick work of his bow tie, letting it hang loose as she quickly freed his buttons and pulled the shirt free of his pants. She slid her hands inside his open shirt, placing kisses over his chest and the trail of hair leading to the top of his pants. His chest and abdomen were even more gorgeous than she'd imagined. Her hand followed behind her kisses, partially satisfying her need to touch as much of him as possible.

She looked up at him, her breath coming in shallow pants at the hunger and lust in his eyes.

His zipper was undone, so she turned her attention to the

still-fastened button. Once it was free, she knelt in front of him and tucked her thumbs into the waistband of his briefs. She slowly slid the fabric of his pants and briefs down over his sexy hipbones, her fingers gliding over his skin. His underwear slid down his erection, and she left open-mouth kisses over his shaft as she made her way down to his scrotum.

When his pants dropped to his ankles, he reached over and put his hands under her arms, pulling her up, her bare chest against his.

His hands were everywhere as he kissed her with a hunger she answered. Then they were on the bed and his mouth and hands were driving her to the brink of madness. He grunted and rolled off her, then practically ran to his suitcase to pull a condom out of his toiletry bag.

When he sank down next to her on the bed, she took it from him and quickly opened the package and rolled it over his shaft, taking him in her hand and stroking. He grunted again and rolled her onto her back, moving over her as he grabbed her leg and wrapped it around his back and plunged into her with one stroke. She cried out in pleasure, arching up to take him. He looked down at her as he took her higher and higher, the hunger in his eyes lifting her even more. They met each other stroke for stroke, a frenzy of passion and fire, need and hunger, until she was sure if she climbed any higher she would pass out from the lack of oxygen. And then she fell apart, letting her love and her need for him overcome her, vaguely aware that he had found his own release. She called his name as she came, wave after wave carrying her somewhere she'd never been before and had never thought she'd ever find.

Home.

Chapter Twenty-One

He stared down at his wife in amazement.

His wife.

Her gorgeous dark hair lay in a puddle on the pillow behind her head. Her eyes were closed as she caught her breath, but they fluttered open to reveal the rich dark brown pools he loved to stare into.

She was the most beautiful sight he had ever seen. And she was his. His chest burst with emotion. "That was . . ." How did he describe the most perfect moment he had ever experienced? "I've never . . ."

She smiled. "Me too."

"I love you." How was it he hadn't told her yet?

Tears filled her eyes. "I love you too."

"It seems a little backward to tell you that now."

She didn't respond, only watched him with hesitation in her eyes.

"I love you, Libby McMillan. When I told you I'd only been in love once, I was referring to *you*. I've loved you for months. I was just too stupid to see it."

She lowered her gaze for a moment before her eyes found his again. "I knew it too, deep down, but I was so afraid to lose you if it didn't work out."

He shook his head and gave her a soft smile. "You don't have to worry anymore, Lib. I'm here. I'm yours."

A shadow of doubt crossed her face, but before he could ask her about it, there was a banging on the door. "That must be whatever Ned was sending up."

She continued to smile, but something was off in her eyes.

"Lib?"

The pounding continued and she pushed his chest. "You better get that."

"No. What's going on inside your head?"

"I'm fine," she sighed with a soft smile. "I'm just overwhelmed. I never knew it could be so . . . perfect."

He felt the same way, but he couldn't help thinking there was something she wasn't telling him.

"*Go.*"

He pulled out of her and grabbed his briefs. After throwing the condom in the trash and pulling on his briefs, he opened the door.

"A special gift for you and your bride, Mr. McMillan," the employee outside his door said. His hand rested on the handle of a room service cart that held a covered plate, a silver bucket with a bottle of champagne, and two champagne flutes. "Although I can see you've already gotten started."

The man started to push the cart into the room, but Noah blocked his path, saying with more force than he intended, "I'll take it from here." There was no way this man was coming into the room where Libby lay naked in their bed.

The employee snickered and Noah had an unexpected urge to throttle him, though he had no idea where in the hell *that* feeling had come from. But he realized it was just another manifestation of his need to protect her from every possible threat, realistic or not. Still, this pervert would have to come through him first to get to her.

The employee had the good judgment to relinquish the cart. "Just set it outside your door when you're done, Mr. McMillan."

"Thanks."

He rolled the cart into the room and stopped short when he saw Libby sitting upright, her legs curled to the side . . . completely naked.

He realized he probably looked like a fool staring at her like that, but not finding it in him to care. "You're so gorgeous, Libby."

"You're not so bad yourself. If they'd sent a woman up with that tray, the sight of those abs and pecs would have melted her."

"You didn't melt," he reminded her.

"Ha! Only because you were already holding me up." Her gaze moved to the cart.

"More champagne?" she asked with a laugh. "If we tour the country with my wedding dress, we'll get all the champagne we want."

"I'll get you champagne every day if you want it."

She laughed again and he reveled in the knowledge he'd get to hear it every day for the rest of his life. "We need to make a toast."

He grabbed the bottle and started working on the wrapper and the cork. "As long as we aren't toasting to you not kicking me in either of my balls, I'm all for it." The cork popped off and he held the bottle over the cart in case it spilled out.

Her laughter filled the room and his heart and in that moment he was absolutely certain this was what he'd been waiting for his entire life. Her. "So . . ." he said with a sly grin as he poured a glass and handed it to her. "About those delusions of grandeur you mentioned . . ."

She took the glass. "Are you referring to the foot-long remark at the hotel in Junction City or the little shake insult in the bathroom at the Golden Cowboy Café?"

He poured himself a glass and she patted the mattress next to her. He sat down next to her and leaned in for a kiss. "Both."

A sparkle filled her eyes. "Let's just say I have nothing to be disappointed about."

He held up his glass, his heart filled with more happiness than he knew he deserved.

She lifted her glass to his. "It only seems appropriate that we toast your manhood."

He burst out laughing, nearly spilling the champagne.

"It's not nearly as huge as Tito's but . . . Hey." She shrugged. "It's no small thing." She winked and he grabbed the back of her head and kissed her, deep and passionate. Then she leaned back and hoisted her glass. "It's not officially a toast until we drink the champagne, you know?"

"Then by all means, let's finish the toast." But she didn't drink when he did. He didn't have time to ask her about it because she slowly straddled his lap and took the flute from his hand and set it on the nightstand.

He got hard again in an instant and a Cheshire cat grin spread across her face.

"I thought you said we needed to drink the champagne for

the toast to be complete?"

She lifted a delicate eyebrow. "Oh, I intend to drink it." She placed her hand on his chest and pushed him back on the bed while she still straddled his legs.

His heartbeat ratcheted up and his breath became shallow as he anticipated what she might be planning. She held her glass over his abdomen and poured a small dribble of the cold liquid on his chest, making him suck in his breath as it spread across the hollows of the muscles of his abdomen.

Libby leaned over and pressed her mouth to his stomach, licking and sucking up the liquid.

"So we've completed the toast?" he asked, his voice strained.

"Oh, no," she purred, her mouth continuing its task. "We're drinking to your manhood, remember?" She sat up and poured more champagne on his erection, then set the glass on the table. His erection jolted in response as her lips covered the head and took him into her mouth.

"Oh God, Lib." He grabbed handfuls of her hair as her tongue and lips sucked and licked, her hand cupping his balls. Within half a minute he was dangerously close to coming again. "My turn."

He pulled her off him and rolled her onto her back in one fluid movement. Laughing, she started to sit up, but he pushed her back down and knelt between her legs. After picking up his flute of champagne, he poured the liquid on her right breast, letting it dribble down to the hollow of her cleavage.

She gasped and her nipple hardened the instant before his mouth covered it, licking and nipping. She moaned as he licked the sticky liquid down to the pool.

"If we're toasting my manhood, we need to toast your glorious breasts."

She smiled. "They're glorious, are they?"

"You have no idea, do you?" He poured more champagne on the left nipple, his erection throbbing as her nipple pebbled. His tongue lapped at the pool between her breasts and then worked its way up the peak to her nipple. "They're perfect. Not too small, not too big. They fit in my hand with a little bit left over. They're soft." His lips skimmed her creamy skin. "And they are so responsive." He took her nipple between his teeth and she gasped, her hips lifting on the bed.

"Your observation is based on very little hands-on experience," she teased as his mouth worked its way down the crest.

"How many times do you have to look upon a beautiful painting to know it's glorious?" he asked in mock disbelief. "You see it and you know. Your breasts are exactly the same. Perfection brought to life. If I could sculpt, I'd make a statue of your beautiful breasts. Now I have a lifetime to enjoy their perfection."

He leaned up and kissed her, the taste of champagne on both their lips. She pushed on his shoulders to sit up, but he guided her back down.

"I'm not done toasting yet."

"I don't see how you could toast my breasts any more than you have."

His eyebrows rose playfully. "It's not your breasts I'm toasting this time."

Her eyes darkened with desire and anticipation as he picked up the flute and slid down her body. He held the glass over the V of her legs and released a slow drizzle, watching as the trickle flowed over her folds and then leaning down to clean it up with his mouth.

"Noah."

He looked up at her, his erection getting harder at the sight of her—her head thrown back, her fists gripping the pillow beneath her head, her nipples peaked on her full breasts. He brought her to the edge of an orgasm before she pulled him up and rolled him over onto his back.

"Condom?" she asked breathlessly.

"My toiletries bag," he answered just as breathlessly.

She left him to get the bag, and it seemed like an eternity before she straddled his legs and ripped open the package. "You need to be more prepared, Noah McMillan. This is your last one."

"Jesus," he mumbled in panic. "That will never do."

She rolled it on him, poised over him. "No. It won't." Then she lowered down and took the length of him inside her, moving slowly and purposely, the evil grin on her face telling him that she intended to torture him.

He sat up and scooted them to the edge of the bed. He cupped her delicious ass and lifted her up before bringing her firmly down on top of him again. "I want to kiss this next time. Your ass and so many other places."

"Yes, next time," she murmured, her eyes closed and her head thrown back, as she rode him, her movements letting him know she was close to coming. He was sure he'd never seen a more beautiful sight in his life—his Libby, unhinged and wild, taking what she wanted from him. Then she released a cry and moaned his name as her fingers dug into his shoulders and her climax washed over her. He pulled her close and she sagged against him, her forehead resting against his.

He kissed her, gently, softly. Wanting to show her how much he loved her. Adored her. Worshiped her.

He scooted backward on the bed, still inside her as he rolled her onto her back. Moving in and out, slowly . . . all the way in and nearly all the way out, again and again.

He reached his hand between her legs, rubbing her. "Do you have any idea how much I want you?"

"As much as I want you?" Her breath hitched, her eyes on his.

Her words triggered something inside him, unleashing a tidal wave of passion and desire.

She locked her legs behind his back as he pounded into her with an intensity that caught him by surprise. Worried he was hurting her, he slowed down.

"Don't . . . stop!" she gasped out.

Instinct took over and he lifted her hips to drive deeper, inflamed by the feeling of her tightening around him.

She cried out and lifted her hips to take him as deep as she could. No longer able to hold back, Noah came hard and fast. After he caught his breath, he rolled her to her side, facing him.

"You're going to kill me," she murmured, her eyes closed.

He kissed her forehead, her cheeks, her nose, and finally placed a gentle kiss on her mouth. "You are everything I could have ever hoped for."

"I love you," she whispered, drifting off to sleep.

Noah held her in his arms, overcome by the knowledge that he had never fathomed what love could be like until he'd held this woman in his arms.

Chapter Twenty-Two

Libby awoke on her side, Noah's stomach pressed to her back. Their nakedness was proof enough that last night hadn't been a dream.

She was married to Noah. Never in her wildest dreams could she hope to have what she'd shared with him last night. And this was only the beginning of so much more.

She shifted and freed her left arm from underneath his, wanting a better look at the wedding ring.

"We can get you another if you don't like it," he murmured, sounding like his mouth was buried in his pillow.

"I love it. It's perfect. What does yours look like?"

He placed his left palm on top of hers and splayed his fingers so she could see their rings together. "They match."

"I never took you as a matchy-matchy guy," she teased.

"Ordinarily I'm not, so don't expect me to wear matching T-shirts."

"How about wearing matching shirts with Tortoise?"

"Maybe . . ."

"What about matching Halloween costumes? We can go as Fred and Wilma Flintstone."

"Only if I get to be Wilma."

She laughed and rolled over to face him as he propped himself on his elbow to look at her. "Good morning, Mrs. McMillan."

Happiness flooded her heart. "Good morning, Mr. McMillan." Then she covered her mouth. "Oh, God. I have morning breath."

He pulled her hand down. "So do I." He kissed her, making her forget all about morning breath.

When he lifted his head, she grinned. "Does this mean I can use your toothbrush now?"

"No."

"We've done much more intimate things that have involved the exchange of just as many germs as me using your toothbrush," she said in a sultry voice.

"Enough of your vixen ways," he chuckled. "You're tempting me when you know we're out of condoms."

She turned serious. "We don't have to use a condom, Noah. I have an IUD. I was with Mitch for five months and no one at all for three months before him."

He shook his head. "I want to get tested first to be safe. I'd never forgive myself if I have something and gave it to you."

"Have you really been with that many women?"

Some of the happiness left his eyes. "Yes. I'm not proud of it, but I realize now I was searching for this—for what we have. Only I went about it the wrong way. Not one of those women meant even a fraction of what you mean to me."

"What about Donna?"

He brushed a stray hair from her forehead. "Donna was a very poor substitute for what I thought I couldn't have. You."

"But why were you so sure you couldn't have me?"

"You shot me down, Lib. Remember? Right before you proposed to Mitch."

Her face grew hot. "We had both been drinking and I thought . . ."

"That I was just hitting on you. Yeah, I know. To be fair, I wasn't really sure what I was doing. Only that I craved you in a way I didn't understand." He tilted her chin so he could look into her eyes. "Honestly, if we had hooked up then, I don't think it would be this. What we have now. I wasn't ready yet. Does that make sense?"

"Perfectly. I don't think I was ready yet either. You've inspired me."

He laughed. "Are you going to photograph me naked?"

"That's not what I was talking about, but hold that thought." She climbed out of bed and dug through the bag Gram had brought her, emerging with her camera bag.

His eyes widened. "You're serious."

She unpacked the camera and gave him a mischievous grin. "We can swaddle you like Tito if you'd like."

"No fucking way."

She laughed again and attached a lens. "I won't take photos of your celebrated manhood . . . or at least not many photos. After all, we've toasted it, so we should capture it in its glory. But those will be just for me."

"Does that mean I get to photograph your breasts?"

She shrugged. "If you'd like."

"You're serious?" he asked in disbelief as he rolled onto his back.

"They're only breasts. It's not like you're going to show

them around to all your buddies, are you?"

"God, no. I don't share well."

She flashed him another grin as she stood up and moved to the window. Bright daylight flooded the room when she pulled the drapery to one side. She turned to study him. "I knew the morning light would work well with your angles."

"Is that photographer dirty talk? Because it's working."

"Be a good boy and I'll tell you all about ISO speeds."

"I knew it was dirty talk. You've given me a hard-on."

She snorted. "You already had one."

"It doesn't take much. All I have to do is think of you."

"Down boy. No condoms. Remember?"

"It's all I can think about."

She laughed. "Roll onto your side and prop up on your elbow. Yes. Just like that."

He held the pose, looking up at her. "Libby, my manhood's hanging out in all its glory."

She held up her camera to frame the shot. "Your manhood's not in the photo. I'll let you know when it is."

For the next twenty minutes she had him pose in multiple positions. With each shot, she got more and more excited. After she and Noah had had their disagreement over her engagement, she'd lost all spark for her art. But now it was back full force. Noah was her muse. "The camera loves you, Noah."

"I'm more interested in the photographer loving me."

"She does. Especially since you're the perfect model."

"So you're basically just using me for my body."

"Do you have a problem with that?"

"God, no. But if you're going to take photos of my manhood, you'll never find it more impressive than it looks now. You have no idea how sexy you are photographing me, both of us naked."

She laughed as she sat down next to him. Leaning in as if to kiss him, she instead held the camera sideways and took several rapid-fire shots of his crotch.

"Hey!" he protested.

"You told me to," she said with a sly grin. "Besides, you're right. It's very impressive. And oh so tempting."

He kissed her slow and gentle, his teeth nibbling her lower lip. It was impossible to imagine being happier than she was at this moment. Could life really be like this?

Noah took the camera from her and slowly pushed her back onto the bed. He guided her onto her side, her back to him as he lifted the camera to his eye.

"You do realize you can't see my breasts," she teased, looking over her shoulder at him.

"I don't want to take photos of your breasts with your camera." He snapped several shots as he moved around her. "That's for my phone. And my eyes only."

He took several more shots before she leaned back against the pillows. "Get your phone. If you're going to photograph my breasts, do it now before I shower."

He slid off the bed and dug around in his suit jacket, then pulled out his phone. "Oh, shit. My phone has blown up in the last twelve hours."

"Why?"

He stood and scanned the screen. "Gram."

Libby sat up, her breath catching with worry. "What about Gram?"

"She tweeted a photo of us at the chapel."

It took Libby a moment to put it together. "Megan and Blair saw it."

"Yeah." His voice was tight.

"Why do you sound so upset?"

He sighed and put the phone on the nightstand. "You need to call them."

Anger simmered in her chest. "Why are they upset? Because they weren't invited?"

He sat on the bed and picked up his phone again, opening his Twitter app. "You need to see the tweet, Lib." He handed her the phone and she looked at the photo on his screen.

It showed the two of them in their wedding attire with Tito in his costume behind them—diaper, wings, and harp.

Oh shit.

"They're pissed at me, and they're worried about you."

"Why?"

"Look at it, Libby." He held the phone up in front of her. "They think we got drunk and I took advantage of you."

"That's the stupidest thing I've ever heard. You've been like the poster boy for anti-marriage."

"Well, maybe they think you only married me because of the curse."

"Why would they be angry with *you*?"

He shook his head and took several steps toward the bathroom before turning around to look at her. "Because no matter what I do, I will *always* be the sleazy bastard."

Libby stood. "Noah."

Some dark emotion covered his face. "I'm going to take a shower." He went into the bathroom and shut the door. The water turned on seconds later.

Her temper raging, Libby grabbed his phone and scanned his messages. Megan and Blair had both sent him texts accusing him of taking advantage of her. They clearly did not take her marriage seriously.

Undecided on who to call first, she settled on Blair, who

answered on the first ring. "You have some explaining to do, McMillan."

"He doesn't owe you a damn thing."

"Libby," Blair said, sounding surprised. "Why are you calling from Noah's phone?"

"Because I left mine at home. Remember?"

"Gram was supposed to bring it to you."

Well, shit. It was probably in her purse, although it was undoubtedly dead. "Look, it doesn't matter which phone I'm using. What matters is you're harassing my husband."

"Libby, listen. I think we can get it annulled."

"Why would I want to get it annulled?"

"You're obviously not thinking clearly. I saw the photo of your wedding. Did you get married in a circus? How drunk were you?"

"I wasn't drunk at all, not by the time we got to the chapel anyway."

"So you're admitting there was alcohol involved? That's good. We can use that as evidence."

Libby groaned. "Blair, what do you want?"

"I want to make sure you're okay."

"I was fine until Noah found the texts from you and Megan."

"What did you expect us to do? You wouldn't answer your phone."

"Here's an idea—how about you try congratulating me?"

Blair was silent for a few moments. "Libby, I know you're confused right now. I know you believed in the curse, so I'm sure you jumped at the chance to make it come true. Especially with the bad influences around you."

"You mean Noah."

She remained silent.

"Okay," Libby said, her voice tight. "So let me get this straight. You think I was so desperate to make the curse come true, I would have married anyone who came along."

"You *were* going to marry Mitch."

"Only because I expected my soul mate to show up."

"Like that sounds any better? Are you listening to yourself? You didn't even know who it was. So then you married Noah."

"I *love* Noah."

"You love Noah," she repeated in a monotone. "*Since when?* You two are *friends*, like two rule-breaking kids who've found a co-conspirator in each other. You never once said you thought Noah was your soul mate. When did you figure this out? Last night when you were drinking? Everything's so much clearer when you're drunk."

"I thought you were my friend, Blair."

"Believe it or not, I *am*."

"No, you just want to lord it over me."

"What does *that* mean?"

"You and Megan love that I'm the irresponsible, head-in-the-clouds, screw-up friend. That way you both can feel superior to me."

"That's ridiculous."

"Is it?'

"Libby." She sounded irritated. "You have a pattern, and if you would just hop off the Libby whirlwind express for a moment and take a breath, you would see it too. You *never* handle a breakup well and you always make some stupid decisions you regret later. That is *exactly* what you're doing now."

Fear bubbled in her chest, stealing her breath. Blair was right about her previous breakup behavior. What if she was right about this too? But there was no way in hell she'd let Blair know she'd gotten to her.

"Libs"—Blair's tone softened—"I love you and I don't want to see you get your heart broken again. Noah is a user. He'll take what he wants and move on. If he doesn't cheat on you first."

"How can you say that?"

"You know he never stays with one woman for more than a week. And yeah, I know he was in a month-long relationship with that woman in Seattle," she said dismissively, "but that only proves my point. He's in a relationship with some woman and then he just up and marries *you*? It won't last."

"I've had my own share of men, Blair. I'm not exactly the Virgin Mary."

"True, but you were always looking for love, deep down. He's just looking for his next lay."

"So if Noah is just looking for his next lay, and we both know I'm an easy conquest, why did he marry me?"

"I didn't say you were an easy conquest."

"Why did he marry me, Blair?" she repeated with more force.

She paused. "I don't know yet. I'm still trying to figure out his angle."

"Well, figure it out without me." She hung up and scowled at the phone in her hand, wishing she could throw it against the wall. Megan would want to hear from her too, but she couldn't deal with her right now. Especially since the claws of Blair's accusations were sinking deeper and deeper into her head.

What if Noah got tired of her? The feelings she had for him were so much deeper and more intense than anything she'd experienced before, but what if it wasn't the same for him? There was no denying he was a good friend. Could he have married her, in part, to make her feel better? And worse, what if this was just another of Libby's many desperate attempts to find someone to love her?

Was she really that pathetic?

But then she thought about everything she had shared with Noah, both before and after their wedding. She could trust Blair or she could trust Noah. Which one would it be?

The temptation to go to him swept her into the bathroom. He was leaning against the wall of the shower, his forehead buried against his arm. His hair was wet and water dripped down his muscled back. He really did have the face and body of a god. No woman had ever held enough of a lure to keep him for very long. Why did she think *she* could?

He heard the door open and looked up, anguish on his face.

Who did she choose to trust?

Staring into his eyes, it was really no choice at all.

She stepped into the shower and pulled his mouth to hers, pressing her body against his chest.

His arms were around her back, pulling her close, his mouth hungry and desperate to claim hers. His hands were everywhere and so were hers—seeking, demanding, begging, claiming. He grabbed her ass and lifted her against the shower wall, entering her as she clung to him. There were no words; their bodies said everything that needed to be said. She came quickly, Noah following right behind her. She buried her face against his chest, still shocked that he was really here with her. That he was hers.

She would believe what she held in her hands, the proof in front of her eyes.

Her friends could go to hell.

Chapter Twenty-Three

"Noah," Libby murmured against his chest, then looked up into his eyes. "I'm so sorry about my friends."

Her words sent a new jolt of fear through him. He stiffened and started to pull out of her and put her down, but she locked her legs around his back and tightened her hold on his neck.

"Don't shut me out. Please."

The fear in her voice caught him off guard. He rested his forehead against hers and her body relaxed.

"I love you. I don't care what they think."

He shook his head. "They're your friends. *Of course* you care what they think."

"I'll admit that Blair infuriated me and hurt me with her judgmental attitude . . ." Her voice wavered. "But she doesn't run my life."

"In their eyes, I will never be good enough for you. They will always be waiting for me to fuck up so they can tell you I

269

told you so."

She flashed him a tiny smile. "That will be a lot harder to do with them in Kansas City and me in Seattle."

"I can't ask you to give up twenty-five years of friendship for me."

She grabbed his face and looked deep into his eyes. "Don't you see? *You're* not asking me to choose. You're giving me the freedom to make my own choice. Blair sees me as an incompetent toddler incapable of making a responsible choice." She took a breath. "I don't think I can ever become the responsible person I want to be because it still won't fit in with *their* vision of a responsible adult. They're always judging me against their standards."

"Libby. I can't be the person who comes between you and your friends."

"Don't you hear what I'm saying? You aren't coming between them and me. *They* are coming between *us*." She kissed him—a gentle brush of her lips against his—her touch full of so much love it took his breath away. "I love you, Noah McMillan."

"And I love you, Elizabeth Gabriella St. Clair McMillan." He forced a grin. "You never told me your name is Elizabeth."

Something flashed in her eyes. Doubt? Did it bother her that he had hadn't known her real name until their wedding? "You never asked. I hate it. It's so stuffy."

He kissed the corner of her mouth. "You're much more of a Libby to me. My Lib."

She closed her eyes. "Yes, your Lib."

His hold on her tightened. He was surprised by the possessiveness rushing through him. He'd thought he would feel more secure about their relationship once they were married, but he was more worried than ever. Now he was aware of what he risked losing.

Her eyes opened and he stared into their rich brown depths. Would he really get to stare into them every day for the rest of his life? The hope and contentment that thought gave him calmed his soul.

"Let's finish washing up, then get breakfast," she said, grinning. "I've worked up quite an appetite." Her hold loosened and she was sliding down his body, slow and sultry, when a new horror hit him.

"We just had unprotected sex."

She shook her head dismissively. "It's okay. I already told you I have an IUD."

"No, it's *not*. I wanted to get checked out first. God . . . Libby . . . I'm sorry. I should have been more responsible." Then it hit him. Maybe he would never be responsible enough to be a good husband. He wasn't sure he could bear it if she joined the long list of people he'd failed.

"Noah. Stop." She said it with more authority than he was used to hearing from her. "You're my husband." The smile she gave him was so sweet and soft his throat tightened. "We can have sex without condoms. But if it makes you feel better, we'll use them until you know for sure, okay?"

Her words soothed the sting of his pain.

"I love you. Please don't feel any guilt about making love to me. It doesn't belong there."

"Okay, but we have to use condoms until I know."

She grinned. "I won't let your manhood near me until it's sheathed. But to be safe, perhaps I should get a chastity belt."

He kissed her again, pressing her against the shower wall as a tidal wave of love and gratitude overcame him. She always knew just what to say to pull him from his dark places.

"Give me your shampoo," she said. "I'll wash your hair."

They were more subdued than usual as they washed each other. The overwhelming fear he'd still lose her was almost enough to drown him. Here in this moment, it was easy for her to want to stay with him. But what about when they got back to real life? When her friends were with her in person? They'd always see him as a fuckup.

He had to prove them wrong and show them he was worthy of her.

He had to close the Abrahams deal.

Something deep inside told him to tell her what was going on. If anyone would understand his decision to impulsively quit his job, it was Libby. But she was so proud of him and the progress he'd made, and he felt like everything between them was precarious enough. He didn't want to risk it. If he could set up a meeting with Abrahams, he'd tell her that he was working on a business deal. But if he couldn't get the meeting, he'd tell her the truth and let everything fall where it would.

He watched her get ready, longing to stay in the cocoon of their room, where they were safe from the rest of the world. When she started blow-drying her hair, he told her he was going to get ice and took the ice bucket and his phone into the hall.

Tiffany answered on the second ring. "I thought you were blowing me off, Noah."

"No, of course not," he said, feeling slimy as he ran a hand through his hair. "I just got tied up." He took a breath. "So, about Scott . . . Can you set something up?"

"Yeah, but I'm more interested in setting something up between you and me."

Tell her. Just tell her you're married. But he couldn't. He needed this deal so he could start his life with Libby, and he wasn't sure Tiffany would set it up if she didn't think she had a shot with him. When Libby moved to Seattle, they'd have nothing. She deserved more from him. "Um . . . I . . ."

"What's gotten into you, Noah? You don't sound like yourself."

"Oh . . . just fighting a cold."

"I can bring you some chicken soup . . . and then feed it to you."

Before Libby, he would have been ready to go just thinking about it. But now, it made him feel dirty. "That's okay, it's just a small one. So about that meeting . . ."

"You are one persistent boy, aren't you? That's something I loved about you," she said with so much innuendo a deaf man could hear it.

He ignored her last statement. "My business *really* needs this."

"And I really need *you*." Her voice was low and seductive.

Shit. *Shit.* What was he going to do? *Tell her. TELL HER.* "I'm not in town for very long."

"We only need a few hours, *lover boy*."

"I thought you were seeing Scott."

She giggled. "Come on. Like that stopped you before."

"*I'm* seeing someone."

Another giggle. "Like that's stopped *me* before. Besides, everyone knows you don't really see women. Lucky for you, I'm not looking for more than a few hours at the most. You know what they say—what happens in Vegas . . ." Her voice trailed off with seductive promise.

He swallowed, knowing he was at a crossroads. If he led her on any more, he'd be cheating on Libby and he refused to do that. He'd support her some other way; hell, he'd get a job as a janitor if need be. "Tiffany, I'm married."

"You're *what*?" She couldn't have sounded more shocked if

he'd told her he was an alien from Mars.

He leaned his back against the wall by the ice machine and heaved out a breath. "I'm married and I love my wife very much. I don't want to deceive you or lead you on any more than I already have. I need this account, but I won't sleep with you to get it. If you don't want to set up a meeting for me with Scott, I understand, but I really hope you can help me out."

"Well, I'll be damned," she mumbled. "*You're* married. Has hell frozen over?"

He released a nervous chuckle. "It very well might have."

"So you love her, huh?"

"You have no idea. *Please.*"

"Yeah, sure . . . why not? If *you* can fall in love, get married and be so adamant about remaining faithful, it gives the rest of us single girls hope." She still sounded dazed. "When are you free?"

"My day is flexible. Just tell me when and where and I'll be there."

"I'll text you when I know something. Tell your wife congrats."

"Thanks, but if we run into each other later, can you not mention the meeting to her? I want to surprise her with the closed deal when it's done."

"Yeah, sure."

He was already on his way back to the room when he realized he hadn't filled the bucket. He turned around and completed that task, then went back to the room. When he walked in, Libby was leaning over her suitcase, stark naked.

He grinned. "You have no idea how happy I am that you aren't self-conscious about your body. It makes me consider becoming a nudist."

She laughed as she pulled a black sweater from the bag. "I

figure this is how God made me. Besides, gravity isn't my friend. One day the girls will go south." She glanced up at him. "I hope you're prepared for that."

"Libby, you will always be beautiful to me. Even when you're nine months pregnant with our baby someday." He hadn't meant to say that last part, but as soon as the words left his mouth, he knew it was true. Libby would be an incredible mother.

Her mouth parted as she turned to look at him. "I thought you didn't want kids."

"I didn't think I did either until you. I love kids. Perhaps unsurprisingly, I seem to have a lot in common with them." He winked. "I just don't want to screw up *my own* kids. But how can they be screwed up with you as their mother?" Then he stopped. "Unless *you* don't want kids."

She shook her head, smiling with tears in her eyes. "No. I do."

"And you married me thinking I didn't?"

"I want you more. Kids are bonus."

He pulled her into his arms and kissed the top of her head. "Finish getting ready and let's get some lunch—it's after eleven o'clock, so I think it's past breakfast. How about I call Gram and see if she and Nana Ruby want to join us?"

"Really?" Her eyes widened in shock. "I thought you'd be upset with her after the whole Twitter incident."

He sighed. "Blair and Megan were going to find out the ugly details at some point, and Gram meant well. If we invite her to lunch, she'll know we're not angry with her. If she even knows things are a mess back home. She might be totally oblivious."

She stiffened in his arms. "You think our wedding was ugly?"

"I think our wedding was perfectly *us*, but we both know that your friends—especially Blair—would have been horrified and offended by it." He bent at the knees to look her in the eyes. "I suspect you got an earful when you called them earlier."

"I only talked to Blair and it was enough."

"I'm sorry."

She shook her head and her eyes lit up with fire. "Their loss, but it only proves that other than Tortoise, there's really nothing left for me in Kansas City. I want to move my things to Seattle as soon as possible."

"I love you, Lib. I hope I'm worth the grief."

A soft smile spread across her face. "I'm not sure I'll ever get tired of hearing you say you love me."

"If I said it as many times as the feeling hits me, I suspect I'll annoy the hell out of you, but I'm willing to take the risk."

She placed a kiss on his lips, her eyes sparkling with happiness. "I like the sound of that. Why don't you call Gram while I get dressed?"

He nodded and watched her ass as she dug her jeans and underwear out of the bag. It was a good thing he was out of condoms or he'd suggest they order room service instead.

He pulled up Gram's number. "Hey, Gram."

"I'm surprised you and Libby are still speaking to me. Megan's about to birth twin cows." She sounded more subdued than usual.

He shrugged even though she couldn't see him. "Libby says it's their loss. We love that you got a photo. For all I know it's one of the only ones. We were supposed to get professional photos, but Angelica broke the camera, so unless one of the homeless guys had a camera, I'm pretty sure that didn't happen."

"I'm not sure why they have their panties in a wad. I thought it was a lovely service."

"Thanks, Gram. We loved it too. Say . . . I know we talked about having dinner tonight, but we were wondering if you and Nana Ruby wanted to join us for lunch instead."

"Sounds good. Then we can go see Donny and Marie tonight."

He laughed. "*You* want to see Donny and Marie?"

"Nah. It seemed like a good compromise. Ruby's a little bit country and I'm a whole lot of rock and roll. What Ruby doesn't know is we're going to a strip club after. I'm hoping to meet my Mr. Right."

"Well, okay then . . . that works out well. Do you have a preference where we eat for lunch?"

"That Food Network guy has a restaurant here. How about we eat at his place?"

"Sounds good. Can you be ready to meet us there at noon? I'll see if I can get reservations."

"We'll see you kids there."

"It's a date." He hung up and grinned.

Libby stood in front of him wearing a pair of jeans that clung to her hips and a black sweater with a V-neck that dipped into her cleavage and knit fabric that showed off her generous breasts. It didn't help matters that he knew she was wearing black lingerie underneath. "I'm ready to go. What are we going to do for the next forty-five minutes?"

He pulled her into his arms, groaning. "Not what I'd like to be doing. You're gorgeous."

She laughed. "How about we find some condoms for later, then wander around until it's time to meet them for lunch."

"That sounds like a fabulous plan. We better get the jumbo package. I hope your purse is big enough."

Chapter Twenty-Four

Gram and Nana Ruby were waiting for them at the entrance to the restaurant. Nana Ruby had ditched the sparkles for a red sweatshirt that said *My grandkid can whoop your grandkid's ass.* Gram wore yoga pants and a T-shirt. Her face was red and she was huffing and puffing.

"Gram, are you okay?" Libby asked, worried. "You don't look so good."

"I'm still sweating from that hot yoga class." She pointed her finger at Libby. "And for the record, hot yoga is *not* full of hot men. I stayed long enough to break a sweat, then hightailed it out of there."

Noah laughed and wrapped his arm around Libby's back, resting it on her hip. She glanced up at him with a smile.

"You girls are stealing all the hot men," Gram teased. "There are none left for me." She pointed over to Nana. "Even Ruby has a man."

"You'll find one," Noah assured her with a wink. "He could be right under your nose and you're too blind to see it."

She wrinkled her nose. "More like I would have to be blind to look at any of them naked. All the fat rolls and floppy skin. Not to mention it's too hard to get to the good stuff." She held her hands in front of her, mimicking holding the fat rolls.

Libby cringed at the thought.

"Good God, Maude," Nana groaned. "We're about to eat."

"Thanks for coming to our wedding," Libby said. "You have no idea how happy we were that you were there."

Gram patted her arm, her eyes soft with affection. "I wouldn't have missed it for the world, Libby, my girl."

Libby gave her a hug, happy that she and Noah had support from *someone*.

The hostess led them to their table. After they ordered and their food was served they talked about the wedding and Libby's friends' reaction.

"I understand why Blair's carrying on," Gram said, sawing on a piece of steak. "She's always had a stick up her ass, but I'm disappointed in Megan."

"To be fair," Libby said, sipping from her water glass, "I haven't talked to Megan."

Gram scowled. "I have."

Well, that confirmed that.

"How long are you kids staying in Vegas?" Nana asked.

Libby turned to look at Noah, surprised by the blank look on his face.

He studied her face. "I found out a potential client is here. I'm hoping to have a chance to meet with him."

"Oh. Okay." When had he found *that* out? He hadn't had his laptop out, but then again, he only needed his phone to check his email.

"I'm hoping to see him this afternoon. We could leave tonight or tomorrow." He leaned over and kissed her temple. "I'm eager to get Libby moved to Seattle."

Gram looked surprised. "You're moving to Seattle?"

Libby gave her a sheepish look. "We'd decided on that a couple of days ago. Before . . . our wedding."

Gram leaned forward, her eyes glowing. "Is that so?"

Noah tried to play nonchalant. "Libby's serious about the artistic side of her photography, not just family portraits and senior photos. The climate is better for that in the Pacific Northwest."

"And who brought this up first?" Nana Ruby asked.

Noah shrugged, keeping his attention on his salmon. "I did."

"Is that so?" Gram asked again, sounding like she knew there was more to the story.

He looked up. "What?"

"You were just being a good friend?"

He grinned. "That too."

Libby gasped and turned to face him. "What else?"

He hesitated, then sighed. "Lib, I decided not to come to your wedding because I couldn't stand the thought of you marrying anyone, let alone Mitch. But then I decided I couldn't let it happen at all. I intended to stop the wedding."

"*You did?*"

He cringed. "Yeah."

She whacked his shoulder with her napkin. "So why didn't you *tell* me?"

He lifted his hands in defense. "You shot me down a month ago. I figured you were going to take some wooing."

"We've already discussed the whole proposition thing. And *wooing?*" she teased.

"Turns out I'm old-fashioned. Who knew?" A huge grin spread across his face. "I didn't have sex with my wife until our wedding night. Go figure."

"Noah," she groaned good-naturedly. She wasn't opposed to people knowing, but heavens only knew what Gram would do with that information.

Gram laughed. "Oh, we already knew. He told us last night."

"*What?*"

"We told him to step up his game plan."

Libby shook her head, trying to make all the pieces fit. "So when you asked me to move to Seattle . . ."

"I figured it would give me the opportunity to convince you I was worth the risk."

"And when I told you I wanted to take a year off from men?"

He grimaced. "I wasn't thrilled, but I was willing to wait."

"While you saw other women?"

He turned serious. "No. Once I put it together that I loved you, I knew there was no other woman for me but you."

"But you said you would move . . . get a two-bedroom house . . ."

"Lib, I fully intended to give you your own room until you were ready. My intention was to show you I'd changed."

Overcome with emotion, she pulled his face to hers for a kiss. "I love you."

He smiled at her. "I love you too."

"And I love that daughter-in-law of mine," Ruby said with a low growl. "But she's a pigheaded fool if she can't see the two of you are meant to be together."

Libby offered the woman a smile. "Thanks, Nana."

Gram patted her hand. "They'll come around."

Libby was so pissed about their lack of support, she wasn't sure it mattered.

Noah pulled his phone out of his pocket and read the screen. "That's the text I've been waiting for. My meeting is set for two." He looked up at Libby, worry in his eyes. "Is it okay if I leave you for about an hour or two?"

"Of course it is. I'm not a child who needs to be babysat."

He shook his head slightly. "I know you're not, but I'm taking time from our honeymoon. That doesn't seem right."

"Oh. I hadn't considered this our honeymoon."

"It's very much our honeymoon, Mrs. McMillan. And while I never really cared for Vegas before, I have a special fondness for it now. Still, after my meeting, I think this city has served its purpose. Are you good with leaving tonight? We can go anywhere you want."

She rested her hand on his cheek. "I want to go home."

His smile fell slightly and she realized he misunderstood.

"*Our* home. In Seattle."

He kissed her again, and when he finally lifted his head, Libby's face burned with embarrassment. He'd practically devoured her in front of the grandmas.

"If only I were twenty years younger," Gram murmured.

"You'd still be too old for him," Nana said sternly.

"It wouldn't matter," Gram said with a grin. "He'd still only have eyes for our girl."

They finished lunch and while Nana and Gram invited Libby to walk the strip, Libby turned them down. "I think I'll grab my camera and see what I can find to photograph."

The two women left and Noah and Libby went up to their room. Noah opened his laptop and studied the screen, his leg bouncing as he read.

"Noah, why are you so nervous?"

He looked up at her and blinked. "What? I'm not nervous. Just a regular meeting."

He was lying. Why was he lying?

All the doubts from earlier came rushing back. She knelt in front of him. "I need you to promise me something, okay?"

"Anything, Lib," he answered with an earnestness she was still getting used to.

"I need you to promise to tell me the truth. You know I've had a history with men who have been untruthful. I need to know I can trust you."

"You have to know I'd never purposely hurt you."

"I know, but this is a deal-breaker for me, Noah. I need you to always tell me the truth."

He looked into her eyes, an uncharacteristic seriousness setting into his jaw. "I will. I promise."

"Thank you."

He pushed out a breath. "This deal is important. I've been talking to this guy in Seattle and getting the runaround. I found out he's here, so I'm hoping to seal the deal this afternoon. With the merger . . . the business needs this."

She kissed him and smiled. "That wasn't so bad, was it? Why would you hide that from me?"

"I don't want you to worry."

"Noah, we're married now. If you're nervous, then it's my job to worry. Just like it's your job to be nervous when we go to New York for my exhibit."

He pulled her onto his lap, evoking a surprised laugh from her. "You've decided to finish your project?"

She grinned. "Let's just say this morning's photography session inspired me."

He lifted his eyebrows in mock recrimination. "I know it's a New York exhibit and they're much more liberal there, but I strongly discourage using the photos of my penis, no matter how impressive they are."

She laughed. "You've ruined my theme. I planned to photograph the penises of men all over the country. I could group them by region. Or would it be better to organize them by length?"

"The only penis I plan to let you near is mine." He looked up from his laptop. "And if I had more time, I'd let you get even closer to it now."

"Later," she murmured.

"I know we've paid for the room tonight, but I'd still like to go home this evening if it's okay with you. I'll book us tickets when I get back from the meeting." He grinned. "But there will be plenty of time for you to get reacquainted with my penis before we go."

She laughed. "Sounds perfect."

He stood and set her on her feet. "Wish me luck."

She gave him a kiss. "Good luck, my love."

"You're all the luck I need." He gathered his laptop and put it into his bag. "Are you sure you're okay by yourself?"

She picked up her camera bag. "I'm fine. I'm going to explore outside the hotel. I have some ideas about capturing the fountains at the Bellagio."

He grabbed her left hand and kissed her wedding ring. "Flash this at any man who gets within six feet of you."

She laughed.

"You think I'm joking. You're the most beautiful woman I've ever known and I'm not the only one who notices. When we get home I plan to get you a huge-ass diamond to blind any man who comes near you."

She tried to keep a straight face. "Huge-ass. I think I heard they added that to the list of diamond sizes."

He looked into her eyes, all teasing gone. "I love you, Libby."

That caught her attention. "Noah, what aren't you telling me?"

He hesitated and then flashed her a smile. "In full disclosure, my apartment is a total bachelor pad. I think I even left dirty laundry on the floor when I was throwing my clothes around in my haste to pack. I hope it doesn't scare you off."

"Just take me home and we'll sort it all out when we get there."

He gave her one last look, the seriousness in his eyes scaring her, and left the room.

Chapter Twenty-Five

The beauty of Las Vegas was it was warmer than Kansas City, but the wind still nipped through the weave of Libby's sweater. She hugged it tight, wishing Noah was with her to keep her warm. But she knew this meeting was more important than he was letting on. Why hadn't he told her about it sooner? When had he found out the guy was in Vegas?

She lingered in front of the fountains, waiting for them to turn on. She knew they were on timers, but they seemed to be lagging behind.

While she waited, she photographed people on the strip and found herself concentrating on couples. There were two distinct groups—those who were simply there together and those who wanted to be with their significant others. The ones in the former group filled her with sadness. With one couple, the husband wore a look of irritation while his wife stared at him with a yearning that broke Libby's heart. But there were others. A wife on her phone while her husband lagged behind. And another couple that had clearly had a recent argument—the wife in tears, her husband with a set jaw and a hard look in his eyes.

But the couples in love filled her with hope. Those couples had to touch each other in some way, even if only with their eyes. She watched as a couple in their forties stopped next to the fountains, probably waiting for them to turn on. The wife wore a light jacket and shivered when the wind gusted, so her husband pulled her into his arms. After wrapping his jacket around her back, he kissed her gently. The moment reminded her so much of her and Noah during their visit to the Czechoslovakian egg. Other than the kissing, had they looked like that? She remembered his gentleness and realized he'd already known he loved her. He'd planned that entire day out of love for her. How had she been so blind?

The familiar insecurities rushed in out of nowhere—her worn, faithful companions. They whispered into her ear, telling her that she was doomed, that she couldn't keep Noah's love. And maybe it was true. So many men—men she'd never even loved—had left her. And if her string of lost lovers wasn't proof enough that she might be unlovable, her parents were icing on the cake. Her mother may have been physically present in her life, but she'd always made it clear that Libby was more of a nuisance than a blessing. And her father had left her when she was a baby.

And then he'd left a second time.

The memory she'd never shared with anyone—not Megan, not Blair, and not even her mother—washed over her, sickening in its clarity.

He showed up at their front door one day after Libby came home from school. Her mother was still at work. She wasn't supposed to answer the door when her mother wasn't home, but she recognized him from the photo she kept in her underwear drawer. She pulled it out often enough that she would have recognized him anywhere, even if he now had wrinkles around his eyes and streaks of gray in his dark hair. She'd dreamed of this day since she was little. In her fantasy, her dad would show up and tell her that he'd never intended to leave her for so long. He'd been kept from her by some overpowering force—he'd been in a coma, or he'd been lost on a deserted island, or he'd been held prisoner by pirates—and now that he'd come to his senses he'd searched high and low for his little girl.

But suddenly there he was, standing on her front porch, glancing at the landscaping under the picture window with a look of disgust as he pushed the doorbell repeatedly.

Libby's stomach tumbled with nerves and she swallowed her nausea as she opened the door, prepared for him to swoop her into his arms and shower her with love.

He eyed her up and down dismissively before looking over her shoulder into the living room. "Is Gabriella here?"

Libby stuffed down her disappointment. He hadn't seen her since she was a tiny baby. How would he know her now? She held on to the doorknob and twisted it nervously. "She's at work."

"Oh." He took a step back as if to leave.

He couldn't leave! He'd just shown up! She scrambled to come up with a reason for him stay. "She'll be home any minute if you want to come in and wait!" It was a flat-out lie. Her mother was going out with friends after work, but he didn't have to know that.

He eyed her again, as though appraising her trustworthiness. She flashed him a warm smile and he gave a slight nod. "Well, I can wait for a few minutes."

She backed up and opened the door wider for him to cross the threshold. "Gabriella's done good for herself, huh?" he said walking around the room, picking up a knick-knack and examining it before setting it back in its place.

Libby shut the door. "Yeah, I guess."

He turned to study her, his right hand twitching. "You say she'll be back in a few minutes."

"Yeah. Can I get you something to drink?"

He hesitated.

"A beer?"

She knew she'd made the right offer when a grin spread across his face. "Yeah. Sure. Gabby still drink Miller Light?"

"Uh . . . I think she has Corona and Boulevard."

He sat on the sofa and crossed his legs, releasing a sharp laugh. "That's Gabby. Always thinking she's better than where she came from."

Libby had no idea what he was talking about, but this wasn't going how she'd dreamed it would. "Which one?"

Annoyance filled his eyes. "Get me the Corona, kid." Libby was on her way to the kitchen when he called after her. "You got a lime? Ain't that how the high and mighty drink it? With a lime?"

"Uh . . . I don't know . . ."

He rolled his eyes. "You ain't too bright, are you? Never mind." He waved his hand dismissively. "Just get me the damn beer."

She stumbled into the kitchen, resisting the urge to cry. Why hadn't he told her he loved her? That he missed her and wanted to make up for lost time? She considered calling Megan, who lived closer than Blair. If her friend hopped on her bike, she'd get there in five minutes. But Libby looked at the clock on the microwave and realized that Megan was at a piano lesson and Blair was shopping with her mother. Libby could have called Gabriella—her mother made her use her first name so men wouldn't think she was her kid—but she would be furious to hear Libby had let a stranger in the door. But he wasn't a stranger! He was her father!

"Hey, kid! Where's the beer? You get lost in the fridge?" He chuckled at his cleverness.

Libby pulled herself together and pulled a bottle of beer from the fridge, popped the top open and walked into the living room.

He was still on the sofa, his arm draped over the back. When she walked into the room, his expression changed. His hard, dark eyes softened and he licked his bottom lower lip.

She stopped in the doorway and took a moment to study him. There was no doubt he looked older than his picture, but it *had* been twelve years. He was thinner, and his face was covered with salt and pepper stubble. His jeans were filthy and his T-shirt was stained. He'd worn holes into the elbows of his black leather jacket as well as his white athletic shoes.

"How old are you?" he asked.

"Twelve." She waited for him to connect the dots.

His eyes blinked wide. "Twelve. You look like you're fifteen."

She didn't answer. She was used to her mother's friends assuming the same thing.

"You're a pretty thing."

She was used to hearing that too. She shared her mother's thick, dark, wavy hair and olive complexion, and was already showing the promise of her mother's figure. She'd been the first girl in her class to need a bra.

"You gonna stand there all day or bring me that beer?" He

grinned, but the leer on his face reminded her of her mother's boyfriends. The ones she avoided.

Tears stung her eyes again, but she blinked them back as she took a few hesitant steps toward him, holding the bottle out.

He reached for it, but wrapped his hand around her wrist instead. "Didn't get one for yourself?" The smile that spread across his face wasn't friendly.

She jerked back out of instinct and the liquid in the bottle sloshed onto both their hands.

He let go of her like she was dirty. "Now look what you did, you stupid bitch." He jerked his hand back, and for a moment she thought he was going to backhand her, but then he dropped it.

Libby took several steps back, still holding the bottle in her hand, prepared to use it as a weapon if need be.

He licked the beer off his hand and leered at her. "Why don't you come sit by me."

This man might be her father, but she wasn't stupid. "I don't think so."

He gave her a look that said suit yourself, then glanced around the room. "Your mother keep any money in the house?"

"*No.*" She was pissed and she didn't try to hide it.

He grinned. "Not even in her room? Under the mattress maybe?" He got up and made a move toward the hall, but Libby moved faster and blocked his path.

"I don't think so."

A sneer covered his face. "Let me teach you a few things about life, Elizabeth."

Her breath stuck in her chest. *He knew her.* He knew her and yet he was still being an ass.

He laughed as if reading her thoughts. "Yeah, I knew you were Gabby's brat."

"I'm yours too," she pushed out, barely audible.

He released a short bark. "By no choice of my own. I gave her the money to get an abortion, but she used it to go to Mexico for a week."

"What?"

He towered over her. "I bet Gabby never told you that, did she?"

"No."

"I'm not surprised. I bet there's a lot of things she never told you."

He was close enough for her to smell his odor of stale cigarettes and sweat. His eyes were slightly unfocused. He was high. He must have come looking for drug money.

Libby took several steps backward into the hall. "I think you should leave now."

He laughed as he advanced on her. "Why? We're just getting reacquainted. I bet you've had dreams of this day. Am I right? All kids want their parents to love them. You thought I'd show up and bring you a pony or something, huh? Just let me get the money and I'll take you out for an ice cream cone."

She was an idiot. Every dream she'd ever had of their reunion shriveled up and died. She narrowed her eyes and said with as much force as she could muster, "You need to leave."

"What are you going to do, *little girl*? I'm not leaving until I get the money Gabby owes me."

"Then come back when she's here."

An evil gleam filled his eyes. "You said she'd be back in a few minutes."

She squared her shoulders. "You need to *go*."

He paused, then laughed. "You're just like *her*."

She knew who *her* was and his words hurt more than if he'd slapped her in the face. She *never* wanted to be like her mother. He laughed when he saw he'd gotten to her. "You know, since I *am* your father, I suppose I owe you a legacy. Am I right?" He grinned wide, showing her a mouth full of broken and rotting teeth. "I'm fresh out of ponies, but I've got something better."

Whatever he had, she didn't want. Not anymore. "*Leave.*"

"You don't want my gift?"

"If you don't go, I'll call 911."

"You won't because you want to know what I have to say. Well, here's my legacy to you: words of wisdom. Isn't that a father's job? To prepare his kid for life?"

No. A father's job was to make his daughter feel protected. To dry her tears and hug her when she was hurt. His job was to love her no matter what and always, always be there for her, but that was a mother's job too, and Gabriella had never done any of those things for Libby. So why had she expected any different from her low-life father?

"I don't care what you have to say!" she shouted through her tears. "Go!"

He laughed, a harsh bitter sound that sent a shiver down her spine. "Men will only be interested in one thing, Elizabeth. Your body." He touched her cheek and slid it down her neck.

She slapped his hand away with enough force to push it off her.

He released a peal of laughter. "Ah, you got some fight in you, girl. That comes from me. That'll serve you well. But you got things from both of us."

"Get the hell out of my house!"

He ignored her, leaning so close she could smell his rotten breath. "Your mother and I, we're both fucking messes, and guess what, girlie? You got our genes. So let me give you a heads-up no one ever gave Gabby: No man will ever really love you. They'll want your body and your looks and they'll lie through their teeth to get you. But when they've used you up, they'll move on. That's what I did with your mother and every woman ever since. And your mother, she's the same."

Libby shook her head. "No."

"She ain't been with one man longer than a few months, am I right?"

She gripped the beer bottle so tight it was slippery in her hand.

"And don't be thinking you can escape it. You're just like her, from your face to your fiery temper. The sooner you accept that you'll never keep a man, the less heartache you'll have." He stood up straight. "So there you go, Elizabeth. My legacy for you. Get used to a lonely fucking life." He backed up into the living room and kicked a chair, making it fall over backward. "Get used to being alone, because no one fucking wants you. Not me. Not your mother who planned to abort you. *No one.*"

Without a second thought, Libby swung the bottle into the side of his head, beer and glass spraying everywhere. "You're lying! Someone will love me! Someone who deserves me, and that sure as hell isn't you. Now get out of my house, you fucking *loser!*"

He stumbled backward, looking dazed. She pushed his chest as hard as she could and he lurched toward the door, blood streaming down the side of his face.

She opened the front door and shoved him onto the front porch. "If you ever come back here, I'll *kill* you."

She slammed the door shut and locked it, pressing her back against the wood and fighting the sob lodged in her throat.

When she heard his car start and pull away, she slid to the floor, her tears bursting loose. After she'd cried herself hoarse, she decided she had a choice. She could let the asshole who'd contributed half her DNA steal her dreams, or she could give him a big fuck-you and believe in them more.

She chose her dreams.

She ran to her room and dug out his photo, which she set fire to in the kitchen sink. As his image burned, she burned any hope of a relationship with him with it. As far as she was concerned, he was dead.

Already a firm believer in magic and destiny and fairytale endings, she latched on to them even more. She was determined that every boy and then man she met was *the one*— the exception who would prove her father wrong. In high school, she wrote off the broken relationships to immaturity and youth, but it was the cross-country road trip with Barry, the surfer, that made her question her real destiny. By the time they hit New Mexico, it was clear that she was a short-term relationship for him. He would never take her home to meet his mother.

Had her father been right? Was she so screwed up no one could love her?

And until she met Mitch, a long string of one-night stands and month-long relationships seemed to support that idea. But then Megan's wedding reminded her of the curse, and she was sure *that* was her destiny. That was why her soul mate hadn't shown up yet. It just hadn't been time. So she kept Mitch around to spur her own substitute groom.

And to her surprise, he turned out to be Noah.

Only she wasn't sure why she'd been surprised. She was glad they'd started out as friends, otherwise she doubted she would have spent the time to get to know him so well. And she *knew* he loved her. She could see it in his eyes. But she had to keep in mind that he was still Noah. What if Blair was right? Staying with women wasn't something he did. Was he capable of changing for her? Was she capable of changing for him?

What if her father was right? What if her genes were her destiny and she would end up alone?

If she lost Noah, she knew she'd give up on love completely.

Chapter Twenty-Six

A ringing phone broke her out of her thoughts and she was surprised to discover it was her own phone since she'd assumed it was dead. She dug it out of her purse and stifled a groan when she saw the name on caller ID.

Megan.

Figuring she might as well get this over with, she answered before it went to voice mail. "Hello, Megan."

"Don't hang up on me. I'm not going to give you a hard time."

Libby didn't quite believe that, but she decided to hear her out. "Okay."

"First, I want you to know that I *do* believe you and Noah love each other. Blair has a hard time seeing it, but it's been clear as day to Josh and me."

"So why do I hear a but in there?"

Megan paused. "I just wish you two had slowed down a bit

and talked things through more. But that's not who you two are. You're impulsive."

"That didn't come through as a compliment, so I'm presuming that's your but."

"Libs, you know I love you and I want you to be happy, but there are things you need to think about with a marriage. Logistics."

"What are you talking about?"

"Where are you going to live?"

"I'm moving to Seattle."

"Even though Noah quit his job?"

She blinked, sure she'd heard Megan wrong. "What are you talking about?"

"Libby, Noah quit his job on Friday." She hesitated. "I take it he hasn't told you."

She didn't respond. Her silence was answer enough.

"Don't you think that's something a husband should tell his wife? Especially before they get married?"

"That doesn't make any sense, Megan." She knew she sounded short, but panic was bubbling in her gut. "He's in the middle of a business meeting right now."

"In *Vegas*? His offices are in Kansas City and Seattle. Why would he have a meeting in Las Vegas?"

Oh, God. Please don't let this be happening. She wasn't sure she could handle his betrayal. What was he up to? "I have to go."

"Libs, I'm sorry. I thought you should know."

"No." Libby started hurrying toward the hotel. "You wanted to gloat."

"Libby! How can you say that? We love you!"

"You may love me, but you've never tried to understand me." Not like Noah had. No one had tried half as much as Noah had. "I have to go." She hung up on Megan's protests and turned her phone off so she couldn't be reached.

Noah had to have an explanation. She just needed to let him tell her what was going on.

But what if he lied? He hadn't said a thing about quitting. How could she trust him?

She was close to hysteria when she got back to the hotel room, equally relieved and upset that he hadn't gotten back yet. She packed up the few things she had removed from her suitcase, then began to pace the room, waiting for him to come back.

Out of the corner of her eye, she saw a light blinking on and off on the room phone. She ignored the message, worried Megan or Blair had found out which room they were in, but what if it was Noah? He didn't know her phone was working, and besides, she had just turned it off.

With shaking fingers, she typed in the code to hear the message, sucking in a breath when she heard a woman's voice. "Noah, sorry to call you on this phone since I know you're trying to keep this from your *wife*," Libby heard a hint of jealousy in the word, "but just in case you didn't get my message, come to room 1470."

No. God, no.

She held the phone in her hand for several seconds, shell-shocked. What was she going to do?

She found herself in the elevator before she realized what she was doing.

Think this through, Libby, she told herself as she pressed the button for fourteen on the number bank. *Once you do this, it can't be undone.*

But what couldn't be undone? Her finding out he was in a business deal for a business he wasn't part of? Or finding him fucking another woman in a hotel room while on his honeymoon with her?

The elevator stopped on the fourteenth floor and she headed down the hall, her heart pounding in her chest. The reasonable, sane part of her told her this was a mistake. Noah loved her. He wouldn't betray her, but Blair's voice played in her head on repeat: *Noah is a user. He'll take what he wants and move on. If he doesn't cheat on you first.*

Her father's voice joined the party next: *No man will ever really love you. They'll want your body and your looks and they'll lie through their teeth to get you. But when they've used you up, they'll move on.*

Not Noah. Please, God, not Noah too. Anyone but Noah.

Then knock on the door and find out.

Her body had been on autopilot while her mind was busy taunting her and she found herself in front of the door to room 1470, her hand suspended to knock. What if he wasn't in there? What if he was? What would she do?

She'd put it together as it played out.

She rapped on the door and took a step back, preparing herself for what was on the other side.

A perky brunette opened the door. She was dressed in a pencil skirt and blouse unbuttoned enough to show her cleavage, and she held a champagne flute in her hand. "Can I help you?"

Suddenly, Libby felt like a fool. "I'm sorry. I think I have the wrong room."

"That's okay, I thought you were room service," the woman said, then looked over her shoulder. "Noah, it's okay. The food's not here yet."

Noah.

White spots danced in front of Libby's eyes. She shoved the woman aside and marched past her.

Noah sat on the made bed, a champagne flute in his hand. His face paled the moment he saw her and he jumped to his feet.

A thousand and one possible reactions filtered through her head—screaming, crying, throwing things, pitching a royal fit—but all she could manage was to turn around and walk out of the room.

"Libby!"

She ran down the hall and pounded on the up button.

"Libby! Let me explain!"

As soon as the doors opened, she ran inside and pushed the button for their floor.

Noah was running after her, panic on his face. "*Libby!*"

She ignored the pleading in his voice as the doors shut on his face.

She couldn't think, couldn't react. She could only run. When she opened the door to her room, it occurred to her that she had to figure out what to do next. What was she going to do?

Home. She needed to go home.

When Noah burst into the room, she was already dragging her suitcase toward the door.

"Libby. You have to let me explain."

She tried to get around him, but he grabbed her shoulders and held her in place.

"Libby! Talk to me!"

She shook her head, trying to string the words together to form a sentence. "What do you want me to say?" she finally spat out.

"Don't you want to know why I was there?"

She shook her head, tears burning her eyes. "I already know."

"No, you *don't.*"

She jerked free from his hold and looked up into his pleading face. "Then let me tell you what I saw. You were in a hotel room drinking champagne with a woman—*in a hotel room!*"

"Yes! But it's not how it looks. We were celebrating a business deal."

"In a *hotel room?*"

"Yes!"

"For a job you quit last Friday."

His face paled even more. "Yes, I was trying to get it back."

She put her hand on her hip, some of her fire returning. "Why didn't you tell me you quit? How could you keep that from me? I begged you to tell me the truth before you left."

"I wanted to tell you—I was dying to tell you—but your problems seemed more important than mine. And then I figured if I could get the deal, it would be a moot point."

"My *problems.*"

He ran his hand through his hair. "Libby, I didn't mean it like that. I meant you were so upset over Mitch and the wedding, it just seemed like your issues took precedence over mine."

She ran over the details of the last couple of days in her head, looking at everything in a new light. "That woman was Tiffany."

He sucked in a breath. "Yes. How did—"

"You sent her a Facebook friend request." How could she have been so stupid? "*She's* the reason we came to Vegas."

Fear filled his eyes. "Yes, but it's only because her boss was coming too."

"Her nonexistent boss."

"Libby, *please.* You *have* to believe me. Nothing happened. I met with her boss and presented my proposal, then, thank God, he accepted."

"In her room."

He cringed. "Yes. *Their* room."

He was unbelievable! Did he really think she was that gullible? "So where was her boss, Noah?"

"He was in the bathroom."

She shook her head. She'd heard enough. "Whatever." She tried to walk around him, but he blocked her path.

"How can you assume the worst of me after everything?" he demanded, sounding angry.

"Are you fucking kidding me?" she shouted. "I caught you cheating and you're accusing *me* of doing something wrong?"

"I wasn't cheating on you!" He groaned in frustration, then paused. "How did you even know where I was?"

"Your girlfriend called and left a message with her room number."

"*She's not my girlfriend!*" he shouted, pounding his fist into the wall.

"You're telling me you weren't screwing her?"

"No! If you would just listen to what I'm telling you, you'd know that!"

Suddenly she had a moment of doubt. What if her insecurities were causing her to overreact? God knew Megan and Blair had her worked up . . . not to mention the memories of her father. Noah and the woman had both been fully clothed. But this was clearly not the first time they'd met. The woman had accepted his friend request while they were on their trip. "You knew her already. Have you screwed her before?" He started to protest, but she pointed her finger in his face. "Think carefully about your answer."

Fear washed over his face. "Libby."

Oh, God. "Answer the question, Noah."

"Yes. But it was last January. There is nothing going on now. *I swear.*"

"You swear. *You swear!*" Her voice broke and she shoved his chest, but he was so much larger he barely moved, which only pissed her off more. "You lied to me!"

"Only about my job, Libby, but I was trying to get it back. *For you.* So we could start our new lives together."

"How can I believe you?"

"What reason have I given you to not trust me?" He grabbed his head with both hands. "Oh, my God, Libby! I love you! Can't you see how much I love you? I would sooner die than cheat on you. You have to believe me!"

"Why do I have to believe you?" she demanded. "So I can look like even more of a fool?"

His eyes lit up like a struck match. "You're just looking for a reason to break up with me."

"*Excuse me?* Are you really trying to pin this on *me?*"

"I've never given you a reason to not trust me. Not one."

"*You lied to me about your job!*"

"I didn't lie, Libby! I just hadn't told you because I was hoping to get it back. You kept telling me how proud you were of me and I knew I needed to get my job back to take care of you. I didn't want you to look at me with the same look of disapproval I always see in Josh's eyes. I was planning to give the stupid account to Josh as a peace offering. *For us.*"

She shook her head, more confused than ever.

"This is what you do," he said, his voice tight with anger. "You sabotage your relationships so they'll never work out. It's a self-fulfilling prophecy."

"*Are you kidding me?* You think you have me all figured out, Mr. I-Sleep-With-Every-Woman-I-Can-So-I-Don't-Have-To-

Commit."

"You're wrong about one thing," he said, quietly. "I made a commitment to you."

"I wished you'd never committed to me at all."

His mouth dropped open. "You don't mean that."

"You are incapable of making a commitment, Noah McMillan, and I refuse to stick around so you play me for even more of a fool."

He couldn't have looked more hurt if she'd pulled out a gun and shot him. "My father was right," she said, her voice breaking. "No man will ever stay with me. They lie to get what they want, and once they get it, they're gone. I'll save you the trouble of slamming the door in my face." She grabbed the handle of her suitcase again. "I'll just leave first."

She rolled her case into the hall, fully expecting him to follow her, but he didn't. Disappointment sucked the air out of her chest, making her light headed. What was she so upset about? She wanted him to leave her alone, right?

She hit the button for the elevator, silently pleading with him to follow her, to fight for her. To convince her she was wrong.

Then she heard him call out to her. "I thought you said you hadn't seen your father since you were a baby."

She turned around to see him standing in the hall outside their room. "I guess that makes us both liars."

The elevator doors opened and she walked inside with her suitcase. When she turned around, Noah stood in the hall about thirty feet away. "Don't leave me, Libby. Please."

"Wrong answer," she whispered. But damned if she knew what the right one was.

Then the elevator doors closed, Noah's pain-stricken face disappearing behind it, and she felt more alone than she ever had in her life.

Chapter Twenty-Seven

The elevator doors closed and Noah felt the bottom of his world drop out—the sucking void threatening to swallow him whole. Did he run after her? Did he let her go?

You don't deserve her, the little voice in his head told him. *You don't deserve to win her back. This was how it was always going to end.*

Somehow he found himself back in their room. The bed was made. The used towels replaced. All evidence of her was gone.

It was as though the last few days—the absolute best days of his life—had never happened.

He wasn't sure he could go on without her.

What the fuck did he do?

Part of him was devastated that she thought the worst of him. He wanted to be angry that she didn't trust him, but how could he blame her? She was right. He'd never told her about quitting. How had she even found out?

What did it matter?

She knew he'd kept something huge from her, so why *wouldn't* she think he was cheating? The kicker was that he'd closed the deal. Scott jumped on board as soon as he listened to Noah's spiel. Turned out the competition had flaked out anyway. Tiffany had ordered a room service lunch for her and Scott, and to celebrate, they'd opened a bottle of champagne. And then, much to Noah's misfortune, Libby had arrived at the exact moment Scott was in the bathroom.

Would she have been this upset if she'd seen him? Maybe not, but he'd still kept the job situation from her.

The phone in his pocket vibrated and he pulled it out, praying it was Libby calling to tell him she'd changed her mind.

It was Tiffany.

"Noah, did you get the misunderstanding resolved?"

"No," he said, his voice breaking.

"Would it help if I called her and explained?"

Would it? He shook his head even if she couldn't see it. "No. I think it would make things worse."

"I'm so sorry. I should never have called your room."

He wanted to be angry with her, but he just couldn't find the energy.

"Let me do something, Noah. Tell me what to do."

"There's nothing *to* do."

"She probably just needs time to calm down. Then you can work it out."

He wasn't so sure that was possible. That look on her face...

"Well, congrats on the deal."

"Thanks." But now it was all for nothing. He'd mostly done it for Libby . . . and now she was gone. He knew he should be happy to have helped the business, but he couldn't muster much emotion for that either.

He considered leaving—he'd found a flight to Seattle for that night—but what if she changed her mind and came back? So he didn't leave the room for the rest of the night. He found her wedding dress in the closet, puddled on the floor. Hope rushed through him. She loved the dress. Maybe she'd come back for it.

He ordered room service in the evening and steadily drank all the bottles in the mini bar. By three a.m., he knew it was hopeless and passed out on the bed. When he awoke, she was the first thing on his mind. The wedding dress wasn't next to him on the bed where he'd left it.

Had she come back?

He bolted upright and looked around the room, but the only thing he saw was the room service tray and half a dozen empty mini bottles of alcohol. The dress lay on the floor. He must have kicked it off in his sleep.

Libby was really gone.

He was back in Seattle by mid-afternoon and he headed straight to the office. Josh was sitting at his desk when Noah walked in.

Josh looked up in surprise, a grin spreading across his face. "What are you doing here? I didn't expect to see you for at least a few days." His gaze took in Noah's rumpled clothes and his smile faded. "Why do you look like death warmed over?"

Noah ignored him and tossed a file on his desk. "The Abrahams deal. Signed, sealed, and delivered."

Josh sat upright and his eyes widened as he opened the folder. "How'd you pull this off?"

"What the hell does it matter? It's all there. The payment schedule is worked out in there too."

Josh started thumbing through the papers. "So do you want

to handle this here or in K.C.? Megan said Libby was moving here, but I figured I'd check."

Noah shook his head. "I'm not handling it at all."

Josh pushed back his chair and stood. "Wait. You just got this account. Why wouldn't you want to handle it?"

"In case you forgot, I quit last week."

"But the deal . . . ?" Josh sounded confused.

"I got it for you. I thought I'd bring it in as a peace offering to get my job back, but now I don't give a fuck." He turned around. "Congrats."

"Noah!" Josh called out after him, his voice worried now. "You look like you've been on a three-day bender. What happened?"

Noah spun around, furious. "As if you and Megan haven't been laughing about it."

"What does *that* mean?"

"Look, Megan and Blair made no secret of the fact they don't approve, so I'm sure they're happy that Libby left me."

Josh's mouth dropped open and his eyes widened in shock. "*What*? *When*? What happened?"

"What does it matter? She came to her senses. Everyone's happy."

Josh shook his head. "That's not true, Noah. What happened?" His face went as pale as skim milk. "Oh, God. Megan. She told Libby about you quitting. She was upset you hadn't told her."

His chest squeezed tight with her betrayal. "Megan hates me that much?"

"No, Noah. That's not it at all. She was just worried you two got married so quickly." He held up his hands in defense. "And yes, I reminded her that she and I were married a hell of a lot faster."

Noah found it difficult to breathe.

"But if Libby left you, where is she?"

The answer was obvious. She would have gone to the only place she would feel completely safe. The thought that he'd hurt her so much brought a lump to his throat he found difficult to talk past. "She went home to Tortoise."

Josh blinked in confusion before recognition registered in his eyes. "Oh . . . her dog."

He nodded, then turned to leave.

"Noah," Josh called out in alarm. "Stop."

He stopped in Josh's doorway. Their receptionist's worried glance reminded him that he looked like a mess. He'd slept in his clothes from the day before—the smell of Libby was still faintly in the weave of shirt, and he couldn't bear to change. That was the last part he had of her and once it was gone, she would be lost to him forever. The thought brought him close to a breakdown, but he didn't even care. Let them think the worst . . . they probably already did.

Josh grabbed his arm and pulled him back into the room, shutting the door behind them. He pushed Noah into a chair and then sat on the edge of his desk. "Noah, you have to go after her."

His brother's words broke down his last layer of control and his chest heaved as he struggled to keep it together. "She hates me." He heaved out a shortened version of the story, then said, "I tried to tell her nothing happened between Tiffany and me, but she refused to believe me." A sob rented from his chest. "I deserve it. After everything I've done, all the people I've hurt, I deserve every bit of it." He looked up at Josh with tear-filled eyes. "She's the one good thing in my life and I hurt her so badly. I don't deserve *her*."

Josh leaned toward him. "No, Noah. That's not true. You

deserve every bit of happiness and more."

Noah gritted his teeth as tears spilled from his eyes. "If you knew everything I've done, you wouldn't be saying that."

"The women?" Josh shook his head. "They were all consenting adults who knew what they were getting into. You never lied or led them on, Noah. I know you well enough to know that."

Noah released a harsh laugh. "No, not the women."

Josh was silent for a moment. "Are you talking about Dad?"

Noah's eyes swung up to meet his brother's as his heartbeat ratcheted up enough for him to hear it.

"I know you and Dad didn't get along. I know I was his favorite. It made me uncomfortable that he gave me more attention than you, but you had Mom."

Guilt clawed at Noah's chest and some feral part of him decided it was finally time Josh knew the truth. Noah needed his brother to hate him as much as he hated himself. "I killed Dad."

Josh stared at him like he was trying to sell him property on Mars. "Dad died of a heart attack here in the office while you were at school over a hundred miles away. You did *not* kill Dad."

He shook his head, nearly choking on the bitterness in his heart. "I may not have been here, but I killed him anyway."

"What in the world are you talking ab—" Recognition filled his eyes. "Dad never called you."

Now it was Noah's turn to be confused. "What are you talking about?"

"Dad told me about his visit to you at school. He was really upset that you were buying drugs for your ADD and he thought you were dealing too. He told me he'd changed his mind about making you partner and he wanted to give the whole business to me."

"*You* knew? You knew he told me I was no longer his son?"

"He told you that?" Josh reached forward and grabbed his shoulder. "No. He never told me that part. Only that he'd discovered the truth. *Oh God,* Noah. I had no idea . . . otherwise I would have told you what happened when he came to me."

"What are you talking about?" Noah choked out, pulling away from Josh's comfort.

"Mom had already laid into him by then. I think he hoped I'd take his side, but Mom and I both told him off for guilt-tripping you about taking medication for a documented medical condition. Would he deny insulin to a diabetic? Mom told Dad he'd forced you into it." Josh's voice broke. "And I made sure he knew I didn't want this business without you. It was the McMillan Brothers or nothing at all. I think he realized then what he'd done. He said he was going to call you and apologize. The morning he died, he told me that he had. He said he'd called and told you he was sorry and he'd taken it all back."

Noah shook his head. "I had a voice mail . . . I discovered it after I found out he died." His voice cracked. "I heard his voice and I deleted it. I couldn't bear to hear him berate me from the grave."

Josh took a deep breath, tears in his eyes. "Noah, he swore to me he apologized. He must have done it in the voice mail."

Pressure built in Noah's chest.

"If anyone is responsible for his death, it's him. He didn't exercise or take care of himself. Maybe when he realized how much he'd hurt you, his grief pushed him over the edge."

Noah leaned forward, covering his face with his hands.

Could that be true?

Josh put his hand on Noah's back. "He said he was going to call you and apologize, and that was a full day before his death. I guess I got so caught up in my own shock and grief that I never thought to ask you if he had. Plus you never mentioned it, so I . . . I guess I thought it was resolved. And I didn't want him to hurt you any more than he already had."

It was all too much. Libby. His father. He jumped to his feet, intending to run far, far away—where didn't matter—but Josh stood and pulled him into a hug.

"I'm so sorry, Noah. I see things a lot more clearly now and I'm sorry I've been such a prick. You really came through with this Abrahams account, even after I treated you like shit. For what it's worth, your job would have been waiting for you whether you brought in the account or not."

Noah pulled free and shook his head. "I don't know what I want anymore. The one thing I wanted most in the world is gone."

Josh grabbed his shoulders, his fingers digging deep. "She's not gone. You just have to fight for her."

"I still think she's better off without me." He turned around and opened the office door.

"You two are perfect for each other," Josh said, his voice tight.

Noah turned to face him in disbelief.

"I saw it the night of my wedding. I know Libby was with Mitch, but she never looked as happy with him as she did when she was with you. Megan and Blair didn't get it, and honestly, I never tried to explain it to them because I figured they'd amp up their campaign to warn Libby off you. But I could see you were meant to be. The day you told me she was engaged, I think you might have misunderstood my response.

When I told you to examine your own life, I meant it was time for you to realize you loved her. I worried if I told you straight out, you'd resist it. So I kept my mouth shut. I'm sorry for that." He rubbed the back of his neck. "God, I'm sorry for a lot of things, Noah." His voice cracked when he spoke again. "Can you forgive me?"

Noah stared at him dumbfounded. He had no idea Josh was willing to give up the business if he wasn't included. He'd spent the majority of his life feeling like he was failing his brother; it never occurred to Noah that Josh felt the same way.

Josh pulled him into a bear hug. "I love you, Noah. You think you don't deserve happiness, but you are *so* wrong. And besides, did you ever consider that Libby is probably telling herself the same thing? That *you* are the happiness she doesn't think *she* deserves?"

Noah broke free, panic welling in his chest and making it difficult to breathe. He wanted to be that man for her, but he'd screwed up after less than twenty-four hours of marriage. A zebra couldn't change its stripes. What made him think he could be any different? "No. I'll only hurt her in the end. More than I already have, and I can't live with that."

He jerked the door open and strode though the office toward the exit.

"Noah! Where are you going?"

He had no idea. He found comfort that he and Josh were mending their relationship, but in less than two weeks, Josh would be gone. Libby had Tortoise to run to, but now that Libby was gone, he had absolutely nothing.

Chapter Twenty-Eight

"Libby! Open up," Megan shouted. She and Blair had been pounding on the front door for several minutes, but Libby couldn't bring herself to answer. Instead, she kept rubbing the head of her anxious dog. Tortoise—sensing her emotional crisis—had barely left her side in the week she'd been home.

"Libby, I know you're in there. Please let me in."

Megan was supposed to be in Seattle, so what was she even doing here? But she'd completely ignored her friends' phone calls, so she wasn't totally surprised.

There was more pounding, harder and more insistent this time. "Open the damn door, Libby St. Clair!" Blair shouted. "You live in the damn ghetto and I'm pretty sure I'm about to get shanked."

"Blair!" Megan protested.

Libby climbed to her feet and moved to the door, Tortoise at her side the entire time. After releasing the deadbolt, she swung the door open, revealing Megan in jeans and a plum peacoat and Blair in her business attire—attaché case and all. This didn't look like a friendly visit.

Blair's mouth dropped open, but she quickly shut it and waved her hand in front of her face. "Good God. When was the last time you showered?"

Libby leaned against the doorframe. She couldn't remember, but she didn't really care. The yoga pants and T-shirt she was wearing had been intimate companions for several days now. "Go away, Blair."

"Sorry, Libs." Blair pushed past her and walked into the house. "This is an intervention."

Tortoise hunched down next to Libby and released a low growl.

Blair stopped in her tracks. "Your new dog's really friendly. Is it part pit bull?"

Libby's shoulders stiffened. "*He* is a Lab mix. And you just pushed your way into my house. He's protective."

"Well, I guess it's a good thing you have some sort of protection in this neighborhood."

"What do you want?" Libby asked, already exhausted from this exchange.

Megan followed Blair inside, eyeing the dog. "Libs. We just want to talk to you."

Ignoring them, Libby bent over and rubbed Tortoise's head. "It's okay, boy." Then she stood upright and headed back to the sofa, where she plopped down next to her nest of pillows. "Let's get this over with. Say whatever it is you have to say, then get the hell out. I'm sure you feel vindicated."

Tortoise sat on the floor in front of her, keeping his gaze on Libby's friends.

Megan shut the door and eyed the messy room. She opened

the lid of the pizza box on the coffee table and cringed, then carried it into the kitchen. "That's not why we're here."

"*Obviously.*"

Blair grabbed a kitchen chair and dragged it into the living room in front of Libby. "Sarcasm won't help."

"Nothing will help." She hadn't meant to sound so defeated, but it was true.

Megan sat in the overstuffed chair between Libby and Blair. "We're worried about you. This isn't like you."

"You expect me to be all sunshine and rainbows? Sorry to disappoint you there too."

"Libby," Megan said apologetically.

"Enough," Blair barked, pulling a legal pad and a pen from her case. "I'm here to get the facts. Are you legally married to Noah?"

"You saw the photo," she sneered. "What do you think?"

Blair put the notebook on her lap. "From what little information Josh was able to get from Noah, you left him less than twenty-four hours after your wedding. Did you mail the marriage license to the courthouse?"

Libby stared at her in shock.

"*Was* there a marriage license?"

"Well, of course."

Blair gave a half-shrug. "Not necessarily. If you were drunk, you might not have thought about it, although the chapels out there usually ask."

Libby groaned and leaned her head back against the sofa. "I told you. We weren't drunk. We were perfectly sober when we got married."

"So what happened to the license? Did you take it?"

She sighed, thinking back to the best night of her life. How had it crashed and burned so quickly? "No, we didn't take it. In fact, I forgot my dress there."

"Your wedding dress?" Megan asked.

Tears filled her eyes. "No, the black dress Gram packed in my bag."

"What black dress?" Megan asked, but then she shook her head and smiled. "She wanted me to pack that sexy cocktail dress she found in your closet. She must have snuck it in when I was grabbing your makeup bag."

That and several other things she'd never needed. Tears spilled down her cheeks before she realized it. "I left my wedding dress in the hotel room in Vegas."

"Oh, Libby," Megan's voice broke. "I'm so sorry I was such a bitch. I've been a terrible friend."

"That's not what we're discussing at the moment," Blair said in her no-nonsense voice, but she sniffed and kept her eyes down on her legal pad. "What was the name of the chapel?"

"Little Heaven. Why?"

Blair scratched notes on her legal pad. "I'll have Melissa give them a call to see what happened to it."

"Why?"

Blair looked up and gave her an exasperated look. "We need to file the annulment papers as soon as possible, although I suspect we won't have grounds if you continue to insist you were sober. It could end in divorce instead, but given your career, it shouldn't adversely affect you."

"Annulment?" she asked in surprise.

"Libby. You're here. He's there. It's obvious this is over. Let's put an end to it as quickly as possible."

"But . . ." How had she not considered the legal ramifications? Of course they needed to file for a divorce, but the thought had her on the edge of a panic attack.

"Do you have a physical address for Noah?"

"Why?" Her voice sounded as panicked as she felt.

Blair shrugged again, writing on her notepad. "It's okay. I can use the address of their office in Seattle. It's probably better to serve him there."

"Serve him what?"

She looked up and rolled her eyes. "Divorce papers, of course."

"But . . ." More tears fell.

Blair looked up and pinned her gaze on Libby, although Libby could barely see her through her tears. "Do you love him?"

"Blair," Megan admonished as she sat next to Libby and pulled her into a hug. Megan stroked her hair. "Libs, do you love him?"

She nodded, breaking down into sobs.

"Then why are you here instead of Seattle?"

"Because . . . I'm so . . . stupid," she forced out.

"What did you do?"

She took a breath to settle down. "I accused him of cheating on me."

"What?" Blair demanded. "Is there something I don't know?"

"Blair. Enough. We've caused enough damage," Megan said softly, keeping her eyes on Libby. "Libs, what happened?"

"I started freaking out after you called me. It didn't make sense for him to be in a business meeting if he'd really quit his job. There was a message on the phone in our room . . . from a woman. She called Noah by name and asked him to meet her in a hotel room. I freaked out and went to the room."

"And?" Megan asked.

"A woman opened the door with a champagne glass in her

hand. I thought I had gotten it wrong since she was fully clothed and so perky, but then she said something to Noah—calling him by name again—and I marched in and found him sitting on the bed drinking champagne."

"Naked?" Blair asked.

She shook her head. "No. He had all his clothes on."

"So what was his excuse?" Blair asked.

"He said it was a business meeting. He said he'd closed some deal for Josh. I accused him of lying, especially when he admitted that he'd slept with her before."

Megan took her hand. "He was telling the truth about the business meeting. He was working on that deal for a couple of months and the whole thing fell apart on the Friday he was supposed to fly in for your wedding. Josh wasn't very nice to him about it, so Noah quit."

Libby's chin quivered. She was such a fool.

"But that doesn't explain why he didn't tell you about quitting his job," Blair pointed out.

"He said it was because of everything I was going through."

A soft smile lit up Megan's face. "He was thinking about you instead of himself. He was being selfless, Libs."

"I know that now." A sob broke off the last word.

"I was wrong." Megan glanced over at Blair. "*We* were wrong. We couldn't look past Noah's history to see what was right in front of our faces." She paused and squeezed Libby's hand. "He loves you, Libby. I had no idea how much until I saw him yesterday. He's a mess."

"He is?" she asked, feeling guilty at the relief she felt over his pain.

"He knows he screwed up by not telling you about his job, and I'd bet my life that he didn't cheat on you. He loves you too much to think about another woman."

"I love him too."

"Then what's keeping you apart?"

Before her plane took off from Vegas, she'd realized how wrong she'd been. A small part of her hung on to the belief that Noah had cheated on her, but now Megan was bashing that belief to smithereens. It made her heart ache for him even more . . . all the pain she'd caused him. "I—I hurt him. I was horrible. He'll never forgive me."

"Do you know how he answered when Josh and I asked him why he wouldn't just come talk to you?" She paused. "He says he doesn't deserve you. He doesn't want to hurt you any more than he already has."

"You have a choice, Libby," Blair said, her voice softer than before. "You can keep running away from love or you can live your life with a man you clearly love—a man who loves you just as much." Her voice broke. "I almost missed that chance with Garrett, Libs. Don't let Noah go. You'd regret it for the rest of your life."

Megan squeezed her hand. "Libs, Noah is your soul mate. The man who showed up and saved you from the marriage you weren't meant to have. You can't give him up. He's the man the fortune teller foretold. The one you're destined to marry."

She shook her head. "You don't believe in the curse."

Megan smiled. "Don't you see? You've made us believers. We were just too obstinate to admit you were right. There *is* magic in the world." Her eyes shimmered with tears. "What I have with Josh is magic, and what you've found with Noah is magic too. I mean, come on. Noah McMillan, confirmed bachelor, is holed away from the world because he can't handle losing you. Who could have predicted that? You changed him, Libby. And he's miserable without you."

"She's right," Blair said softly. "What were the chances of

me seeing Garrett before my wedding, let alone him being in the wedding party?" She leaned forward. "You spent weeks convincing us to admit the curse was real. It's our turn now. Noah is the man you're supposed to be with. Don't throw that away."

Libby started crying again. "I don't know what to do. I don't know what to say."

Megan smiled through her own tears. "Go to him. I bet you don't have to even say a word. Just show up and that will be explanation enough."

"So?" Blair asked.

Libby nodded. "Yes. I'll go."

Megan beamed as Blair pulled an envelope out of her bag and handed it to her. "Then here's a wedding present from me and Garrett."

Libby opened it and gasped when she saw an airline ticket voucher. "This is for this afternoon."

"Which is why you better get your sorry ass in the shower. I know the man loves you, but there is a limit to how much one person's olfactory nerves can take."

Libby launched herself at her friend, throwing her arms around her neck. "I love you, Blair."

"I love you too." Her voice broke. "Thanks for not kicking me out after being such a bitch. Especially given my bad-cop role in this part of the intervention. But Megan and I figured we needed to shock you into going to him."

"How did you know it would work?"

"Because, if someone had suggested that I divorce Garrett after our first fight, I would have freaked out just like you did. I had to make sure you really loved him."

Megan snorted. "Because the fact she looks like shit wasn't proof enough."

"And don't forget the way she smells."

Libby laughed. "Hey!"

"We're so sorry, Libby," Megan said. "You did everything in your power to help the two of us find the perfect partners and we let you down."

"I still haven't decided if I'm going to forgive you," she said with a grin.

"Which is why I'm hoping your wedding gift from me and Josh will bribe us back into your good graces." Megan gave a sheepish grimace. "We bought Tortoise a ticket to fly with you in the baggage compartment. He's too big to ride with you." She held up her hands when she saw Libby start to freak out. "It's perfectly safe. I stopped at the pet store before we came and got the carrier they recommended for him to fly comfortably."

Libby shook her head in shock. "Why would you do that?"

"Because Blair and Garrett got you a one-way ticket, and we know how much you love your dog."

"You better get in the shower," Blair said, sounding gruff. "Megan and I will start packing your clothes. I've paid for you to bring three bags and I figured you'd want to bring your camera equipment in your carry-on. You and Noah can come back and get the rest later."

Tears flooded Libby's eyes. "I don't know what to say."

Blair swallowed, but a tear fell down her cheek. "Just promise you'll come back to see us more often than Megan did before she married Josh."

"We'll probably be back for business."

"Not necessarily," Megan said, subdued. "Noah refuses to take his job back."

"Oh."

"Does that change anything?" Blair asked.

She shook her head. "No. I just need to get to him."

Her friends pushed her toward the bathroom and she climbed into the shower. They kept barging into the bathroom to ask her which clothes to pack. Tortoise sensed something was up and began to pace nervously.

"Oh! Food for Tortoise!" Libby exclaimed once she was packed and ready to go.

"I know this may come as a shock," Megan said. "But we have dog food in Seattle."

Libby stuck out her tongue as she scooped some of Tortoise's dry food into a Ziploc bag and slipped it into her purse.

"I think I'm ready."

They rode to the airport in silence. Tortoise sat quietly by Libby's side in the backseat of Megan's old Explorer, eyeing the crate in the back with suspicion. He wasn't very happy about getting inside the box when they checked him in at the airport, but Libby rubbed and kissed his head. "I'll see you in no time," she cooed. "And then we'll go see Noah. He'll be so happy to see you."

She only hoped he'd be happy to see her too.

Megan and Blair walked her to security and they shared a moment of awkward silence.

Megan handed her a slip of paper and a key chain. "This is the key to my car. The lot where it's parked is written on this paper. Take my car from the airport and I'll pick it up later when I get home. The address is where you can find Noah. He's not at his apartment."

"Where is he?"

"He's at his grandfather's house on Bainbridge Island. My mother-in-law sent him out there to inventory the house and his granddad's workshop. Something to keep him busy." She paused. "She also said he used to love it there when he was a kid. I think she was desperate to do something to make him feel better. I saw him there yesterday, so I know he's still there."

"Thank you." She stuffed the paper and the key in a pocket inside her purse.

"Oh!" Megan's face lit up. "Have you heard from Gram?"

"No. Why?"

"She got married in Vegas."

"*She what?*"

Megan grinned. "A hot yoga instructor from some class she took out there. Nana Ruby had to fly home without her. Knickers is fit to be tied."

Libby laughed. She could only imagine. But it reminded her of her own situation. "I don't even know if we're still married. I don't know what happened to the marriage license."

A soft smile lit up Blair's face. "You are. I called Melissa while you were in the shower. She just texted a few minutes ago that she'd gotten ahold of the owners and they mailed it in. Also they're sending your dress and some wedding photos to my office."

The wedding photos. Libby laughed. "If you look at them keep an open mind, okay?"

Shaking her head with a grin, Blair reached into her bag and pulled out a picture frame, then quietly said, "One more thing. I forgot to give you this."

Libby's throat burned when she realized what it was—a photo of the three of them at the carnival on the day they'd been cursed by the fortune teller. The three of them were hamming it up for the camera. They were happy and carefree and sure they'd have each other forever. She was with her two best friends, the only two people who had made her feel truly loved until Noah. It was so perfectly *them*.

Blair wiped a tear from her cheek. "The day this whole curse nonsense was born. I should have never doubted you, Libby, but you believed enough for all of us. Thank you for that."

"We used to be inseparable," Libby said, regret in her voice.

"We can be again," Megan said through her tears. "Living in different states doesn't have to change that."

"We can Skype," Blair said. "I do it for business. We can conference call."

Libby nodded, then the brunt of her fear hit her full force. "What if I get there and he doesn't want to see me?"

Blair smiled through her tears. "There's only one way to find out. Go to him. But no matter where you go or what you do, know that we will *always* love you. We will always be your second home."

"You need to hurry," Megan said, pulling her into a hug. "They're about to board your flight."

She hugged them both again, then went through the small security line, ready to break down into tears again. She didn't think she'd ever been so scared. Her entire life was about to be decided in a few hours and she wasn't sure she was ready to face it.

She took a deep breath and smiled to herself. She'd figure out a way to make him forgive her. She'd camp out on his doorstep if that was what it took.

They were meant to be together. She only hoped he believed that too.

Chapter Twenty-Nine

Noah stood in his grandfather's workshop, turning a piece of hickory wood over in his hand. When he was a kid, he used to spend weeks at a time here with his granddad. It was one of the only things that always set his hyperactive mind at ease. He knew that's why his mother had sent him here. Her busy-work for him was a flimsy excuse. Not that he was complaining.

The peace this place usually instilled in him was elusive, but at least he felt a sense of belonging here. At the moment he'd take any kind of relief from his demons he could get. They were back in full force. The sense of worthlessness. The belief that he deserved all this pain and more. He knew Josh was concerned, but Megan's visit the previous morning had caught him off guard. She'd shown up out of the blue with a bag of groceries and a six-pack of his favorite beer.

After setting the groceries on the kitchen counter, Megan had popped the top off one of the bottles and handed it to him.

"A little early for beer, don't you think?" he'd asked as he took it from her.

"Never too early for a good beer. Besides, it's nearly noon." And she took out a bottle for herself too.

They ended up sitting on the back porch for about ten minutes, drinking their beers in silence.

He waited until he opened a second beer to ask, "Is this a peace offering?"

She turned the bottle in her hand, then set it on the arm of her Adirondack chair. "I screwed up, Noah. But I intend to make it right."

He shook his head and sighed. "Don't. Just don't."

"She won't take my calls. Or Blair's. She's alone and miserable. Go to her."

He lifted the bottle to his mouth and didn't set it down until he knew he could swallow past the lump in his throat. "She left me, Megan. She believes the worst of me."

"She was just scared, Noah. You have to know that. She's terrified you'll break her heart."

"I know. All the more reason to leave her alone. I'll just hurt her again. It's what I do." He took another swig then, drinking down a large gulp.

"I don't believe that."

He shrugged. "It doesn't matter. It's done."

"So how long are you going to stay out here?"

"I don't know. It's quiet. Lets me think."

"About going back to work with Josh? Or about Libby?"

"Both." Libby was an easy choice. He couldn't have her, so it really wasn't any choice at all. But the business was another matter. He couldn't deny that he'd found a sense of accomplishment over the last few months, but he wasn't in any shape to go back to work yet. He still needed more time to nurse his wounds. And he sure couldn't handle going back to Kansas City, knowing Libby was there. He'd consider opening his own firm, but he would never want to be in direct competition with his brother, which left him where he was. Jobless.

"Josh and I are moving to Kansas City in a few weeks and I'd really like him to spend most of his time at home," she said quietly. "Which means he needs someone to run Seattle. He wouldn't be back much. The entire thing would be yours. Like it was supposed to be from the start."

He turned to look at her.

She gave him a weak smile. "I'm not above begging. I want you to be happy, Noah, but I think working for the business *does* make you happy. It's Josh's micromanagement that drives you crazy." She laughed and took a sip of her beer. "Yes, I know my husband very well."

He grinned.

"So what I'm saying is, we can both get what we want. Josh will stay home with me in Kansas City with occasional trips to Seattle, and you can run the Seattle office with no interference. It's a win/win, don't you think?"

He sucked in a breath and blew it out. "I don't think I can handle it."

"Bullshit," she said with a grin. "You handled it until Josh graduated from college. You just let him take over because you didn't believe in yourself. But you *are* capable and we both know it. And I know someone else who believes in you too."

His grin fell. "I don't want to talk about Libby."

"Fair enough, but tell me this: Do you love her?"

Tears filled his eyes, which pissed him off. He'd never been a crier before the last week. How did he answer that question?

It was like she'd asked if he needed air to breathe, or water to survive. The answer was so obvious, yet a simple yes seemed so inadequate.

Megan stood. "Let me make you lunch."

She made them sandwiches and helped him clean up the kitchen before she left. She pulled him into a hug after he walked her out to the car. "Don't give up on yourself, Noah. And please don't give up on Libby. She misses you just as much as you miss her."

He'd spent nearly every minute after she left thinking about Libby and fighting his desire to run to her. The knowledge that he might never see her again was more than he could bear.

In addition to the stockpile of food Megan had left him, there was a bottle of champagne with a sticky note on it.

Save this for when you know it's time to open it.

Fat chance of that.

Now here he was, a day later, still just as bereft, holding a piece of wood in his hands that begged to be shaped into something useful. It struck him that he had something in common with the block. This was how he'd been before meeting Libby—unformed. From the very beginning, she'd helped him determine what type of man he wanted to be. It might be too late for him, but he could shape the wood into something functional and beautiful.

He set the piece of hickory on his grandfather's workshop table and examined the grain in the block. The day before he'd used the lathe to make a spindle out of a piece of pine. When he examined the piece of hickory, he could see the promise of a candlestick.

Then it hit him.

He could make the candlestick and give it to Libby as a peace offering. On the surface, it seemed lame, no contesting that, but if anyone would appreciate a handmade gift, it was Libby. And if he told her his analogy . . . maybe it would work. Besides, now he could tell her in person that he'd just gotten the results of his tests, and they had come back clean. Maybe that was reason enough to go to her.

At least it gave him the ghost of a plan.

He worked on it all afternoon and into the evening, fumbling a couple of times, but altering the shape enough to accommodate his mistakes. When he took it off the lathe, he decided it wasn't half bad. He squared off the ends with a band saw and then sat in his grandfather's chair. He was sanding the piece when he heard a dog bark.

He hadn't seen or heard any dogs at the neighbor's house, but he supposed it could be a visiting dog. He didn't think much of it, until a large animal burst through the partially open workshop door.

He jumped in surprise and gasped. "Tortoise?"

The dog spun in circles with happiness, then put his front legs on Noah's lap, begging for attention.

"How . . . ?" If Tortoise was here, then Libby . . .

She stood in the doorway, more beautiful than he remembered her. Her long hair was loose and wavy, skimming over the top of her breasts. She wore a green sweater paired with dark jeans that clung to her hips, and a pair of brown boots. He couldn't believe she was there. How?

Megan.

He still sat in the chair, Tortoise excitedly licking his face. Without thinking, Noah nudged the dog down and stood.

Libby stayed perfectly still in the open door, worry in her eyes. "Noah, I'm so sor—"

He didn't let her finish. He scooped her into his arms and kissed her hard. This had to be a dream.

When he lifted his head, tears streaked down her cheeks and fear filled his chest. "Lib, what's wrong?"

"You still love me. I was so scared you'd hate me."

He shook his head in disbelief. "Oh God, Lib. I could never hate you. Never in a million years."

"I was so wrong. I should have trusted you."

"Shh." He kissed her into silence, his tongue seeking hers. Her arms tightened around his neck as he lifted her up. She wrapped her legs around his waist and he carried her across the yard and in through the back door, Tortoise following on his heels. He took her to the master bedroom and set her on her feet, cupping her face in his hands. "I never thought I'd see you again, much less touch you."

"I was miserable without you, Noah. I need you."

"I need you too." He pulled her sweater over her head, then paused. "I got my test results today. I'm clean."

"So no condoms?" she asked hopefully, giving him a sly look.

"No condoms. Thank God. I don't have any here."

They undressed each other, then made love in a combination of passion and reverence. Afterward, he held her in his arms.

"You were right," she whispered.

His hold on her tightened. "Those are my second three favorite words," he teased.

She laughed. "And your first three?"

"Hearing you say I love you." He gave her a long leisurely kiss. "But what was I right about?"

"You said I was looking for an excuse to leave you first. My dad's words were ringing in my head, and I wasn't thinking straight." She looked up at him. "I saw him when I was twelve. I never told anyone." Then she told him about the horrible visit that left her more scarred than she'd realized.

"You kept that to yourself all these years." His voice broke. "Oh, Libby. The man was a fool. You are the most lovable person I've ever known." He cupped her face and kissed her again, then smiled against her lips. "I can't believe you came back to me."

"Blair and Megan helped me come to my senses."

He chuckled. "Megan worked some of her wiles on me yesterday." Then he realized how well his sister-in-law had orchestrated their reunion. "Wait here." He stopped in the doorway and looked back at the most beautiful woman in the world, still in disbelief that she was naked in his bed. "Are you hungry?"

"Only for you," was her husky response.

He felt his own body respond. "I plan to keep you very busy that way, but I'm talking about actual food."

Her teasing fell away. "I only want you, Noah."

"I'm all yours."

He came back a few minutes later, grinning ear to ear. "Megan must have had a lot of faith we'd work things out." He held a tray stacked with cheese, crackers, and fruit, along with two juice cups and the bottle of champagne. "She left a note saying I'd know when to use this."

Libby sat upright in bed, letting the sheet pool in her lap, and the sight of her bare breasts was tantalizing enough for him to want to make love to her again. "She was always the one of us who was the most prepared for anything. Don't let her innocent face fool you. She's a schemer."

He gave her a wicked look. "It's the quiet ones that always fool you." He popped the top of the champagne and filled the juice cups, handing one to Libby.

"Look at this," she laughed. "Someone gave us champagne

334

and I didn't even have to wear my wedding dress."

Her smile faded, and guessing the reason, he cupped her cheek in his hand. "I have your dress. It's back at my apartment. I couldn't leave it."

She looked down at the tray on the bed. "Thank you."

He lifted her chin and searched her eyes. "Promise me that you'll never leave me again. I don't think I could survive it."

Tears filled her eyes. "Never."

"And I'll never leave you. It would be like ripping out my own heart."

They made love again, this time more playful, and he marveled how every time seemed to be better than the last. Then they lay in each other's arms and Libby told him about her friends' intervention and how miserable she'd been without him. He told her about his talk with Josh and the possibility of taking over the Seattle office.

"What do you want to do?" Libby asked.

"I don't know yet." He looked down at her. "What do you want me to do?"

"I want you to be happy. Whatever that means."

"I have to provide for us, Libby. I want you to focus on your photography."

"You don't have to provide for me. We're partners. We'll figure it out. Together. Okay?" she asked sleepily. He realized it was after midnight in Kansas City. No wonder she was tired.

He gazed into her eyes and kissed her softly. "I made you a present."

That got her attention. "What is it?"

"I'll show you tomorrow."

She propped herself up on her elbow. "You can't tell me that and expect me to wait. I want my present now, Noah McMillan."

He leaned over and kissed her again. "I'll give you anything you want, Libby McMillan."

She grinned against his lips. "You'll regret that promise."

"Probably." He grinned back. "But it's worth it." He stood and stepped into his jeans. "I need to take poor Tortoise outside anyway. Don't fall asleep."

But she was dozing when he got back, her hair spilled on the pillow behind her head. He stared at her for several seconds before she roused.

"Stalker," she murmured.

"I couldn't help myself," he laughed as he sat down beside her, hiding the candlestick behind his back.

"Where's my present?"

"Am I not present enough?" he teased.

"You're everything I need, but you promised me a present. Where is it?"

He loved this about her. Her excitement over the littlest things. She made him feel that same giddy happiness. He had no idea how he'd gotten lucky enough to have her, but he would never deny his need for her again.

He fingered the grooves of the candlestick, suddenly nervous. "I made it for you this afternoon. I was going to bring it to you as a peace offering. I'm still rusty, so keep that in mind."

"You were going to come to me?"

"I couldn't live without you, Lib. Even if that makes me a selfish bastard."

She grinned. "Then I'm a selfish bastard too." She sat up, practically bouncing with excitement. "Now back to my present. You *made* it? Give it to me!"

He put it into her open hands. "It's a candlestick. Like I said, I'm rusty so it's a little uneven on the left—"

She kissed him and pressed the candlestick into his chest in her excitement. *"You made this?"*

"Yeah."

"It's the most beautiful gift I've ever gotten. It's even better than the one Blair gave me before I got on the plane, so that's saying something."

He wanted to ask what Blair had given her, but she distracted him with that beautiful mouth of hers. They showered each other with kisses, and he marveled that he could be so deliriously happy.

As he drifted off to sleep, her voice broke into his thoughts.

"Oh, my palm was right all along," she murmured, half-asleep. "And I was scared I'd gotten it wrong."

He roused awake, determined to never let her down again. "What did you see on your palm?"

"You. I was so worried it was someone else." She looked up at him when he tensed. "I'll explain it to you tomorrow. Just know that your candlestick is the most perfect present to chase away my last lingering doubt."

"You still doubt us?"

She shook her head. "No. Not anymore. Just promise to love me even when the girls go south and we're good."

He smiled, kissing her forehead. "I promise to love you no matter what."

It was the easiest promise he'd ever made.

Epilogue

Libby paced the floor of the New York art gallery, feeling like she was about to throw up. Her exhibit was opening in half an hour and she wasn't ready.

Her husband's arms pulled her back to his chest and his lips found her neck. "It's going to be great, love," he whispered in her ear. "Your exhibit is amazing."

She laughed. "You're just saying that because you're in every single photo."

He laughed with her. "Well, I'm sure having an amazing model helped." He spun her around, looking down at her with so much love it sucked her breath away. "I'm so proud of you, Lib. You did it."

"Only because of your encouragement."

Garrett groaned. "Are you two newlyweds about to attack each other again? Because you have a room only a couple of miles away. *Use it.*"

"Like you're one to talk," Noah laughed, keeping his arm around her back and tugging her to his side. "I just saw you feeling up *your* wife a few minutes ago."

To Libby's surprise, Blair blushed.

"Okay, okay." Josh squeezed Megan's hand as they walked toward the group. "We're all newlyweds and we can't keep our hands off each other. May we always be this way."

"Hear, hear," Noah agreed and motioned toward the entrance to the room.

A waiter walked up to Noah, carrying a tray of champagne. "As you requested, sir."

Noah winked at Libby and she felt herself blush as he started to hand out the flutes. "I think all six of us have something to celebrate, so Libby and I thought it would be good for all of us to say what we're grateful for." He held up his glass and looked into Libby's eyes. "Libby. I wouldn't be half the man I am without you. Thank you for standing by me while I tried to figure out what I wanted to be when I grew up."

He'd struggled with his decision to stay in the office, but Libby had encouraged him to try, assuring him he'd have her full support to quit if he felt pressured or overwhelmed by Josh. But Josh had stuck to his promise to stay out of Noah's office. He'd flourished in his position over the last couple of months. Libby was so proud of him, some days she wasn't sure she could contain her happiness.

They'd moved into his grandfather's house, and he spent part of his time in the workshop, creating things out of wood. She'd confessed her fear that her palm had said she would marry someone creative, and he'd told her that if woodworking wasn't creative enough, he had all sorts of creative ways to make love.

"I'm so proud of you, Libby." His eyes glistened. "You did it, baby. Even though I tease you about your success being linked to your ridiculously handsome model, this was all you. And it's just the beginning of many great things."

She reached up on her tiptoes and kissed him, smiling against his lips before she lowered back down.

"I never would have finished if not for you. Not just because you were my model," she teased. "But because quitting was never an option. You fed me, gave me coffee, and encouraged me when I was sure I'd never make the deadline. Thank you." Tears filled her eyes. "I never knew I could be so happy until you loved me."

Garrett coughed and said under his breath, "Get a room."

The group laughed and Noah kissed her anyway. When he lifted his head, he shot his friend a grin. "Okay, hot shot. Your turn."

Blair lifted her eyebrow in expectation.

Garrett's grin turned mischievous for a moment, like he was going to make some sort of joke, but then he said, "I'm grateful for second chances." He turned to his wife and held up his glass. "Blair, these last few months have been a whirlwind, but I wouldn't trade them for anything. I can't believe you're mine after everything that happened, and I can't wait to spend the rest of my life with you."

He wrapped his free arm around Blair's waist and pulled her in for a long kiss.

"Get a room." Noah laughed.

The others joined him in laughter.

Blair blushed again, trying to regain composure. "I was going to say I was grateful for this ass—" Garrett leaned into her ear and whispered something that made her smile. "I'm grateful for my friends who tolerate my brisk behavior and love me anyway. And I'm also grateful for second chances. Both in love and in friendship." Her gaze settled on Libby. "I wouldn't have missed this for the world, Libs."

Libby smiled at her friend.

"My turn," Josh said, glancing first at Noah and then at Megan. "I'm grateful that I sat down next to a drunk woman on a plane who told me her sad tale. And I'm so glad I took a chance and pretended to be her fiancé." He smiled down at her. "I couldn't imagine my life without you."

She looked up at him with adoring eyes. "Neither can I."

Everyone clicked their glasses together and took a sip, with the exception of Megan, who had an ornery grin on her face as she held her glass in place.

"Why aren't you drinking?" Blair demanded, her question an accusation.

Megan's grin grew wider.

"Oh, my God!" Libby shouted. "Are you *pregnant?*"

Megan cringed. "I wasn't going to say anything until after your exhibit, Libs. It's *your* night, but Noah figured it out yesterday so this was all his idea. I hope you're not angry. I didn't want to take the spotlight away from you."

"Angry?" She shook her head. "I'm going to be an aunt. A *real* aunt since you're my sister-in-law now, not pretend like before. This is perfect."

"Sure," Blair said drily. "Rub it in."

Megan pulled both of her friends into a hug. "I love you both the same. I want you *both* to be godmothers."

"You realize this is the end?" Blair asked. "No more date nights. No more cute outfits. Nothing but sleepless nights and spit-up."

Megan's eyes filled with fear, but Libby squeezed her arm. "Don't listen to her, Megs. It's not the end. It's just the beginning of something wonderful."

Then she gave Noah a knowing smile as she held the glass of champagne she'd pretended to sip. It was a new beginning for *both* McMillan families.

And Libby had never been happier.

About The Author

New York Times and USA Today bestselling author Denise Grover Swank was born in Kansas City, Missouri, and lived in the area until she was nineteen. Then she became a nomadic gypsy, living in five cities, four states and ten houses over the course of ten years before she moved back to her roots. She speaks English and a smattering of Spanish and Chinese which she learned through an intensive Nick Jr. immersion period. Her hobbies include witty Facebook comments (in her own mind) and dancing in her kitchen with her children. (Quite badly if you believe her offspring.) Hidden talents include the gift of justification and the ability to drink massive amounts of caffeine and still fall asleep within two minutes. Her lack of the sense of smell allows her to perform many unspeakable tasks. She has six children and hasn't lost her sanity. Or so she leads you to believe.

Made in the USA
Columbia, SC
02 December 2020